DAMAGED GOODS

JE MAC

Published by Dying Media Press
Copyright © 2014 J.E. Mac
Print Edition October, 2014

ISBN: 978-0-9914625-1-3
Cover art by Ray Dillon

10 9 8 7 6 5 4 3 2 1

For Nick,

For being the role model.

"It is easier to build strong children than to repair broken men."

—Frederick Douglass

PROLOGUE

Splinter shrapnel bounced off the stupid grin on Virgil's face.

Cutter coughed into his hand, forcefully clearing his throat. At the very least, he had expected a response. Something other than the viscous ribbon of drool hanging from Virgil's slack maw losing its fight with gravity.

Must've been some good shit.

On a threadbare sofa in the middle of the darkened apartment, Virgil rocked back and forth oblivious to the intrusion. His eyes were clamped shut, fluttering with REM rhythm, as he spasmodically hugged himself deep in the throes of his current download cycle. Jacked into his forearm, a Tibro500 vibrated in noisy circles, yipping like a mop-dog tethered to a too short leash.

Cutter shook his head in disgust.

Virgil was a heap in the latest cybernetic tech bolted to a life form once claiming to be human. The department typically referred to them as mods, but Cutter preferred calling them something else entirely. He hated mods. He was no fan of tech in general, but at least synthetics like Roy never had a choice in the matter.

Cutter nudged the barely humanoid synthetic to his right. "You believe this guy?"

"Insufficient information," said Roy. "The suspect will have to make a statement before I can assess if it is fact."

Cutter inhaled long and deliberate, feeling the corners of his eyes tighten. He fought his natural reaction to roll them at his binary partner. It wasn't Roy's inability to decipher figures of speech that bothered him. Sometimes he just plain forgot.

In front of them, a technological zombie swayed to the music of a whirring hard drive. "Excuse me, Sleeping Beauty!" Cutter shouted. "L.A.P.D! Ringing any bells?!"

The hairs on Virgil's ear moved ever so slightly as the concussive wave from Cutter's voice knocked them down in single file. Cutter flipped on his Mag-light and drowned Virgil in its beam. Virgil's eyes fluttered open. Fully dilated pupils puckered shut like shower-time at the big-house.

Without missing a beat, Virgil bolted for a room in the back, but not before stumbling over the sofa. It was almost comical.

A blue glow lit up the room. Lightning coursed through Virgil's tech raining an electrical storm of blue sparks throughout the apartment. Unable to heft the weight of his lifeless tech, he slammed face first into chipped plaster drywall and collapsed to the floor.

"Room secure," said Roy. At the sound of his partner's haunting monotone, Cutter couldn't help himself. He actually rolled his eyes this time.

The heap of metal-meets-man struggled against his dead

weight, trying to flee from underfoot. Cutter kicked Virgil's shorted-out tech like tires on a new car.

"You're one ugly technophile, you know that? Hate to think all this is actually an improvement."

Virgil helplessly flopped on the floor, anchored by what he probably, and proudly, called his body. "What the fuck, man?! I can't move."

Cutter pointed his still sparking taser at the darkened backroom. A high pitch whine cried from the device like the song of a dying whale. Sparking ribbons of electric blue static danced in a halo around the muzzle and then dissipated into darkness.

"Anyone else here?"

"Just me, piggo."

Attitude.

One more reason Cutter hated using the taser. Give him something with a little more kick and he'd show technopunks like Virgil manners and decorum the likes of which hadn't been seen since the Victorian era.

He slid a thumb into his waistline, pinning his leather jacket open, revealing the Wesson & Colby ZeroTwelve pulse pistol bulging out of a shoulder holster. Much more his style. Too bad the department frowned on the use of black market weapons— even for its officers—and in his case, that rule was *especially* for its officers.

Cutter reattached the taser to his belt and knelt down next to the incapacitated mod. His jacket hung open. The ZeroTwelve swung in its holster, tapping against Virgil's temple. Cutter loved this variation on Chinese water torture.

It didn't always get results.

But he loved it just the same.

Dead tech clattered against the floor. Beads of sweat

cascaded down Virgil's forehead, cutting lines through months of accumulated grease. From the looks of him, Cutter figured it was the closest thing to a shower Virgil had since first augmentation.

"You should really wipe yourself," said Cutter. "That's disgusting." He reached into his jacket, nudging the ZeroTwelve out of his way, and offered a handkerchief to Virgil.

Virgil had an offer of his own. He spat in Cutter's face.

Cutter calmly wiped his brow and twisted with enough force to send the butt of his ZeroTwelve into cheekbone leaving behind a blooming purple orchid.

"You can't be doing that man!" Virgil yelped. "I got 'ing rights!" He writhed back and forth, but his metal bulk pinned him in place. "So lucky I can't move! Lot more I'd do than that too! Ain't 'ing you can do 'bout it neither! You got your book and your bot keeping an eye on you."

"You know what, buddy? You're awfully insightful." Cutter turned to Roy. "Hey Roy, you hear something in the backroom?"

Roy perked his sensors. "Negative."

"You don't hear shit you mod-needing motherfucker! I told you, it's just me in here!"

"Maybe you should check it out, Roy?"

"Affirmative." Roy disappeared into the darkened room on command.

"Ya 'ing piggos are so damn stu—"

Without forethought and absolutely no hesitation, Virgil's hands glommed onto his nose in a pathetic effort half-trying to stop the stream of gushing blood and the other half simple instinct protecting it from being hit again.

"What the 'ing shit, man?!" Virgil screamed in disbelief. "Tinhead, you see that?!"

Roy's metallic inflection bounced off the walls from the

backroom. "I do not see anyone in here."

Cutter smiled, teeth gleaming dingy yellow, poking through a triangle of lip that turned the corner of his mouth. "Roy, try running a full inspection. Leave no stone unturned."

"There are no stones in here."

The smile vanished from Cutter's face. "Just run the damn inspection."

"Roger that."

Cowering beneath him, Virgil scooted along the wall, desperately trying to drag his metal bulk to safety. Cutter placed a boot on scraps of Virgil's frayed jeans pinning him in place.

"What's the rush?" said Cutter.

Holding his nose, ineffectively damming the blood waterfall, Virgil pressed himself into drywall. If anyone could have pushed himself through physical material, Cutter thought Virgil just might have a shot.

"Hey circuitboard!" Virgil pleaded. His voice went up an octave in the middle.

Cutter snorted. "Good luck with that."

When no answer came, Virgil pointed at Cutter with a shaking hand. "Your book... your bot..."

"Yeah? What about 'em?"

"But—" Unable to find words, Virgil violently shook against his dead tech, twisting toward the back room, desperately shouting. "Hey! Black and White! Look at this 'ing shit man! You can't let 'em treat me like this! I got 'ing rights!"

Roy poked his head into the room. "You are bleeding."

"No shit I'm bleeding! This 'ing piggo broke my 'ing nose!"

"Should have modded your face," said Cutter, slapping Virgil on the backside. "Nosebleeds are an all too common side effect of jacking in."

With an arm around Virgil, he waved at Roy with his other. "Don't worry, Roy. I'll make sure our friend gets the attention he deserves. Why don't you continue tagging and bagging any evidence you find in the other room?"

"Roger that."

Horror clung to Virgil. He turned his gaze from the darkened room to the man hovering inches away. Roy's servos whined from the back room, a faint reminder of his presence.

"You… you can't do this, man."

"Maybe so. Maybe not. Not much you're gonna do about it either way."

Cutter watched Virgil mentally scramble for an escape, an excuse, anything that would get him out of his current predicament. Mods like Virgil bored the hell out of him. It was the same old routine. The same problems repeated time and again. New faces making the same old mistakes. The augmentations may have been different, the technology newer, but they all spelled the same thing.

Trouble.

Criminals like Virgil thought they were reinventing the wheel.

Hey, lookit this, its round. Imagine what we could do with it. We're geniuses. We'll be rich. Why has nobody thought of this before?

They had. Just—you—hadn't. Those that had been around long enough saw things start to repeat endlessly.

Cutter figured he had been around for way too long.

He placed a hand on Virgil's shoulder. "Now that we have some privacy, why don't you and I have a little one on one?"

Cutter leaned against the wall and slid down into a sitting position. With a flick of his wrist he pulled out a pack of American Spirits. He smacked the bottom. A cig poked up and he pulled it out with his teeth, letting it dangle from his lower lip. He reached into his jacket to replace the pack, but stopped halfway through the motion.

He held the pack out to Virgil. A filter jutted out like a golden finger. "Want one?" The cig hanging from his lip danced as he asked the question.

"What?"

"Okay, suit yourself. Don't say I didn't offer." He pocketed the pack. Seconds later, an orange glow ignited from his cupped hands. He inhaled deeply and blew out a cloud of smoke followed by two rings. They expanded and deformed before disappearing.

"So tell me a little about yourself," said Cutter.

"What the 'ing is this?"

"Don't want to talk, that's fine. I got enough on my mind for the both of us." Cutter puffed and another smoke ring drifted out. "I'm wondering what a modded up shitbrick like you is doing with a Tibro500. Little out of your league. You don't seem the type to be running a full blown jack-op out of your apartment."

"I—" Virgil hesitated. "I was jus' usin' it to get high, man! I swear!"

"Uh huh."

Cutter picked up the Tibro500 from the floor and turned it over in his hand. "What's this one do? Teach you Kung Fu?"

"I ain't into that shit. Just reversin' the flow for the ride."

Cutter eyeballed Virgil. He could believe that. Virgil was altogether wrong. His fashion choice and pawn shop mod job reeked of a techno junkie on a bender. Still, a Tibro500 was not common in the lower dregs. It was more common in organized crime rings and fully operational jack-op distilleries. But he figured any excuse was a good excuse to give another scuzzo mod the third degree.

Cutter removed Virgil's wallet from his pant pocket and flipped it open.

Virgil Cooper—picture of a sixteen year old kid, pre-mod work, pre-junkie, likely pre-puberty too.

He held it up, comparing it with the mix of tech and flesh he saw before him. He couldn't tell anymore. All mod jobs started to look the same. Practice found it easier to simply describe them by their accessories.

Left arm, right leg, a couple sparking shorted-out implants in the chest, a cybo-spine—that was all Virgil was to him—a short list of spare parts.

"Sad. Such a good looking kid. Bet you made your parents proud." He flipped the wallet shut. "So tell me, Virgil," he put extra emphasis on the kid's name. "Why do this? This whole thing. What's it about?"

"The fuck you talking about?"

"You hate yourself or something? Maybe hate your parents?"

"Who the fuck are you?"

"Maybe it's a grudge against the whole human race?"

"You're one of those, huh?" Virgil snorted. "Jealous?"

"Sure looks that way." Cutter stubbed out his cigarette on Virgil's cybernetic shoulder.

"So here's where we're at—I'm supposed to take you down to the precinct, call up your folks, tell 'em what you've been up to. Tell them how you've improved upon their design. Book you for all these very, very illegal augmentations you got going on here. Charge you with grand theft e.l.e. and the possession of one really badass drive."

Virgil said nothing.

"No words? No foul mouth? No smart lip? Is this what I have to look forward to Mr. Next Step In Human Evolution?

Dumb silence?"

An implant broke free from restraint and hopped back and forth on Virgil's chest, spitting sparks. The rat's nest of exposed wires tethered the malfunctioning tech to his body, preventing it from flying off completely.

"Word of advice, kid. If you're going to invest in all this garbage, you should at least get good work. Your pawnshop repo tech is still on the fritz from the short-out."

Virgil laughed and immediately stopped himself. He met Cutter's gaze for a brief instant, then flicked his eyes to the floor. After a moment he said something low, almost a whisper. "So what's stopping you?"

"Hmm?"

"What's stopping you from hauling me in?"

"Oh, nothing. That's our next stop. I just wanted a cigarette break."

Cutter removed the cash from Virgil's wallet. He tossed the empty wallet into his lap. Virgil scowled at him. If his eyes were fangs his would be dripping venom.

"There a problem? You look like you want to say something."

Virgil held the defiant gaze. After a moment, he softened and said, "Can't you let me off with a warning or something?"

"Warning?" Cutter climbed to his feet and dusted off his butt. "That's a good one."

"That's the problem with you piggos. Think you're above it all. Think you don't have to answer to nobody."

Cutter let his words stew.

"Well… we don't."

He pulled a pair of cuffs off his belt and reached down for Virgil's arm.

"Aren't you forgetting something?"

"You have the right to blah, blah, blah."

"Ain't what I'm talking about."

"Why don't you enlighten me."

"Backup juice," said Virgil.

Servos shrieked, as motor function returned. Virgil lit up like an addict sparking an unlimited supply of rock. A blaster pistol ejected from a hidden compartment in his cybernetic leg.

Cutter went wide-eyed. The involuntary spasms from Virgil's electroshock therapy had not been involuntary at all. Shoddy workmanship, yes. But the vibration came from a secondary power cell recharging the downed tech. A backup power supply that fed juice to the main power, jumpstarting the whole system.

God damn it!

Cutter knew this. It was rookie knowledge. Back to Basic 101. How could he have been so careless? Maybe the fucking checkups—no, he wasn't about to think that.

Not many had the good fortune to look down the barrel of a Sig-7 and catch a glimpse of plasma particles dancing in orange light milliseconds before they ignited. This rare opportunity was one that Cutter could have gone an entire lifetime without seeing.

He rammed his shoulder into the technological behemoth rising up in front of him. The shot went wide, filling the room with an overpowering stench of burnt leather. The blast singed his jacket and blew a hole through chipped plaster clear into the hallway.

Cutter reached into his jacket. Virgil swung, knocking the ZeroTwelve across the room. He lowered the Sig-7, finding Cutter in his sights.

"Three point seven terabytes of photographic evidence stored," said Roy, entering from the back room. Virgil turned. Cutter lunged. They tumbled.

On the floor, Cutter wrestled for the Sig-7 in Virgil's cybernetic grip. It wouldn't budge. He settled for punching the smile off his face instead.

Reeling, Virgil grabbed Cutter by the wrist and flung him across the room. He hit the floor with a thud and slid to a stop next to his ZeroTwelve. He reached for it and rolled out of the way as an orange energy pulse shredded linoleum.

Cutter came to a stop with the ZeroTwelve centered between his legs, sights leveled, trigger finger itching for action. Virgil was gone.

* * *

Pressurized doors exhaled a final breath and coughed Cutter onto the earthquake tortured streets of Los Angeles. The city was painted in grotesque monotone and sprinkled with shattered glass and barred windows. Skyscrapers like jagged teeth buried a grid of concrete gullies in shadow transforming the otherwise harsh California sun into something more sinister than shade.

He often wondered what had happened to the city he had once loved. Wondered whether the dreams of utopia had been intentionally placed in the middle of the city landfill or if time simply backhanded the hopes and dreams of those longing for an impossible ideal. He found himself running through the promise of a 1920s vision that had gathered mold and deflated with rot.

This was not the Los Angeles he could remember in the dog-eared scrapbook of his mind. But it was the Los Angeles he had grown to call home.

Cutter sprinted under a smattering of overhead jumbotrons that backlit the street with neon highlights, giving everything an artificial glow. From them, a lilting female voice tongued his ear with promises of a better life, paid for in monthly installments.

This was supposed to be routine.

A scuzzo mod getting high. Most of the time these busts weren't even worth the paperwork. Rough them up a little and send them on their way, knowing full well they would be getting high off the flow the instant authorities left.

It wasn't even a game. It was just the way of things.

But if word got back…

That he had been careless.

It would mean more checkups. Lots more.

Or even worse. No checkups at all. Just a pink slip and, if lucky, a piss poor severance package.

Half a block ahead, Virgil plowed through pedestrians.

"Roy, where are you?!" Cutter shouted into his com. "I'm losing him!"

"In pursuit. Heading off the suspect at San Vicente."

"Good! Do that!"

Through a cluster of thoughts, one surfaced crystal clear: *Please don't turn onto 3rd. Please don't turn onto 3rd. Please don't turn onto 3rd.*

"He turned left onto Third," Roy said over the com.

Great. He was headed toward The Grove.

The Grove was people, people, and even more people.

In some distant past it had been a farmer's market. Somewhere along the line, the idea of a farmer's market in the middle of a major metropolitan city became kitch. Every weekend, stuck up Beverly Hills snobs hightailed their personally trained Botox injected selves to The Grove to talk about how *quaint* it was. After decades, simple economics stepped in and The Grove no longer resembled a farmer's market, rather one of the most pretentious strip malls in the country. If other strip malls held a contest to vote on Miss Strip Mall USA, they too would think The Grove was a stuck-up bitch.

In short, The Grove contained an orgy of very vocal, obnoxious targets for a mod evading arrest to choose from. A hostage situation was low on Cutter's current To-Do list. He pushed past the ache burning in his legs and lengthened his stride.

What was taking Roy so long? He should have caught up by now.

Ahead of Cutter, an old lady weaved between cars as fast as her walker would allow. Her minor misdemeanor reminded Cutter why he hated synths in the first place. Roy was probably distracted by a similar infraction. Some poor bastard who happened to be walking his dog without a license. Or some punk kid playing hooky from school. Definitely high priority stuff.

The jaywalking old woman had bigger problems than making sure she crossed at a crosswalk. Even bigger than the cab driver getting out of his car to quote-unquote give her a hand.

Virgil had seen her and was bearing down on her location. The roof of an Accord crumpled beneath his weight, as he bounded from car to car, lengthening his lead on Cutter.

Cutter hoofed it between alleys of gridlocked traffic. He huffed, breathing heavy, running out of steam. He clutched the ZeroTwelve in his hand, lot of good that was doing. He couldn't get a clear shot even if he wanted to. He was winded, exhausted, and—was it his imagination, or was Virgil actually getting faster?

The boys at the station would have a field day. If only Cory could read his mind now—no way he would let him live this one down. There would be mod pamphlets on his desk for weeks: Intro to Augmentation—in only four short weeks, you too could be the you, you only dreamed of. Cory thought that shit was hilarious. Especially knowing how much Cutter hated it.

And maybe they were right. Maybe if he had mechanical

legs, Virgil wouldn't be eight car lengths ahead and on a collision course with an unsuspecting old lady and her walker. Maybe Cutter wouldn't have been overpowered in the apartment if he had cybernetic arms. Maybe if he had a targeting chip implanted like so many others in his precinct, he could make the shot, and save the day.

He raised his weapon, still on the run. His sight shook, unsteady. Virgil disappeared behind a van and reappeared on the roof of a sedan.

Cutter lowered his weapon. His sights shook. *That ain't happening. Not in this lifetime. Sorry lady.*

Virgil leaped from the hood of a Ford. Metal flexed beneath his feet with a popping sound. The old lady turned her attention from the cab driver she was busily swatting with her purse, toward the noise.

A horrific coalescence of metal and man flew at her with a sneer on its face.

A fraction of a second before impact, Roy slid to a stop in front of the old woman, chest out, bracing himself for impact.

Thank God, for that. Explaining how an old lady had been used to spray paint The Grove with her guts in a written report to the Chief was the last thing Cutter wanted.

Virgil smashed into Roy, sending him skidding backward. The old lady and the cab driver dodged to their left. Roy fell backwards in the space they had been inhabiting. Virgil rebounded, fleeing in the opposite direction.

Perfect.

Cutter ducked behind a car and lined up his ZeroTwelve. It wasn't much of a covert hiding spot, but all he needed was a clear shot.

Virgil made eye contact and turned hard right into the

shopping center.

Cutter sighted down the barrel. Just one shot would drop Virgil, no question. That wasn't the holdup. Cutter knew better. The blast would pass clean through Virgil and probably hit one of the yentas behind him. It wouldn't stop there though. It would pass through her and keep on going into the Pinkberry behind her, explode out the backside into an adjacent Banana Republic, and keep right on going.

Probably why the department didn't let him use the ZeroTwelve in the first place.

Fire now and risk hitting innocent bystanders? Or let Virgil get lost in a sea of shoppers to tear them apart as he saw fit. Lose-lose.

Cutter pulled the trigger.

He was trained to aim for center of mass. Unfortunately, center mass was not where the shot was heading. It was low and behind the target, way off course.

Virgil darted between cars. There was no chance for the shot to hit center mass now. His left foot kicked back in stride. The energy bolt connected scattering metatarsal and meat pulp across the high shine of a brand new Caddy.

Bull's-eye.

Virgil misplaced his lack of a foot on the pavement, searching for support, like thinking there was an extra step at the bottom of a staircase, but finding none. Virgil crumpled to the asphalt. His bloody ankle stump hit pavement, providing no support for his extra subhuman tonnage.

Cutter closed in on him, weapon drawn. Virgil tried to stand and collapsed under his own weight. He gave up on walking upright and dragged his body along the sidewalk.

The spectacle had not gone unnoticed. In fact, it went by

very noticed. Shoppers gawked in a semicircle around Virgil, as he dragged himself within arm's reach.

People are so dumb, Cutter thought. *Run the hell away? Nope. Let's gawk and stare. Maybe pick up a stick and poke at him too. Good ideas all around.*

Cutter trained his weapon on Virgil.

And there it was—the Sig-7.

The down angle was perfect. He'd love to think it was a precision shot, but the ZeroTwelve did most of the work. The weapon was a surgeon. And really, he only needed to aim close enough. Whether he hit gun or hand it didn't matter. Virgil was disarmed all the same.

The crowd of shoppers let out a unified gasp, and backed off the scene. *Probably would have been smarter to have done that before some crazed mod jacked up on the flow waved a weapon around, ya think?*

Cutter stalked across the street. His crosshairs locked on Virgil's very human face. "Any other tricks you want to tell me about?"

Virgil pulled out the Tibro500 and drew it back, as if he was going to throw it at Cutter.

"Seriously?" Cutter said. "What are you going to do with that?"

Virgil brought his arm down and smashed it on the ground.

Cutter slid behind Virgil and wrestled his arms behind his back. With a quick motion from inside his jacket, he slapped handcuffs on Virgil and plugged them into his tech, bringing it under control.

Cutter shook his head. "Not too bright are you?" He shoved Virgil's head into the pavement, using it as leverage to stand. Swiping the drive off the ground, he flipped it over so that the display was visible. 'DELETION COMPLETE' was written in green.

Rifling through his pockets, he removed a small device and jacked it into the Tibro500. The device spit out a steady stream of ones and zeroes.

"You can't destroy information," said Cutter. "There's always a trail. Always a way to recover. These things never forget. Hell, it's why we use synths in the first place. Ain't that right, Roy?"

"In the future," said Roy, "I would suggest crossing at a crosswalk for your safety." He handed a jaywalking ticket to the old woman with the walker.

ASSEMBLY

1

Celia watched from the hallway, knowing full well her presence was unwelcomed. If she was spotted, she would be in serious trouble, but she couldn't help herself. She peered into the nursery, bright eyes shifting from mother to daughter and back again.

Juniper spun in the middle of the nursery, holding her sweet baby Jessica in outstretched arms. She pulled Jessica to her bosom and kissed her forehead. At the touch of her lips, Jessica squealed with childish glee. Giggling, Juniper scrunched her brow together and made googly eyes. She leaned in close, nuzzling her daughter's neck, and whispered nonsensical gibberish in a comforting tone.

Jessica swiped at the invisible words and missed. Unable to grasp them, she answered her mother with a gurgle and gibberish all her own.

Celia clumsily swept a strand of dark hair behind an ear and leaned into the room for a better view of the activities. The room's décor had changed. The familiar pink tones she had grown accustomed to remained, but the bed where she once slept had been removed and a chested drawer put in its place. The crib was new as well, the focal point of the room, draped with a mobile that casually spun as air stirred past. The ceiling had been covered in cottage cheese spray foam, but now was scraped bare, repainted lavender matching the rest of the room's pastel tones, and dotted with glow in the dark stars.

Juniper blew a raspberry into Jessica's tummy, "Who's gonna git you? I'm gonna git you!" She tickled the child's belly to her ceaseless delight.

This wasn't the first time Celia had secretly watched Mommy

and Jessica together. Sometimes when Jessica was sleeping, she watched Mommy take her from the crib and rock back and forth in the large armchair in the corner. Jessica would nestle against the warmth of her mother as Mommy softly hummed a lullaby.

That was only sometimes, though. Usually when Jessica slept, Mommy would too. But most often the play was like it was now, Mommy wheeling in circles, flying Jessica through the air.

She could remember when Mommy used to play with her like that. Twenty-two months, three days, sixteen hours, forty-three minutes, and twelve seconds to be exact.

Celia felt her body go rigid as a lyrical melody filled the nursery. Before she could be spotted, Celia withdrew into the hall.

"Daddy's home!" said Mommy.

Through the vertical crack between the door and wall, Celia watched Mommy gently place Jessica in her crib. She wrapped her in a blanket and gently stroked a wisp of hair.

As Mommy headed toward the door, Celia ran across the carpeted hall on tip toe. She opened a slatted door and hid inside the linen closet seconds before Mommy set foot in the hall. Her timing had been practiced to perfection.

From her slatted view she watched Mommy walk past. The third step from the top creaked as Mommy went downstairs to greet Daddy.

She heard the heavy oak door in the entrance swing open and her parents exchange warm greetings. A surprised, "Oof," came from Daddy, and Celia was sure that Mommy had thrown herself around him in a loving embrace.

She listened to Mommy offer to whip up an after work snack for Daddy, listened to their warm tones dissipate as they moved through the living room into the kitchen. When Celia was certain

Mommy and Daddy were out of earshot, she crept out of the linen closet, silently tip-toed down the hall, and poked her head into the nursery where Jessica was sound asleep.

The nursery was quiet and the potpourri scent of lavender permeated the air. An invisible hand gently nudged the mobile in the otherwise motionless room.

Celia approached the crib. Her feet sank into the dense carpet, muffling her footsteps.

"Hello, little Jessica," she said, taking hold of the wooden bars that separated her from the sleeping child. She lowered the wooden railing flush to the soft pillow-top mattress. Jessica slumbered, sucking her thumb. Drool collected in her curled palm.

Celia hovered over the infant, watching in silent contemplation.

After a few moments, she said, "Who is going to get you?"

She watched Jessica. Her features so pink, her entire body inflating in and out with every breath, completely unaware that anyone was lurking over her.

"I am going to get you!"

She grabbed Jessica's feet and slid her to the edge of the mattress. A chubby leg dangled over the precipice. Jessica's eyes snapped open.

Celia yanked her off the mattress and lifted her high above her head. Her childish gait stomped uncertainly with each step. Top heavy, high above her head, baby Jessica dictated movement, rather than Celia's own motor control. She waddled side to side, spinning in an effort to keep up with the off-centered weight that led her in haphazard circles across the nursery.

Jessica squirmed, kicking her feet, and caused Celia to swing to the right. She sprinted beneath Jessica searching for the center of gravity to keep her upright, until the process repeated itself. As they swung to the left, Celia compensated. Too far to the left, and now Jessica was falling to the right and she ran in the opposite direction to keep up.

Celia laughed joyously at the upside down pendulum they created. She wished Mommy could see what fun they were having.

See Mommy, we can get along fine.

Jessica wiggled, and gravity sent her in a direction Celia had failed to anticipate. Her hands adjusted for a better hold on Jessica, her feet moved to find balance, but the weight was too far in front of her.

Jessica fell fast.

They came crashing down into the crib.

Celia lay face down, arms extended forward. Her knees were on the carpet, chest resting against the lowered crib bars, head buried in the mattress. She groggily raised her head, finding her bearings. And then a giant smile spread.

She giggled loudly.

Again!

Pale features flushed red. Tears leaked from Jessica's tightly shut lids. Celia turned her attention to Jessica, who was in the middle of the soft mattress, amidst a mountain of pillows. Her tiny features contorted transforming into a ghoulish mask.

Celia cocked her head to a side. "You have sprung a leak."

But that wasn't a problem for Celia. She knew what to do. She had seen Mommy do it a thousand times and it always resulted in a smiling, giggling Jessica.

Celia placed her lips on Jessica's belly and began to blow. She stood up with a smile beaming across her face.

Silence filled the room. Jessica held her breath. She cocked her head to a side, looking intently at Celia.

And began to wail. Her screams filled the room and echoed into the hall.

Celia couldn't believe it.

What had she done wrong? She did everything Mommy had done. But the result was so different.

Celia patted Jessica on the head and wrapped the pink blanket around the struggling, bawling infant. "It is okay Jessica. Everything is all right."

Jessica screamed at decibels louder than seemed possible from her tiny lungs. Tears streamed down her cheeks.

Mommy was at the door in seconds. She bolted to the crib, knocking Celia down in the process. She lifted Jessica and cradled her in her arms, cooing soft reassurances to abate the screaming child.

Daddy was at the door moments later.

"What happened? Is everything okay?" said Daddy.

"Charles!" screamed Mommy.

Celia cowered. Mommy only called Daddy by name when she was in trouble.

"I was just going to get her," said Celia.

"I can't do this anymore!" Mommy's face burned red. The purple vein in her forehead thumped a blistering one hundred and twenty-three beats per minute.

Celia stayed absolutely motionless. When Mommy got like this, it never ceased to frighten her. But this time, something was different. Usually during an outburst, Mommy would leave the room without a word.

But not tonight.

Streaks of sweat spotted her scarlet face. She towered over Celia, and if her hands hadn't been preoccupied holding Jessica to her chest, Celia got the impression that she would have thrown something at her.

Or worse.

"Honey, let's talk outside," said Daddy. "She hears everything."

"I don't care! I want it out! I can't take it!"

"She's our child. We have a—" Daddy paused and looked right at Celia. His face looked the way she had seen so many times before. So sad.

"Celia, will you be a good girl while Mommy and Daddy talk? Wait in the hall, please."

Celia nodded and quietly obeyed.

"That's a good girl," said Daddy, closing the door and cutting her off from view. Through the wall, Celia could make out the muffled argument.

"We have a responsibility," she heard him say.

Cutter stirred a cold cup of coffee, mindlessly watching a television that had been bolted to the ceiling. A cigarette shrugged off ash onto the table. He raised his arm, a motion that began somewhere between stretching and wafting away the gathering smoke and ended with the cigarette dangling from his lip.

On the television, volumetric light refracted through rippling water. Fibrous tendrils drifted in front of a pale white object. A lilting female voice chimed in with a reminder too friendly for Cutter's liking.

"Ready for a fresh start? Wish that every day could be better than the last? With over three hundred new locations to serve you, InSight strives to provide the relief you are so desperately seeking."

Cutter exhaled, watching the images flicker through a veil of swirling smoke.

"*Every day does not need to be a struggle.*"

The tendrils turned into strands of hair. Behind them, two pale blue eyes opened, and a face rose to the surface.

"*Let InSight help you clear your mind.*"

The face broke the waterline, revealing Mayor Benjamin Foster, the current, and he hoped—next Mayor of Los Angeles. Somehow, he repelled the water, not appearing the slightest bit wet.

The images flashed to an American flag proudly flapping in the wind, as Benjamin Foster, well-dressed and iconic in appearance, rose on a rotating pedestal with a smile and a glimmer in his eye.

"Join us today at M.J. Square," said the televised Foster, "and participate in the future."

"*This message is brought to you by the city of Los Angeles mayor's office. Bringing you a better tomorrow, today.*"

"Hiding?" asked Cory.

Cutter kept his back to him and stubbed out his cigarette on the table.

"No," Cutter scoffed.

He quickly placed his coffee cup over the butt, hiding the evidence.

Cory grabbed a mug from an overhead cabinet, flipped it into the air with a cavalier flourish, and caught it behind his back. Cutter watched as his worst nightmare placed the mug on the counter and poured coffee from the pot.

Maybe nightmare was a bit strong. Cory was a good cop and his general take no shit attitude was something that Cutter appreciated.

His problem had more to do with one simple fact.

Cory was a mod.

He was not an intimidating sight, devoid of weapons and attachments fitted to his tech, as stipulated in the Augmentation Laws of 2064. He was registered, as required of all legal mods, but something about him rubbed Cutter the wrong way.

Cutter guessed that Cory couldn't have been more than a buck-thirty before the procedure. The cybernetic arms on his miniscule frame reminded Cutter of a gorilla. He quietly sniggered to himself at the thought of a teched out knuckle-dragger.

Maybe it was the visual that set him off. The cybo-spine lined Cory's back, a frightening metal exoskeleton that mirrored the appearance of what was beneath. Hydraulically linked vertebrae worked in conjunction with the implanted chest chassis to support the extra weight of his arms.

All that work, and for what?

From what Cutter could tell, the tech did not encumber movement, nor did it overtly draw attention to itself, unlike the blackmarket mods he was used to dealing with. Cory's tech was *very* unlike Virgil's version of low-budg-high-tech. Cory's work was professional and appeared to be a general extension of evolution rather than appendages built for mayhem.

"Heard about your little shopping incident," Cory chimed. "The whole department has."

"Yeah?"

"Yeah."

"And?"

"Chief's looking for you."

"Commendation, huh?"

Cory laughed. "Sure buddy, sure. Just giving you a head's up is all."

Cory walked out, sipping his coffee. Cutter watched him

plow through the bullpen towards his desk. He had left a technoperp cuffed to it. A friend of sorts was paying the thug a visit. A mod-whore gussied up for a night on the town was busy slapping the poor restrained bastard.

Air hissed from Cutter's nostrils whistling a half-hearted chortle. Typical Cory.

"Hey sugah," he heard the mod-whore say. "What say you lose my number next time, kay?"

"Hey!" Cory yelled at a nearby officer. "You mind keeping your mod-whore off my scumbag?"

"Would hate to see him catch a virus," the officer said and restrained the woman.

"Ha, you hear that? Everyone's a comedian." Cory swatted the officer on the backside. "Shut up and get her to holding, will ya?!"

Cutter returned his attention to the television. He caught the images just in time to see them fade from daytime soap to black and another cycle of adverts.

So much for a distraction.

A familiar baritone tickled his ear. His gaze was drawn across the bullpen, over the heads of a half dozen officers, to Police Chief William Parks.

Parks was in rare form. His presence left behind a wake of scattered officers, scrambling to complete tasks that should have been completed days, if not weeks ago. His uniform looked like he had it dry cleaned, pressed flat, and starched daily. His image of perfection was unblemished by a single stray wrinkle.

His chest overflowed with medals and bars, most of which Cutter hadn't the slightest notion of their significance. Service, duty, honor, something like that, he could only guess. It wasn't like they were labeled. They could have been for helping old ladies cross the street for all he knew. Maybe one for lighting camp fires?

Behind Parks, and tripping over his own feet, was Earl Pinkerton. Pinkerton had a uniform unique to the department. He wore a lab coat, unbuttoned, with long tails that floated with each step and a high tech eye loupe over his left eye.

Cutter grimaced. They were at his office. It didn't take a detective to realize they were probably looking for him.

"Who else knows about this?"

"Just you and me so far, Chief. I barely had enough time to verify the data, but it all came back legit."

Parks peeked through a windowed door demarcated from other identical windowed doors by a stenciled name: Cutter.

You aren't gonna find me in there. Cutter smiled and sipped his coffee. His eyes flitted down to his cup of joe. He sneered at it, choking down a gulp.

It was ice cold.

Parks scanned the precinct. This was his precinct. His officers. He was the boss, and Cutter was only here for one reason—to do exactly what Parks told him to.

But he had no interest in getting his ear chewed off today.

"Where the hell is Cutter?"

A few officers turned towards Parks, and then returned to their work without an utterance.

"Anybody got eyes on Cutter?"

Cory laughed.

"Stetler!" Parks hollered. "You know anything about this?"

"No sir. I don't know a God damn," he said muffling laughter.

Parks grumbled to himself. Cutter could barely make it out. Something about all the good for nothings that worked under him. An army of law enforcement at his disposal and he couldn't even locate one of his detectives in his own precinct. That's like the firehouse burning down, or some shit.

Parks peacocked through the bullpen, walking the length of the far wall. Behind him, the city's criminal processing database blinked and blooped with work that Cutter wasn't particularly keen on getting done. Not today anyway.

Parks stopped at a corner desk, tossing a glance back at Cutter's office door.

Not a good sign. Whatever Parks had on his mind, he definitely wanted to give him a piece of it.

Any other day, Cutter thought. *If it got the job done, who cares? Right?* On some other day, he might march up to Parks and tell him that. Just not today. There was his coffee, and the solitude of the break room, and, well—the fact that they'd had that conversation in all its million incarnations before. Cutter knew the Chief's response by heart.

Parks could turn a blind eye to his officers' liberties with the law. As long as nothing reflected back on him or his department, he cut his officers a lot of slack.

However, a rampaging mod provoked by one of his detectives—that little bit of slack would vanish like so many underage girls into the back of windowless vans.

Cutter had been reprimanded before, chewed up and spit out. He knew it didn't bother him as much as Parks thought it should.

But it didn't mean he liked it. And it certainly didn't mean he wouldn't try to avoid it if at all possible.

Wait things out long enough and something new eventually took its place. Put a little time between anything and people tend to forget. A murder, a kidnapping, hell, even a string of parking meter thefts was enough to go from suspension without pay to back on the job, especially in this underfunded, understaffed department.

One of the perks of the job.

Cutter hunched down, out of view through the break room window, as Parks scanned the bullpen, a lighthouse beam sweeping darkened waters. Cutter silently scolded himself. He probably could have picked a better place to lie low. The break room in the middle of a police department was not the most creative or secret of hiding spots.

He waited until Parks and Pinkerton moved into the corridor on the far side of the bullpen that led to holding.

He dumped the frigid coffee in the sink and set his mug upside down, unwashed of course. As he passed the break room table, he noticed the desecrated remains of his cigarette. He pocketed the smashed butt and scattered the ashes with a swipe of his hand, leaving no trace of his indiscretion behind.

Slipping into the bullpen, he worked his way left, past the interrogation room. The door was open. He peeked in out of habit, but neither criminal nor officer occupied it. Too bad, some of his fondest memories had been birthed in that room.

He threw a sideways glance toward the hallway that led to holding. So far, so good. Parks and Pinkerton were nowhere to be seen.

Pushing a low wooden door that swung at his knee on double hinges, Cutter entered behind the front desk kiosk. The area was more secure than the rest of the department. A wall blocked off those in the waiting area from seeing deeper into the department. This was by design, both for privacy and safety.

It was the department's front entrance, the entrance for anyone that wanted to pay a visit without an appointment. Cutter never understood why anyone would want to visit in the first place, but it happened.

Sitting in the lobby was a man, about forty, hunched over on the waiting bench, his head wrapped in bandages. There was a story there, Cutter was sure, but it didn't interest him.

A rookie cop manned the front desk. Cutter didn't recognize her, but that was common. The turnover rate was high. Sure, the job was dangerous. But it was mostly because the pay was shit. Her mousy brown hair was drawn back in a tight bun.

He absent mindedly took in his own wardrobe, the stark contrast that it was. He tried to remember the last time he washed his clothes. Not clothes in general, but the ones he was actually wearing—today—right here in the precinct. Three, maybe four days he'd gone in the same attire. He didn't think anyone would notice. His leather coat was clean, or at least looked it, and did the better part of hiding the sweat stains on his undershirt.

He made a mental note to do laundry when he got home. The same mental note he made every day, but seldom remembered.

The girl, fresh out of Academy, acknowledged his presence by meeting his eye, and then returned to filling out stacks of paperwork. *A ho hum dismissal of his very existence,* Cutter thought. She had better things to do than chat it up with a detective skirting the chief. Cutter couldn't help taking it personally.

Maybe it was his clothes. Maybe he really should do laundry today.

Cutter dipped his nose into his armpit and sniffed, short and deep. He snapped back at the foul odor. Yeah, laundry—and a shower.

A large hand clasped onto his shoulder.

"We need to talk."

The deep baritone made Cutter jump.

Guess laundry will have to wait.

Parks' grip on his shoulder was firm and authoritative, with a hint of street that begged for resistance, and the resultant throw-down that was sure to follow.

Cutter declined the invitation to fisticuffs. "So talk."

"Your office."

His office was a hurricane of paperwork. Papers and file folders were strewn about. Cardboard boxes were stacked four and five high, crammed into every nook and corner of the office. The bottom boxes buckled under the weight, Atlas holding the world on his shoulders. A volcano of file folders erupted from the middle of Cutter's desk. A few file folders hung off the edge, pushed there from the surge of new folders spewing from the crater.

Cutter had left three floating display monitors open. This wasn't a practice in laziness, simply practicality. The job never ended. There was always a new report in desperate need of transcription into the system. He would get around to it, eventually.

Parks knocked a handful of stray reports off the chair facing Cutter's desk. He slid the chair back, gave it one good smack causing dust to rise, and took a seat. Pinkerton lined up behind the chief, awkwardly fidgeting over his shoulder.

Cutter leaned back in his chair, a big high backed number that pivoted as he leaned, and tossed his feet on top of piles of paperwork.

"So what's the deal?" Cutter prodded. "They finally run out of work for you?"

"Don't I wish," said Parks.

"This about the mod at The Grove? I already filled out a report. It should explain everything."

"Not exactly. Was glad to see that you brought Roy back in one piece, though. If you aren't careful you might start a trend."

Cutter smiled. Humor on the part of the chief spelled relief in capital block letters. Still, if he wasn't in trouble, it had to be something serious.

But that didn't stop him from tossing a barb of his own.

"At least that's a problem I can easily rectify." The corner of his mouth turned in a tight smirk. His eyes gleamed, issuing a challenge to his superior.

"Keep talking like that and I might assign you a partner that gets upset when you use them as a blast shield."

"That only happened once. I used the last Black and White to prop open a vault door."

"Yes, Carl," said Pinkerton. He didn't seem amused. In fact, he seemed kind of pissed, Cutter thought. "You returned him to us in quite a state of disrepair. We couldn't even salvage him for scrap."

"Damn, did I forget to send flowers again? Next time. Promise."

"Let's cut the wise," said Parks. "Earl found something you might be interested in."

'Interested in' was code for, "Here's your next assignment."

Pinkerton's demeanor softened. He seemed to perk as Parks handed the reins of conversation over to the socially awkward scientist.

Pinkerton grew, stepping out of the shadows from behind his boss. He placed a busted-up Tibro500 on Cutter's desk. His hands slid inside his lab coat and removed a long metal cylinder that had a cord for a tail. He placed the cylinder in front of Cutter and plugged the tail into the Tibro500. A turquoise button lit up with a faint glow. He pressed it and a holographic projection leaped into existence. Laser lines anchored it to the metal cylinder.

"And what do you want me to do with that?" said Cutter.

Pinkerton's boyish smile faded. How could Cutter not understand? Just look at it. "This is the readout from the Tibro500 you brought in."

"I'm sure there's a point somewhere."

Pinkerton snorted, shaking his head at Cutter.

"Check this out." He pressed a series of buttons that were arranged in rows beneath the glowing turquoise button causing the display to jump and flicker with new screens filled to capacity with data. His boyish enthusiasm regained momentum with each scrolling wall of text that presented itself.

"I'm sure this all means…" Cutter searched for the word. "…something."

"It's a simulation holo-program. Every conceivable piece of data one could want. These plans are beyond detailed."

"Plans for what?"

Pinkerton abruptly halted. He shot a worried look at Parks, looking more apprehensive than shocked, like a little kid with a secret he couldn't wait to share. His gaze seemed to beg Parks for permission. Was it okay, could he tell him? Could he, could he?

"An assassination attempt," Parks said.

Pinkerton's expression fell. He wanted to break the news to Cutter and see that smug look wiped off his face.

Cutter eyeballed the drive.

"An assassination attempt?" Cutter's thoughts drifted to Virgil. Good ol Virgil and his pawn shop mod job. "Somehow I don't see our technoperp having a political agenda or the brains to carry out something that elaborate."

Parks nodded. "Not him. This is much bigger than a jack-op dispensary."

"He probably got ahold of the drive in the aftermarket and was using it to get high," said Pinkerton. His head bobbed for emphasis.

Cutter looked at him blankly, staring through the scientist until he became so self-conscious that he had to look over his shoulder to confirm that Cutter was indeed looking at him and not something behind him.

Parks picked up the Tibro500, gesturing with it in his hands. "We got lucky, Jack. This looks to be the start of something much larger."

"You going to tell me that thing was responsible for the JFK assassination?"

"Better." Pinkerton grabbed at the Tibro500 in Parks hands and then instantly hesitated. "Uh sir… could I… uh…?" Parks shrugged and handed the Tibro500 back to him.

Pinkerton placed it on the desk and excitedly ramped through a series of readouts. "All the data is current."

"How current?" asked Cutter.

"Like—today current."

On the holographic display, walls of text gave way to blueprint after blueprint of technical data. Pinkerton giddily scanned through the device at light speed. He pointed out key locations on the blueprint scans, as it rapidly moved and resized pertinent information.

Cutter nodded, not really following along.

"This here is the civic center," Pinkerton said, pointing to a series of abstract lines that were replaced as quickly as they had appeared. "M.J. Square is here, and these are all the adjacent buildings, complete with floor plans and—"

Cutter abruptly sat up. "It's for today's rally?"

3

"We keep having these problems," said Juniper.

Gary was not a man to blindly ignore another living being, especially when addressed directly, but his focus was on the task at hand. What came out was an incoherent grumble, seemingly dismissive at that.

He cranked on a bent piece of metal lodged behind a circuit board. If he had been a more chatty man, he might have uttered a friendly, "Now, here's the problem." But he wasn't. He was methodical and the only reassurances he needed came from his confidence in his work. Whether he was found personable or not, he could care less.

The job got done.

Gary plopped the foreign mass into his toolbox. It clanged and echoed through the kitchen, startling the newborn that had been wrapped in a pink blanket and pressed against her mother's bosom.

The newborn cracked open puffy eyes and tried to wipe sleep away with a tiny hand. Slumber had her, and a lion's roar yawn returned her to the comfort of sleep.

Juniper smiled at her little girl, so precious. She pulled the end of the blanket tight around her, preventing even the slightest chill from penetrating the blanket cocoon.

"My husband and I are thinking of returning it," said Juniper.

"Tampering voids the warranty." Gary succeeded in draining the last remnants of friendly banter from the conversation.

"We've had it for five years."

"Then you won't have a problem telling her what silverware was doing crammed behind the circuit board."

Juniper's mouth fell, her brows arched, and her nose scrunched into an expression that reminded Gary of a community theater actress, vaguely trying to express some specific emotion, but failing to accurately portray it. Surprise? No, that's not what she was going for. She was definitely reaching for something else. Indignation was the likely candidate. Gary had dealt with enough housewives to know the beats, even if the cues were slightly off.

He could tell that no one had been so blunt with her, not in years, anyway. But he really didn't care. It wasn't his job to care. Not about people anyway.

He tapped the circuit board with an oblong probe tipped by a red light. Green lights lit up inside the casing and the faint hum of life returned as the rest of the system powered up.

He grabbed the hatch cover by its flowing black hair and parted matching hair on either side of the case. Biting his lower lip, he squinted at the opening and lined up the cover with the assembly. *And now for the tricky part,* he thought. If a stray strand happened to get trapped inside it could potentially damage the circuitry. Furthermore, from the outside it would reveal the seam of the hatch and shatter the illusion.

With a final twist of a locking mechanism buried from sight, the hatch cover snapped into place. He ran his hand down the length of the seams, double-checking his work for snags. Not a one.

Gary nodded and placed the probe back in its form-fitted holster on his belt. He secured his toolbox and climbed to his feet. His work here was complete.

The machine was back in working order. Two visors raised simultaneously on the unit, revealing two black holes against a backdrop of white. As light broke darkness, the holes contracted into pinpricks revealing a ring of hazel surrounding each one. The hazel rings tracked the room, jittering from side to side before locking onto a target.

"Mommy!"

Celia sprang to her feet scampering to Juniper's side, and excitedly hugged her leg.

"Did I do good?" she asked, looking up at Juniper.

Gary could tell 'good' was not the word Juniper had in mind. But Celia was all smiles, and in truth, that was all that mattered to Gary.

"Sign here," Gary said matter-of-fact. He held a sensor pen and an electronic work order out to Juniper. She pretended not to see it. Instead, her gaze was fixed on Celia.

"So, if we have more problems, I should call you?"

"I ran a full diagnostic. She's in perfect working order. I shouldn't have to come by for another eighteen months." Gary shook the sensor pen, trying to grab Juniper's attention. "I just need you to sign that the work has been completed."

Celia giddily tugged on the hem of her mother's dress.

She was good as new. In fact, better than new, if Gary had anything to say about it. With proper care and maintenance, little Celia would be six years old forever.

"Yeah, but what if—do I call the company?"

"Like I said, she's perfect. I wouldn't worry about it."

He lowered the pen, correcting his aim, almost placing it directly into Juniper's hand. She had both hands wrapped around the newborn. But it seemed that was more of an excuse for not taking the pen than an actual problem.

She had no intent of signing and no amount of pen wagging was going to change her mind. Gary shook his head, returned the sensor pen to its slot on the electronic work order and tucked the whole thing under his arm. If she didn't want to sign, fine by him.

There were procedures in place for difficult clients.

"I don't want to get stuck with a lemon," said Juniper. "With all the problems we've been having lately—and you're telling me that my warranty might be voided? What kind of service are you providing?"

Gary noticed her posture. The entire time he had been working, Juniper stood rigid, baby in arm, in the corner of the kitchen. Now, she was closing in on him, suffocating him with her presence. Her movements were swift. As her motion grew flamboyant, the sleeping baby took no notice of the gravity defying effects that her mother's centripetal motion was creating.

"We've been loyal customers for years. If anything happens, I just think I should know the best way to handle it. Whether it should be something I have my husband fix, or if I should call someone about the problem."

Not his problem, Gary thought. Not anymore.

He was halfway out the door, while Juniper continued yammering about her rights as a consumer. He probably should have held his tongue—but sometimes the work wore him thin.

He stopped at the front door and turned face to face with Juniper. He was not surprised to find that she had been on top of him every step of the way.

There was little space left between Juniper and Gary. He simply pretended that talking two inches away from another person was normal. Pretended that her ranting and posturing did not bother him at all. He rolled his neck, snapping the crick he had felt all afternoon with a loud popping sound.

"Well, I'll tell you what. It's rare that these things breakdown. Rare to have problems of any kind. Truth be told, they're built to go an entire lifetime without needing a checkup. The eighteen months are more or less so old codgers like yours truly have something to do that justifies a salary."

He smiled and leaned forward almost imperceptibly. Juniper took a step back to keep from toppling over.

"Should she break down again," said Gary, "I s'pose we could send out a team to investigate the problem. Get right down to the root of it and have you taken care of."

Gary could see the thought process work its way across her face. Her eyebrows were doing the math. They scrunched and arched and danced, never finding a single expression, but jostling between many.

It was simple arithmetic—a) An inquiry into the cause of the damage, plus b) Who was likely responsible? Equaled c).

Gary had already done the math.

Years of dealing with situations much like this one left him with the appearance of outer calm, despite feeling quite the contrary. His face was stoic, while his eyes gleamed with fire.

"No..." said Juniper. "No, I don't think that will be necessary."

"Yeah, I'd hope not."

She whipped the electronic work order from Gary's hand and signed on the hyphenated line. Gary nodded out of habit. Courtesy was not something he meant to grant her. She handed the work order back to him, trying her best to avoid direct eye contact. No matter. He didn't want to look at her either.

He tucked the work order under an arm and showed himself the door.

"Thank you for stopping by. My husband and I appreciate it."

"Mm-hmm."

He made sure the door closed with enough force to rattle the house. Once again the newborn was startled from slumber. This time she was unable to return to the land of Nod and protested the only way she knew how; with shrill cries that filled the household.

Celia excitedly jumped up and down, tugging on Juniper's dress.

"Did you miss me, Mommy?"

4

"If you were planning to kill the mayor, where would you hide?"

"That building, third story, window farthest left," said Roy with a deadpan only a synthetic could deliver.

The miniscule M.J. Square was flooded with InSight supporters waving banners. In the dead center, a temporary stage had been erected and a podium placed atop like a pulpit for Sunday mass. Bleachers lined either side of the stage, and makeshift barricades that reminded Cutter of bike racks had been placed at the foot of the stage. A wall of security guards kept the path between stage and barricade clear, holding off a bay of reporters and overzealous supporters.

Cutter and Roy stood in the back, statues amidst the chaos. Cutter's eyes flitted across the crowd. Somewhere in the writhing, whirling sea of supporters, someone had plans. Never a good thing. Not at an event like this.

The square was walled in by dilapidated apartment complexes. Most were condemned due to lack of upkeep, falling apart at the mortar. Mayor Foster probably chose this place as a symbol.

The setting was depressing, but probably the point, especially for someone who was likely to be issuing a message of hope and revival.

Maybe Cutter was too cynical, but he found the whole

situation painfully ironic. The M.J. Square projects had been a failed attempt at urban rejuvenation during Foster's first year in office. Now, a decade and a half later, they were abandoned and left to ruin, already showing signs of irreparable wear that came with selling out to the lowest bidder.

"That was quick," said Cutter.

"Extrapolating proximity, crowd size, wind conditions, and humidity, that location provides the most direct line of sight while also providing several adequate routes of escape."

"What did we ever do before synths?"

"Detectives would gather evidence and then based on a suspicion would—"

"It was rhetorical."

Cutter turned the knob and pushed inside the complex with the barrel of his ZeroTwelve. Roy followed with a team of six SWAT officers carrying riot shields and plasma rifles.

The lobby of the poorly aged apartment complex was in shambles. The bannister from the archaic stairwell rested in splinters. The only apparent residents skittered across the floor and along the walls.

Cutter worked his way through the debris to the staircase. The slats were rotten with mold. He climbed, hugging the wall. The stairs moaned in protest.

At the top of the stairs, daylight flooded in from a single overhead skylight. Cutter circled the landing, and disappeared into the darkness of a narrow hallway. Roy and the SWAT team followed close behind.

Cutter stalked to the end of the corridor. He pulled his handkerchief from his pocket and held it over his nose and mouth. The rancid smell of decay bit at his nose.

He stopped at the end of the hall, turned toward the door

on his right, and shot a look to Roy. Roy nodded. Third story, window farthest left. The SWAT team fanned out in tactical positions on either side of the door. Roy butted up behind Cutter, holding his forearm blaster readied.

Even though it was part of Roy's programming, at least someone had his back, Cutter thought.

He inhaled deeply, letting the building stench fill his lungs. He rocked back, gathering momentum and kicked in the door.

"L.A.P.D—" was all Cutter managed to get out.

He burst through the front door. Roy and SWAT fanned out behind him, securing the room.

The apartment was empty.

Concrete poked through holes in the scuffed parquet floor, revealing a thin sheen of plastic, shattering the illusion of real hardwood.

In the far corner, a faded olive green armchair sat threadbare, exposing tufts of stuffing. Yellow drapes with cheesy daisy patterns drifted leisurely in front of the window on the far side of the room.

All that was left in the apartment were remnants of a life, now long gone.

Cutter brought the handkerchief to his nose once again. The stench wasn't any better in here than in the hallway. It was just different.

"You sure this is the spot?" asked Cutter.

"It is where I would be," said Roy.

Cutter pulled back the curtain. "Nice unobstructed view."

It was a straight shot to the stage. He watched two stagehands prep the podium, finishing a final sound check. After a moment, Mayor Benjamin Foster took the stage.

Even in person, he looked like his picture from the adverts—

shined, and polished, and too good to be true. In short, perfect.

He climbed the stairs, chit-chatting with several people in the crowd. He went from one to the next seamlessly, while maintaining a casual gait toward the podium. It was a friendly gesture, Cutter thought, showing what a man of the people he was.

Cutter wondered how many hours Foster had spent honing his personality. Clearly, it had been an acquired skill.

Foster adjusted the microphone to an appropriate height without a single squelch of feedback. The maneuver only took him a second. He knew exactly where the microphone needed to be so that he could stand with perfect posture and still harness the full resonance of his timbre.

"Well, all right. Wow. Look at this turn out," he said into the microphone. "It's hard to believe you are all here to see me."

A small chuckle spread through the front few rows.

"Oh, that's right. You aren't here for me at all. We're really here for InSight. And the immense contributions it has brought to the city. Who here hasn't benefited from a little InSight?"

The crowd roared in response.

Cutter had to hand it to Foster; the man knew how to work a crowd.

"All right. Well, I'm glad. I'm glad. The city has been working hard on a new program. And I'm happy to say, I finally have a little announcement to make. Okay, okay. It's not so little. In fact, I think that when you hear what we have in store, you may have to rethink your entire future."

Foster paused, letting his words reverberate from the PA and echo through the square. Nice and dramatic. Even hooked Cutter's interest.

"Working in conjunction with InSight, the city is proud to

announce—starting immediately after the rally InSight is going to be free to everyone."

The words echoed through the small square dissipating into silence. Foster held a perfect smile on his face. A lesser man might have faltered, might have panicked at the silence. But Foster waited.

Quiet commotion spread over the hushed crowd like a receding ocean before a tsunami. Something began to surge forth from the rear, starting small—a sound that grew out of nothing.

The wave of sound hit full force, surging forward, rippling through the crowd in rows until it enveloped Foster. The raucous roar filled the square to deafening levels. Cheers of joy joined with cries of disbelief in a collaborative screaming gasp. If Foster could have managed a bigger smile, a physical impossibility for a man who had perfected the business of the smile, he would have. Instead, a cool calm washed over his expression. This was the outcome he had expected. The outcome he had planned. Everything was as orchestrated.

Cutter turned from the window back to the apartment and the six SWAT members, adrenaline coursing through their veins with no outlet.

"Sorry boys," said Cutter. "False alarm, looks like."

One of the men in the rear was already heading for the door. Two in front lingered. Really itching for some action, Cutter thought. He always felt bad when he had to call men for a job that didn't pan out. It wasn't fair to tease them. But what could he do? He couldn't conjure crime out of thin air.

Roy finished cataloguing the room, a quick, easy task considering.

Cutter held the door for the remaining two SWAT members, waving his hand in a leading manner. One of the men gave the room a final once-over, seemingly unwilling to believe that they had been pulled aside for nothing.

With a sigh the man holstered his plasma rifle, slung the riot shield across his back, and sullenly slinked out the door.

Cutter entered into the darkened hallway with Park's words rattling in his head. Private enterprise going public was certainly nothing new. Not that he kept close track. Politics and business were well outside of his admittedly small realm of expertise. Most of his encounters with corporate entities were the criminal highlights, access granted through work. He knew full well his opinion was likely bias. For all he knew, this new announcement was business as usual.

Still, he had a problem with the announcement—he didn't believe in altruism, but he couldn't figure the angle.

There were mounds of people willing to throw away large sums of money on an ill-conceived effort to feel better about themselves and their meaningless little lives. Every dollar spent was peace of mind that they could rest assured in the newly discovered fact that life was okay—only after the payments cleared, of course. Sweet little bit of business Insight was running.

And it wasn't a personal grudge either. Cutter had nothing against the company itself, just an opinion of those who used it. But even that wasn't a fair judgment either.

The department used InSight to keep its officers in line. 'In line' was not the term the department used. The term they used was 'sane.' Cutter despised the checkups.

Okay, so maybe he did have an opinion, he told himself.

He hated that InSight regularly sent salesmen to the precinct every month or so. The InSight officials would eschew the company motto—fresh and healthy, or something like that. He didn't really pay attention when he was forced to listen.

But it wasn't all bad. The work InSight did with the department was free. Maybe that was what raised red flags in the first place. He assumed the move had been strategic to get in good with law enforcement. There were obvious advantages to making officers of the law happy, especially if you were a large company that had plans on pursuing the highly illegal.

Or InSight could have just thought that the officers of Los Angeles were overworked and underpaid. That if anyone needed the services InSight provided, it was these poor schlubs, working from an outdated office in a city of ever increasing crime, fueled by poverty and technology.

Still, it nipped at Cutter's consciousness. Why would any company give up a lucrative revenue stream without an obvious motive?

Cutter needed something he could understand. And action performed out of the kindness of one's heart wasn't it.

He squinted in the darkness. Only a single beam of light from the overhead skylight sliced through the shadow, hinting at the forms trudging through the landing. Roy rounded the bannister and led SWAT downstairs.

Cutter stopped and peered through the skylight, watching a plane thunder overhead. It drew a line of cloud, cutting the blue sky.

Maybe it was his imagination, but it appeared as if a tiny speck had separated from the plane. Great, he thought. Exactly what he didn't need. Somewhere a loose piece of plane part was sailing through the sky on a collision course with—well, it didn't really matter what it hit.

He prayed that it would land outside the city limits. Please land in someone else's jurisdiction.

He grabbed the railing and took a step downstairs to join

Roy when something caught the corner of his eye. He turned toward a warm glow that emanated from the corner.

The darkness effectively masked peeling wall paper. It shrouded dust bunnies piled high, assorted scraps of wood, shredded wallpaper ribbons, and torn carpet covered in fungus from years of neglect. But underneath it all, the darkness highlighted a red glow pulsing in the corner.

Cutter walked over, head cocked, as the faint light illuminated the debris. He swept his foot, kicking up dust and exposing a small red light that blinked with metronomic regularity.

"Roy, I got something," he shouted over the bannister. In the lobby below, Roy was systematically ushering SWAT out of the building.

Cutter pulled out a pocket knife from his jacket and flipped open the blade. He knelt down, scraped the flashing red light off the ground, and held it close for inspection on the blade's edge.

"Looks like a beacon of some sort," he said so quietly that it was almost to himself.

What was it doing here?

"I think you may have been right," shouted Cutter. "Looks like this was the place. Guess, we scared them off."

Glass shattered, raining down on Cutter with a shrill pitch. He turned, too late. Only enough time to gather sparse detail on the shape plummeting through the skylight surrounded by shimmering glass.

In that split instant, remnants of detail were slotted together in a strained effort to form a whole.

It was made of metal. Large and heavy. Flat, black, and matte in finish. Hydraulics and tubing encased a larger machine. An engine off the plane?

No. It had form. A specific shape. A hauntingly familiar

shape that tugged at Cutter's notion of very bad things.

Metal in the shape of a man.

Cutter knew what it was, only too late.

A synthetic.

A soulless creation mindlessly following a preprogrammed routine. Whatever the significance of this assassination, an attempt for personal glory could be ruled out. There was nothing personal about sending a synth. This was cold hard calculated business.

Cutter should have been thinking about his own safety, about moving out of the way, about reacting to the synth falling at terminal velocity, but his thoughts wandered to the mayor. *Boy, he had really stepped in something here, hadn't he?*

Before it hit the ground, the metal man spun with a flying kick that smashed Cutter in the face and sent him flying against the far wall.

It rebounded, tucking into a ball, and back flipped away, landing on all fours like a jungle cat. It absorbed the full impact without the slightest indication that it had just fallen several miles.

Cutter shook the cobwebs from his rattled brain and reached into his jacket. On instinct, he found the grip of his ZeroTwelve.

The synth was on him.

A deft swipe of a cybernetic limb knocked the ZeroTwelve from Cutter's hand. An equally eloquent move, ballet-like in execution, plucked the blinking red beacon from the other.

Face to face with the metallic Grim Reaper himself, Cutter felt time slow to a standstill. He had never seen a synth move the way this one did. Synths were powerful, strong, and occasionally fast, but always had a certain clunkiness about them. Their movement was noticeably inhuman, weighed down by their tech.

This synth wasn't just fast. It was agile. Its lithe form sprung from obstacle to obstacle, reacting as if it could see into the future. It moved following some preordained drill it had run many times before and only now was executing a final show—the live version.

This was it. This was the end.

Cutter smiled at the inevitable irony of his life. A metallic skeleton, mocking him with its man-shape, was going to end it all—of course that's how it would end, fulfilling his worst nightmares.

His death would be no different than an assembly line worker that accidentally fell into an automated sorter. Cold steel would crush the life out of him without forethought or hesitation. Not a single person would blame the synth or hold it accountable. It was only running its routine.

Perhaps at his funeral, in an effort to console each other, mourners would say that the synth couldn't do anything more than follow its programming. That it was a shame no one got to it in time. Maybe, just maybe if someone had the foresight they could have changed its programming and altered the all-too inevitable.

But these sentiments would be mere afterthoughts taking flight as a result of the incident, soon to be forgotten, and rarely if ever acted upon. The cycle of life—it is what it is, they would say.

Cutter winced at its weight on his thighs. The hand on his shoulder dug into flesh, preventing him from fleeing.

Cutter looked up at the faceless creature hovering inches from him. It leaned in close. If he had been in a more sardonic mood, he may have joked that it was leaning in to kiss him.

It had no eyes, no mouth, no nose—nothing that gave it expression. Its face was simple horizontal slats that reminded Cutter of a hockey mask. His search for any semblance of humanity was fleeting.

A hiss of air sounded from the synth's mask, as if breathing a sigh of relief that Cutter could not. Its metallic faceshield unfolded, revealing a very human face. Wires and circuitry marked what, at first sight, Cutter mistook for a hairline.

"Good to see you again, Jack," it said.

5

"Get away from there!"

"Why?" asked Celia. She kept her cheek pressed against the glass. Warm puffs of breath fogged a halo around her mouth. She blinked, eyes set in wonder, staring at rows of lifeless mannequins that wore the latest trends.

"Because I said so, that's why."

"Why?" Celia asked again.

She was grabbed by the wrist and yanked away from the display window leaving behind an oily impression where her cheek had been.

Celia struggled to keep pace. A pink stroller led the way, carving a path through scattered shoppers. She peeked over the stroller lip at her baby sister, Jessica, sound asleep, thumb inserted.

"When I tell you to do something, I expect you to listen."

Celia knew there was only one thing to say when Mommy got like this.

"Sorry."

She saw her mother's eyes flick down in her direction. A programming subroutine ran a scenario that indicated such a reaction was a human trait that would indicate empathy.

Celia wasn't so sure.

When she met her mother's gaze, Mommy's eyes snapped

forward. Celia crosschecked her internal dicto-thesaurus.

Empathy – the intellectual identification with or vicarious experiencing of feelings, thoughts, or attitudes of another.

She had to trust her internal programming that tried to decipher human behavior into terms she could understand. It provided the only hint into the puzzling actions of humans she had at her disposal.

But empathy didn't seem right.

Mommy never seemed able to understand what she felt. She never could assume, emulate, or otherwise discern Celia's attitude. In fact, Mommy was almost always at a loss over the things Celia said and did, which further confused her.

Celia thought her actions were precise and crystal clear. Her thought patterns and subsequent responses were dictated by logic, a simple mathematical programming language that followed a strict rule-set. Mommy's programming seemed to be derived from something else entirely.

When Celia asked, "Why?" it was because she was curious. It was because she didn't know an answer. In her mind, there was no other reason to ask a question. Her questions were simply part of her learning routine.

Instead of answering them, Mommy's reaction often splintered into even more questions.

Overhead flashing lights interrupted Celia's train of thought. An alarm siren sounded and an automated voice, hauntingly emotionless, broadcasted over the mall PA system.

"Please move to the nearest designated safe zone. This is not a drill."

Mommy paused, looking up at the ceiling, as if she expected to see someone with a microphone hovering over her, issuing the warning. With a sudden jolt, she bent over, thrust her hands into the stroller, and wrapped Jessica under a mountain of blankets. Jessica began to cry at the disturbance, wails matching the pitch of the echoing sirens. With Jessica secured, Mommy put her weight on her front foot and leaned into the stroller handle. Without warning, she froze in place.

Celia cocked her head to a side.

Was Mommy broken?

Mommy slowly turned and looked down at Celia. A strange blank expression was on her face.

"Please move to the nearest designated safe zone. This is not a drill."

Mommy bent down on a knee, placing her hands on Celia's shoulders.

"Celia," she said, her voice taking on a tone Celia seldom heard. Solemn and sincere. She only spoke like this when it was really important.

"Stay," said Mommy.

"Why?"

"Stay here."

"But why?"

Mommy looked at her, struggling to find the exact right words. After a moment, she said, "I am your Mommy and I say so."

Mommy slowly stood up, eyes never leaving Celia. The stare pierced through her, making her feel uncomfortable.

Mommy nodded and as soon as she broke eye contact, she shoved the stroller down the long corridor towards a row of flashing lights marking a designated safe zone.

Celia calculated the distance between Mommy and the door, her travel speed, and approximate time of arrival. She hung her head and quietly followed at a meandering pace to not overtake her mother.

The designated safe zones were makeshift bomb shelters, designed to protect shoppers from a variety of attacks. Decades prior, the Augmentation Wars had crippled business. The mall commission decided that implementing designated safe zones within the mall itself would allow shoppers piece of mind in trying times, allowing them to continue on with business as usual.

Juniper followed the emergency runway lighting. Her hurried steps click-clacked through the quickly emptying mall.

Celia padded several feet behind.

Ahead of them, a man in a denim jacket held the thick steel doors open and frantically waved to Mommy.

Mommy glanced over her shoulder. At the sight of Celia, she turned bright red. Tears welled at the corners of her eyes. She spun on heel, her jacket and scarf whipped around, making her appear large and monstrous.

"God damn it! Just do as I say! Please! Look—I just—good girls obey their mommies, okay? And you are a good girl, aren't you Celia?"

Celia nodded. She was a good girl. Or at least she had always tried to be. Sometimes Mommy got mad at her, but that was never because she had intentionally meant to upset her. Sometimes Mommy just got mad. Like now. Like how she could not understand why her Mommy acted so peculiar—so opposite of everything her internal subroutines indicated as human behavior.

Celia looked at her mother in bewilderment. The only thing she could figure was, like her mother, empathy was a trait she did not possess either.

"Then stay right here. For Mommy. You are a good girl, right?"

"I am a good girl, Mommy."

"Good. Stay."

Mommy held out her open palm, flat. Celia recognized the gesture. When she was first introduced to her new home, Mommy and Daddy had a dog named Bruce. It was the same gesture Mommy used when they were training Bruce to 'stay.' She saw the same apprehension in Mommy's eyes, unsure whether Bruce would remain still, or loyally follow his family. She remembered how angry Mommy got when Bruce didn't obey, and the elation when he finally learned.

Celia's gaze wandered from the open palm to her mother's eyes. They flicked back and forth waiting for the slightest movement. Mommy slowly backed away, straightening from her hunched position, and allowed her open palm to recede until it was at her side.

Celia stayed.

She watched Mommy turn away. She watched her push the stroller to the nearest designated safe zone. She watched Mommy not look back.

"That's a good girl, Celia," Mommy said over her shoulder.

The man in the denim jacket lifted the stroller inside and placed his arm around Mommy's waist, ushering her into the confines of the safe zone.

"*Please move to the nearest designated safe zone. This is not a drill.*"

The steel doors slid closed with a resounding clang that echoed through the empty mall.

Celia was alone.

5

Cutter wracked his brain for signs of recognition. The face was a few years older than his. Blonde eyebrows hinted at their owner's former hair color.

He had arrested many men and a handful of those to which that status no longer applied. In this day of modification and augmentation, appearances changed. The twinky twerp he busted for hack-fraud one day was tomorrow's mod bashing through brick walls ripping vault doors off hinges.

But he had a pretty good eye, even when things weren't readily apparent, and a gut instinct for putting the pieces together.

He knew one thing for certain.

I have never seen this guy before in my life.

He had never seen the crooked yellowing teeth that peeked through a crooked smile, hovering so close that he could see remnants of this morning's breakfast wedged between them. He had never smelled the rancid breath that burned his nostrils, as the metal man violated his personal space. He did not recognize the ice cold blue eyes that stared through him with familiarity he found extremely unwelcome.

A blaster shot rang out.

Cutter tried to steel himself, fighting the urge to flinch, but how could he not? He had been expecting it.

He had been expecting pain too.

But there was none. *Thank God for that.*

He gave himself a quick pat-down, in search of any holes that hadn't been there this morning—a quick inventory of limbs and digits. They were all present and accounted for.

He was whole. No blaster burns, no fresh wounds, and no blood spatter decorated his body. Most surprising was that the synth-man-thing was no longer on top of him.

Roy was at the top of the stair, his gauntlet blaster trained on the synth that now scurried across the floor in search of cover.

"You have the right to remain silent," said Roy, his automated Miranda rights kicking in. "Anything you say…"

Cutter heaved, breathing a sigh of relief. His eyes darted toward the ZeroTwelve on the other side of the landing.

The synth flipped to its feet.

"…can and will be used against you in a court of law. You have the right to an attorney…"

The synth regained its footing and pointed its forearm at Roy. A hunk of metal flipped up and snapped into position—looking like nothing Cutter had seen before.

"Roy! Shut up and take him down!" he shouted.

The synth shot—something—not bullets—at Roy.

They were large and tore apart the bannister when they hit. One clanked into Roy's chest with enough momentum to drive him into the railing, forcing him to find his footing. Another ricocheted off Roy's leg and thudded to the ground near Cutter. It was a metal ring larger than his hand, cut into the shape of a 'U.'

Bullets, plasma bolts, laser beams, and now this—large metal U-rings. Despite the need for full attention on the dilemma unfolding in front of him, his inner voice still quipped: *What will the wonders of technology bear tomorrow?*

A barrage of U-rings flew through the air, hitting Roy, driving him down the stair for cover. The wooden slats creaked under every backward step.

Staying low, Cutter sprinted to his weapon on the far side of the landing.

The synth rotated on its hips, tracking Cutter's movement. It reached out with a forearm, trying to lock on to the sprinting form. Plaster spat at Cutter from the walls as U-rings embedded themselves into it, narrowly missing their intended target. A stray U-ring connected with the ZeroTwelve sending it spinning off the landing.

Cutter dove. His shoulder hit the bannister, forcing him to a stop. He reached out as far as he could and felt the ZeroTwelve land in his palm. He squeezed tight.

He needed to find cover. He needed to get out of the line of sight. But movement on the floor below distracted him.

In the lobby, the six SWAT members poured through the front door, two at a time, shoulder to shoulder. The front two rushed up the stairs. The remaining four took tactical positions, quietly signaling each other for a surprise attack.

At the top of the stairs, Roy fired at the synth, forcing its attention on him. The synth returned fire, toppling the remaining railing, sending it tumbling into the lobby.

Cutter watched as the heavy metal U-rings tore chunks out of the rotten staircase, pockmarking its surface and support struts. Underneath, a beam split in half and fell to the floor.

Two SWAT officers raced to the landing, hopping up the stairs two at a time.

"No, wait!" Cutter shouted.

The officer on the right turned toward the scream. The other didn't have that luxury as he put his foot through a rotten slat and sank down to his thigh. Shock gripped his expression. He reached out for his partner, scuffing his shoulder with a wildly flung arm that landed with enough contact to grab attention. They locked eyes, and in that brief moment, they knew what was coming next.

The staircase collapsed, kicking up a cloud of ancient foul-smelling dust. The two men disappeared into a cloud of chaos.

At the base of the stairs, the two SWAT that had been next in line were buried up to their waists in flying wood and crumbling plaster. The last two that had been guarding the entrance, hurried to the disaster area. They dug through broken two-by-fours and mold encrusted drywall.

The staircase fell out from beneath Roy's feet. His chest hit the landing, while his bulk hung over the edge. The hydraulics in his arms whined, straining to pull his immense weight back onto solid ground.

The synth rounded, for a clear shot at the dangling Black and White.

Cutter raised his weapon, set his sights, and fired.

The blaster bolt sizzled through the air, racing for the back of the unsuspecting synth.

The synth swayed, pivoting with smooth grace, allowing the ZeroTwelve's beam to pass over its shoulder.

How in the hell?

In a fluid motion it kicked off the far corner and spun to face Cutter. It charged, arm raised, the metal contraption on its forearm aimed squarely at him.

The events happened so quickly that Cutter hardly had time to recover. His mind still clung to the notion that he hadn't missed. But he had. And somewhere else his log-jammed mind was still trying to answer the question—how?

Neither questions nor answers were important, at least not right now, with a programmed killer bearing down on him. His instinct kicked adrenaline into overdrive, giving his consciousness the swift kick in the ass it needed.

Cutter raised his weapon. There wasn't time to aim. Barely enough time to squeeze the trigger.

Pain ebbed through his wrist. The shot sailed high, charring an overhead rafter.

Not even close.

He tried to bring his arm back to his body, but discovered a large U-ring had caught his forearm and pinned it to the drywall.

The synth barreled down the landing on a collision course. With his free hand, Cutter desperately tugged at the U-ring to free himself. He felt the flimsy drywall flex as he pulled, but the U-ring would not release its bite.

Heavy footsteps thundered on decaying wood, growing louder with each resounding thud. There had already been too many close calls. He had been lucky far too many times today. He stopped struggling with his pinned wrist, mustering what little dignity he could. He turned to face the synth, resigned to his fate.

It would be over soon.

The synth didn't break stride. "Sorry about the rush reunion, Jack," it said. "Maybe some other time." And darted past Cutter into the darkened hallway, to the room, third story, window farthest left.

Relief wasn't the first thing Cutter felt. In fact, it was far down the list of emotions. The first emotion was sheer and utter bewilderment.

What the hell had just happened?

Roy ran past, snapping Cutter out of his perfunctory daze. Regaining his senses, he turned his efforts to his pinned hand.

Roy ran down the hall in pursuit, slammed his shoulder into the apartment door, and burst through the threshold.

WHAM!

The synth had been waiting and drove a loose piece of rebar straight through Roy's chest. Roy reached for it, but a low thud pinned his right hand to the cinderblock wall. Three more thuds followed, hitting with precision at his ankles and wrist. He was attached to the wall by four deeply embedded U-rings.

Underneath the horizontal slats on his faceshield, the synth sneered at Roy. If Roy could have seen the synth's exposed teeth snarl, an internal thesaurus would have popped up with the word 'Feral' and a brief list of synonyms. 'Feral' would have been cross-referenced with his onboard facial recognition and expression interpretation software, and the words 'aggressive' and 'handle with caution' would have tipped off the otherwise clueless Black and White that he might be running headfirst into a trap.

With Roy immobilized, the synth turned to the window and pulled the daisy-laden curtain aside.

Benjamin Foster was still at it.

Banners waved and flashbulbs blinked. The crowd roared with seemingly unending enthusiasm. Foster played to the crowd, and they ate it up.

"What started out as a social experiment," Foster boomed over the loudspeaker, "has proved too invaluable to keep from the community at large."

A plasma rifle unfolded from the synth's back and craned over its shoulder. A scope met its eye.

Damn stupid ring-thing! Give me back my hand, Cutter thought. His wrist was red and swollen from repeated attempts to pull his hand through it. "Stupid, piece of…" A long string of unintelligible gibberish finished Cutter's thought.

He placed a foot against the wall, using it as leverage, and pulled as hard as he could.

The U-ring didn't budge.

He made up his mind. Either this damn U-ring was going to give, or his wrist was. Either way, he'd be free.

He interlocked his fingers, giving support to his bruised wrist, and placed both legs on the wall. He straightened his legs with all his might. His face burned red-hot, as he gritted his teeth and grunted in agony.

The entire force of his efforts were focused on a single

point—his wrist. He twisted his flesh against the metal restraint, using the bones in his forearm as a lever to pry the U-ring out of the wall. He pictured the claw end of a hammer in his mind, tough rigid stainless steel plucking a stubborn nail from a stud, but other thoughts kept creeping in—a living hammer with nerve endings, made of porous material, too fragile for its intended job.

When positive visualization began to fail, he simply pictured snapping his wrist in two over the steel ring—and pulled harder.

He didn't care how the job got done. All that mattered was that he succeeded.

He held his breath. Wrist or ring—with enough force, he'd be free soon.

The U-ring turned slightly.

Cutter heard the sound of individual splinters snapping in slow succession. The sound of a snow laden branch that held more than it could bear.

He let out a fierce scream, prepping himself, and channeled all of his resolve into a short, intense burst of strength.

Cutter fell to the floor, landing on his tailbone.

He was free.

The metal U-ring clanged next to him. He rubbed his wrist. Pain pulsed through it, but it was still attached. He picked up his ZeroTwelve. His wrist held the weight of the weapon with some effort, but he would be fine—at least good enough.

He ran down the hall and into the room, third story, window farthest left, just in time to be blinded by a large blue-green pulse that surged out the window.

"Happiness is no longer for the rich. It is now—" The shot tore through Benjamin Foster. His final words "for everyone" rang through the square with a metallic tinge.

The blue-green bolt hit with such force that Foster's body

exploded outward. Torn shreds of wardrobe, flesh, and smile rained on expressions of terror and surprise in the crowd.

The crowd fled from the epicenter of the explosion like ripples in a small pond, only to rebound off the edges, pinned in by the small confines of M.J. Square.

Several turned back, watching in horror, as others were pelted with shrapnel. A hawk-eyed supporter caught a glimpse of shiny reflection. The explosion tossed bits of scrap metal and circuitry.

At the window, the synth spun responding to Cutter's presence. As the plasma rifle folded into place on its back, four U-rings sailed at Cutter in loose formation.

He dove headfirst through the middle. One flew so close that he heard the whisper of air as it whipped past. That was why the Academy always aimed for center mass. Get too cheeky with placement and the intended target had more options for survival. And even more for counterattack.

Cutter rolled to his feet.

Before he could draw a bead, the synth had already fled through the open window.

Cutter sprinted to the window. He jumped on the sill, grabbing the frame with his left hand and swung onto the ledge to give chase. He stopped short, halfway out the window.

There was no ledge, no awning, nothing to support his weight. He twisted, trying to hold on to the sill, as he fell. His legs pumped, frantically windmilling for traction. He caught the sill with his hand, as his weight tried to yank his shoulder out of socket. But he had managed to stay his fall.

He looked down. The only available footing was scattered divots here and there where mortar had fallen apart.

The crowd below caught sight of his acrobatics. Someone

pointed at him. "The shot came from up there."

Yes. Yes, it had.

He clambered back inside and fell to the floor. He wasn't built for this. He lay on the ground heaving, trying to catch his breath.

The sound of concrete grinding and servos whining assaulted his ears. Seconds later, Roy freed his right arm, and methodically removed the remaining U-rings holding him prisoner.

"Where were you Roy? I could've used the backup."

"I was right here," said Roy, removing the last U-ring from his ankle.

Exhausted, Cutter rolled onto his side, unable to dish a snarky comeback.

"He headed west. Hurry."

Roy bolted out of the room so quickly that his response to the affirmative was almost inaudible by the time it reached Cutter.

Roy would plot the most direct route to intercept the synth. If that was all it took, Cutter could count on Roy and Roy alone to apprehend the assassin. But he knew better. This synth, this man, this whatever it was—wouldn't make it easy for them.

Cutter went to the window.

"There he is!" someone in the crowd shouted.

Yeah, yeah. You got the wrong idiot, idiot, Cutter thought, as he dismissively waved to the crowd.

From his vantage, he made out the chaos that the synth had created. A single black loafer smoldered on the stage. From what Cutter could tell, the rest of the mayor was scattered in pieces across the majority of M.J. Square.

Well, shit.

Any way you sliced it, this was going to look terrible in his forthcoming report.

A glint of something buried in the scattering crowd caught his eye. He tilted his head, trying to get a better glimpse of the object, but the shine twisted, rotating rays in the late afternoon sun. His eyes skipped to another object that was catching a high-shine. And another. Dots of light peppered the crowd like seashells on a beach in the early morning.

What should have been on his mind was the synth-man-thing-whatever it was—and apprehending it before it could get away.

But he was distracted by a more pressing question.

Mayor Benjamin Foster was a synth?

WORLDS COLLIDE

"A hole in the heart
Of our Mother, we made
Inverted the playgrounds
Where scientists played
The future was bright
Gazing upon stars
By ignoring the present
We created new scars"

—Verse 1 of Swiss Children's Nursery Rhyme
Coined after the events of the Hadron disaster

1

A dull drone reverberated off the concrete. Trash stirred in the gutter shaking in anticipation of some unseen force. A streak of flashing red and blue zipped past kicking a discarded candy wrapper into a rising frenzy.

As the droning echo faded, locomotion dissipated leaving the wrapper to the wind. It drifted from side to side casually losing altitude. A brief updraft teased the wrapper with flight before returning it back to its place in the gutter.

Three cambots streaked past, hovering a few meters above the sidewalk. Tiny lights flashed in red and blue on either side. A small high-powered spotlight waggled back and forth, cutting through daylight, as a large camera eye lens scoured the streets. The one-eyed orbs spread in loose formation, zeroing in on their target.

A U-ring knocked one out of the sky.

Cutter checked a holo-display projecting from his sleeve. Three cyan rings—now two—pinpointed a red blip on the display, herding it towards a yellow triangle.

The synth's zig-zagging through the street did its job, throwing Roy off the trail. However, its haphazard path had allowed Cutter to catch up.

"Just stay on him!" Cutter yelled into his com.

A cambot bleeped in response.

Another cyan ring fizzled on Cutter's display. Not good. If the last cambot went down, that would be game over. The synth would be long gone by the time anyone with authority showed up.

The yellow triangle bee-lined on a collision course with the red blip.

Cutter ducked under an automated arm that stacked an automobile in a vertical parking structure and cut through the Oakridge Mall parking lot. He weaved between rows of cars, checking his wrist display, making sure he was on target.

If his hunches were worth a damn, the synth was going to cut through the lot, perhaps even into the mall to ditch the last cambot. If Cutter hurried he could cut off the synth before it could get away.

When the icons drew so close that the encounter of the real thing was inevitable, Cutter pressed his back flat against a blind corner. The mall towered above him, a glass and steel monument to capitalism. He held his weapon at the ready, taking a deep breath. The clanking pattern of footsteps drew ever closer. Procedure mandated that he issue a warning first—give the technoperp a head's up and the opportunity to yield. But that was only procedure.

Cutter spun around the corner and fired.

Like before, the synth moved out of the path of the beam. Unlike the previous encounter, in doing so it slammed against the wall with a horrific screech of metal against brick, narrowly avoiding the red stream of superheated particles.

Cutter had caught him off guard, but not helpless. Too bad.

The synth's U-ring launcher snapped into place on its forearm. Cutter laid down a steady stream of beam blasts.

The synth stumbled, twisted sideways, and barreled through

a side door into the massive mall structure.

Shit.

Inside the corridor, a freckle-faced security guard lifted a Dixie cup to his nose. He inhaled deeply, letting the hazelnut aroma permeate his nostrils. Wisps of steam swirled off the wax paper cup. A chubby hand brushed shaggy orange hair from his eyes. He pulled tight on a door latch that led to the main shopping concourse, checking to make sure he was alone in the narrow hallway. It was secure.

His gaze drifted up to a ceiling towering three stories above his head. Exposed pipes and electrical lines hugged a poorly constructed soffit. Despite the corridor's cramped five foot width, the triple high ceilings made his private little break room seem more spacious than it actually was.

He raised the cup to his mouth, almost tasting the caffeine when the door at the far end of the corridor swung open blinding him with daylight.

In the glare he made out the silhouetted form of a man.

"Hey!" the young security guard shouted. He raised an arm and pointed toward the door. "You aren't allowed in here. You'll have to go around to the front."

The figure ran at him on an unfaltering course.

The door smacked the wall, flung open a second time and another silhouette ran in, close behind the first. This one had a pistol in his hand.

The cup of coffee bounced off linoleum as the security guard reached for the weapon in his holster. The safety strap held it in place. He looked down, panicked. With both hands he pushed the strap off the weapon. Shaking, he brought the sight level to his eye.

"Stop! Or I'll shoot!"

"Get out of the way!" Cutter shouted.

Synthetic laughter echoed down the narrow corridor. Shards of metal twisted away from the synth's body like a locust swarm of balisongs. Razor sharp blades locked into place. Low powered shots thundered and impotently bounced off the synth's frame. Fear registered in the security guard's eyes. The synth plowed through him at full velocity with the force of a freight train. Blood and guts decorated this private sanctuary to routine.

The synth barreled through the double doors into the main concourse.

Cutter ran through the bloody chaos with his face buried in his sleeve, covering his nose from the copper stench. As he sprinted into the mall, the scent gave way to another—a startling mixture of body odor, deodorizer spray, and the faint hint of pine.

Sirens sounded, lights flashed, and an automated recording assaulted Cutter's ears. Despite the distraction, Cutter was grateful for their function. The mall was deserted of potential victims.

Without breaking stride, he quickly scanned the layout. The right dead-ended into a Macy's. Not a whole lot of options in that direction. The left forked into a hub around a fountain.

Cutter ran toward the fountain, catching sight of the metal skeleton in full sprint. It hugged the left wall, disappearing down a corridor.

About time he caught a break, Cutter thought. The synth made a wrong turn. Dead end, sucker.

The corridor led to an abandoned department store. A once universally known brand that had either gone under or been assimilated into an equally, and now larger, department store. What was once the showpiece of that end of Oakridge Mall was now walls of white plywood and boarded up windows. Signs hung, congratulating shoppers for their support over almost a century, but sadly it was time to move on. Move on to what, Cutter had no idea.

Cutter slowed to a fast walk, holding his ZeroTwelve at the ready. Maybe there was time for procedure after all. He strained to hear metal footsteps, but was only deafened by the blaring siren and automated voice that constantly reminded him that this was not a drill.

He poked his head around the corner, taking careful bead on the synth. The synth stood in the center of the corridor. Apparently, it realized its mistake too.

"On the ground now," Cutter shouted.

At the sight of Cutter, the synth ran straight to the nearest wall and bounded up a support column to the second level.

Cutter stopped short at the base of the column and looked up, watching the synth scamper over a second story bannister.

"Fuck me."

2

"June?!" a voice echoed through the tin can.

Juniper held Jessica tight to her bosom, rocking back and forth. She hummed lightly, almost without thought. The sound soothed her as much as it did the infant cradled in her arms.

"June," the voice echoed again. A hand found her shoulder. She craned her neck in the direction of the touch, keeping her back to it, protecting her newborn.

"June, I'm so glad you're safe." Charles wrapped his arms around his wife and newborn. She reciprocated his warmth and smiled at the gesture. "Is everything okay?" he asked.

"The baby and I are fine."

"Where's Celia?"

Juniper looked at her feet, averting his gaze.

Lizard-like, Charles's head made small movements from side to side. His tongue poked through his lips at the left corner of his mouth. He looked from Juniper to Jessica, to the pink stroller parked in front of her, to the large bag stashed underneath overflowing with the baby's needs. He turned around, scanning the small container stuffed with shoppers. Celia was nowhere to be found.

He turned back to Juniper, searching for answers in her expression—answers he already knew to a question he asked anyway. "You didn't?"

Juniper held her gaze on the floor. That was confirmation enough.

He shouldered past his wife and headed toward a nearby hatch. He suddenly stopped when he felt the soft caress of her hand on his.

"Charles…" she whispered. He looked back at her. She pleaded softly, "Don't."

His lower lip hung slightly open. He searched her face for signs of recognition. Who was this woman that stood before him, that held his child in her arms? Was this the same person he had married? The same woman he had fallen in love with? What happened in the course of their relationship that created this— this thing that he could not stomach looking at?

He snapped his hand from her grasp, shrugging it off, and pushed toward the designated safe zone wall. He plowed through a semi-circle of shoppers that seemed to pay no mind to their current encapsulated predicament. A blonde woman, perhaps mid-twenties, held a teal top in outstretched arms, flipping it around on display for another twenty-something to gander at. Charles barreled between them, nearly knocking over a brunette.

The blonde's brow furrowed, jaw fell to the floor, but the words, "How rude," couldn't find their way out in time. Charles was on a mission. He reached an emergency hatch and looked out the small porthole window bolted dead center.

Outside the confines of the safe zone, he saw Celia standing in the middle of the empty mall corridor. Her back was to him, an easy target to spot in the otherwise empty mall concourse.

"Celia!" Charles shouted. She didn't move. The walls were soundproofed, a fact that Charles already knew, but he yelled anyway, "Celia!" He tugged on the emergency release handle. It rattled, stuck in place.

The jammed lever took him by surprise. There was nothing wrong with the lever as far as he could tell. He placed both hands firmly on it, leaned forward for extra purchase, and yanked. It didn't budge. He cocked his head at an angle and shook the like a vending machine that had stolen his last dollar. Nothing. When brute force proved unsuccessful, he double-checked the graphical release instructions painted on the side of the door, a large swooping red arrow accompanied by minimal text: *Turn and Push*. Again, he tried to twist the lever in the direction indicated, but it held firm.

His mind juggled two thoughts simultaneously, both equally alarming. Celia was by herself outside the safety of the designated safe zone—at the same time several hundred shoppers were shoved into this sardine can of protection with an inoperable escape hatch, its lever jammed into a locked position.

A hand grabbed his. He whirled to face Juniper, feeling his temperature boiling red-hot. He was already shouting at the top of his lungs, "How could you do this?! How could you leave her out there?!"

But it wasn't Juniper.

A man in a denim jacket snapped his hand away from Charles like he had touched something he didn't expect to be scalding. The man put his hands up defensively. "Hey buddy, don't be getting any crazy ideas, okay?"

Charles cocked his head back. He felt the need to vent, to punch something, but this guy clearly was not his intended target.

Over the man's shoulder he could see Juniper. They locked eyes only long enough for her to look away. Even at this distance, he could see her eyes were puffy, swollen pink, fighting tears.

She delicately inserted her finger into Jessica's mouth, allowing the baby to suckle. He saw her whisper something to their child. Something quiet, under her breath. He watched her lips move, forming words, something softly to reassure the newborn, perhaps even herself. He mouthed the movement, sounding out the words.

In a soft tone to their sleeping child, Juniper whispered, "It's for the best."

3

Cutter bounded up the stairs three at a time. Doubling back on itself, the staircase continued back and forth to the upper levels of the mall.

Breaths came in puffs. Cutter reminded himself, *in through the nose, out through the mouth.* The chase had left him winded, but the stairs were pure torture.

At the switchback, Cutter grabbed the handrail and whipped around a hairpin turn. Faster than thought could register, he flung himself up the next tier of stairs. For reasons unknown, he pictured a captain of some titanic ship shouting, "Full astern!" at a panicking helmsman. Captain and crew stared into the distance, eyes bugged out of their heads, unable to stop the massive vessel as an iceberg loomed ahead with certain horrific doom.

At the top of the second floor landing, the synth stood with its plasma rifle craned over a shoulder, aiming down the narrow stairwell.

Blue-green light flashed.

Cutter's speed left him in precarious position as he tried to full stop in midair. His momentum clearly had a mind to get him killed, and was doing a damn fine job of it.

In flight, he squatted into a sitting position, franticly trying to dissipate his forward thrust. His left foot was three steps ahead of the rest of his body, right tucked under his buttocks. He leaned back, trying to put on the airbrakes. Unfortunately, those were not standard issue on this make and model.

He tumbled backwards, left arm raised over his head, a self-conscious effort to protect it from the fall. His right arm shot out at the solid floor behind him; all his weight rested on that monopod of right arm desperately trying to return him safely to terra firma, as a rushing orb of aquamarine death pulsed down the stairwell.

His back crunched on the corner of the second stair pinging agony down each vertebra along his spine in painful succession. With a thud his shoulders hit the switchback, his head pivoted at an awkward angle, and the rest of his body flew ass over teacups.

He collapsed face down, flat against the switchback floor. The blue-green pulse cratered into the wall inches above his head, spewing stucco into his face and hair.

He tried to think through a cloudy haze of thought. What was he doing here again? But only one word came to mind.

"Christ!"

Cutter picked his fatigued body off the ground and hauled

himself up the middle tier of stairs. His right leg dragged behind him. The fall had twisted something. The extent of the injury wasn't clear. What was clear was that it hurt like Hell.

He reached the second floor landing, almost laughing as he painfully raised his ZeroTwelve. There was something funny about being greeted by a cybernetic crotch dangling from an upper balcony. Some thirty yards away, the synth stood on a handrail, top half hidden by ceiling, as it pulled itself up and disappeared onto the third level.

Cutter doubled back into the stairwell.

Tile shattered beneath a metal pronged foot. As quickly as the destruction occurred, the destructor moved on, leaving behind a trail of spider web fractures in red tile.

High above the food court, a canvas awning provided airy ambiance to the interior below, protecting those normally seated beneath from undesirable weather. Sunshine filtered through a sizeable gap between canvas and mall ceiling, flooding the massive dome with soft light.

The synth sprinted towards the opening, closing quickly. Cutter fought his way up the stairs to the third floor. The synth leaped for the opening—for escape—for freedom, when a metal hand grabbed his foot and whiplashed him to the floor.

"You have the right to remain silent," said Roy, training his forearm blaster on the synth. "Anything you say—"

The synth punched Roy in the face, knocking him backward.

A winded Cutter reached the top of the stairwell. Level three—he had made it. And just in time. Roy was getting the piss knocked out of him.

Roy blocked a punch meant for his head with his forearm, saving himself from permanent damage, but sacrificing his forearm blaster in the process.

Cutter fired. Again, the synth's sixth sense kicked in and it moved behind Roy, keeping the Black and White in direct line of fire, allowing the shots to go wide.

Smart, Cutter thought. He was using Roy as cover. *That's fine. We can play.*

Cutter fired four rounds. Once again, the synth moved, keeping Roy between Cutter and itself. Only this time, it didn't help.

The first shot ricocheted violently off Roy's shoulder. The second hit Roy at mid arm, splitting a hydraulic tube (the synth equivalent of triceps). The last two shots punched a hole clean through Roy's back. These two shots burst through Roy's chest and sizzled through the technoperp's shielding on the other side.

The synth looked at Cutter for only the briefest of seconds. Crucial information. It had hesitated.

Cutter smirked. *There's that human brain.*

The reaction time to adjust to new input was slow—well, slower than a real synth. That was the problem with mods. Their human parts were always going to be their downfall. Subduing a mod was more or less about exploiting its humanity. Synths had a different set of problems—like inflection, for starters—but a real synth would have readjusted to the new variables immediately. It took this "synth" an extra millisecond or two to realize that the cover he thought so certain was nonexistent.

Cutter fired a steady stream of blasts without thought or hesitation. The blasts tore clean through Roy, ripping his partner to shreds. Little did that matter. Without cover, the peppering blaster fire was ripping the synth to shreds as well.

The differences between synth and mod were becoming glaringly obvious.

Roy didn't falter. The technoperp did.

It didn't matter how many times Cutter sent superheated particles through Roy, how much destruction it caused, how much it interfered with his ability to do his job, Roy always put his objective first. And his current objective was the apprehension of the steel encased assassin.

The synth pushed Roy forward, his living shield proving ineffectual. He rolled back, frantically scouring side to side to for cover, indecision quickly adding up to seconds he didn't have.

4

Distant noises echoed down the long corridor. Celia's ears perked at the sounds. Despite her curiosity, she did not dare move toward them. She was a good girl.

Her internal audio monitors tried to place the rhythmic clanking. Her HUD came back with images of men working sledgehammers, pounding spikes into railroad track. As the pace increased, images of pots and pans swatted together filled her internal viewscreen. They morphed, quickly realigning themselves into an image of chain-link fencing unrolled and nail-gunned to rows of metal posts.

A high pitch shriek tore through the air. Celia looked up to the upper balcony. In the smudged reflections on the ceiling she could make out movement. Another high pitch shriek rang out. A red beam sparked off the railing on the balcony directly across the opening overhead.

Sounds of metal battle crept closer, only maintaining a safe distance vertically, three floors above her head. She tracked the movement best she could, tinging clashes drawing ever closer, the distorted reflection of smudges on the ceiling pinpointing an approximate location.

A loud crunch, not of skin, or metal, but of plaster thundered above her. A crescendo of steel maracas that failed to find a rhythmic beat. Again, the thundering crunch repeated. Nuggets of spackle floated down in front of her, followed by heavier bits of debris that fell to her feet too fast to register exact contents. She bent down and picked up a brownish chunk. Rubbed her thumb and forefinger together. The brittle object crumbled between her fingers. Puzzled, she looked up at the source.

Overhead, a silvery metal man burst through a plaster guardrail, scattering white chunks of used-to-be railing. Another metal man, a dark black skeleton with horizontal slats across its face, was ramming the first off the ledge. The silvery metal man fell, reached out, and grabbed onto the dark skeleton's neck. They lost balance, tumbled, and went over.

Celia watched unflinching—she was a good girl—as the twisted forms of dark metal and silvery chrome plummeted toward her.

They whiplashed to a full stop in midair. The chrome man held onto the ledge with the dark metal skeleton dangling from its foot.

5

Charles rattled the door handle.

"We have to do something," said Charles. "We can't leave her out there."

The man in a denim jacket nervously fidgeted, as Charles tugged on the escape hatch lever. He saw the commotion outside—a fight ensuing between two synths and another man in a leather jacket with a high powered pulse pistol. And, of course, Celia out there by herself.

He saw the fight raging three stories up, aligning itself with the little girl on the concourse far below—a little girl that for whatever reason refused to move.

He also saw all the reasons to stay safe and sound inside the designated safe zone. All the reasons not to help.

Frustrated, Charles kicked the lever. It had occurred to him that the lever might not even be broken. The defiant erection protruding from the escape hatch may have simply been for show. What's higher liability for a mall—having an escape hatch that doesn't work or one that does, allowing any anxiety ridden claustrophobe the ability to pop the hatch in the middle of an attack exposing everyone inside to quick searing death?

He threw his shoulder into the hatch's porthole window. His efforts were as impotent as the lever, but in his mind, they were more than show. They had to be. His instinct did not heed to his rational mind. No, it was the other way around.

He said it before. He had to do something. He could not leave her out there. He turned to the man in a denim jacket. "Well, what are you waiting for?! Help me, God damn it!"

6

Cutter ran to the railing and looked down, sweeping his weapon across the faux mahogany and aiming at those dangling below.

Roy clung to the ledge, his right hand clasped around a bent railing strut. His left hand pushed at the synth that was reaching up, trying to pull itself up and over his body.

At the sight of Cutter on the overhead ledge, the synth slinked into a low position. It let go of Roy's midsection and slid to his foot letting its weight dangle from the end of the Black and White.

Cutter put his eye to the sight and steadied his breathing. A whole lot of Roy blocked his shot. If only he could get a clear line of sight, pop the technoperp in the head, this whole mess would be over.

Cutter moved to his right to get a wider angle. The assassin pulled himself up and monkeyed behind Roy. Cutter fired through Roy. Red sparks rained off the assassin on the other side. Its head peeked out from behind Roy.

Didn't like that, did ya?

Without hesitation, Cutter fired at its exposed head.

The assassin ducked behind, causing Roy to swing.

This was Cutter's chance.

He ran across the balcony, aiming down. Any second—his moment would appear. He slid his sweaty finger inside the trigger guard. There would be one chance.

As he ran past, the synth pulled itself up, reaching for the balcony and solid ground.

Roy's head, arm, foot—the assassin's hand and head all fell into perfect alignment.

And something else.

Something below them.

Cutter backed off the trigger.

In the middle of the mall concourse, directly below the dangling metal skeletons, was a small dark haired girl. She couldn't have been more than six years old.

What in the hell was she doing here?

Cutter scanned the mall for signs of her parents, friends, anyone that could lay claim to this little girl and get her out of the way. Except for her presence, the mall was a ghost town.

He looked down, scanning for the nearest designated safe zone. He found the steel doors. They were shut tight. To the left, a glimmer of frantic motion caught his eye. Through a porthole window on the side hatch, he saw several men tugging on a lever attached to the door.

This was not good.

He waved his arm in a large sweeping motion at the little girl. "Get the hell away from there!"

The dangling synth followed Cutter's gaze, discovering the dark haired girl below. It was a curious sight. She looked up at them with big brown eyes, head tilted to a side, saying nothing. A shudder caused him to almost lose his grip. The Black and White he clung to was struggling to pull itself up.

"Move!" Cutter yelled.

The assassin clambered up the back side of Roy, using blaster scars, divots, and battle damage as hand holds. He reached for the ledge.

The weight proved too great for Roy. The Black and White's hand slid down the bent railing strut onto the crumbling concrete ledge. The assassin's hand covered Roy's, also grasping for purchase on the slick polished floor, preventing Roy from attaining a better handhold.

The non-skid on the tips of Roy's fingers grated across the surface under the weight of the two heavy metal machines.

They went over.

Cutter turned from the girl to the noise.

Shit shit shit.

He glanced at the stairwell, thirty yards behind. "Fuck me."

And ran for it.

Roy and the synth plummeted on a collision course with the girl below, fighting in mid-air, exchanging blows the entire way. The synth blocked a punch and yanked Roy forward, managing to rotate his body and climb on top. He shoved an elbow into

Roy's face as gravity hurled them toward the girl below.

They collided with a cracking thud, kicking up a white cloud of debris that cloaked everything from the second story down. As the cloud settled, a single silhouette stood in the dissipating dust.

It was Celia.

She hadn't moved. Not a single step.

She was a good girl.

She giddily bounced up and down, applauding the show. "Again, again!" she cheered.

White dust swirled, departing. On the floor in front of her, a tangle of silver and black was twisted together. A faint whine barely audible under the pitter patter of falling debris cried out to her.

She smiled, bouncing in place. Her claps echoed down the long corridor. Her weight shifted forward, as she raised a knee, about to take a step. She paused and looked down at the toe of her pink Converse kissing the red tile—and firmly stomped it flat to the floor.

The whine grew louder. Parts moved, black and silver alike. A smell lit up her olfactory sensor: the stench of rotten cabbage mixed with a hint of burnt rubber.

From the crater rose a black skeleton. Metal creaked. Electricity hissed and sparked from a shoulder that was carried low. With a clumsy step, it staggered out of the shallow divot and suddenly stopped to look down at its leg.

Celia beamed. She had just done the same thing.

Maybe he was a good boy too!

A silver hand clung to its ankle.

A haunting reverberation oscillated from the dark upright figure. Celia raised a brow.

"Just won't quit, will ya?" it said to its foot.

With unexpected speed, it stomped.

Celia's jaw dropped. *Something moved!*

The debris had averted the powerful crushing stomp. Not only did it move, but it was rising up out of the rubble, and now stood before her.

Another man of metal had risen from the crater. *This one did not look so good*, she thought. It was pock-marked with blaster fire. Golden sparks hissed and sizzled. Pieces fell from it as it circled with a funny twitch in its step.

The dark one charged the newly risen silver man. Lowering a shoulder into its chest, the dark man drove the silver one toward her. The silver man's heels dug trenches across the floor.

She looked down at her feet. She was getting good at this whole "Stay" thing.

Dark limbs flailed, obscured by the silver man closing in on her. It rocked back, nearly clipping her.

She reached out and touched a sliding piston on the silver man's back. The oiled metal disappeared inside a metal tube. She giggled. The silver man twisted, looking over its shoulder at her.

"Hi!" She waved.

Its head jostled—a nod, perhaps. Very polite. However, the dark man was not as friendly. It punched her new friend upside the head while he was distracted. Both fell toward her.

The silver man bent over backwards, an inverted arch support. The move forced her to crunch down into a ducking position. No matter, her feet were still in place. *But still, that was rude.*

With intense curiosity, she peeked out and looked at the dark man pounding a torrent of fists against her new silver friend.

"What are you doing?" she asked quizzically.

She had never seen men, or even men made of metal, act

in such peculiar manner. They were—playing? Was it a game of some sort?

"I like playing games," she said.

She startled, as the silver man twisted to its left and tossed the other across the floor, then rose to its feet.

She reached out and tugged on its arm. "What's your name?"

The silver man looked down at her, head spasmodically jerking from side to side.

"Roy," it said after a beat.

"I'm Cel—"

He fell into her. She swayed, keeping her balance and thankfully her footing too. *Mommy would be so proud.*

The dark one had jumped onto Roy and wrapped its legs around his chest, forcing him to bear its full weight. It pushed Roy's face away with the flat of its palm, grabbed a thin hydraulic tube supporting Roy's shoulder like a collar bone, and yanked. His shoulder sprayed coffee-colored liquid that stunk like rotting cabbage. He pushed at it with both hands, trying to shake off the metal man pulling him apart. He took a stray step backward, encroaching on what little space was left between them.

The dark man grabbed Roy by the wrist and stood straight off his body, perpendicular to the floor. With brute strength it ripped Roy's arm clean out of its socket. The dark man tumbled to the floor, and skidded back a few yards before recovering its footing and the trophy in its hand.

Roy stepped forward, circling slightly to the left, staying between the dark man and Celia.

Celia's right hand drifted to her left arm, clasping around her fleshy bicep. She tugged on it.

"My arm doesn't do that," she said.

Wielding Roy's busted arm over its head like a club, the dark man charged.

Roy dodged the first wild swing of his own arm. The arm whirled, snapping back for a rebounding second swing. From the angle and speed, he calculated that he could avoid the attack—but Celia could not. The broken club-arm hissed through the air. He held his ground, absorbing the full brunt of the attack. The dark man lowered a shoulder, drawing back for a third strike.

Just as Roy had hoped.

As the club-arm came down, Roy grabbed the dark skeleton by the wrist, whipped him forward, using their momentum to flip them both backward into the air.

Celia looked up, her eyes stapled open and glowing, lower lip dangling, as Roy and the synth sailed upside down over her head. She craned her neck in a hundred and eighty degree arc, watching until they slammed down into the tile on the other side of her.

Before Roy could stand, he was swept off his feet.

The dark man held Roy by the wrist and ankle and lifted him off the ground. One-armed, Roy kicked out with his free leg, but was a puppet, strings being pulled by an assassin.

"Just—give—up!" said the dark skeleton.

Like ringing a gong, he swung Roy into the steel reinforced doors of the designated safe zone.

Inside the designated safe zone, the wall leaped in at Charles with a reverberating thud.

"That's not good," said the man in a denim jacket.

Charles shot him a look. *No fucking shit.*

After all the pleading for help, the man now sidled up next to Charles and grasped the lever. "On three. Ready?"

Asshole, Charles thought.

They counted to three and heaved together. Charles wasn't

surprised when it didn't budge.

Another thud pounded somewhere to their left. The wall bulged inward, eating up valuable real estate.

Sweat poured from the other man's forehead in dirty rivulets, as they yanked on the lever together. "We gotta get out of here, man."

Charles shook his head. There was nothing to say.

Big man, unable to help a stranded girl, but now that your safety doesn't seem quite so safe—NOW, you're ready to help.

A tiny projectile sailed across Charles's field of view, pinging off the hatch. He picked it up: a tiny nub of metal. Grinding sounds and low pops were followed by another barrage of projectiles. He looked up at the safe zone structure for its source.

And saw the problem.

His worst fears were coming to fruition. Like the lever, the designated safe zone wasn't designed for anything other than show. When push came to shove, it crumbled.

Another thud shook the container.

The ceiling sagged above their heads. Rivets rocketed out of place under the immense load. The weight of the upper levels squashed a support beam, revealing flimsy aluminum innards.

Anger coursed through his body. He didn't have time to distinguish it from what he felt for Juniper, or Celia, the situation, the shoddy workmanship, the contractor—no doubt sunbathing on some tropical island paradise. His anger coalesced into a single thought, one big ball of rage blurring his vision red.

He looked at his palm—at the shiny bent rivet.

This was useless.

He threw it at the hatch, turned, and headed deeper into the safe zone.

"Hey man, where are you going?" the man in the denim

jacket pleaded.

To my wife and child, that's where.

He grabbed Charles by the wrist. "You aren't going to leave, are you? We gotta get out of here!" His temperament had gone from ice cold to sweaty panic, verging on irrational. Charles shook off the man's hand. The danger had the reversed effect on him.

"Yes. Yes, we do," he said, and walked deeper into the safe zone without looking back.

Another thud shook the container. Fine particle debris sifted through cracks in the ceiling, creating dust waterfalls, pouring on those below.

Juniper coughed into her fist and turned her head away from Jessica. As the coughing fit subsided, she covered the infant in a pink blanket and gently stroked her head.

"Everything's going to be okay," she cooed. "Mommy's got you."

Despite her words, she wasn't so sure. Her casual *oh this is just another drill* attitude had vanished. People were pushing and shoving, herding toward the doors and walls that confined them. Others huddled under support beams, watching in horror as the ceiling jerked towards them, locked inside a human trash compactor.

Juniper couldn't fight the threshing, elbow-tossing, mosh pit—not with Jessica to tend to. She stood exposed, in the middle of the safe zone, the ceiling dipping low several feet from her. If it got any lower she would be forced to crawl. She debated moving, debated pushing through the crowd for an exit—it wasn't much of a choice—she *had to move*—for her safety and the safety of Jessica.

A voice called her name.

She turned toward the sound. It was Charles. And he still looked mad, she thought.

"What's happening?" she asked. It was more than a question. She wasn't looking for the answer, rather an action. *What do we do?*

Charles loaded the stroller with the belongings that had spilled out of Jessica's carry-all. He grabbed Juniper by her elbow, and yanked her forward with enough force that she almost fell. "We have to move. The roof is going to cave in."

"But this is a safe zone."

"Not anymore."

Charles barreled through frenzied shoppers, pushing them aside, using the stroller as a makeshift cow-catcher. He dragged Juniper by the arm at a clipped pace. "Come on. The escape hatch is sealed shut."

"What? What do you mean sealed shut?"

"I don't think it was meant to be opened."

Not meant to be opened?

She didn't have time to ask as she was yanked deeper into the safe zone.

"We have to find a safe place *inside* here," said Charles.

He pulled them through the shrinking confines. Juniper's head bobbed, watching those well aware of their predicament scramble for safety.

A violent shudder nearly rocked her off her feet. Daylight blasted in from the wall hugging the steel entrance doors. People flocked toward the opening, grasping at jagged metal edges that looked like something ripped open by an oversized novelty can-opener.

The ceiling crashed to the floor where Juniper had been standing moments ago.

Charles placed his hand on a vertical steel red I-Beam. "We'll be safe here."

She had always found Charles's confidence reassuring. His ability to make snap decisions on the fly helped calm her nerves. How the solution to any problem always came to him with ease, without hesitation or need for deliberation.

If she hadn't been looking at him, she would have felt secure. Safe.

But his eyes betrayed him. Charles made deliberate eye contact, holding his gaze for an exaggerated moment. His wide open eyes, were locked on her with self-conscious effort, trying to prove there was truth behind his words. A truth he hoped for, but could not actually fathom.

She knew her husband too well to be fooled. The simple fact that he felt obligated to reinforce his words with anything more than sheer confidence drained hers. His guise of certainty sent shivers down her spine.

They weren't going to find safety—in here, or anywhere.

Hands reached out through a hole that had formed where the metal wall buckled over on top of itself. A horizontal crease scarred the metal, six feet across, but not much taller than a fist. Hands shook, stretched, and reached for an escape from the fate of those they were still attached to.

Roy hit the wall, inches from desperate reaching flesh, nearly smashing hands flat. Something or someone pressed his busted metal face flush against the steel door. Roy twisted violently, trying to escape its clutches. Sparks flew from his shoulder, and oil collected in puddles beneath him. Servos strained as he reached for the metallic fingers digging into his cheek hydraulics and pushing into an eye socket. And then they were gone. Moved of their own cognizance. Without the support, his dead weight collapsed to the floor.

Roy tried to drag himself away with his good, and only arm, but the toll of the fight and the gunfire left him helpless.

"Here, let me help you with that." The dark skeleton grabbed Roy by the ankle, spun him around so he was once again facing the wall, and casually pulled him away from the designated safe zone. He proceeded to pick up Roy for another whack at the steel doors.

"That's not how you play nice!" Celia shouted.

Her voice carried across the empty mall corridor. For a moment, the dark skeleton paused and looked over his shoulder at her. A metallic chuckle rang out.

"Oh, it isn't?"

Straightening her posture, almost standing on her tippy toes, Celia shook her head in defiance, furrowed her brow, and jutted out her lower lip. "No."

"So, none of this?" While Roy clawed at the ground, the dark skeleton swung him by the foot into the steel doors that sealed the designated safe zone. Roy rang like a gong.

"No," said Celia with absolute certainty.

"What about—" With both hands, he raised Roy over his head and brought him down. Roy wasn't even fighting anymore. He couldn't. He limply smacked into unforgiving steel. Scraps of metal flew in all directions. A large metal mesh, somewhat reminiscent of a pectoral muscle, hung from his body.

"No." Celia leaned forward. She wanted to move; she wanted to help. But she was a good girl. "Stop it! Play nice!"

"Oh... all right." But it didn't look like he was going to play nice. He picked up Roy, lining up for the coup de grace. Roy reached up, fingers grasping for contact. His hand fell on the dark skeleton's shoulder, but found no purchase and limply fell away, a completely ineffective gesture.

Celia's HUD lit up with icons accompanied by reams of streaming data. Calculations slotted figures into advanced algorithms, displaying dozens of potential solutions emblazoned across her display, but they all returned the same result. There was nothing she could do to save Roy.

A red blast exploded off the dark skeleton's back, pushing him forward. He collided face first into the designated safe zone wall. Roy slipped from his grasp, dead weight collapsing onto red tile.

Bewildered, Celia turned toward the source of the red beam.

A man with grizzled features, wearing a leather jacket, limped across the concourse. He held his arms out, forming a triangle in front of him, a pulse pistol mounted at the apex.

"Down on your knees *NOW!*" he shouted.

Celia obeyed, crouching down.

The man ran past her, as if he hadn't even seen her.

Strange, she thought. He didn't seem to care if she got on her knees or not.

"I will fire," he said, with his pulse pistol aimed at the dark skeleton.

Oh.

He hadn't been talking to her at all.

The man limped towards the dark skeleton, but something was happening with its back. Celia cocked her head for a better angle. A long metal tube was rising over its shoulder.

"Put it down!"

The protruding contraption arched over the dark skeleton's shoulder and came to a rest in its hands. The tip charged blue-green.

Celia watched, blue-green light reflected in her eyes.

The man's pulse pistol blazed red, tearing chunks of metal from the dark skeleton. It staggered from each hit, but forced itself forward, step by step, under the barrage of blaster fire.

Celia could see the man's grizzled features turning pale white. He didn't look as rugged or as tough as only moments ago. In fact, she knew this expression. She had seen it on Mommy during the few times Celia had played with Jessica. He was afraid.

"Put it down now!" he yelled.

The dark skeleton laughed.

She thought she saw panic on his face, but it was hard to tell under the strobing red of blaster fire, increasing in speed, as the dark skeleton staggered toward him.

With nowhere to turn, nowhere to run, his only hope was the blaster fire he layered on thick, or the unlikely turn of events that the dark skeleton would simply give up.

The mall shook with a roar. As the high-pitched blue-green pulse discharged, a sparking conglomeration of frayed wire and blaster-burned plastic wrapped itself around the dark skeleton.

The shot backfired in a ball of aquamarine fire.

Despite all the damage he had sustained from the would-be assassin, from Cutter, from the fall and the fight, Roy had managed to execute his most basic of programming—to protect and serve. With the last ounce of electricity cycling through his dying systems, he reached up, wrapped himself around the technoperp, and bore the full brunt of the blast at point blank range.

Roy rocketed through the air at Cutter. The dark skeleton sailed backwards into the dented safe zone door. The door buckled, and the upper story jerked forward under the load.

Inside the designated safe zone, rivets spat at those clawing for freedom along its walls. Juniper turned her head at a crackling sound. To her right, a support beam bent in half buckling under the immense load and sagging ceiling. Inch by inch, the smooth concrete beam bowed, edges crumbling like Play-doh. Rebar poked through weak spots in the concrete, the beam swelling and extending spines like a puffer fish. Then a hideous sound filled the room drowning out cries for help; the beam snapped in half. Released from overwhelming pressure, rebar and concrete innards sprayed projectiles in a shotgun blast at those in its path. Where the beam had stood, the second story came rushing down, ceiling collapsing, taking the entire right side of the designated safe zone with it.

Charles grabbed Juniper's shoulder. "Stay here."

She wanted to tell him, "No. Don't go. Don't leave. Think about me. About the baby."

But she knew he would go anyway. People were in trouble. Those that hadn't been killed outright were struggling to find shelter somewhere, anywhere amidst the chaos. Others were half buried, some pinned under fallen beams and debris, unable to free themselves.

She knew her husband too well. He couldn't leave them helpless.

Looking into his eyes, the strangest feeling shot up her spine—instinct, premonition, foresight—somehow she knew that if he left her side, it would be the last time she ever saw him. Tongue-tied, she was unable to find the words to respond to what she was certain were the last words they'd ever utter to one another.

Juniper nodded, but Charles was already on his way across the enclosure, pushing a fallen block of cement off a trapped woman.

Juniper felt the rumble. She didn't need to look to know

what it meant.

She held Jessica against her chest and neck, cradling the child's head. She looked back, tears glazing her eyes, just long enough to see the ceiling collapse and swallow Charles whole, burying him alive under rubble.

The force of the collapsing ceiling split the designated safe zone's steel doors. Emergency lighting from the mall concourse flooded into the safe zone through the triangle of debris propped up by the twisted left door.

Hope poured into her like a waterfall. She and her child had a chance. She ran for the opening. The ceiling above her split, reminding her of the parting of the Red Sea. Except, this wasn't the part where Moses led his people to freedom, rather she was on the receiving end, an Egyptian giving chase as the waters closed in around her. She sprinted as the second story fell into the safe zone that was now, more or less a sinkhole for the upper stories. The floors above fell creating a giant bowl and causing debris to funnel toward the exit. A steel girder that had been a support on the second floor fell on its side and slid down the half pipe.

Juniper sprinted for the opening, for her and her baby's only chance at survival. The walls closed in around her, trying to once again seal off the designated safe zone from the rest of the world. She wasn't going to let it beat her. She couldn't. She had her child to think about.

She reached the mangled doors crushed under the weight of the collapsed second story. Rebar jutted across the opening like a net, blocking her exit. She reached forward with Jessica in her shaking hands, as she tried to fit her child through the largest opening. The gaps were too small. Her child was too big. They were trapped.

"Please! Somebody help!" she screamed.

She turned back watching the mall eat itself, floor after floor, folding into the safe zone, pushing the remains of an entire building toward her. The steel girder bounced down on a collision course.

She held Jessica to her chest, kissed the top of her head. "I love you, Jessica. Always know. Mommy loves—"

Juniper turned her back to the I-beam taking the full brunt of the force. The I-beam smashed into her, bending the rebar netting and pushing her body through a widening gap in the mesh. Her body maintained an upright gait and the false appearance of animation.

The I-beam came to rest outside the designated safe zone, sealing off those inside from hope. Momentum sent Juniper's form sprawling through the air like a rag doll. Her body limply bounced off the ground a few feet from Celia. Celia tilted her head toward the body. Juniper was piled up on top of herself, limbs at angles that shouldn't be possible.

The collapsing second story pushed debris through any remaining holes and openings in the shredded safe zone wall. Hurtling concrete and metal tore across the concourse like buckshot. A large square of paneling flew at Cutter. He hobbled out of the way losing grasp of his ZeroTwelve in the process. The paneling caught him in the shoulder, knocking him to the ground. Pain ebbed through his body. With a groan, he rolled over and inspected his shoulder. Scuffed leather on his sleeve. He had been lucky.

The dark skeleton turned, just in time to catch an oblong metal shard to the face. It fell to a knee, cupping its head in both hands. With a primal roar, it tugged on the metal shard. The shard didn't budge.

The faceshield opened and Cutter saw a deep cut carved in

red on the assassin's cheek. The shard had lanced the horizontal slats in its faceshield and nearly the man behind it as well.

The shifting rubble came to a standstill, leaving the concourse in eerie silence. In the distance, footsteps faintly echoed down the corridor, rapidly approaching, growing louder with each footfall.

The dark skeleton turned. Cutter followed his gaze and was greeted by the sight of the boys in blue. Parks led the charge. A smile grew on Cutter's face. *Bout time they showed up.* "It's all over for you, now."

The dark skeleton grunted in his direction, gripped the metal shard, and yanked it free.

"Freeze!" yelled Parks. He held a pulse pistol in his hand.

The dark skeleton threw the metal shard at him. Parks dove for cover.

Sprinting for the opposite side of the concourse where the mall was still standing, the dark skeleton climbed up a column to the third story. It hopped the railing, ran fifty meters across the third floor and disappeared out the opening between the canopy and mall ceiling.

Cutter could hear Parks huffing, trying to catch his breath. He pointed toward the stairwell, directing three officers toward it. "After that synth!" He signaled a group of six other officers to head back the way they came from.

Cutter doubled over and spat on the floor, checking to be certain. Blood swirled in the puddle of spit. He looked up at Parks.

"It wasn't a synth," Cutter said.

"Then what the fuck was it?"

"It was a mod." Cutter looked up at the gap between canvas and ceiling three floors above their heads.

Parks followed his gaze. "Never seen a mod that looked like

that before."

"Me either." Cutter nodded, almost imperceptibly. "And that's not the worst of it. He knew me by name."

A quick glimpse failed to indicate whether the tangled mass of metal lying on the floor was ever more than scattered debris. Black smoke coughed from gaping holes in its chassis, protruding wires sparked, and chrome finish was scarred with blaster burns.

Fluid gurgled and sputtered from a ruptured hydraulic tube, leaking onto fused metal rods that were bent and twisted. A mangled protrusion poked through a cavity at midsection. Perched on top, a metallic hand appeared to grasp for something that wasn't there at all.

Roy had come to his final rest.

Standing in the middle of the mall concourse, Celia craned her neck, straining for a better view. She rocked to a side. Then the other, trying to make out what was lying on the other side of Roy.

Her gaze drifted down to her feet and her pink Converse that were planted exactly where they were supposed to be. She was a good girl.

She scanned the mall corridor searching for a familiar face. For anyone that could help.

More specifically, for permission.

There were people of all sorts, shapes, colors. Different uniforms. Some dark navy. Others yellow with orange reflectors. Some people in white had set up a tarp near the designated safe zone. They dragged others out of the remains of the collapsed second story.

Most stood in huddled groups. All seemed to ignore her.

She returned her gaze back to Roy. Back to whatever it was on the other side of him.

She lifted her foot and placed it in front of her, cautious, afraid, as if she were walking on ice that might give way at any second. After a single step she looked around. No one, not a single person, stopped or in any way deviated from their previous tasks.

She took another step.

Still, no one noticed.

And another.

She was walking.

And the world kept right on spinning.

She walked past the decaying ruins of the Black and White. She paid no mind to the electrical sparks that snapped and popped and leaped out at her.

Her gaze was set on something else. Something beyond Roy.

"Mommy…?"

The words barely passed her lips. She already knew. Her internal sensors had put the pieces together. She had seen the action unfold. The results were all but conclusive.

Still, she had to see for herself.

"Mommy…?" she said again, slightly louder than before.

Juniper laid before her, sprawled out and motionless. Celia slumped down on the mall floor, falling back into a sitting position. She nudged her mother's shoulder. When no response came, she poked her mother in the chest.

"Mommy, wake up."

She leaned forward, crouching onto all fours, reaching across her mother's body and tugged on her shoulder. Mommy's head flopped toward her, looking up with glazed eyes. Blood streaked her right cheek like colored tears.

Celia put the palm of her hand flat on Mommy's arm and
gently rocked.

"Wake up Mommy. I was a good girl. Please, wake up."

Footsteps approached. She turned to see two officers loading
the remains of Roy onto a cart. One turned, making direct eye
contact. Without a word, he turned back to his partner and
quietly wheeled Roy away.

In the distance, Celia saw a huddled group of men in police
uniforms that had separated from the others. They were too far
away to make out exact words, but one was yelling and pointing.
Several others scattered at his flamboyant gestures. There was
another—a man she had seen previously—a man with grizzled
features wearing a weather-worn leather jacket. He was looking
up—at what, she didn't know.

He seemed caught up in predicting the future. As his gaze
fell upon her, she watched his contemplative expression change.
It seemed to her, that he was now reflecting on a sad past he had
just discovered.

She turned back to Mommy and once again gently rocked
her shoulder.

Mommy was so quiet.

Celia leaned down and whispered in her ear. "I was a good
girl."

A shadow eclipsed her. She looked up. The man with grizzled
features wearing a weather-worn leather jacket stood towering
over her.

"What's your name, sweetheart?" the man asked.

Her gaze returned to Mommy.

"Celia," she said.

She placed her hand on Mommy's cheek and softly stroked.
When Mommy once again failed to respond, she dragged a finger

across her mother's mouth. Her lower lip clung to the passing finger and slowly recoiled as it slid past.

Celia turned to the big man lumbering over her.

"Can you wake my mommy?"

SOME OF THE WHOLE

1

"No," said Cutter.

Thin intersecting lines of cyan sketched a piece of hardware that spun on its axis. A detailed technical hologram floated in the air a meter or so above a glowing blue power source. With a dull flash, the hologram cycled to another outline, an equally gruesome looking weapon attachment.

"That's not it." Cutter absent mindedly pressed a button. A new hologram blinked into place.

"Nope."

The image flickered. One by one, layouts for arm attachments, leg prosthetics, and every piece of hardware that had ever been catalogued in the city's database cycled in front of Cutter with the rock steady beat of a metronome.

The modded weaponry was always a good place to start. There were only so many places that could do mod work. The weaponry had to come from somewhere and that made it easy to track. Easy to ID. Easy to put together which pieces had been attached to what scumbag. It often led to when and where and who. At least, who a scumbag was before he decided to augment his humanity.

"Nope."

Unfortunately, that only helped when you could match mod-job to recent work.

The case was beginning to annoy Cutter.

But more than that, the man in a nice suit ceaselessly pacing back and forth behind him was batting his last nerve like a tetherball. Despite the man's iconic appearance, Cutter had a mind to give him a black eye just to make him stand still.

Rather than give in to the impulse, he leaned back in his chair, interlocking his fingers behind his head and let out a long sigh. "We aren't going to find it in here."

"What the hell do you mean?!" yelled Mayor Benjamin Foster. His suit strained against its top golden button, threatening to catapult it at Cutter. "I want that fucker found!"

"Anyone ever tell you," said Cutter, "you're awfully bossy for a dead man?"

Foster's face went bright red. Cutter smiled. Watching Foster forcibly try to control his temper was fun. Foster clenched his fists into tiny delicate stones. They looked soft. Probably felt like being punched with tiny pillows. If it really came down to it, Cutter wouldn't mind finding out. Foster was a politician—a man trained in keeping his cool under pressure. Seeing how far he could push him was a cheap thrill—really, the only kind he could afford.

Chief Parks put a firm hand on Foster's shoulder. "We're working on it, Ben."

"Working on it?!" Foster rained spittle at Parks and thrust a pointed finger into his chest. "Elections are less than a month away! I can't have any modded up mercenary shooting at me with the InSight deal on the line! Do you have any idea what this is going to do to my political career?!"

"Boost morale?" said Cutter.

A strange small man in a brown business suit, with a briefcase at his hip, slid a piece of paper loaded with statistical information in front of Cutter.

He was Foster's lackey. He had introduced himself as Josh Yeoman, but lackey was really all the information Cutter needed.

"Actually," said Yeoman, "the polls dipped significantly after the Mayor was shot in a public venue."

Cutter shrugged. "Could have something to do with thinking he's dead."

He shot a look at Foster, fishing for a reaction, but Foster was already collecting his cool—that professional distance devoid of any real personality. With his back to Cutter, Foster unbuttoned his suit jacket, smoothed out the wrinkles, and with a newfound calm, turned back to the conversation.

"Yes there is that," said Yeoman without a hint of irony. "The general public also perceives the use of synth decoys as a sign of weakness."

Cutter leaned back in his chair. "If only it could have been the real thing."

"Can it!" Parks snapped at Cutter. "I assure you, Ben, we're doing everything we can to track this guy down. Pinkerton is working on a new synth replica as we speak. This incident is something you can recover from. But you're going to have to take a break from your campaign until we get this resolved."

"That isn't a possibility," Yeoman interjected. "We're on a very tight schedule. The most important rally of our campaign is tomorrow at Staples Center. The seats are going to be filled to capacity. To back out now would be very detrimental to the Mayor's reelection campaign." He nodded at his own words. "Very detrimental indeed."

Yeoman's attitude stumped Cutter. The fact that Foster seemed to go along with the plan was another mystery. Cutter understood the need to follow a schedule and the desire to keep the gears spinning, but to do so at the risk of one's life seemed counterproductive to that agenda. There had already been an attempt on this man's life, and he wanted to further tempt fate?

If it were his life on the line, Cutter thought, he wouldn't hesitate to postpone the campaign indefinitely.

"And two days after that," Yeoman continued, "there is the venue in the harbor where InSight will officially open its doors to the public. If we don't maintain the schedule, we can kiss any chance of reelection goodbye. And that is if this most recent incursion hasn't already lost the election for us."

"Ben," Parks said. "That is a very bad idea."

Foster nodded at Parks, a simple admission that he had heard. It looked to Cutter as if Foster wanted to say more. A whole lot more. Instead, he stormed out of the office. Despite his calm facade, the door crashed into the jamb behind him, rattling the small window with Cutter's name on it. Yeoman politely bowed, collected his papers, and neatly returned them to his attaché.

"It's been a pleasure, gentlemen," said Yeoman, as he made for the door.

"So melodramatic, don't you think?" said Cutter.

Parks held his head in his hand, and sighed. Breath hissed from him like air from a deflating tire. He leaned over holding out a shaking fist (whether from nerves or anger, Cutter wasn't sure) and extended a finger almost grazing the tip of Cutter's nose. "I shouldn't have to tell you who that man is. Everything he has done for the city. Hell, for this department."

Parks' reaction didn't come as a surprise to Cutter, but he wasn't exactly expecting it either.

"This guy, his tech, it was something new," Cutter said. "Something I've never seen before."

"If it wasn't for Foster there wouldn't even be an L.A.P.D," said Parks, unwilling to let Cutter change the subject.

Cutter clicked a button. The blue-line hologram hovering between the two men blinked out of existence. "Why was I kept in the dark about this?"

Parks peered down his nose at Cutter.

A chill filled the room and ran down Cutter's spine. Parks settled back, head swaying slightly to the right and away from Cutter. Cutter stared down his superior officer, waiting for answers.

The Chief's secrecy didn't make sense. At least, none that Cutter could figure. Why go to all the trouble to keep him out of the loop? Why put him on the case at all if he wasn't going to be privileged with the finer details?

Parks broke the silence. "What do you mean?"

"You know exactly what I mean." Cutter leaned forward. His chair creaked as it returned to an upright position. "Why wasn't I informed that we were using a synth replica? That the Mayor's life was never in any real jeopardy?"

The Chief, a master in the nuances of the silent stare, assumed a new one—a gaze of granite. Cutter wasn't going to get anything from Parks with a direct tactic. But then again, the blunt approach had always been his favorite.

"Really?" said Cutter. "That's your response? Nothing? Not even going to feed me an obligatory 'it was a need to know operation and you didn't need to know' bullshit?"

"I'd never say any cornball shit like that."

"You put me on the case, didn't inform me that we'd be using a synth decoy, didn't bother to fill me in on the details, and here I am finding out that there was more to this."

"I never said there was anything more."

"No, no you didn't. And I think that's the God damned problem, don't you?"

Parks rubbed the tip of his nose with his index finger scratching an itch that wouldn't go away. After a moment, he sat down in the chair across from Cutter, and folded his arms. "What would you like to know?"

"How about a nice soft one for starters—Why?"

"You brought in the drive."

Cutter leaned forward, resting his elbows on the desk. "What are you implying?"

"I'm not implying anything. I'm stating fact. You brought us the drive."

"I got the case because I brought in the drive?"

"Exactly."

That was standard procedure all right. *My evidence, my case.* But something wasn't ringing true.

"That still doesn't explain why you cut me out of the intel."

Parks pursed his lips and stroked them with a single hand. "I suppose it doesn't."

"You can cut it with the cryptic bullshit already. What the hell is going on?"

Parks nodded. "You're right. I should have told you."

Cutter tensed. He was ready to leap across the desk and smack the every-loving-shit out of his superior. "So tell me already!"

"He knew things he shouldn't have."

"Care to be more specific?"

"Not really."

Cutter slammed his fist on the desk. "If you want me working this case, I need to know what's going on." Cutter pointed through the windowed door into the bullpen at no one in particular. "You brought your Mayor buddy in here. It's clear there is something you aren't telling me."

Parks leaned back in his chair, studying Cutter, still stroking his mouth. After a moment, Parks said, "He had information he shouldn't have had access to."

"And that means?"

Parks shifted in his chair, restless. Cutter could see the floodgates beginning to open. "This does not leave this room."

Cutter nodded.

"This mod, he knew how the stage at M.J. Square was going to be set up. Which direction it was going to face. Where the stands were to be unfolded. He knew where the most direct line of sight would be before we had even begun. He knew how security was going to be arranged. He knew that it was a small enough venue that we would not be able to bring in a mobile forceshield. He knew our procedures for an event like this and how we would react to a threat.

"In short, Jack, he knew things he shouldn't have."

"So why cut me out?"

Parks squinted at Cutter, refolding his arms across his chest. Cutter was so close. But the Chief was still holding back on a crucial piece of information—the only piece of information Cutter really cared to know. Why were they playing musical chairs with information that could possibly save the Mayor's life?

Cutter thought about cases he had worked. He thought about times that Parks and the department had withheld information that had been pertinent to the cases of the detectives and officers working them. There was only one reason the department ever froze out an officer from his case, but—

"Oh," said Cutter. His brow furrowed, as he looked up at Parks.

"We had to be certain, Jack."

They thought I had something to do with it.

Cutter thrust his body across the desk, stopping nose to nose with Parks. He felt a vein in his forehead thumping and the cords in his neck drawing taut. His hands clamped into fists on the edge of the desk. "You get your desired results? All clued in to my allegiance, now?

"You're getting worked up, Jack. You would have done the same thing if you were in my shoes."

"Bullshit!"

"I think it's time for another checkup, Jack."

The color left Cutter's face. A forced calm washed over him. "I'm fine," he said automatically.

Cutter hated himself for the reaction. The simple mention of a checkup was like mentioning the veterinarian to a castrated dog. But there was little he could do about it.

He hated the checkups.

And being told what to do.

Parks played on both.

Cutter steered the conversation back into a more productive direction. "I'm going to need a new partner to help me track down this guy."

"So you can make Swiss cheese out of another Black and White?" Parks shook his head. "I don't think so, Jack."

"When will he be ready for active duty?"

Pinkerton laughed. It was an answer to Cutter's question, but not the one he wanted to hear.

The room was speckled with mottled light. Wires and thick cables clung to the walls and hung from the ceiling. The room was the sum of the precinct's tech department, but really it was Pinkerton's turf.

Cutter walked through an aisle. Two racks faced each other, overflowing with tech, plastic, wiring, circuitry, odds and ends, bits and pieces. Some of it was whole—the old fashion atomizer to his right for instance looked like something out of a cartoon. Piled next to it were other scraps and spare parts, pieces of things he didn't recognize. A large toolkit sat on the floor at the end of the rack to his left. Its facade was a matrix of tiny plastic drawers. Several hung open, showing off their wares: small bolts, screws, washers, some even housed transistors.

Cutter moved into the depths of the room, finding a hidden cavern within, illuminated by a single and surprisingly strong directional light. Spotlighted in the beam, Pinkerton sat on a high stool at a workbench tinkering with a new metal monstrosity. With a blow torch in hand and his eye loupe lowered, he looked like a jeweler that preferred to buy his wardrobe at the mad scientist's Gap.

Pieces of synthetic, multiple arms, a leg, several torsos—maybe four or five different synthetics in all, but barely enough parts to scrape together a whole—sat on top of the tempered Masonite workbench.

Cutter recognized a hunk of metal—Roy. Or what was left of him anyway. Not much to look at. He picked up Roy's left arm and twisted it into a shoulder socket.

"So… soon, I take it?"

"You're kidding, right? Thanks to you, Roy is nothing more than a handful of spare parts. You can't keep treating your partners like they're disposable."

"Ouch, that hurts. I recycled."

He let go of the arm. It fell out of the socket and clattered to the floor.

Pinkerton turned at the sound, blow torch still burning heat ripples in the air. He looked at Jack with a condescending glare. "You really are something, Jack. Some damage is beyond repair."

Cutter picked up the arm and placed it back on the

workbench. Pinkerton returned to his task, a metal bot that looked extremely familiar.

Cutter sifted through some debris. It wasn't just Roy that was familiar. Here was a face he knew well—only the version he knew didn't have a giant gash through the middle of it and was slightly more irate. He picked up a piece of the damaged synth-Mayor's skull and held its eye to his. "Alas, poor Yorick, I knew him well."

"Horatio," Pinkerton corrected, whipping the metal skull from Cutter's hand.

Cutter held his hand in the air as if the skull was still atop it, and said, "Pretty sure, it's Yorick."

"It's not 'well.' It's Horatio."

"Huh?"

"That's the quote."

"What is?"

Pinkerton shook his head. "This"—he held up the metal skull—"is not a toy"—and placed it next to a half constructed Mayor-bot two-point-oh, a striking resemblance to the real-deal.

Cutter slid an eight by ten glossy off the workbench before Pinkerton could swat his hand away. It was photo reference of Benjamin Foster for the new Mayor-bot.

"Jesus, Jack. You're like a little kid." Pinkerton yoinked the picture from Cutter.

"Big fan? I could have gotten him to autograph it for you."

"Leave my stuff alone."

"So you got a new Black and White lined up for me or what?"

Pinkerton laughed again. His nasally tones echoed in the small room. Cutter found it an all too common answer to his many questions.

"You're on the blacklist. Chief specifically said you are not to get another. Roy was your last one—Thank God."

"C'mon now, Earl. How am I supposed to do my job? No concern for my safety?"

"About as much concern as you've shown for your partners. In fact, not giving you a Black and White makes *my* job that much easier."

Cutter pointed at the new Mayor-bot, nearly sticking his hand into burning flame. "Nice fuckup there. Black eyes your choice? Going for that completely soulless politician look?"

A flash of heated blue whipped past Cutter's face. Pinkerton grabbed him by the collar. A raging blue arrow of flame reflected in his eye loupe.

Cutter had pushed things a step too far. He knew it. It was one thing to make fun of this milquetoast poindexter to his face, but to insult his work—that had been a mistake. Cutter leaned away from the heat, but Pinkerton held him close, surprisingly strong for his meager size.

With a tone that was calm on the verge of psycho, Pinkerton spat through gritted teeth. "When you learn how to build an exact working replica of a public figure, then you can comment on the lack of life in the eyes, kay, smart guy?"

Cutter held up his hands. "Easy there, sparky. Didn't mean to offend."

Pinkerton eased his grip, letting Cutter's jacket slide through his fingers. Cutter took a step back and unruffled his coat.

"So no bot?"

Pinkerton glared at him. Unbelievable.

Cutter stood in the awkward silence, awaiting an answer.

"No! Bot!" said Pinkerton.

Cutter shrugged, regaining his cool. Pinkerton watched impatiently. After a moment, Cutter nodded to no one in particular and headed for the door.

Pinkerton picked up his blowtorch and returned to the work at hand: the Mayor-bot. He was near completion. Its new face was an exact likeness, a real accomplishment. Pinkerton was the "tech guy," but there was real artistry present in his work. The remaining final touch-ups had less to do with artistic flourishes and more to do with welding its legs into place.

"Oh Pinkerton, one last thing," Cutter said. He held up a finger as if an idea had suddenly popped into his head.

"What?!" snapped Pinkerton.

"The mayor's eyes are blue."

Pinkerton scrunched his brow. Hot hatred for this cocky bastard surged through his body. He turned toward the door in time to see it swinging shut, but Cutter was long gone.

He swiped the eight by ten off his workbench and held it to the light.

Sure enough, the mayor's eyes were blue.

His Mayor-bot's were black.

3

"Didn't your parents teach you no manners?"

"No."

"It's not polite to stare."

"Oh."

Celia broke eye contact with the elderly woman sitting in the police station lobby. Her eyes drifted down to the gauze that tightly wrapped the woman's left hand.

"What's wrong with your hand?" Celia asked.

With a blur of motion, fast for a woman so seemingly old, she rapped Celia on the head with her cane.

"Ow! What was that for?"

"Go on! Git!"

Cory manned the front desk, leaning back in a squeak-plagued chair. His feet were propped up across the sign-in sheet, as he leafed through a zine casually strewn on his lap.

"Catch desk duty?" Cory turned toward the sound of the voice.

Cutter strode up behind him.

"Requested it," said Cory. "Bit chilly in the Ozarks, don't ya think?" He flipped the zine toward Cutter revealing a double-page spread. From it, a hologram of a naked woman jutted out. She ran her hands down her sides, seductively swaying in slow dance. Hands inching toward—

Cutter had other things on his mind. He needed a Black and White. Failing that, a partner would suffice.

"You got plans?" asked Cutter.

"Not a fan of pop-up books?"

"At the moment, I got better things to do. And I see you got your hands full."

Cory smiled. "Not yet. Give me a minute or two." He nodded at Cutter, prompting a new question. "Any word on our mystery assassin?"

"Other than he seems to have never existed in the first place? No, nothing yet. Actually, I wanted to talk to—"

He stopped midsentence. Something in the lobby caught his attention.

Cory said, "Really? You don't say?"

Cutter looked over the divider into the lobby. He saw the dark haired girl from the mall.

What was her name again?

She had told him. It was on the tip of his tongue. He could

almost hear the knowledge rattling between his ears.

"You wanted to talk to…" Cory said, trying to lead Cutter back into the conversation.

Cutter nudged Cory's chair with his foot. "What's she still doing here? No next of kin?"

"She's going up for police auction." Cory peeked over the divider and pointed in her direction with his chin. "It's all preprogrammed responses. Scary-real though, isn't it?"

Celia—that's what she had said. Her name was Celia and she had wanted his help to wake her Mommy.

Fuck that.

That was some heavy shit, right there.

"She's a synth?"

"Top of the line. Expensive as hell too. Avery-Dennison was putting them out a few years back. Mostly for couples that couldn't conceive. Made to order. Composite DNA skin over a synth body. No two were alike."

A synth—could work in his favor.

Celia was looking at a man in the lobby, probably six-six. He was tall, but also lanky, a string bean. Cutter could take him in a fight, no contest, he thought.

She watched the tall man plug quarters into a vending machine. She looked up, arching her back. Her eyeline moved from the quarters in his hand up his chest, to his face. She had to lean back to see his features. Back, back, back, and—

She toppled over.

Cutter shook his head.

Maybe this was a terrible idea.

He pushed through the double hinged wooden door that hung at his knee and walked into the lobby. He stood behind her in silence, watching the miniature automaton figure its way off its butt.

She sat on her hindquarters, legs half folded in loose Indian style. Leaning forward onto her hands, she pushed herself onto all fours, and carefully stood upright.

The move seemed childish, like it belonged to someone younger than her.

"How old are you?" said Cutter.

Her head whipped around at the sound of his voice. Scanning the room, she found only kneecaps. She tilted her head back, listing slightly to the left. Her curious pout morphed into a beaming smile as her eyes drifted up to his face.

She raised her right hand, holding it up with her fingers splayed. After a moment, she looked at it, her face scrunched as if to say *that isn't right*. She raised her other hand, a balled fist with a single finger, her index, pointing straight up.

"This many."

Cutter nodded. "You're six."

She mimicked his nod, only faster and more self-assured, a childish flourish. "I remember you."

"Do you know why you're here?"

"I'm waiting for Mommy."

Cutter briefly mulled over a response. He wasn't one for tact, but given the circumstances, his conscience shoved what little decorum he had to the forefront.

He ignored it; this wasn't a little girl. He didn't know how much decorum was actually required.

"Your Mommy isn't coming back."

"But I was a good girl."

"I'm sure you were."

"I was." She nodded, no doubt about it.

"Can you do me a favor?"

She rocked on her heels, arms swaying behind her back. "May—be." Her voice went up in the middle with a playful lilt.

Cutter knelt down in front of her, holding up his index finger, a gesture reminiscent of the little girl's hand math. "Track my finger."

She looked at his finger cross-eyed.

When he ran similar tests, usually sobriety, it never occurred to him that the perp's response could be funny. But with a wide-eyed girl staring cross-eyed at his finger—he hated to admit it, but it was slightly adorable.

He swung his hand to the right.

She turned her head, tracking the motion.

Cutter wagged his finger. Her head bobbed.

"With your eyes only."

"What?"

"Keep your head facing me, but track my finger with your eyes."

"Oh."

Cutter swung his finger to the left.

She held her head motionless, eyes following his moving finger.

"Tell me what you see."

She jumped up! She knew the answer to this one. "A finger!"

"Is that all?"

She leaned in closer for a better look. Cutter shook his head at her. She was supposed to stay still, but whatever. He wasn't checking for sobriety.

"There is a swirly pattern."

"Good."

He stood, walked past a crotchety old woman nursing a bandaged hand. She held it out to Cutter, silently pleading for anyone to take a look. One, this wasn't a hospital. Two, he was busy. Three, he didn't care.

He grabbed a magazine from a small basket next to the bench, ripped a page out of it, and traipsed across the lobby to Cory.

"Toss me a pen will ya?"

Cory obliged. "What are you up to?"

"Investigating a crime. What's it look like?"

"Sudoku? I dunno."

Cutter ignored the remark and handed the pen and ripped magazine page to Celia. "You think you can draw what you saw?"

She took the pen and torn page, sat next to the elderly old lady (who grunted at her) and began to draw.

Cutter didn't wait for her to finish. He could already tell. The accuracy probably wasn't enough to identify anyone in the field, but he wasn't testing for that. Her precision and memory after the fact was there. Her attention to detail and recall was what Cutter was after.

"You're an observant one, aren't you?"

Her head bobbed, slowly gaining steam, speeding into a confident nod.

"Would you like to go for a ride?"

Her eyes lit up.

The last thing Cutter heard as he exited the precinct was Cory's voice. "Jack! You can't take her out of here!"

The cruiser hummed through damp city streets, kicking water out of the occasional puddle.

Cutter looked at Celia seated in the passenger seat. Her head swiveled with excitement, as she gazed out at the blur of buildings whipping past outside the window. He had seen the signs before, but never in a child so young (or a synth for that matter). A typical shut in. No exposure to the outside world. Now, set free, nothing escaped her view.

Cutter returned his eyes to the road and more pressing matters. An assassin was loose, gunning for the mayor. Why?

The InSight deal seemed the only logical reason—but still—what made InSight special? And why single out the mayor? He was just a figure head, and really had nothing to do with InSight's day to day operations.

Maybe the whole setup had more to do with the mayor's reelection campaign.

Or maybe it was personal?

He had been quick to rule that out when he first saw that the assassin was a synth. But it wasn't a synth at all.

It was a mod.

A mod on a first name basis with yours truly.

Maybe somebody just didn't want to see the mayor back in office. Or breathing—ever.

Cutter figured the best place to start was to cross reference those that had a beef with both InSight and Mayor Benjamin Foster. Gotta start somewhere.

"Could you look up—" He looked over to Celia. She was elbow deep in the glove box. He shook his head. "Never mind."

How did the Chief expect him to do his job without a synth?

He needed the kind of help that only the analytical, personality devoid mind of a synth could provide. Or maybe that was just his excuse. But anyway, he had to figure out who this guy was and help of any kind was welcomed. Cutter was running out of ideas. Who was this mystery assassin? The guy behind all the modification. What was in it for him? He wasn't a pre-programmed killer. He wasn't a machine mindlessly following a routine. He had been *someone*.

Clearly, a man at one point in time.

Now, he was a thing. He had lopped off every bit of flesh, down to a nub of face, presumably saving the brain behind it, and hardwired himself into tech the likes of which Cutter had never seen before. Had to have balls of steel to do something like that. Cutter scoffed at the accidental pun. It wasn't even a good one. Stupid, he thought. Balls of steel—the perp very well may have had them installed as well.

A clattering of plastic made Cutter jump in his seat. Celia held her head low, peeking up through her bangs. Stacks of instruction manual discs and a case that contained his vehicle registration form were scattered at her feet.

"Sorry," she said.

Cutter grumbled. "Can you make yourself useful?" His tone was a statement more than a question.

Celia froze. Her head slowly pivoted in Cutter's direction. "Like how?"

"Do you know how to use the dashcomp?"

Her eyes flicked down briefly. She looked at Cutter and shrugged. "I don't know."

"Have you ever tried before?"

She tilted her head, furrowing a brow. After a moment of intense silence, she shook her head.

Cutter swung the dash-mounted keypad in front of Celia. "No better time to learn," he said. A display flipped down from the overhead comp unit.

Celia looked at it. "What do I do?"

"You type into it."

She looked blankly at the monitor. Cutter cracked a smile. He didn't mean to, but her reaction was so sweet and innocent, so untouched by anything.

"With your fingers. Here, uh, spell cat."

"C-A-T," she said, touching the tips of her fingers like a child might to prove that she could count to three.

"With the keypad," said Cutter. He leaned across the center console and clumsily placed her hands over the keyboard. They hovered perfectly motionless.

"Then what?"

"You type."

Cutter stole a glance in her direction. She was looking at the keypad, confused. He sighed. This was not so cute anymore.

"You press the key with the corresponding letter that you want to appear on the screen."

She poked at the 'C' key and said the letter out loud. She repeated the process with each letter. All Cutter could think was how painfully slow this was turning out to be.

"And you're a top of the line synth?" Cutter said.

"What's a synth?"

"A synthetic. You know—a robot."

"What's a robot?"

Seriously? Cuteness over. Long gone.

"I could do it faster if I plugged in," she said.

Cutter stared at her. *Kid doesn't know she's a synth, but knows she can plug into the dashcomp.*

"Uh, okay? You can do that?"

Celia nodded playfully. Was she mocking him? Of course she can you old fuddy-duddy. What do you think she is? A six year old girl? Pfft, times have changed old man.

She reached behind the display and pinched a fiber optic

cable, disconnecting it from the dashcomp. She tilted her head, flipping her hair to a side, and ran her hand down the back of her neck. She found a nearly invisible slit that contained her external access port and plugged herself in.

A horn blared, and Cutter returned his eyes to the road—the wrong side of the road and oncoming traffic. He swerved hard, barely missing a McDonald's delivery truck. The driver was kind enough to give him the finger as they drove past each other.

Static hissed over the radio as a report came in. "*Triple homicide reported at fourth and main's InSight distribution facility. Local units, please respond.*" Cutter reached for the radio receiver.

"There!" said Celia.

The letters C-A-T appeared on the display.

"*Probable connection with the suspect in today's rally shooting. Local units, please respond.*"

Cutter held the receiver to his mouth, finger hovering over the down button. Turning toward Celia, he held it to a side.

"Type antidisestablishmentarianism," he said.

He flicked his eyes to the display just long enough to see the word appear onscreen at a record setting pace.

Celia bounced in the seat next to him. "Did I do good?"

"How about—Peter Piper picked a peck of pickled peppers. If Peter Piper picked a peck of pickled peppers, where's the peck of peckled pippers that—ah, hell. You know what I mean."

He navigated the narrow city streets, radio receiver in his left hand pinned against the steering wheel. When he deemed it safe, he peeked at the display.

The words were there. All of them. Including the flubbed line and his own editorial, *Ah, hell. You know what I mean.*

Celia giddily bounced in her seat.

"Soooooo…" she said, a long drawn-out question. "Did I

do good?"

"Yeah, kid. You did good."

Celia beamed, grabbed the keypad, and played with her new toy.

Maybe he had been mistaken. Maybe Celia could be more useful than he thought. Maybe she could lend a personality bankrupt eye to the case, a point of view that he had come to expect on the field. He never imagined that she could actually replace a Black and White, but maybe—

"Let's try something," said Cutter. "Do you see a file folder marked, 'Training'?"

A vacant expression came over Celia. Her eyes blindly scanned thin air. "Yes."

"Open it."

Her head fell to her chest. She hung lifeless, a broken marionette. Instantly, Cutter regretted his decision. He should have known better. The proprietary Black and White training programs were heavy duty. She was just a consumer model.

"Celia?" He reached over, and nudged her shoulder. She fell against the passenger side door.

"Great. Just great."

She bounced up, returning to her normal childlike self.

"You okay?" asked Jack.

"Yeah, why?"

He held his tongue. Celia looked up at him. Her big brown eyes caught the moonlight and reflected the streets back at him.

"No reason."

"*Jack!*" the radio screamed. It sounded annoyed. "*I know you can hear me! GPS has you pegged two blocks from the scene. Get your ass over there.*"

He brought the radio receiver to his mouth, eyes never leaving Celia. "Cutter here. I'm on it."

5

About a million keys jangled on an enormous keyring. A mid-twenties security guard inserted one after the other, an arduous process, trying to remember which one opened the door.

Cutter tapped his foot. Watching this kid fumble with three dozen keys wasn't his idea of a good time.

"Uh, no, I guess, maybe it's this one," said the security guard. He hunched over, shaking in the cold, and jammed another key into the deadbolt.

A cyan glow from an overhead InSight billboard illuminated the loading bays. Beneath it, Celia ran down a lowered concrete ramp, arms extended making monorail noises. At the bottom she banked a hard turn letting loose a Doppler sound that exaggerated her motion.

She skipped back up the ramp towards Cutter and the security guard. At the halfway mark, she abruptly stopped. Her gaze fixed on Cutter. "Jack! Jack! Look!" She spun in circles. "Look!"

"That's great, kid," said Cutter, with his back to her.

The security guard looked up at him with a panicked half smile. "It's one of these."

A key turned the tumbler.

Finally.

Cutter stepped forward, encroaching on the security guard as the door cracked open. He leaned forward, attempting to peek inside, but the security guard stopped short in the doorframe. Cutter damn near toppled the kid. He thrust a hand against the jamb to right himself.

"What's the holdup?" grunted Cutter, collecting what little

patience he had left.

"Uh…" The kid looked at Cutter. Or rather off into the distance somewhere over Cutter's shoulder.

Cutter followed his gaze, landing upon Celia. She spun circles in the loading bay, making a racket. The only noises for miles in the otherwise silent warehouse district.

"I don't think you have to worry about waking the neighbors," said Cutter.

A half-chuckle escaped from the security guard. "Yeah, uh, that's not what I meant."

"Want to clue me in?"

"You sure she's going to be okay?"

"Her?" Cutter looked back at Celia. "Yeah, she'll be fine."

"It's really bad in there."

Cutter shrugged. "She can handle it."

The security guard nodded, but didn't seem convinced.

"Celia," Cutter shouted. "C'mon."

She veered her imaginary monorail towards them and scurried inside.

A dull chug of electricity thundered, echoing through the building. The lights flickered, as each section in the warehouse blinked into existence from the darkness. Powerful fluorescents illuminated sections with a faint green tint.

The building was arranged like most warehouse distribution centers. Aisles large enough to drive a vehicle down were flanked by large green shelves. Crates stacked upon crates reached toward the ceiling. From what Cutter could see, there wasn't much notable to speak of.

He nudged the security guard with his elbow. "Did the intruder take anything?"

"No," said the security guard. His head bobbled back and

forth, an aftershock from the question. "Not from what I could tell anyway. Everything's bar coded and tagged. If anything tried to walk out the front door or through the loading bays an alarm goes off. I'd know about it."

Cutter stopped at the opening of an aisle, looking for—he didn't even know. A reason, perhaps?

The security guard waved a hand at Cutter. "It's uh… This way, please."

"I was expecting something a little more…" Cutter searched for the word. "I don't know—a little more."

"Yeah, we get that a lot. I mean… Not a lot, but… This is one of our warehouses. There's not much tech here. Mostly raw materials. Chemicals. Stuff that makes the process work. All the high tech gadgetry is at the portside facility. Application and whatnot is there too. This is mostly extra storage space."

The security guard hesitated at the end of a row. He found his breath and turned to Cutter with a pleading look. Cutter couldn't quite read the expression, but he had his hunches.

"Uh… Here we are."

The kid's gaze once again fell upon Celia. With a deep breath and a deliberate step, he rounded the corner.

Cutter followed.

Through the dim light he could see red splashed in patches, gathered in pools on the concrete.

Flesh was scattered down the aisle in pieces making it difficult to tell one from the other. Or even how many workers had fallen victim to the attack. According to the security guard's initial 911 call there had been three workers on duty.

Cutter couldn't be sure.

A torso hung from a shelf about two meters high. The right arm dangled onto a lower level. A ribbon of blood twisted around it like the primitive design of a tattoo. The right hand limply hung, touching the index finger on its other hand. Only this left arm was no longer attached. It sat upended on the concrete, leaning against the green shelves, resting on torn shoulder muscle, and gently grazing index finger against index finger in what Cutter considered a disturbing reimagining of Michelangelo's "Creation of Adam."

An orange forklift was on its side. Hazard lights blinked, as its wheels hummed, spinning but finding no purchase.

The scene was brutal. Raw.

These men hadn't been murdered.

They had been butchered.

Cutter had seen worse before. But not by much.

On the hills cutting through Laurel Canyon, he had seen auto accidents that were reminiscent of this. The city never bothered to iron out the tight turns and slope of the canyon drive. The solution to ever increasing vehicle speed, traffic, and general impatience saw flashing lights added to centuries old twenty-five mile an hour speed limit signs.

Lot of good that accomplished.

Countless times that bypass had spilled blood. He had witnessed a battle that pitted man against machine with an outcome that was all too predictable.

The deformation and ruin of the human body he had seen was definitely worse than this. But it had not come at the hands of another. At least, not directly.

To see a scene like this, was surprising to say the least.

Homicide these days was fairly clean. Prevalent and running rampant, but clean.

Laser beams instantaneously cauterized wounds, advanced medical techniques preserved those that really didn't deserve to be, and the general proliferation of augmentation saw the majority of human weakness eradicated. Most damage these days came from rust, glitch, or computer virus. Even when perps went old school, there wasn't much to it. The fights were short. Tech pinpointed exact weaknesses, shattered joints, and disabled foes at speeds that curbed the occurrence of any overly morbid works of art. A Dick and Jane story written in blood and battered bone.

See Spot.

See Spot run.

See Spot run from a gaping chest wound.

Run Spot run.

See Detective smear Spot into a baggy for DNA testing.

This…this was something else.

Someone had something to say.

This was art.

"What happened?" asked Celia. Cutter had almost forgotten about her. Celia stood next to him, eyes peeled, taking in the horrific scene.

"That's what we're here to find out," he said. "See anything you like?"

Celia leaned to a side, and then stood up on her tippy toes. "I will have to look around."

Cutter smiled. Her reaction vaguely reminded him of Roy: unmitigated unaware naiveté. Funny by accident.

Celia strutted down the aisle, catching Cutter slightly off-guard. He assumed he would be the first to inspect the crime scene, but here was this little girl with unbound curiosity trudging into the middle of bloodshed and chaos. Her input sensors were on full, internalizing all the new information that lay before her in scattered bits and pieces.

Cutter turned to the security guard. "You find them like

this?"

The security guard nodded, glassy-eyed, avoiding eye contact with Cutter. In fact, the extent he went to avoid eye contact waved more red flags than the Communist Party's Honor Guard.

He was fixated on something in the distance. Something beyond the scene. Cutter couldn't tell what he was looking at, but maybe it was something only the kid could see.

"When did you discover them?" asked Cutter.

"I'm sorry?"

"The bodies. When did you discover the bodies?"

"The bodies…" He reached out, pawing the air, pointing at nothing in particular. "I… I think it was… It was right before I called." The guard tucked his nose into his elbow. "Can't you guys look that up in your records or something?"

"Was there any indication what he was after?"

"They were… Well…" The security guard staggered to his left. "They…" he muttered incoherently, bracing himself against a nearby shelf for support.

And puked.

Cutter folded his arms.

"I—I'm sorry," the security guard said. Remnants of lunch dribbled down his cheek. "It's just…everything, you know?"

"I can take it from here," said Cutter.

The security guard blindly shoved the massive keyring into Cutter's chest and waddled toward the exit holding his belly.

Cutter turned his attention toward Celia, not expecting her to respond. "So what do you think, huh? Got any ideas? Opinions?"

Celia was crouched down, staring intently at something on the floor. At the sound of Cutter's voice, she looked up at him. "About?"

Cutter raised both arms and spun in a slow circle. "This. All of this. Any thoughts?"

Celia nodded. "Yes. Many."

Cutter shook his head, continually amazed by the simplicity of a synth answer. "Well, I guess that's a start," he said.

He headed toward the nearest torso, squatted next to it, and withdrew a pen from his jacket. With the pen, he gently lifted up the torn blood soaked jacket, inspecting the contents beneath. This guy was a mess.

The technoperp must have had a reason for coming here, not taking anything, and dismantling these blue collar workers. Workers, from the looks of it, that didn't put up a fight or stand in his way at all.

Celia picked up a bloody lump of something off the floor and held it up for Cutter to see. "What is this?" she asked.

"You got something?" Cutter stood, and looked over her shoulder at the object she was playing with.

Disappointed with her find, he said, "Pancreas." And then gave it a second look. "Maybe."

He returned to his investigation of the limbless torso.

"Pan-kree-us." Celia sounded out the word. She held the damp mass to her eye, inspecting the slimy oozing piece of flesh. Intersecting blue and oddly discolored green veins revealed a cityscape of blood highways. She made a "Harumph" noise and then tossed it down with a splat before skipping over to the next gruesome bit of flesh.

She bent at the hip, and poked at something new with her index finger. "And this?"

Cutter turned, once again distracted from his investigation. "That—is a little disturbing, Ceil."

"What?"

"Don't poke at them. They're dead."

"Like Mommy?"

He walked straight into that one. "Yes. Like Mommy. Let's look for clues, kay?"

Celia sprung to her feet with excitement. "Kay!"

Cutter was trying to focus on the investigation at hand and the dismembered warehouse workers that had been murdered for apparently no reason. However, he counted his blessings for her response. At the mention of the death of her loved ones, her parents no less, a human child might break down into tears. Having to console a sobbing heartbroken child would have seriously hindered his investigation.

Celia, on the other hand, glossed over the subject as if he had asked her what outfit she wanted to wear for the day. The mention of her parents, their death, their non-existence didn't seem to faze Celia in the least.

He walked over to the used-to-be man hanging from the shelf in an assorted arrangement of human spare parts. There was a lot that struck Cutter wrong with this scene. Was it InSight that the assailant was after? Was it the raw materials? Or was it the workers themselves?

Cutter wasn't about to completely rule out theft as motivation, but it seemed unlikely. Had he wanted something, the intruder had time and opportunity to take it.

This whole mess could have been a show; a statement made to let InSight know that this guy was serious. Serious about what, though? Cutter had no idea. There was no motivation, and this guy wasn't leaving any overt messages behind.

The most logical reason was the workers themselves. But that didn't make any sense at all. What did they have that would warrant such an attack?

They were manual laborers. Sure, they worked for InSight in a fairly high security facility, and thus were likely compensated with decent pay (probably more than Cutter made, he figured) but that wasn't reason enough to tear them limb from limb. A mod as teched-out as the guy that attempted to assassinate the Mayor could easily aim for a higher profile wealthier target if robbery was his end game.

"Jack?" Celia said.

What was your plan here, buddy?

"Jaaaaa-cK!" The shrill pitch vaporized his thoughts. "Jack Jack Jack Jack Jack Jack Jack—" He slowly turned, watching Celia wear his name like a bandolier across her chest, pelting him with machine gun fire.

"—Jack Jack Jack Jack—"

Really? She needed this much attention? "Can I help you?" asked Jack.

"What is a clue?"

He wasn't sure if she was putting him on, or if this was just some childish game, part of her programming to give her the appearance of a real little girl. "Evidence," he said. "Something that can tell us who did this."

"Oh." She bit her lower lip and swayed, arms spinning freely. "And you want me to look for that?" she asked.

"It's just a thought," said Cutter, returning his attention to the shelf. To something he hadn't noticed before.

On the shelf next to the dangling right arm was a sensor pad. The display was still on, cyan glow cutting through the green overhead fluorescents. Cutter picked it up. On display was a checklist of serial numbers cross referenced with other serial numbers. Cutter looked at the crates stacked to the ceiling. In their upper corner they had been tagged with a bar code. Beneath it a serial number.

These workers did have something useful. Something specific.

They had information.

They knew the shipping schedule. They knew when new shipments were coming in and going out because they had to load and unload each and every item onto and off of the delivery trucks.

It was a safe bet that they also knew where the shipments were coming from.

And better yet—going to.

"Jack?"

"Uh huh?"

"Why would someone do this?"

"Cause they're a sicko, perv, or psychopath. Take your pick."

Celia reflected on the answer.

"Jack?" she asked again.

"Uh, yeah." He was starting to get irritated by the constant distraction. He was close to figuring out what the technoperp had been doing here. He needed a minute to think it through and put it all together.

"But *why?*" she asked.

Immediately dazed, his brain was a hollow void. The comment. So innocent. So to the point. Like she had access to his thoughts over an entire lifetime. He asked himself the very same question at the start, middle, and end of every case he had ever worked. *But why?* He turned toward her, looking into her eyes. Those large inquisitive eyes searching for the answers to the world and all the world's problems. Answers that he too so wanted to possess. "Really wish I had an answer for you, kid."

He fought to regain his previous train of thought. "Wish

we had a Black and White too. Would make things a whole lot easier."

"What's a Black and White?" Celia asked.

"You met one at the mall. Roy was a Black and White."

"Roy!" Her eyes lit up. "I liked Roy. He was funny."

Funny was not how Cutter would have described him. Or any synth for that matter. "You got some imagination, kid." Cutter ran a finger over the sensor pad. "We don't have a Black and White. All I've got is you. So just look around for anything that seems out of the ordinary."

Celia nodded, two swift confident movements confirming her certainty. One up and one down. She was on the case.

Just because there wasn't a Black and White, didn't mean she couldn't be of use. Somewhere inside her, the Black and White protocols were running. She was going to make use of them; make Jack proud.

She accessed the information.

A laundry list of files scrolled behind her eyes. Something in here had to help with the current case. After all, being a walking, talking crime laboratory was what Black and Whites were designed for.

She stopped on a file listed as 'Scan mode.' And selected it.

Would you like to enter 'Scan mode?'

Yes, she thought she would.

Her HUD popped up with a red overlay on her graphical interface. Yellow reticle squares flickered and moved in what seemed a random pattern. One pinpointed the nearest corpse and bombarded her memory with a string of data. Another reticle scanned the ground, resizing into an ellipse over the pools of blood. The blood analysis led to more information than she had anticipated. It separated blood type, cholesterol levels, guessed at eating habits and personal vices, split the pools into categories, and opened a new port, arranging the information into four separate categories.

The information confirmed it: there had been four people present. The program amassed information about each individual.

The scans picked up pace. A double helix was assembling on the screen in her head. A second double helix formed, attached to a separate dataset. And then another, followed by another. They were generated from the data disseminated from the information inherent in the blood, cross-matched against the corpses, assembling individual differences.

But Celia quickly noticed that something wasn't adding up.

The data built four DNA strands. It put the pieces of the scene together reassembling the men that had been working at the warehouse that night. She double and triple checked the work, but it always came back the same. Parts were missing.

"There's four separate DNA signatures, but only three bodies," Celia said. "Is that out of the ordinary?"

Cutter was stunned. "You can do that?"

"Do what?"

"Never mind," he said. "Remotely access the police database and cross reference the DNA you found here with the DNA of the workers from their worker ID. Exclude them, and see if you can match the unknown DNA with anyone in the database."

"How do I do that?"

Cutter sighed. "Kind of like you did with the dashcomp in the cruiser. Only remotely."

"Oh."

Celia stood rigid for a moment that seemed too long, reminding Cutter how inhuman she could be at times. It was somewhat haunting to watch this child become an empty shell.

"Ceil…?" said Cutter.

A screech-hiss of a modem belted out from Celia. "Okay," she said.

"Okay what?"

"It worked! Easy peasy!"

Behind her eyes, Celia was looking at the police database. The structure was unfamiliar to her. It resembled a tree, she thought. Branches of information spread out from a central trunk. One of the branches led to a veritable catalogue of bad guys and criminals.

"Now what?" Celia asked.

"Search for the workers' DNA. Exclude them. Check to see if the unknown is already in the system. If not, we'll make a new profile."

One at a time the four double helixes enlarged in her vision and slowly spun next to a series of mugshots, pictures cycling like images in a flipbook. Vital statistics, height, weight, hair and eye color, accompanied each picture at a speed only a computer could interpret. Celia easily kept pace.

POSITIVE MATCH.

"Done!" she said.

The outlier had blonde hair and blue eyes. He was six foot three and one hundred and ninety pounds. She figured the last number was invalid now. He was trimmer, a skinny skeleton, but constructed of high density combat alloys. She would have to update this information when she could get a better assessment.

Besides his weight, another bit of information captured her curiosity. It was the picture. Not the man in the picture, who appeared normal enough. Just a regular guy, pre-mod work.

The oddity was the picture itself.

Unlike the majority of pictures in the database, this one was not a mugshot.

"Yeah, it was a long shot," said Cutter. "At least we have the DNA on file now. It'll help link any future incidents with this one to build a case."

"I matched the three workers with the pictures from their IDs. There is also a match to the fourth DNA strand."

"You gotta be shitting me," said Cutter.

Celia shook her head. She most certainly was not!

Cutter rubbed his chin with the back of his hand. "That's almost too easy."

"His name is Costas, Ryan," said Celia. "Age thirty-eight."

Cutter placed his pen back in his pocket and dusted off his hands. He had extolled as much information as this scene was willing to divulge. "Let's pay him a little visit."

Celia skipped to Cutter's side, stepping on something that let out a squish noise and oozed bodily fluids onto the floor. As she followed closely behind Cutter, she left a tiny bloody footprint trail as they headed for the door. Neither seemed to notice.

She looked up at Cutter, excited for the first time in her short life that someone had actually taken an interest in her. Excited that someone had taken the time to show her how to do something new, something that hadn't already been programmed into her.

She was proud of her new skill. She read off the internal dossier overlaid across her vision. "Ryan Costas," she said with a playful tone. "Last known residence: 10736 Magnolia Blvd. North Hollywood, California. Occupation: Detective. L.A.P.D."

Cutter stopped dead in his tracks. "He was on the force?"

Celia nodded. "Last partner assigned: Cutter, Jack."

6

With weapons readied, the detectives kicked in the door and rushed into the apartment. Dark shapes moved in the dim light; people scattered in all directions like roaches. Apparently, the blinding light pouring in from the entrance gave them reason enough to flee. The detective in front held up his left hand. A piece of paper dangled from it giving them another.

"We have a warrant for the arrest of J.J. Slim," he shouted. He brought the warrant down, pulled out his Mag-light, criss-crossed it beneath his weapon, and sighted down the barrel. He swept the crowd, illuminating faces of those fleeing, searching for one in particular.

Behind the detectives, two cambots hovered through the doorway, gliding to a point position in front of them, spotlights scouring the scene, single camera-eyes streaming a live-feed to the surveillance van outside.

These kind of sting operations could always be a nuisance. Too many civilians. Too many possibilities for things to go wrong. It was a simple smash and grab, but simple seldom was.

The lead detective slinked into the room. It was deep and narrow, only lit by the faint glow from the tech that lined the walls. He had hoped for better lighting conditions, but wasn't surprised to walk into a cyber dungeon. The dimmed light and streaking neons added to the experience—or so users said.

"Watch yourself," he said over his shoulder to his partner. "These places can be dangerous."

He had enough to worry about without having to tend to the rookie shadowing him. A rookie, first day in the field, that the precinct had so graciously burdened him with. Whatever may have been lying in wait in the darkened room was trouble enough.

The dull glow from the wall backlit people that were arranged in tightly packed rows like produce on a farm. They were attached to odd looking lounge chairs that turned them into human hardware.

As the lead detective swept the room with light, he noticed a handful of those that were slow to react to their presence. They were in perma-daze created by the halo of blinking lights attached to their collective foreheads blasting their cerebral cortexes with pulsing flashes. They finally noticed the intrusion when power was cut from the devices that helped them trip the light fantastic.

At the sight of the detectives, a man sat bolt upright, and made a break for it. He took three steps before his feet flew out from under him, and he recoiled against the cord he had forgotten to remove from his arm. Staggering to his feet, he tossed the cord aside and ran.

The lead detective shook his head at his partner and pointed in the direction of the fleeing man. His partner nodded.

He had expected people to flee. But to flee through the entrance, behind them. He was counting on each face having to pass them to exit. That wasn't the case.

They were flooding out a door in the back of the room, complicating matters. The detectives and their accompanying cambots rode the flow of those draining through the doors to the rear of the room.

"Keep your eyes peeled for our target," the lead detective yelled over the commotion. He shot a look back over his shoulder and saw the rookie picking up a halo and putting it on for a quick taste of the effects.

He'd have to remind himself to scold the newbie after the

operation was over. Really, he should have done it now, but he didn't want to voice his concerns, give the civvies, or even those that ran this place, grounds for an illegal search and seizure countersuit against the op.

Instead, he settled for instructional commands. "Make sure no one is leaving behind us."

His partner nodded, head swaying like Stevie Wonder mid-song. "You check these things out? Pretty cool."

"This isn't play time."

His partner swung his head from side to side, reacting to whatever program was flashing across his field of vision.

The lead detective headed deeper into the room when something behind him—a faint, but familiar click-click grabbed his attention. *Only one thing made that noise.* And if it was behind him, he was in serious trouble.

He spun, swinging his weapon around, jutting out an elbow in the hopes that he could land a blow on whoever was behind him.

He wasn't so lucky.

A loud high pitch whine rang in his ear. He saw a blur of khaki, but when he completed the turn there was only a man in a trench coat crumpled on the floor. Abstract splatter art decorated the wall behind him and a plasma shotgun lay at his feet.

It happened so fast that the lead detective was trying to put the pieces together, when the rookie said, "Should be more careful old timer. These places can be dangerous."

The rookie held the halo away from his eyes, allowing a bluish glow to illuminate his chiseled features. A much younger, not-yet weather-worn, Jack Cutter held a pulsing ZeroTwelve in hand.

The lead detective exhaled, releasing the breath he had been holding since the telltale sound of a plasma shotgun had been cocked behind him triggering the code red in his head. Without a word, he turned his back on Cutter. With a simple flip of his wrist he signaled for him to follow.

"You know, Costas," said Cutter, a sly grin leaking into his expression. "A thank you would have sufficed."

"A thank you?" Almost under his breath, Costas said, "You damn near shot my ear off."

Cutter smiled. "An ear for your ass? I'd say that's a fair trade."

"Just follow procedure. This is a routine smash and grab. Don't make it any more difficult than it has to be by dicking around."

"Yeah, yeah," said the rookie.

Costas simply shook his head and pointed toward the back door with his weapon. Cutter nodded and followed close behind.

They flanked either side of the door. Costas rocked forward, peeking down a long corridor. Doors lined its length, eight in total. At the far end of the corridor, patrons were high-tailing it out of this fine establishment.

"It's clear," said Costas in a hushed tone. He moved into the corridor with a slow steady pace, weapon held in front of him should anything unexpected leap out. He stopped at the first door on the right and felt Cutter bump up against him. He gave a low three count and kicked in the door.

In the middle of the room stood a man that occasionally flailed his limbs with no real concern for rhythm. If he was aware of their presence, Costas couldn't tell. The man's vision was obscured by the helmet he wore, a big number with tinted blackout glass that covered his face. The helmet was part of the full body experience. However, his pants at his ankles looked more like a personal choice.

"That," Cutter said, "is not a pretty sight."

Costas gave a head nod. "The honor is all yours."

"Ugh," said Cutter, disgusted. He entered, keeping his weapon trained on the target, more habit from Academy training than feeling threatened by this man pointing at him with something other than a finger. As he approached, the man blindly spasmed, wrapping his arms around an invisible (presumably) woman. Seconds later, his right arm reached down to pleasure his invisible partner's parts that were not there, while grabbing on to himself with his other hand to pleasure what was.

"Okay, that's gross."

"Go on," said Costas, watching from the door. "We don't have all day."

Cutter shook his head. He slowly holstered his ZeroTwelve. Mustering his courage, he cringed and tapped the man on the shoulder expecting some sort of reaction. But there was none. He reached out to tap him again, but jumped back when the man started violently thrusting at the air with his hips.

"Hey!" Cutter yelled, grabbing both shoulders and shaking him. A smile peeked out from beneath the blackout visor accompanied by a quiet grunt. Apparently this man thought the shakedown was part of the ride.

Cutter yanked the helmet from his head. The man had grey hair, was probably in his 60s, and eyes dilated to the size of half dollars.

From the doorway, Costas could already tell. "That's not him."

"Wha—What do you want?" the old man said, blindly waving at thin air. "Who are you?"

Cutter shoved the helmet into the old man's chest. "Sorry to have bothered you." And exited as quickly as possible, leaving behind one very confused old man.

"You're doing the next one," Cutter said.

Costas was already lining up on the door across the hall. He kicked the door in leaving a black scuff mark from his boots. Inside, three women were lying on a spinning heart-shaped bed doing a lot more than making out. All three wore blackout glass helmets.

Cutter shook his head. "You lucky S.O.B."

Lucky or not, J.J. Slim was male, and these three weren't. Costas withdrew from the room and moved to the next door. Cutter stood in the doorway, gaze lingering on the activities inside. "You sure he's somewhere in here?"

Costas shot him a look. "Orders say he's here. So I'm likely to believe, he's here."

"You always so by the book?"

Costas answered by kicking the next door wide open.

"These ladies look to be in distress—" Cutter cocked his head at an angle. "—of some sort. We could always stay. Protect and serve, right?"

"Not a good sign if you can't even focus on the operation your first time out."

"Yeah, well…" said Cutter still eyeballing the naked femmes. "I'd say this is a worthwhile distraction."

He turned back to Costas, hoping his partner might join him in some extracurricular activity, but Costas was at the adjacent door, smiling back at him.

"You were saying?" Costas tipped his head in the direction of the new room.

As difficult as it was, Cutter pulled himself away from the attraction and jogged to Costas.

He stared into the room. "What the hell is this?"

In a previous life, the room had been the master bedroom. In the rear corner, an open door revealed a passage into the bathroom, the only remaining hint of the room's prior function.

Now, the room was filled to capacity with tech, blinking lights, monitors, and a wide assortment of surveillance equipment. The equipment was set up in a semicircle around a single chair. On the display monitors, an elderly man pumped his hips at thin air, three ladies were elbow deep in pleasure town, and the entry room and its rows of tech lounge chairs were a cybernetic ghost town. The monitors revealed rooms that they hadn't checked containing people using blackout visors for unknown fantasy wish fulfillment. Several of the cameras were aimed at the street outside. The front door. The alley.

Costas thumped a monitor with the barrel of his gun. "There's our guy."

J.J. Slim, a tall skinny kid, mid-twenties, pushed his way out the back door into the alley behind the building.

"Shit. I'm on him," said Cutter, in pursuit. One of the cambots peeled off from inventorying the room and followed.

Wait, Costas thought, but it was too late. Cutter disappeared through the door at the end of the hall. "Kid's impulsive, I'll give him that," Costas said to himself.

J.J. Slim was small time. Questioning was the main reason to haul him in—an effort to try and find a link to the larger syndicates. Running a rinky-dink dispensary out of an apartment, impressive as it was for a one man operation, was hardly worth the time of L.A.P.D. But if it led to the bigger illegals, well then, Mr. Slim jumped to the top of their list.

Costas moved into the room. Everything they needed was likely here. A gold mine of information lying in wait to be dug out of the computers and hard drives that ran Slim's operation.

A few steps inside the door, Costas began to cough. An overpowering stench hit him like a punch to the nose.

"Shit."

He saw it before his brain registered the source. Ribbons of smoke reached up blanketing the ceiling in rolling black fog. The darkened room had hidden it from plain sight, but the stench was unmistakable. Burning plastic. An electrical fire was smoldering inside the system cases. Costas shook his head at the smoking tech. Slim made sure that whatever they found would look like S'mores before they could salvage it.

Costas stumbled out of the room, half bent over, hand over his mouth, coughing up a lung.

He looked back into the room and watched his case go up in smoke. The tech chomped on itself, cannibalizing anything that could be of use. He wished he had something to stop a fire—an electrical one at that, localized only to the hard drives, computers, and pretty much anything that could nail Slim or his business associates. The only link left was on a display monitor running down an alley and out into the street.

Costas rushed down the hallway, following the trail Cutter had taken moments prior. The layout of the corridor was odd. The corridor flooded into the building's inner stairwell. Apparently, the apartment's owner had knocked a wall down providing an immediate route of escape. No wonder the patrons had been fleeing for the back doors.

Smart.

Costas bolted through the archway, pushing off the hand rail, and barreled down the corrugated steel stairs. The patter of his heavy boots echoed through the stairwell shaft like thunder.

He stopped at the bottom of the stairwell, cautiously approaching the closed door. The remaining cambot buzzed around his head like an annoying housefly. He swatted it out of his way. The device made a high-pitch whine, wobbled, and reset its position to vid-capture the scene a few meters away.

Costas pushed into the alley. Steam rose from between the seams of a manhole cover, obscuring the view of the sidewalk that was beyond it. He crept through the white shroud of vapor and keyed his com with his chin. "You got eyes on him?"

"Eyes, yes. Hands, no." Cutter sounded winded over the com. "But I'm close. Followed him a few blocks."

Costas checked his wrist display. His yellow triangle pointed north. Cutter's blue square marched west. "All the evidence is fried. We need this guy." For added measure, he laid it on thick. "Don't let him get away."

"I know this may be hard for you to believe, Costas, but I wasn't planning on it."

Costas headed west at a clipped pace. The sound of his heel click-clacked off the sidewalk, loud against the ambience of a city sound asleep.

During the day, there would have been a handful of pedestrians on the streets, even in an area as impoverished as this one, but at night the streets were empty. A halo glow hugged every street lamp and traffic light, cutting through an invisible marine layer that transparently coated everything. Unlike fog, the field of vision was still deep, but the atmosphere was thick and wet.

On either side of the street, wall to wall apartment complexes enclosed him. A single wall of concrete—sometimes not even that—sometimes only a single pane of glass—separated the life of the neighborhood from the dead quiet of the streets. Bad things happened at night in areas like this one. Most residents had no idea how bad it could be. Mainly because they didn't want to find out.

"Oh shit," came over Costas's com.

"Oh shit? Oh shit what?"

"Nothing."

"Oh shits are never nothing."

"Suspect saw me. Hung a left."

"Left? He's doubling back?"

"Sort of."

Costas scanned the street ahead. "Stay on him. I'll cut him off."

He trotted down the sidewalk keeping an eye on his wrist display. The indicators lined up several blocks to the west. When they did, he stopped and looked down a nearby alley that would cut across to Cutter, and hopefully cut off Slim in the process.

As he took a step forward, a spotlight lit up the alley like daylight.

Costas looked up at the cambot hovering overhead. "Seriously?"

The spotlight snapped onto Costas, pinpointing him in the center. The cambot hovered back and forth. The faint whirring sounded like an apologetic whimper.

"Do you mind?"

It clearly didn't understand.

"Stealth mode maybe?"

The spotlight blinked off. A few beeps later, its onboard running lights disappeared as well.

Costas shook his head.

Overhead, several light fixtures were now housings for broken glass. Costas looked into the darkness where scattered debris, junk, garbage, and overturned dumpsters were barely visible, making it impossible to tell if the alley went all the way through to the next block.

He took a deep breath and crept into the alley.

Something didn't feel right.

Paranoia. Nothing more than plain and simple fear. Hell, it was okay to be afraid, as long as he acted according to procedure. After all, that's what procedure was for. Training honed muscle memory, alleviating the need for thought. With enough training, input stimuli was all that was needed for a rote and resultant reaction. Thought became secondary.

He came to the first pile of trash damming the alley. Behind an overturned dumpster, a narrow path had been carved out through the debris piled several feet overhead.

He emerged on the other side, only to see another pile of garbage blocking the alley some twenty yards in front of him. *Great,* he thought. He had discovered the Los Angeles version of the Panama Canal. Garbage locks as far as the eye could see.

His more cynical self sniped, *this seemed like a pitch perfect way to end the night.*

Even the rotten alley stink seemed appropriate, but something in his gut was ringing like church bells at midnight. He heard a faint maraca rhythm, like a rattlesnake issuing a warning coming from up ahead.

What frightened him wasn't the dark. It was the fact that had Slim turned down this alley, he should have run into him by now.

Everything looked normal enough. But how much could he really see in the full blackness of night. Slim could have buried himself in garbage and he would have never been the wiser.

Costas found another narrow path in the debris and pushed through to the next garbage lock.

It took his eyes a minute to adjust.

Then he saw him.

Slim was crouched down behind a dumpster, hiding among empty cardboard boxes and piles of garbage.

Costas had been lucky. Slim's back was to him. If it hadn't been for a gleam of chrome reflecting the moonlight, Costas would have walked past oblivious to his presence.

But there it was, lucky him, a gleaming beacon in Slim's hands, a bulbous weapon shaped like a chrome football.

Slim fidgeted behind his makeshift cover, training the weapon on the alley opening. Apparently, he wasn't anticipating anyone approaching from behind. Slim shifted his weight back and forth. The constant erratic movements made Costas nervous.

Static crackled, followed by a voice.

"Flushing him toward you, now," said Cutter.

Cutter rounded the corner, full sprint, directly into Slim's waiting sights. There wasn't time for anything other than—

"Cutter!" Costas yelled. "Look out!"

Cutter had enough common sense, instinct, and trust for his partner to listen. He threw himself against the wall.

Slim spun toward the yell, toward Costas.

"Drop..." Costas began, but Slim had already brought his weapon around. Despite regulation, there wasn't time to issue a full warning.

A bright white light exploded sucking air into the muzzle. Heat rippled in a concentric circle, forming a particle wave of bent light. A wide spray of energy spouted from its center.

The blast pelted Costas in the gut.

Pain ebbed through his body. In that moment, he felt oddly different. The world around him moved in slow motion. His initial thoughts were still on apprehending Slim, on procedure, but somewhere deep inside himself a voice nagged that these things were irrelevant now.

A clattering of metal rang out with resonance like a gong and forcefully stole his attention. He looked down to see his service weapon lying on the asphalt. Had he dropped it? He couldn't remember.

His hands fell, tracing his chest, searching for the source of pain. Warmth poured from him. His hands came back wet. *Odd*, he thought; *I'm leaking.*

He felt a sandpaper ridge he didn't remember on his stomach, and was surprised when his hands didn't stop where they should have. The soft touch of skin was missing. If he had been shot, he expected to feel something—but his hand kept going deeper, until he bumped into a hard rigid protrusion—and immediately paused, struck with horror.

His hands were somewhere between the fourth and fifth lumbar vertebrae. He could feel his own spine.

Repulsed, he snapped his hand away, bumping against the upper ridge, only now realizing that the sand paper feel was his skin, burnt and cauterized by the searing heat from the blast.

It was an odd sensation—finding only what was missing.

He looked up from his dripping red hands at Slim—Cutter behind him, charging down the alley. Slim turned to run, but Cutter was already on top of him, and pistol whipped him to the ground.

Costas fought the darkness veiling his vision. Running steps echoed in his head, out of sync with the visual. Leather boots ran toward him, only the entire world was on its side. *Was Cutter running on the wall?* The dull pitter patter somehow stirred up a feeling of nausea. And then a face. The face of the rookie hovered over him. An expression of panic. He was yelling—at least it looked like he was yelling—but he couldn't hear words.

Costas wanted to tell his partner, *Don't worry. Everything is going to be okay.* But before the words found breath, his world faded to black.

* * *

The serenity was only interrupted by the occasional drip, drip, drip from fluids in an IV bag and the accompanying beep, beep, beep assuring that, despite appearances, the lump of flesh in the hospital bed was still alive.

Cutter looked down at the broken man sprawled out before him. Translucent blue tubes ran from his nose to an oxygen tank, and a second large ribbed tube was jammed down his throat. Blood pumped into his body by a silently humming heart and lung machine, the lung portion rhythmically inflating a chest that could not do so of its own accord. The sight made Cutter think of a human pin cushion. More tubes were jabbed into Costas's arm and torso. He wasn't even sure if the tubes were putting things back in or taking them out.

On Costas's forehead, a strawberry road rash peeked out from the bandages wrapped around his head. Besides tubes, there was a second motif present: bandages were wrapped around his chest and shoulder completing the modern day mummification.

How could this have happened?

Cutter cupped his hand over his mouth. If only he had been more careful. Maybe if he had been paying more attention. Or they had taught him better at Academy—trained him harder—this could have been avoided.

No, that wasn't right. He put the blame back on himself.

If *he* had trained harder—if *he* had paid more attention—maybe Costas wouldn't be on life support, fighting for another chance.

Costas was here because of him.

Why had Costas put his life on the line for one dumb rookie? Two words echoed before, after, and between every thought.

My fault.

My fault.

My fault.

That's not what the Chief had said. Chief Parks was the first person to tell him that these things happen, that good officers go down in the line of duty—that it could have happened to anyone.

But it sure didn't feel that way.

The Chief even went as far as congratulating both of them on a job well done. "Your efforts brought in J.J. Slim," he had said.

Cutter didn't see how that changed things. Costas was still laid out in bed. Still unconscious. Still quietly fighting for his life.

He could no longer combat the voices screaming in his head. *It's your fault.* He couldn't help picturing the expressions on the other officer's faces that had arrived at the scene. No one said the words. They didn't need to. Cutter could read it on their faces.

It's your fault.

Costas was barely breathing, only alive because of the machines attached to him.

This hospital bed…

This is my bed.

I should be lying here, tubes poking in and out of me, monitor blipping my vitals. Not Costas.

"Can I help you?" came a voice from behind him.

Cutter turned toward it. The tone was friendly enough, but contained a hint of suspicion. A doctor stood in the frame of the doorway, folding shut a file folder. He had been scanning it as he entered. Cutter presumed the folder contained Costas's medical chart.

He shook his head. "No. I don't think so."

"What are you doing in here?"

Cutter looked down at Costas. "I was his partner," he said. Then corrected himself. "Am his partner."

A question was on his mind, but he could barely muster the words. He wasn't sure if he already knew the answer or that he simply didn't want to hear it. His dry lips, near cracking, parted and hung open, as he willed air across his vocal chords. He forced the words from his mouth. "How is he?"

The doctor opened the chart, a nervous tick, but didn't bother looking at it. In the past day or so, he had gained an intimate knowledge of the patient. Nine hours of surgery, elbow deep in another man tended to do that. The chart only contained information as a record for others.

Almost whispering, the doctor said, "He's stable now." He placed a hand on Cutter's shoulder, a gesture, feeble as it was, to console Cutter. Cutter didn't meet his eye. His gaze remained locked on his partner. The doctor's voice was barely audible over the ambient noise of the room. "But I'm afraid the damage to his spine was severe." His eyes drifted down to the chart in his hands. "He's paralyzed from the waist down and will never walk again."

Costas was alive. He should have been relieved. But in many ways, the doctor's words only confirmed Cutter's worst fear.

"What are you doing in here?"

The words were lost, somewhere between thought and memory. "What are you doing in here?"

Cutter turned.

"Huh?"

◥

Parks hovered over him, hands on his hips, and took a deep breath. A disgruntled huff poured from his lungs that seemed to articulate this was the last time he would ask.

"What are you doing in here?"

Cutter met his eyes and stared for a second too long.

"Research," he said, casually flicking off the monitor in front of him. "Thought we might have something on file. I can't imagine this guy appeared out of thin air."

"Find anything?" Parks looked at him with a stone facade. Cutter tilted his head, trying to chisel through the expression.

Probably better that the Chief didn't know. At least, until things get somewhat sorted.

Cutter leaned back in his chair and ejected a data stick from the deck.

"Still looking," said Cutter. He placed the data stick among rows of various archival implements lining the walls from floor to ceiling.

The precinct's archives weren't the most up to date information processing and storage center, but it didn't need to be. Cutter sat at a long desk running the length of the room. On it, five terminals and accompanying monitors were set up for official use. The remaining walls were covered in data sticks that porcupined into the room giving it the appearance of a data torture chamber.

He had been so engrossed in the footage.

How long had the Chief been watching?

How much had he seen?

A clacking sound drew his attention away from Parks. Celia

was busy jamming archival sticks into a terminal at the end of the room.

Hard to believe that she had been right.

Costas was his partner.

Or had been at one point in time.

Archived vidfiles showed them working together, hard incontrovertible proof. In addition to the vid-files, Cutter had dug up all of Costas's police reports, many hand written, his signature on every document.

Cutter scratched at a few days' worth of stubble on his jawline.

Once he had uncovered the name, the files hadn't been difficult to find. Hidden in plain sight. Literal reams of information on Costas.

Cutter shook his head, quietly mumbling to himself. The existence of Costas wasn't even the most troubling part of the new discovery. Despite staring the evidence squarely in its pixelated face, he didn't have an inkling of memory of the events he witnessed unfolding on the vidfiles.

Disconcerting, considering he held a starring role.

If the situation had been different, if the files hadn't been preserved, hardcoded, and locked away in the precinct archives, he would have thought someone was pulling a fast one. He wanted to pat the culprits on the back.

Funny gag guys. You got me.

A prank had been his initial thought when he saw himself onscreen with the man that now bore a striking resemblance to the cybernetic Grim Reaper. He even stopped playback, ejected the data stick, and examined the plastic casing wrapped around it. *Stupid. Like looking at the thing would reveal all its binary secrets.*

How could his memory be so different from the reality etched in

1s and 0s?

The Chief cleared his throat. "Earth to Cutter."

"Yeah?"

"Are you okay?"

"Yeah, I need more time is all."

Parks grimaced. "Time is a luxury we don't have. Foster's rally is tomorrow at Staples Center. Apparently, M.J. Square was a warm-up."

"That's exactly what I'm afraid of. Foster will just have to postpone it."

"Believe me, I tried to talk him out of it." Parks rubbed the tip of his nose. "They're going ahead anyway."

Cutter shrugged. "Hope he likes getting shot at."

"What do we know about this guy, anyway?"

His name. Where he lived. That he had been my partner.

But that's not what Cutter said. His eyes flicked up to his boss. "Not much."

Parks chewed on his lower lip. "Keep looking. Something's bound to turn up."

"Yeah." Cutter wasn't so sure.

A plastic crunch caused him to spin in his chair. Behind him, Celia jammed another data stick into a terminal. She punched buttons on the console panel with deliberate focus. With every stab of her finger, the device slid back a few centimeters.

At first, he thought she was being a child, or following the programming that made her act like one. Apparently, she found it more fun to repeatedly press rewind. Then play. Then rewind. Play. Rewind. Than to watch the vidfiles on the data sticks.

Cutter agreed. He often found himself in this room mindlessly pressing buttons and staring through the images on the screen. More often than not, he had to rewind because he had been lost in thought on some random topic. Images and pertinent information blinked past his eyeballs without ever registering. Play. Then rewind. Play. Rewind. Until he found what he was looking for.

Cutter looked down at his own hands perched on the console, his index finger on rewind, middle on play. He had been doing the same thing all afternoon. Pressing play. Then rewind. Play. Rewind. Going through file after file, trying to solve the mystery of Ryan Costas, ex-LAPD, ex-partner, current mod-merc-badass, and lost himself in a sea of thought without ever paying attention to Celia.

She wasn't playing with the equipment. She was copying him.

She had done the same thing at the crime scene. Child-like, she had picked up every clue and played with it. But once he told her what to look for, how to process a scene, she had done so to the letter. He had written off her response as typical Black and White behavior, but she wasn't a Black and White. Synth, yes. But she was programmed for something else entirely.

She wasn't simply functioning as a Black and White automaton, a tool for detectives in the field. She was doing something else. Something in addition. She was learning how to become a detective.

Did she understand what she was doing? Or was it only superficial mimicry?

Was there any difference?

Parks pointed at Celia. "What's that doing in here?"

Cutter followed his finger.

He was already keeping secrets from Parks. *Might as well go whole hog.* Parks not knowing about Celia meant he had access to a Black and White of sorts without anyone chastising his questionable use of city property.

"She was here when I came in. Is this what the baby Black and Whites look like before I get a hold of them?"

"Not funny, Jack." Parks rubbed the tip of his nose with his index finger. "I'll have Pinkerton come take care of her."

"Jack showed me a pancreas!" Celia blurted.

Parks put his hands on his hips. His face turned stone. "There something going on here I should know about, Jack?"

Cutter shrugged, but couldn't manage to keep from looking like the cat that ate the canary. "Nothing out of the ordinary."

▪

"How come you cannot remember your old partner?" asked Celia.

She held her hands clasped, pointer fingers pressed together, and looked out the window. As cars whipped past, she aimed her extended fingers at every fourth or fifth car and shouted, "Bang!"

"That's like asking where I've left my keys when I've lost them," said Cutter, his concentration on the road.

Celia nodded. A second later, she cocked her head to a side and turned to Cutter. "I do not understand."

"If I knew that, I'd know the answer."

Celia looked at him, her eyes scanning his face. Her brows scrunched together just above her wrinkling nose. She shook her head, shaking off the confusion. A giant smile returned to her face, and she turned back to the window almost as if she hadn't prompted the conversation in the first place. With a childish exclamation of joy, she blasted a parked car with her finger gun.

Cutter snuck a peek at the child-bot playing cops and robbers in the passenger seat. Or maybe she was playing assassin and dead people in parked cars. He couldn't be sure, but most cops didn't go around shooting people from their moving cruiser.

He hadn't noticed, but he was also wearing a smile, as he watched the little girl play make believe.

In his time with Black and Whites, he never once smiled along with them. Laughed uncontrollably at their inhumanity, yes. But felt his heart warm, watching them do what they were programmed for, never.

Maybe, just maybe, he might miss this one when he had to turn it back in. Which should have been hours ago.

Cutter overheard a conversation in the hall outside the police archives. The Chief had mentioned Celia to Pinkerton. Mentioned that maybe he should come by and pick her up. Take her back to holding and prep her for police auction. If things had gone according to plan, Pinkerton would have taken her into depths of his workshop. Except, that wasn't what happened. In the real version of events, when Pinkerton arrived in the archive room, he discovered that Celia wasn't there at all.

"Bang!" she said, sweeping her clasped hands in front of Cutter, bull's-eyeing a passing car on the opposite side of the road. She shifted her attention to the dashcomp keyboard, flipped it open in front of her, and hammered away on its keys.

Cutter raised an eyebrow. He didn't remember teaching her how to turn it on.

"Registering a confirmed kill?"

Celia shook her head. "Nooooo." She drew out the word, her voice going up in pitch at the end. She might as well have tacked on '*Duh!*'

"Well, forgive me. Don't let me interfere."

"I am looking up the license plate number."

Cutter chuckled. "Of the car—slash—person you just shot?"

"Exactly," said Celia, rapping on the keys. Cutter looked at the screen. She had brought up file after file on practically every car they had passed since the trip began.

"I could be wrong, but I don't think that's procedure."

Celia shot him a look.

Cutter hunkered down. "But I am a little rusty on these things."

Cutter returned his eyes to the road, listening to the rat-a-tat of typing, a soothingly hypnotic sound. Sliding into a trance, he reflected on the day. In the past couple hours, he had unearthed mountains of new information.

He turned the puzzle pieces over in his mind, none of which seemed to fit. Pieces that didn't seem to belong to the same puzzle.

Once he had a human partner, apparently. One he didn't remember. Who was gunning for the Mayor for reasons unknown.

On the other side of the case, Parks was riding him, but was unwilling to put Mayor Foster under protective custody.

Normally, when he'd hit an impasse, he'd just run the data through his Black and White and see what kind of response it spit out.

"Reporting a two-eleven in progress," Celia said.

Cutter grinned at her. He could always ask his new partner.

Celia had picked up the receiver and was holding it to her mouth, upside down. She didn't seem to notice her mistake. She barked out orders into it, police code—actual police code. Cutter shouldn't have been surprised—the Black and White programming was a crash course in everything related to police procedure—but hearing protocol coming out of the mouth of a six year old girl was interesting to say the least. He watched as she made the kind of adorable mistake that only a child would. Despite an intensity beyond serious and a flawless memorization of police code, she forgot to key the mic on the receiver. Her report would never be heard.

Cutter smiled, faintly shaking his head. "How do you like the new programming?"

Celia perked. "It's fun!"

"I'll bet." Cutter narrowed his eyes, trying to figure out the best way to broach the subject. "Want to try and work something out with me?"

"Sure," she said, turning toward him, her mouth forming the beginnings of a pout. "What does that mean?"

"It means, I'm going to ask you some questions. I want you to think about them and tell me what you think the best answer is."

"Is this a game?"

No. But Cutter nodded anyway.

"Yeah. It's a game."

"Do I win a prize?"

"No."

"Oh." Celia's expression sank. "What do I get for winning?"

"You don't get anything."

Her brow arched. "That is not a very fun game."

A smile crept onto Cutter's face. "No. No it isn't."

She put her head down, looking intently at her hands. Cutter silently watched.

After a few seconds of serious consideration, Celia turned to Cutter, bounced up in her chair, and said, "Okay. Ready!"

Cutter nodded. "First question—this is an easy one."

Celia leaned forward on the edge of her seat, poised to answer.

"Are you up to date on this investigation? Costas, me, everything?"

"I am up to date!" Her entire body radiated with energy and excitement. "Do we keep score? That is one for me."

"No," said Cutter, shaking his head. "We don't keep score."

Celia sulked, but only for the brief moment between Cutter's words. When he spoke again, she was all ears.

"If you were me—"

Celia cut him off. "I am not you."

"Yeah, but if you were me—" Cutter forced the sentence through a second time.

"I am not you." Celia looked at him wide-eyed. Her big brown eyes flicked back and forth scanning his face, searching for understanding.

If anyone else had been pulling the same stunt, he would have thought they were intentionally being difficult. But she was following programming. Being herself—the inquisitive pain in the neck that all children are programmed to be.

Cutter sighed. "Just use your imagination, kid."

"What's that?"

Cutter looked at her. He really wanted to have a word with her creators. Why was her vocabulary so limited in certain places, yet so abundant in others?

Programming a child without the knowledge of imagination? How was that even possible?

Cutter wracked his brain, but it wasn't a question he could begin to answer. He knew there was probably a very good reason she hadn't been programmed with the knowledge. Programming synths was specific and choices like these weren't arbitrary. Someone had deliberately left this information out.

But, as far as Cutter was concerned, the thought process that some egg-head put into programming these things was a baffling mystery.

A little kid. With no concept of imagination. Nor had anyone programmed her with the knowledge or understanding of what imagination even was.

What the hell were they thinking?

Probably the same brilliant logic that created a synth girl that didn't know she was a synth, or even what a synth was, but one that knew she could plug into the dashcomp of his car if she needed to.

"You were just playing cops and robbers like two seconds ago," Cutter said, implying a question he thought obvious.

Celia nodded in agreement. "I was."

"How were you doing that?"

"I saw you doing it on the vid-files."

"Oh. Right." Cutter rolled his eyes, the big dummy.

"So, uh…" He flustered. "Imagination?" He held his right hand open-palmed toward her like a Buddhist mudra. "It's uh…" The words escaped him. "Fuck, if I know. Look, I'm just going to tell you a scenario. It's going to have people in it. Pretend like you're in their shoes."

"Kay!" said Celia, her voice ringing like a bell.

"So, Costas used to be a detective. He used to be my partner. For the life of me, I can't remember the guy. But he seems to have no problem remembering me."

"Okay. I am in his shoes."

"Yeah, and?"

"They are too big for me."

Cutter's hand went to his forehead, a tense movement raking through his hair.

"Not literally in their shoes. In their position. If this scenario…" Cutter struggled for the words. "These, uh, these variables, if these variables were present, and you were there, what would you do?"

As an afterthought Cutter tacked on, "Oh, and why. What would you do and why."

"I do not understand."

Cutter tossed his hands in the air for a brief moment, before gripping the steering wheel, keeping the cruiser on course. "I don't know how I can make it any simpler."

Celia was already shaking her head. "I understand."

"You just said you don't understand."

"If I were in this scenario, I would not understand. It does not make sense."

Cutter nodded, realizing she had been playing along. She took to role-playing, maybe a little too well. She had stepped into his point of view and was at the same degree of loss over the situation as he was.

"Okay," he said. "Then what's the problem?"

"If Ryan Costas was a police officer, then why does Chief Parks not recognize him?"

He glared at Celia. Why had the thought not occurred to him?

Celia continued, "Ryan Costas was an officer at your precinct. You were his partner. William Parks has been the police chief for twenty-two years."

Cutter repeated her words, almost without thought. "He was an officer at my precinct."

"They would be friends." Celia inquisitively tilted her head. "Right, Jack?"

Cutter looked at Celia, and all that insight packed away behind her plastic facade. He absent-mindedly shook his head from side to side. After a moment, he shrugged. "You're the brains behind this operation. You tell me."

Celia sat up straight in her seat. "Chief Parks was at the mall."

Cutter nodded, following along. "And Costas had his faceshield open." There was something there. "Parks saw his face. We all did."

Celia nodded giddily. "Did I win?"

"How come Parks didn't recognize him? Or did he?"

"Maybe he did," said Celia. "Did I win, Jack?"

He dismissively waved a hand at Celia. "No, not yet." He thumped his thigh with his hand. "I can't remember Costas. And neither can Parks. Why?"

Celia jutted an arm inches from Cutter's face. He had to look at them cross-eyed for a brief second to see the two fingers she held up.

"Two reasons I can think of," Celia said.

Cutter waited an appropriate amount of time, before realizing Celia was waiting to be prompted to continue.

"Which are?"

"The Chief is not telling you because he thinks you are involved."

Cutter twisted his mouth into a ball. Wasn't really anything he didn't already know. "Yeah, and the other?"

"Or he is involved."

There was something to taking this case back to its most basic simplistic terms. Everything appeared overly complex and convoluted. But the simplest answers were starting to fit together.

"Okay, so let's go down this road together."

"What road?"

"No road. Parks and Costas, two possibilities. Let's extrapolate."

"Kay!"

"So if Parks saw Costas and recognized him, what would be

his motive for not telling me?"

"Maybe he thought you two were still friends."

"Okay, that's a possibility. So, if the Chief knew that Costas and I were partners that might give him a reason to suspect me in the assassination attempt at M.J. Square. Which would explain what all the third degree was about." He looked at Celia, noticing the confusion in her eyes. Before she could respond, he said, "Uh, third degree, it's… it's just a saying."

Celia smiled at Cutter.

"So, the Chief wanted me out of the loop because he was afraid that I might be in on it. I brought in the drive, the assassin knew police procedure, which gave Parks good reason to think I might be involved."

Cutter squinted, looking at the yellow lines in the middle of the road as if the answers could be found inside the passing blur.

"But that still doesn't make sense. He put me on the case. If he was so concerned why risk it?"

"He did not tell you about the Mayor synth replacement," Celia said, offering the information as a question.

"Which tracks if he suspected I helped plan it. Parks wouldn't want me tipping off Costas that the Mayor was a decoy."

Cutter shook his head. It still wasn't adding up.

"Maybe that explains Parks, but that still doesn't make much sense. Costas didn't need me. If he really was my partner, a detective at that, he would have already known police procedure anyway. And we're assuming Parks recognized Costas. But if he recognized Costas, he would have known that Costas didn't need my help."

Cutter pushed his thumb into his forehead, massaging the spot above the bridge of his nose. "My head hurts."

"There is the other possibility," said Celia.

"That he's in on it?" The slant of his eyes shifted toward Celia. She nodded.

"I guess that makes sense. But we have no motive. I mean, nothing at all. What does Parks gain? And why an alliance with Costas?"

Celia shook her head.

"Someone could have bought him off, I guess. He could be in someone's pocket, but I'm having a hard time believing that one. He's been involved with L.A.P.D. too long. And if he was involved, someone from IA would have noticed by now.

"And the partnering of the two seems odd at best. Costas is an ex-detective gone modded-up mercenary. If Parks is tangled up with him, they would have to be covering their tracks big time. Hiding—I don't even know what, but it would have to be big if he was going to risk his career for it."

"What are you thinking, Jack?"

He stared into the road and oncoming traffic. "No idea." He looked at Celia. "You got any thoughts on that one?"

Celia thrust her lower lip forward and chewed on it at the corner. "None that make any sense."

"Yeah. That's where I'm at too."

"I am sorry, Jack," she pouted. "I tried to help."

"You did good, kid. You'd make one hell of a cop."

Celia looked up from her finger gun. "Really, Jack?"

He nodded. "Really."

She beamed. After a moment, her sparkling eyes drifted away from him and returned to the dashcomp. She hammered out a few more reports on the passing cars.

Adorable, Cutter thought.

But something was still nipping at him, tugging at his conscience. A piece of the puzzle was still missing.

Cutter spoke aloud to no one in particular, only half-heartedly expecting a response. "All that aside, the question still remains—why the hell don't I remember my own partner?"

Celia looked up at him. "That is like asking you where you have left your keys when you have lost them."

Cutter grinned. He felt a warmth he hadn't felt in—ever.

He nodded at Celia. "That it is," he said. "That it is."

"Just, uh… Make yourself at home, I guess." Cutter waved an arm, presenting his apartment like a showgirl on a game show.

What's behind door number only?

Celia took in the sight. It didn't look like Mommy and Daddy's house. Fast food wrappers were piled on the coffee table. A few stragglers were making a run for a broken television stand that was missing a leg. The curtains were drawn, probably permanently judging from the thick layers of dust coating them. A stale musk filled the room; the ceiling fan slowly turning did nothing to alleviate the smell.

"It's messy," said Celia.

Cutter glared at her.

She lowered her head and stared at her feet. *Maybe she shouldn't have said that.* Jack was so nice to her. She knew better than to insult him—even if she hadn't meant to.

"I'm sorry." She peeked up at him. *Was he going to be upset?*

But he only nodded.

"I don't get visitors much." He gestured toward a threadbare sofa. "I'll bring out some blankets. You can sleep on the couch."

He flipped on a light illuminating a small table in the corner. It was easy to overlook on first glance, hidden behind the sofa.

From the scant crumbs and purple jelly residue, there was a high probability Cutter ate his breakfast and performed his morning routine at this table.

"That's my bedroom." He pointed at a door on the far left wall. With a hand on a door to his immediate right, he said, "Kitchen's in here. You hungry?"

Cutter glowered at her, eyes flicking back and forth waiting for a response of some sort. Celia shrugged. She didn't know how to answer. Cutter scratched at the back of his head. "Right, uh… you eat?"

She shook her head. "No."

"Well, I'm starving, so, uh… I'll just be…" He nodded toward the kitchen.

Celia smiled and straightened her posture. "Okay Jack."

The kitchen door quietly swung shut behind him, leaving her to her own devices.

In the corner, on the opposite side of the kitchen was a La-Z-Boy recliner that looked inviting. Celia turned her back to it and flung herself into its deep faux-leather cushions. With a *phoomph*, it caught her and rocked with the landing. She sat upright tightly gripping the arms, readying to throw herself back into the under-stuffed cushions again when she noticed a knob on the right arm. It was plastic, painted maroon to match the color of the chair. She cautiously poked it. The knob was smooth to the touch and sat between two grooves in a slot carved into the arm. With a little tinkering she managed to slide to knob forward.

Something shot out beneath her, knocking her feet into the air. The back fell out from the chair, throwing her backwards. Her first thought was to scream, but everything happened so quickly that by the time she gathered her voice, the ride was over. She was on her back, looking at the ceiling, body laid out flat on the contraption that had been a chair seconds prior.

She looked around giving herself a few seconds to catch her breath. Everything was still. She felt her chest heave up and down with each breath. She was okay.

From out of nowhere, she erupted with laughter.

Jack had such neat stuff.

First the cruiser gadgets, then the training programs, then a room filled with information sticks that she could watch on display monitors, and now it was a chair that converted into a bed.

If Mommy and Daddy could see her now, oh the things they would say. At home, anything she was interested in was always answered with, "No," and, "Don't touch that," and, "That isn't yours," followed by a quick swat to the hand.

But here, with Jack, he showed her all sorts of things that she could interact and have fun with. Things that weren't just dolls.

It seemed to Celia, that all Mommy thought she would ever be interested in were dolls. Celia didn't really like dolls. They didn't do anything. They just sat there. She thanked Mommy, of course, but her enjoyment wasn't ever really about the dolls. It was always about the time she spent playing with Mommy.

For variety's sake, Daddy used to leave a baseball mitt and a softball on the tea table in front of all of her dolls. Any time Mommy saw it, her face would turn a few shades toward red and she would storm out of the room to have words with Daddy. Daddy rebutted Mommy's refusal of his gift with something he referred to as a tomboy, which resulted in a scolding from Mommy. "We're teaching her how to be a lady."

Apparently, ladies wore dresses and played with dolls. Ladies told children to behave and Daddy what to do.

Celia pulled back on the knob. The back straightened and

the footrest disappeared. With a giant grin, she slid it forward. Once again it unfurled from chair to recliner. Celia screamed with delight.

She reset the recliner again, about to go for another ride, when something grabbed her attention.

She could hear the clink of dishes and the high pitched whine of a microwave oven irradiating Cutter's next meal. But she heard something else too; a faint static hummed, like the whisper of electricity through wires. An almost inaudible buzz tickled her ear, a buzz she had not noticed when they first entered the apartment. A buzz that was somehow familiar.

She scanned the room for its source. The television was off, and the overhead lights hummed, but at a different frequency than the foreign oscillation.

The curtain flitted into the room on a slight breeze.

Celia held perfectly still.

Taking a closer look, she saw the ancient layers of dust she had noted earlier had shaken loose from several folds in the curtain and collected in a dirty Rorsarch pattern on the carpet. The curtain brushed the dust aside, dancing in the breeze provided by the open window.

She checked her memory banks and brought up a previous UI screenshot of the room. The curtains had been drawn and the window closed.

"Jack?"

She waited for a reply. When none came, she tried again.

"Jack?"

She strained to hear the muffled noises on the other side of the kitchen door. The microwave hummed a high-pitch squeal, a frequency barely in the human register. It was accompanied by the occasional clinking of silverware and the white noise of a running faucet.

She felt something that she had difficulty putting into words. She turned to her internal logic circuits for answers. It reported what she was feeling was most often associated with a normal fear response. But that couldn't be. She wasn't programmed for fear.

She needed to be brave.

Brave like, Jack, she thought.

She nodded to herself. She could do that.

She needed to work this through logically. That's what Jack would do. When he had to solve a puzzle, he broke it down into pieces. She had seen him do it earlier.

She could do that. She had helped him. She nodded to herself. That's what she would do. She would be like Jack.

She looked at the curtain moving like a specter in the otherwise motionless room. What could cause the curtain to move? She searched her databanks for a list of possible causes:

Wind.

Fan.

Pet.

She paused. Her internal cursor blinked on 'Pet.'

"Jack, do you have a pet?"

Still, no response came from the kitchen.

Any of the things on her list seemed reasonable, except for one small problem. The window had been shut when they entered. Something had to have opened the window. A window does not open on its own—does it?

She began to ignore the more reasonable list, thinking up possibilities of her own.

Daddy used to tell her stories of make-believe about goblins and gremlins and all sorts of things that only came out at night.

It was night.

Outside the window, the now open window, the window she was certain had been closed when they first entered, she could see the pitch black of night.

Her ears strained to hear anything over the hum and occasional kitchen noises. The night was so devoid of other sounds that she was unsure whether she was making up the strange hum to satisfy some innate need for noise.

The hum grew quieter, to the point that she could no longer hear it, but instead only felt its slight tremble mirroring that of her body.

She should join Jack in the kitchen, she thought.

But—what if something reached out from beneath the chair and pulled me under on the run to Jack—to the kitchen—to get help!

Irrational.

Totally and completely irrational her logic circuits told her.

But it *could* happen she insisted.

It was within the realm of possibility.

There *could* be something under the chair. It *could* pull her under. It *could* also want to eat her. *Or worse!*

What was worse than being eaten?!

She opened her mouth to scream for Jack when a hand slid around her neck. Another ran through her hair. A figure knelt next to her, so close that she could feel his breath on her ear. His tongue flicked with a soft shushing sound that begged her to keep quiet, while his hand caressed the outline of her chin, ready to clasp over her mouth should she make a sound.

"That's a good girl," he cooed.

She strained to look and see who was behind her, only moving her eyes. She dared not make any sudden movement, or any movement at all for that matter.

"Ryan?" she said, a soft whisper.

"You're a smart one too."

He brought his hands together in front of her and pressed a metal plate on the back of his right hand. Nestled amidst four splayed hydraulic tendons, halfway between articulating stainless steel, a fiber optic cable sprung from a barely visible opening. With his left index finger and thumb, he pulled the cable until he had a foot and a half of slack.

Celia watched without moving a servo. "What are you doing?"

"It's okay. I'm not here to hurt you."

"Then why are you here?"

He ran his right hand along her chin, drifting to the nape of her neck. His fingertips applied pressure, massaging, searching, and familiarizing themselves with the curves and contours of her slender neck. She let her head fall forward as he worked his way back and forth. She found his touch surprisingly gentle despite fingers like ice. His hands slowed, focusing on one localized spot on her neck. He fingered the barely visible slit hiding her access port.

"To see the world through your eyes, of course."

He inserted the cable. With a faint click, it locked into place.

In the infinite span of a second everything she knew faded away. The sounds of the kitchen, the hum of the microwave, Costas's soft breath warming her ear, his fingers kneading her neck, every sensation she once knew—all vaporized into the moment as if she was remembering them as nothing more than insignificant details from a lifetime long lost.

She opened her eyes. The world she once knew was gone. In contrast to this new shining vision, the old had been a world draped under a thin plastic sheet that dulled vision, muffled sound, and suppressed aroma. Her nostrils flared at this new world, eyes dilated, as the thin membrane of the past ripped away leaving her with the unmistakable knowledge that the journey only moved forward and she could never go back. Her body swam with sensation. A flood of electricity surged through her port, carrying a dull thrum into her head, alighting every welded synapse along the way.

Celia settled into the La-Z-Boy, the only thing anchoring her to reality. And even that was slipping. She sunk into it, feeling it swallow her whole.

Bleak columns of ones and zeroes rained in front of her. She shook her head side to side and watched the numerals fall from the sky in scattered reaction. A falling zero smiled at her and waved as it floated to the ground. *Odd*, she thought. But not as odd as watching her right hand already waving back at it.

A one landed on her shoulder. She dabbed it off with the tip of her finger, holding it up for inspection. Crystal formations like tiny sand castles composed its microscopic numeral structure.

Another one landed in the palm of her hand. It too, had similar sand castle crystalline structure. She pushed the second one along her palm with her fingernail. She compared the two. While similar in origin, no two ones were alike.

She brushed her hands together, clapping the gathered ones and zeroes from her hands and clothes. They whispered cheerfully as they floated to the ground and collected in drifts. They said things about Mommy and Daddy, reminding her how she felt when she was with them. The next wave of ones and zeroes chanted messages about Cutter, a vague nod to how things had changed.

She looked toward the clouds, searching for the source of snowing numerals. There wasn't a cloud in the sky. To her surprise, there wasn't even a sky. Just a vast emptiness filled with a singular voice.

A voice that belonged to Costas.

His voice thundered across the lack of sky, but she couldn't make out the words. She had a feeling that the 1s and 0s knew what he was talking about.

She felt the rigid plastic connector withdraw from her reciprocal docking port.

"There. That wasn't so bad now, was it?"

She looked up at Costas with new eyes, searching.

"Do you see?"

She nodded. "What are they for?"

"Later."

The moment was shattered by a sharp noise.

10

"Hands on your head, now!" Cutter barked.

How had he gotten in here?

Cutter's eyes narrowed to slits. He tried to avoid the grimace he was sure was plastered on his face. In a time like this—of all times—he was thinking stupid thoughts. The how was easy enough to answer. His apartment was a shit-hole. Getting in wasn't difficult by anyone's standards. What he really meant was—*Why?*

"What are you doing here?!"

Cutter stood in the kitchen doorway in Academy stance, feet spread shoulder width, arms outstretched, with the ZeroTwelve resting at the apex of his hands.

He stepped forward, scattering shards of a shattered plate with his foot and mashing his dinner into the yarn field of cheap shag carpet.

Costas pursed his lips, forming a grim smile. "I heard rumors you'd given up on human partners. This one isn't quite department regulation. Little young, even for you, Jack." Costas rested his head on Celia's shoulder. "You planning on shooting through this one to get to me like you did with your last partner?"

"I know who you are—Ryan."

"Very good, Jack. That's not really impressive though, given our history." Costas stayed behind Celia, keeping her directly between them. He only let his head peek out occasionally, teasing Cutter with a clear shot. Bastard.

Costas unfurled his metal fingers and delicately caressed Celia's chin. He leaned in close to her ear and in a soothing tone, soft, just above a whisper, said, "You know why they are called Black and Whites, don't you, Jack?"

"Cause they're cops."

Costas tossed his head back with a hearty laugh. "Silly naive Jack. That's how they see—in black and white." Costas nuzzled the back of Celia's neck. Cutter could hear his breath, could see the hairs on the back of her neck standing straight up. "Isn't that right, sweetheart?"

"Back away from her." Cutter surged forward, circling for a clean shot.

Costas held out his right hand flat, and wrapped his left arm around Celia's neck. "I wouldn't come any closer Jack. You wouldn't want to see what I'm capable of."

Cutter planted his feet and pulled back the hammer on his ZeroTwelve. The chambered round pulsed with a flashing light. It was tempting. He could fire. Maybe hit Celia. Maybe not.

"Keep talking like that," Cutter said, spittle raining, "and it will take an army of forensic scientists to catalogue your remaining parts."

A haunting metallic cackle filled the room. "We are all just hardware, Jack. Interchangeable parts."

Uh oh. That's not good.

A vivid portrait was being painted in Cutter's mind illustrating just how far gone Costas was from reality. Tech sickness was common among mods. The more soft flesh was replaced with infallible metal, the less the original man existed and the more the stainless steel god took its place.

One of the litany of reasons he hated mods. *Like he needed another reminder.*

Cutter felt the right side of his face tighten. His eye squinted, nostril flared, mouth raised unevenly exposing the hint of canine. "The tech has gone to your head."

"Funny you should say that," said Costas. "My head is the only thing that's mine anymore. Can you make the same claim?"

"Buddy, that is quite possibly the stupidest thing I've ever heard. And I've heard some doozies."

"I know about the treatments, Jack."

Cutter's blood turned to ice, frozen solid in his veins. A shiver ran down his spine.

He didn't know how Costas knew about the treatments. And he didn't care. The mere thought of the treatments was enough to set him on edge.

"I don't have a clue what you are talking about."

Costas nodded. "Perhaps not."

Cutter waved the ZeroTwelve at Costas. "We can play this game of rhetorical questions all day, but I'm not the one who turned myself into a monster."

"I assure you, it wasn't my first choice," said Costas. "But you wouldn't know anything about that, would you?" Costas folded a hand under his chin. "No. Perhaps not."

"I hate to burst your bubble, but until yesterday, I didn't even know you existed."

"They came for me in the hospital, Jack." His words dripped with bitterness. "I did what needed to be done to protect myself." Costas wafted his right arm over his cybernetic body.

Cutter had seen enough black and after market mod shops to know what the procedures entailed. He could picture the telltale blue glow of a cybersaw. He could smell the scent of grease mingling with the unmistakable stench of rotting flesh. Human flesh.

Mod shops weren't exactly known for their hygienic practices or pain-free conversions. Their specialty was illegal modification. Secrecy, lack of records, and high tech gear were abundant. Cotton swabs and pain killers, not so much.

"It was your choice, buddy," said Cutter. "No one forced your hand."

Costas raised his leg and put it on the arm of the La-Z-Boy, showing off the hardware. His work couldn't have been cheap. State of the art all the way. Not even military cast offs—his tech was new. Made specifically for him.

"The legs were the easy part," said Costas. "They were useless. That decision was a no-brainer." Costas's tone began to change. His voice lingered with a hint of nostalgia. "But the arms... Now that was a different story."

Cutter could only imagine.

Not that he wanted to.

He had read the reports. He saw Costas in the vid-files. He had enough run-ins with the upgraded version to know what had been sacrificed in the augmentation process.

He simply didn't want to think about it.

What a conversion like that would cost.

Not in any monetary figures.

But in more important terms.

From the reports, Costas's legs were dead weight. He was paralyzed from the waist down. Costas was probably right; the choice to replace his legs probably was a no-brainer.

His upper limbs, however, had been quite intact.

As much as Cutter disliked mods, he could stomach the thought of cutting through useless extremities—but to imagine fixing what ain't broke…

The excruciating pain. The deafening high pitched roar of the cybersaw. A blue glow flickering like something out of a Frankenstein movie, while the patient's arm buckled and shook and spasmed against the restraints—

Until it didn't.

Until it was one more useless reminder of humanity lying motionless on the operating table, a lifeless thing, swept off into a Hefty garbage sack in queue for the dumpster.

Cutter felt Costas's stare burning into him.

"I sacrificed my body to protect what was left of my humanity."

Cutter tried to look away, feeling this man-thing pry up the windowsill of his soul, Peeping-Tom that it was. A rude, deliberate invasion of privacy. An intrusion he thought he was impervious to, but for some reason this man-thing could take a stroll into his noggin, uninvited.

It left him feeling defenseless.

This thing in front of him, this mound of technology barely attached to its remaining humanity had been his partner. That alone was enough to frighten Cutter, but the fact that he couldn't remember Costas terrified him in a manner he couldn't even acknowledge in the deepest chambers of his soul. And now this thing was peering into those darkened recesses.

An electrical charge leaped up his back, arcing from one vertebra to the next.

Maybe this used-to-be-man knew him better than he knew himself.

Costas was shaking his head as if he was disappointed with what he had found. "Interesting. You don't remember me at all, do you Jack?"

Cutter ground his teeth. His hand tightened on the grip of his ZeroTwelve.

"They've sure done a number on your head," said Costas.

It happened.

In that moment. Cutter had no idea why.

Barely even remembered doing it.

Sheer impulse.

Cutter fired.

A red beam scorched the air with a burnt toast smell.

Costas's faceshield snapped shut, deflecting the blast. He staggered backward from the impact, before slowly returning to an upright position.

Cutter couldn't see it, but he was sure that underneath its horizontally slatted faceshield, Costas was smiling a sick twisted little grin. The shot had done nothing. Like hitting the school bully with everything you've got, only to realize it wasn't enough. His helplessness made him hate Costas even more.

"Impulsive as ever, Jack." Costas leaned down to Celia's ear. "I'll be seeing you tomorrow at the Staples Center, sweetheart."

He backpedaled to the windowsill, and with a gentleman's salute, tipped his hand toward Cutter. Without turning to face the sill, Costas hopped up on it, took a backwards step, and fell to the street below.

Cutter ran to the window. By the time he got to the sill and looked down upon the streets, Costas was nowhere to be seen.

He turned back inside the apartment. Celia was curled up on the La-Z-Boy, hugging her knees to her chest.

"Are you okay?"

Celia looked up with glassy eyes. Her teeth sunk into her bottom lip. She slowly rocked back and forth.

"Jack…"

He sat down on the arm of the chair. After a moment he patted her head.

His brain kept telling him there was supposed to be an emotional connection. This incident would have been difficult for anyone. A modded-out killer, the killer of her parents, had come to pay a visit and she was freaked out by the event. Of course she was. Who wouldn't be? His detachment from the mismatching information left him in a hazy trance, only broken by Celia's quiet whisper.

"Hold me," she said.

Cutter took a deep breath.

He could do that.

He leaned into her and wrapped his arms around her. "It's going to be okay," he heard himself say. He was even more surprised by the words that followed. "I won't let anything happen to you."

BROKEN PIECES

1

The stadium erupted into frenzied pandemonium, leaping to life the way a time lapse of moldy bread grants the illusion of movement to an otherwise inanimate object. Ten thousand tiny blobs of color shimmered with excitement.

High above the activity, Cutter watched from a skybox that clung to the underside of Staples Center's domed ceiling.

M.J. Square had been bad. This was much, much worse.

The light inside the stadium was dim except for a circle of yellow that snapped on in an instant, illuminating a transparent blue dome that spread from the visitor's locker rooms to the home team's locker rooms. The field deep within the bowels of the stadium was normally a battlefield for the highly paid, built to remind us what great warriors we once were.

But not today.

Today a metal pod sprouted from a raised platform where center court belonged. For speaking events and conventions, the basketball court and occasional hockey rink, were converted into a raised platform with a podium and a mic-stand. Only today, those putting on the show seemed to be striving for a little more fanfare than a stagnant platform situated under the protection of a transparent blue dome. Expectant cheers of the crowd roared, as a metal pod surfaced, taking place center court. Steel petals wilted from its sides and a stage blossomed from its center, rising on whining struts reminiscent of metal spider legs. The mechanical monstrosity came to rest with a hissing sigh. While dazzling in its production, the spectacle would not have normally garnered such ruckus response from those filling the stadium to capacity. From the center of the pod, a stage in-the-round bloomed. On it stood the crowning jewel, Mayor Benjamin Foster.

"Thank you! Thank you. I really, I couldn't be more elated by the warm reception. This is all too much."

Foster waved, a practiced gesture that belonged only to politicians and beauty queens. An effortless smile, which could easily be mistaken for the genuine article, held his lips in place. He showed no sign of the effects of the glaring spotlights that likely blinded him. He simply paced back and forth across the stage smiling and waving. Smiling and waving.

Cutter grumbled to himself. Such a corny crafted display. Foster never kept his back to any single side for too long. Always the politician.

On the far right of the stage, there was a strange chamber of sorts that towered over Foster, easily double his height. It was a cylindrical metal tube with an opening in the front and a plush velvet lined chamber inside, like something a computer might dream up if it were putting together a magic act. After a moment soaking in applause, Foster acknowledged the contraption with a subtle sweep of his arm and glided toward it.

"First, I feel I must clear the air."

Of course you do. You're supposed to be dead.

He waved a hand in front of the machine with delicate care, as if proving he had nothing up his sleeve. Reaching over to a control panel on the face of the chamber, he pressed a single button in a matrix of buttons. A green light illuminated from within the cylindrical contraption.

"Despite rumors to the contrary, I am, in fact, quite alive and well."

It took Cutter a moment, but he knew the device. He had never seen this model. Frankly, he didn't know they made them so large—this had to be an industrial version.

"I'm sorry for the deception," Foster said.

No, you aren't.

"But as you can see, and probably have already guessed, it was quite necessary. I would not be standing here tonight, speaking to all of you, if certain routine precautions had not been taken."

Foster's hand rocketed up, finger pointing toward the heavens. "However," he said, with the reverence of an Evangelical preacher, "my colleagues urged me not to come tonight."

Cutter choked on a laugh. *Bullshit.* The whole idea on how to properly deal with the PR ramifications of the M.J. Square fiasco had probably been his idea in the first place. Or possibly Yeoman's. He didn't want to give Foster too much credit. *Urged not to come? My ass.*

If anything, Foster's colleagues, backers, supporters, whoever it was could give two shits about his well-being. They just needed to paint him in some light other than pussy. In fact, being here tonight, his speech, his newly manufactured machismo, may have even been his colleagues' ideas as well.

"Yes, friends—there have been reports that another attack on my life will take place. Soon. That whoever wants me dead will attempt to finish the job." He hung his head in a faux moment of silence for himself. After an appropriate amount of time he extended both arms out to the crowd. "But I would not let that keep me from all of you."

Cutter shook his head. *Man, Foster could milk his own cowardice and twist it into theatric heroics.*

"When my colleagues realized that I was undaunted, that I had to be here tonight, they vehemently requested that I once again use a synth decoy." Foster stepped through the opening in the cylindrical device. A transparent sheet slid closed trapping him inside.

"That, I will not do."

Through the transparent sheet, his silhouette was speckled with color. A heat scan of large red, orange, and blue blobs against a backdrop of green mimicked his beauty queen mannerisms.

His silhouette cycled from heat scan, to underlying skeletal structure, to lymph highways, to pulsing blood throbbing through veins en route to a beating heart. Cutter found this last image startling. It wasn't the overall health of Foster's heart that surprised him, rather that Foster had one at all. The transparent sheet slid open and Foster stepped out.

Cutter had been right about one thing: the machine was a bioscanner. Many airports and places of high security had long ago replaced metal detectors with them. Generally, they were a little less obvious than this one; the newest models were nothing more than six inch wide strips that could be mounted to the underside of any door frame. Cutter thought this one was a showpiece for lack of a better word.

"No, friends—how can any man truly support his beliefs while hiding behind a synthetic decoy?"

Yeah, easy for you to say now, safely hidden behind the transparent blue glow of a plasma forceshield.

This stadium's forceshield (and most stadiums for that matter) was the same high-grade low energy-efficiency plasma shield that the Pope used in his Pope-mobile. God himself couldn't fire a projectile through this sucker.

Foster paused for dramatic effect.

"One can't." He paraded across the stage. "As you can see, despite an attempt made on my life, I am here tonight, in the flesh."

He turned toward one of the guardbots on the edge of the

stage, a standard issue synth bodyguard, a big dumb machine that looked like death on inverted haunches. "Could you..." Foster said, and pointed without really pointing in that way politicians do, at the nearest heavily armed automaton on his left. "Could you do me a favor?"

At first, it appeared as if there had been a little mix-up. The guardbot pointed to itself, as if to say, "Who me?" A human guard to his right slapped him on the back, nodded his approval, and nudged his mechanical partner over to Foster. With shy apprehension, it slinked to the side of the mayor, almost comical for a heavy-duty guardbot with machine gun turrets for arms.

The whole setup was beautifully orchestrated, Cutter thought. It lent credibility to the impromptu nature of this bioscanner routine, despite how scripted it was behind the scenes. There was no way Foster or Yeoman would have come out here tonight without a plan to redeem the image of Mayor.

"If you don't mind," Foster said, indicating toward the bioscanner. The guardbot looked at the mayor, then at the bioscanner, and finally back to the mayor before settling upon its final decision.

Cutter self-consciously shook his head. He thought Foster was bad, but these bots could ham it up just as good as the rest of us.

The guardbot stepped toward the bioscanner and turned sideways, twisting its broad shoulders to fit inside the chamber.

The bioscanner repeated the earlier routine, scanning from heat signature, to skeletal structure, to lymph pathways, to circulatory system, with several marked differences. Where Foster's heat scan had been primarily warm colors, reds, yellows, and oranges, the guardbot's scan was almost entirely blue, save a brightly glowing red splotch in the center of its chest. The skeletal structure, while vaguely human in form, under the revealing eye of the bioscanner was anything but organic. The lymph scan was the most similar, revealing the circuitry on which electricity ran through the bot's body. And lastly, similar in look, but completely different in function, the circulatory system showed only a labyrinth of tubes. These carried fluids that kept the guardbot running, a circulatory system of oils, lubricants, and hydraulic fluids.

"As you can see, there is no deception here tonight. There is—" Foster shot a quick glance at the guard bot. "Thank you. You can step out now." The guardbot did, and clunked across the stage returning to its previous post.

Foster swelled, addressing the tens of thousands jammed into the stadium. "There is only me, Benjamin Foster, here to impart a very special message. I am here to speak to you tonight, in the flesh, despite any threats to my safety, because that is how important this message is. The message is too important to be stopped. Too important to…"

Cutter felt a tug on his sleeve.

"What are you looking for?" asked Celia.

"Him," said Cutter.

Celia placed her hands on the lip of the sill, pulling herself onto her tip-toes. She peeked down at the swirling whirlpool of people below. "He's down there?"

Cutter nodded. "Somewhere."

"How do you know?"

He didn't. Not for sure. It wasn't exactly a hunch, though. Short of giving them a seat number, Costas told them where he would be—what to expect. He gave them an invitation to his next assassination attempt. At least, Cutter was hoping it was only an attempt.

"Celia," said Cutter. "I have a special task for you. Think you're up to it?"

Celia's eyes brightened. "Like a case assignment?"

"I guess you could call it that. I need you to be my eyes."

Celia went cross-eyed for the briefest of moments, trying to look at her own eyes. "Okay, Jack."

"I have to go down there, talk to Foster and Yeoman. Probably get the third degree from his personal bodyguard service, as well. I need you to look everywhere. Not just in the crowd, but at places where Costas could be hiding."

Cutter pointed at the steel support beams that arched across the domed ceiling like ribs. "Places like that would give him a clear shot at the Mayor. Keep your eyes peeled. If you see anything out of the ordinary, anything at all, you contact me on the com. Do you remember how I showed you?"

Instantly, her voice boomed loud in his ear. "I remember, Jack!" Cutter reeled, gripped his com, and quickly adjusted the volume.

"That's good," he said over the ringing in his ears.

"I wouldn't worry about it," said the security camera operator.

What a strange thing to say, Celia thought. She wasn't worried. Not about Foster. Or Costas. Or even Jack.

She watched the strange man press buttons at a computer console. He flipped several rows of switches before pulling a slider that changed the main viewing monitor to a different camera angle. Thirty-two touch-screen monitors, stacked in a rectangular shape, eight by four, ran the entire left wall of the skybox. The camera operator shifted in his chair, reaching out and sliding a finger across a nearby touchscreen. As he moved, it seemed he carried his weight with an air his girth was something earned through rigorous self-indulgence, rather than lack of self-control.

"Stuff's all state of the art," he said. "I doubt we'll see any trouble tonight. Or any night for that matter."

Celia liked his confidence. She also liked the way he talked. He had a strange accent, barely pronouncing his vowels, and spoke in choppy phrases.

"And 'sides, even if this guy did turn up, he'd have to get through the forceshield, and that sure ain't happening. Ya could drop an H-bomb on it, ground-zero, and it'd repel the attack with only a flicker."

He turned toward her, every feature on his face smiling. His grin was comforting and effortless. His eyes turned into upside down U's, colored by his blushing cheeks. Even his nose seemed to swell, taking joyful perk mid-face.

"Unless your would-be assassin has firepower the likes of which I ain't ever seen, not saying that stuff doesn't exist, just sayin' it's unlikely outside of a space station, then tonight is going to be totally, thoroughly, and one-hundred percent uneventful. And if he does have that type of firepower—" the security camera operator threw up his hands "—well then, God help us all."

"You talk funny."

"Thanks? I guess," he said with a shrug.

Celia surveyed the display screens over his shoulder. Her internal Black and White programming lit up her UI with a handful of tiny blue targeting squares. Strings of numbers ran calculations inside the blue squares. She wasn't aware of the math behind them, just the result.

With camera angles measured and relative distances compared, Celia marked the probable locations of all the stadium cameras and applied them to a blueprint on her secondary UI overlay. A third overlay popped up with the cameras range of motion, placing thirty-two green cones on the blueprint, allowing her to see any blind spots in the coverage.

The security camera operator fiddled with a circular knob on the console. Screen twenty-four panned to the left, giving a slightly wider view of access tunnel C. He flipped a switch and it was screen twenty-five's turn to be adjusted.

"What is your name?" Celia asked.

Over his shoulder, he said, "Everyone calls me Gus." He tilted his head, nodded, approving camera twenty-five's new position, and then turned toward Celia. "But you can call me Gus."

Celia scrunched up her nose, and raised her head to nod, but failed to complete the motion. Instead, she let her head fall limply to the left and arched a brow, before nodding. "I will," she said.

His full facial smile rolled, as laughter burst from somewhere deep within his belly. He leaned forward and tweaked her cheek leaving behind two red impressions where his fingers had been. "And you're Celia, you adorable lil thing."

"How did you know my name?"

"I got ears, don't I?"

What an odd question. He had so many strange things to say. Celia looked at the side of his head. Indeed, he had two ears. "Yes, you do."

"Well then, I used 'em." He gestured over his shoulder at the spot where Cutter had been earlier. "Heard your buddy talkin' to ya. He always such a stick in the mud?"

"No," said Celia, shaking her head. "As far as I am aware, he has never been a stick in the mud."

Gus exploded with laughter, louder than before. "You're too

much, lil one."

Celia looked around, puzzled. The two men standing guard at the blast door smuggled smiles.

"What?" she said.

"Never stop being yourself, lil one." Gus returned to the display screens, turned the circular knob on the console, and made minor adjustments to the cameras one by one.

Celia heard the two men at the blast door mention her name. When she turned to look at them, the one on the right abruptly stopped, while the other began talking about a local sports team.

Celia thought they could be brothers. They had a similar look, slightly above average height, five-foot ten or eleven, broad shoulders, and athletic builds. Both had high-powered semiautomatic blasters slung over a shoulder, hanging down to their buttocks by a strap. They wore uniforms, light in color, off-whites and greys with blue piping. The same uniform Gus wore.

A yellow triangle popped up in her UI field of view with an exclamation point. She mentally clicked it, and it unfolded into a message providing her with an automatic background check that the Black and White programming ran at the sight of the uniforms. It informed her that their dress belonged to SecureTECH, a private company that hired out security guards. Reading on, the wiki also pointed out that many of SecureTECH's employees were closer to mercenaries than Rent-A-Cops.

On the far right side of the room, a brunette was perched behind a large plasma sniper rifle. It was aimed at the crowd below. She too wore a similar uniform. This one, slightly more form fitting, hugged her curves in a way that the male uniforms did not. Her hair was drawn back into a ponytail, and she hunched over the ledge, eye never leaving the sniper rifle's sight.

Celia wanted to know more about her, but she didn't think it was a good idea to disturb her. What if she spooked the brunette and she discharged her weapon, or she missed, or worse—shot the wrong person. Celia didn't want to take that chance. Whatever the brunette woman was doing or looking at appeared to take all of her concentration. Not only was she the antithesis of Gus, Celia thought, but she seemed to enjoy not being part of the conversation at all. If Gus was the embodiment of jubilation, the brunette manning the plasma rifle was his exact opposite.

Celia startled at the sight of a man standing perfectly still behind her. He was wedged in the corner beside Gus's giant wall-sized display monitors. No wonder she hadn't noticed him.

He was tall with rugged features and a heavy five o'clock shadow.

Celia smiled at him. "What is your name?"

If it wasn't for a brief glance in her direction, she would have thought he hadn't heard her.

Celia tried another tactic. "I am Celia," she said, and extended a hand toward him.

He snorted in response.

Celia arched a brow. Maybe she had been wrong. The brunette wasn't the exact opposite of Gus. This man was.

"Don't mind Trev," Gus said. "He's always like that."

"Oh…"

"Some of the more seasoned vets like Trev here, think cushy jobs like this one make you soft."

"They do," said Trev. Celia jumped. The gruff bass of his voice sounded like he chewed on gravel and that gravel had a habit of smoking two packs a day. She found herself taking a step away from Trev.

A voice blurted in her ear. "Celia, I need you to check on something for me."

Celia curtsied politely excusing herself from the conversation. "How can I help, Jack?"

"I need you to run an ID scan. Some of Foster's goon squad reported suspicious activity coming from the access tunnels. Of course, they didn't bother to investigate it."

She ran to the window and looked down at the crowd filling the stadium. "Why not?"

"Not their job. Least that's what they said. Lazy assholes. They didn't seem too thrilled to have me butting in, either. Like they'd rather take a bullet for Foster than prevent the shot in the first place. They said they saw someone offloading goods in access tunnel D. I'm here, but I don't see what the hell they were talking about."

Celia looked at the monitors. Unable to discern what Cutter was talking about, she ran up behind Gus and tapped him on the shoulder. He had been watching her whole routine and managed to stifle a laugh.

"Yes, sweetheart?"

"Which one of these monitors is access tunnel D?"

He pointed to a screen in the upper left, top row, fourth from the corner. Gus gave extra scrutiny to the crowd on display. "What's up, sweetness?"

The screen showed rows of people sitting in bleachers around the access tunnel. Handfuls of people milled about, coming and going. Dozens of possible suspects, but how was she supposed to single one out?

"What am I looking for, Jack?"

"Hell, if I know," said Cutter. "Let's look for Costas, for starters."

A blue targeting reticle twitched across her UI jumping from face to face of those in the bleachers. When it completed scanning static targets, it tracked those moving across frame with startling precision. "I do not see anyone that looks like Costas."

"Yeah, me either."

Celia bounced up and down on her toes. "But I see you, Jack!"

Cutter had walked into frame on camera four.

"Wonderful," he said, but from his tone, Celia doubted he meant it.

"Do you want me to—"

"Hang on a sec," Cutter said. "I may have something."

Cutter walked offscreen. Celia watched him appear on camera three. He was looking at something in the distance, something that wasn't on camera three. She scanned adjacent screens, trying to pinpoint what Cutter was looking at.

A man tussled the hair of a young boy, yanking a ball cap so low on his head that the boy had to raise it off his forehead to see. Celia doubted that had caught Cutter's attention. A woman in a festive sweater with bright red lipstick leaned into a man at her side, tucking herself into the nook of his arm. The man took the opportunity to place his arm around her shoulder. No, Cutter would not be interested in them. On camera eleven, a row of college age boys shook signs with slogans: "InSight for Everyone!" and "About Time!" An opposing row on camera twelve held opposing defamatory signage, like: "It Lives!" and "Out with the Old and That's It!"

"Okay," Cutter said. "You see the guy in the hooded sweatshirt about twenty meters to my left?"

Her eyes flitted back to Cutter on camera three. She didn't see who he was talking about on camera three. Nor on camera four. But on camera five she saw a man in a hooded sweatshirt. She cross-referenced the positions with her three-dimensional blueprint and camera coverage overlays confirming that that this man was twenty-four point five-seven meters to Cutter's left.

"I see him, Jack."

"Is it Costas?"

On her HUD, blue targeting reticles swarmed the man in the hooded sweatshirt, searching for something, anything to lock on to.

"Sorry, Jack." Celia said. "The angle is too steep and the hood blocks off my facial recognition software."

"How about ancillary matchups?"

Celia shook her head. "What are those?"

Over the com, his voice came off gruff, impatient even. He was under pressure. Celia could understand that. "In the Black and White routines, they let you make approximate matches. Not a positive ID, but matches of probability. Height, weight, build, gait, things like that."

"One second." Inside her head, she entered the Training file. An offshoot of the initial launch program was labelled 'Ancillaries.' She mentally dove into the files. "Found it. Downloading the program now. It will take a minute."

"Get back to me. I'm gonna see if I can get in closer for a face to face."

"Okie dokie," Celia said. Her cheeks turned rosy with an ear to ear smile.

She liked this. Liked feeling part of something larger than herself. Being able to help made her feel worthwhile. Mommy was always afraid to let her do anything.

She didn't know if this was the first thought she had ever had of her own, but she came to the realization that she liked learning. Not just gaining knowledge, but the process. New information led to new abilities which in turn led to doing new things that only moments prior were a mystery.

Something else excited Celia, too. She was discovering new aspects of herself, interests in things she didn't know she enjoyed—like police work, investigating crimes, putting together clues. It was like the puzzles Daddy and her assembled when Mommy was too busy tending to Jessica.

Somehow, being with Cutter, putting together his puzzles felt different. Her process never changed, she still followed a methodical pattern, but the time spent with Jack was not the same as time spent with Daddy.

With Mommy and Daddy, she always did what she was told. But Cutter gave her a freedom and responsibility all her own. He counted on her to assemble the pieces of the puzzle that he could not. He had given her specialized tasks, things that only she could do. Cutter's attention made her feel special.

And with those thoughts in her head a brand new thought occurred to her.

Celia walked up behind Gus and tapped him on the shoulder.

"Erm?" he said, hammering away at the console controls. Celia patiently waited for him to finish. After a moment he turned and faced her. "S'up lil one?"

"Do you know the blast rating on those doors?" She pointed at the blast doors that sealed them inside the room.

"Uhm—?" Gus spun in his chair. "I really wouldn't worry about it, angel. Like I said, anything short of Armageddon ain't getting through the forceshield."

"So no one can get through it?"

"You can bet your bottom britches."

"I was thinking," Celia said, hesitating for a moment as she gathered her thoughts. "If I could not get through the forceshield I would go to the place where you could turn it off." Again, she pointed at the blast door. "Which means the forceshield is only as strong as those steel doors, right there."

Gus paused, taking a long look at the blast door. She saw his Adam's apple slowly bob. He shifted his eyes from the blast door back to her. "You got quite an imagination, kid."

He spun his back to her, returning to his station and the thirty-two display screens in need of monitoring. Celia couldn't put her finger on it, but something about the way Gus was acting seemed different than before. His smiling features evaporated; his jubilation waned. Where warmth previously emanated there was now a cold void.

"Celia!" Cutter's voice barked over the com. "Anything yet?"

"The download just completed, Jack."

"And…?"

The man in the hooded sweatshirt was moving quickly between cameras, in and out of blind spots. She ran to the ledge of the skybox and looked down at the stadium below, at Foster giving a speech, at the crowd, at Access Tunnel D.

She pulled her upper body onto the ledge and peeked over. Her HUD zoomed in on the man in a hooded sweatshirt and pinpointed her target.

"Okay, I got him, Jack."

"And…?"

From his flat tone, Celia got the impression that Jack would keep asking "And…?" until she came back with an answer, but it was a theory she did not want to put to the test.

The new programming adhered a transparent blue overlay on the man in the hooded sweatshirt. Celia strained to keep up with the graphs and charts tracking his movements and comparing them to previous encounters with Costas.

"Height and build are an approximate match to Costas. But

the angle still makes it difficult to gather more data."

Jack didn't respond.

She filled the silence with, "Sorry, Jack."

She waited another moment that seemed painfully long, but her internal clock said only three seconds had passed.

"I'm getting some strange interference," said Cutter. "What is that?"

Celia checked the graphical display of their conversation. It was split into fine lines of blue, green, and red. White dots, like snow thrown into the air, rhythmically pulsed every few seconds.

"Static," Celia said.

"I know it's static. I mean, what's causing it?"

"Not sure, Jack."

Muffled distortion screeched through the line. Cutter was saying something, but she couldn't make out the garbled words through the rushing static. His tone had sounded urgent. *He lost him?*

Was that what he said?

But her thoughts directed towards Cutter's plight didn't last long.

She wasn't listening to him anymore.

A new voice drifted through the static calling her name.

She could hear the voice apart from the casual chatter of the security guards. Her eyes flicked down to Mayor Benjamin Foster giving a speech on the field far below. The words did not belong to him either. She tried to distinguish the voice from the general white noise blanketing her auditory system. It was different, not belonging to the crowd. She checked her onboard UI. Her com connection to Cutter was closed.

Again, she heard the voice call to her, words clear as her own thoughts. The haunting call echoed around her, drowning her in a single voice emanating from everywhere and nowhere.

She spun, trying to pinpoint its location.

Celia.

She scanned the room, the security guards, the monitors, and the field below.

Nothing.

I know you can hear me, Celia.

The soft caress of his voice. The polite manner. The intonation. She recognized it.

"Jack is looking for you."

Gus pricked up his eyes from rows of display monitors and glanced at her. After a moment's hesitation, he returned to his work.

Any luck?

"Where are you?"

Gus once again turned toward her, making eye contact. His brow arched up and pushed together over the bridge of his nose.

Celia's internal subroutines ran an expression check. He was likely puzzled. Perhaps even frightened. A little girl that appeared to be talking to herself certainly must have been a strange sight. No doubt, her earlier predictions of doom's day scenarios and the infallibility of the forceshield coming only at the expense of the lives of those inside the skybox had unnerved him.

He cleared his throat. "Don't worry sweetheart. Tonight will be uneventful."

But she knew better. The voices in her head told her a different story.

I'm close. Very close.

Celia looked out the window, checking the cross-beams and support struts. They were hidden in shadow, but from what she could see no one was perched on them. There was no hidden figure prepping a shot that would single out and kill the man speaking to tens of thousands below.

She scanned the crowd, using a few tricks she had picked up from the Black and White programming to accumulate as much pertinent information as possible. The routines began categorizing data. Useless heaps of information complied long lists amounting to a whole lot of nothing.

Celia watched Foster pace around the flattened flower of stage in the dead center of the stadium. The voice was coming from somewhere down there. She did not need the Black and White programming to tell her so. She didn't know how or why—she simply knew. He was down there.

She felt it.

Celia…

Celia took an uneven breath and found that odd, as she didn't need to breathe in the first place. The voice was doing something to her—or had already done it.

"What do you want?!" she said, her voice louder than before.

This time Gus wasn't the only one who turned. They were all looking at her.

The two men that guarded opposing sides of the blast door, the woman with her brunette hair drawn back into a tight ponytail holding a sniper rifle, the man posted up next to the surveillance equipment, and Gus—they all stared.

At her.

A bead of sweat dripped over Gus's brow, missing his face, and falling to the floor. He wheeled his chair around, facing her. "Is everything okay?"

She barely heard him. Saw his lips move. Could have read them if she was paying attention. Her mind was elsewhere. The ambient noise of the room was drowned out by the confusion between her own thoughts and the voice in her head.

Well, Celia… is it? Is everything okay?

"Where are you?!" she shouted, stomping around the room. "Where are you?! Where are you?! Where! Are! You!"

She saw the security guards react to her, startled with fright. She wasn't trying to scare them, but she didn't like the feeling of Costas inside her head.

It was more than that. Worse. Something else. Her thoughts weren't her own anymore.

The lack of control made her feel something she had never felt before.

What was it?

Her internal monitors ran a quick diagnostic.

Anger, it told her.

Anger?

That didn't make sense. She had never been angry before.

Are you ready, Celia?

"Tell me what you want!" she shouted. "I don't like this!"

You know what I want, Celia.

She grabbed at the hair above her ears and pulled hard. "Get out! Get out! Get out!" With each shout, she stomped a pink Converse'd foot down, a crazy march, pacing in aimless circles.

If only she could look at it—see the voice in her head.

She tried to roll her eyes back as far as they would go. Roll them up and into her head for a better look at what was inside. But it was no use. Even with her eyes filled to the brim with white, it wasn't enough. She couldn't get them to look inside.

Gus reached out to her. "Celia, calm down." She slapped his

hand away.

He turned to Trev with a bewildered look. "The hell is wrong with this one?" Trev shrugged.

Celia...

"Leave me alone!"

Gus defensively pulled his hands back.

Do you see all the pretty faces?

Her body went rigid.

She did.

Mommy. Daddy. Cutter. Costas. Foster.

Anyone she had ever met.

She saw all the faces.

The faces streamed across her field of vision, warped and distorted. Bass sounds thumped. Speech from some language she could not understand poured from their mouths, out of sync with their lips. The faces peered down at her, spinning, surrounding her, closing in. They grew large in her sight, a strange rainbow array of mismatched colors on speckled skin. The colors mixed into muddy yellows and sickly greens and browns. She felt her stomach churn. The faces turned ghastly horrific, grotesque. Rotting pustules formed before her eyes, filling, bursting, melting away, and leaving behind blackened craters and pockmarks.

She saw Mommy, blood streaked tears painting a river down her cheek, pooling at her chin, bubbling until the weight was more than it could bear. The blood bubble detached forming a perfect sphere for a split second, then flung itself to the floor, splatter explosion sending the perfection of the sphere into irreparable chaos.

She saw Daddy too.

Sadness was in his eyes. Behind them, a weeping man whose expression was quickly eaten away by a dark fungus spreading across his lip from ear to ear. Teeth peeked through the forming hole, a sickening skeletal grin. Flecks of skin floated away from his chin, defying gravity, as the fungus spread along his jaw, a burgeoning beard feeding on what was beneath, chewing flesh to bone, until his jaw fell to the floor at her feet.

Cutter was also there.

His face was beginning to distort, change, and rot. But she fought it. The images were in her head. *Her* head. This was her mind and she was in control. She did not want Cutter to change in her mind. She did not want to lose the new friend she had just made.

Cutter.

The new friend that taught her things she didn't already know. The new friend that introduced her to a different world she had never seen before. A world, while harsh, that was beginning to provide answers to her *oh so* many questions.

Cutter. The only one that treated her like an individual. The only one that saw her for what she was. The only person that gave her the tools to think for herself, to come to her own conclusions, to find her own solutions, to chip in her own opinion.

As simple as it sounded, Cutter had given her a first taste of independence.

And she liked it.

She gritted her teeth, fighting back tears.

Green-black stalks, like tiny shrubs on an impressionist landscape, sprouted around Cutter's eyes. She clenched her fists and held her breath. Her face turned red. She couldn't stop it. She couldn't stop him from transforming too.

The fungus spread, scattering flesh to the wind. In the blink of her eye, Cutter's eyelids vanished, his eyes drooped and lulled in their sockets. The fungus wrapped around in a spiral, consuming his nose and leaving behind two dark slats, a terrifying peephole into his brain.

Tears streamed down her cheeks, as Cutter melted into an amalgamated mass of pulsing, writhing people she thought she knew.

She turned, wiping her eyes with the back of her hand and found herself looking straight into the face of Costas.

The sickly smiling face.

She scowled, brows furrowing, pointing little arrows at her nose.

He had been nice to her. Polite even.

But...

She did not trust him.

Not one bit.

This image, this face—Costas—he didn't look like the others. He looked almost normal. His lips moved, mumbling something soft, incoherent. She leaned forward, cupping her hands behind her ears. Costas kept talking so low she could only hear the buzz of sound.

His image fell back into the distance, appearing almost normal amidst the others now crowding her. But his words had become the dull white noise that contained all other sounds.

The faces melted together in a liquid flowing form, like the disturbed waters of a lagoon catching the downpour of a waterfall. They were saying something all at once.

She tried to ignore them, but they were too loud. The sound was a deep reverberation, repetitive and difficult to decipher.

She felt them.

They were all there. In her head. They always had been. And. Always would be. Impossible to ignore.

The sound became clear. The faces laughed. A deep voice

echoed, rising out of the rumbling noise pollution, not sounding like Mommy, but Celia was certain that it was her. Words poured from Mommy's mouth in nearly visible streaks of light. Distorted groans croaked an undulating rhythm of sound. "You are a good girl aren't you?" They weren't asking. The faces rolled in waves, rolled with laughter.

No Mommy! No! Celia roared

Her eyes blinked laser beam red.

Do you see all the pretty faces, Celia?

"I see all the pretty faces," she answered.

Scattered glances bounced amongst the security guards.

Before Gus had time to react, Celia jumped on top of him and ripped his throat out of his neck. His body collapsed beneath her and fell off its chair sending it spinning into a corner.

"Holy shit!" said one of the remaining security guards. The brunette turned, lifting her eyes from her sniper rifle sight.

Celia's UI lit up with dozens of small blue targeting squares. This time they weren't latching on and processing the data of people she observed on the screens at Gus's workstation. They were locking on to those in the room, calculating angle, distance, and line of sight, determining who posed the greatest threat.

Rather—she was.

She was doing it.

It was all happening inside her head.

She had no control. But she was doing it.

A blue square morphed into a large red rectangle, highlighting the weapon in Trev's hand. Icons flashed in reds and yellows. Her targeting squares swarmed his body, high speed calculations, yielding percentages, odds, and targets of opportunity on Trev's person that would provide the quickest remedy to the situation.

Trev already had his weapon lowered and leveled at her.

She twisted toward him, lowering her shoulder, trying to make herself as small a target as possible. She charged as a plasma blast sizzled through the air. A splash of red energy ricocheted off her shoulder, melting plastic, and exposing wire. She staggered from the impact, but kept up her momentum and leaped at him. Trev raised his weapon to finish the job. Her tiny fist connected with his eye and exploded out the back of his skull.

Trev crumpled to the floor in a lifeless heap.

The nearest guard by the blast door scrambled for his weapon, for cover, for his life. The other security guard grabbed at his blaster rifle. The brunette hefted her sniper rifle off its perch and brought it around in a cumbersome sweeping motion.

Celia could read the data and incoming calculations. She knew the distance she had to cover to complete the mission objective she saw flashing before her eyes. She knew she wouldn't make it in time before the sniper rifle drew a bead on her or the guard pushing his partner out of the way had a clear shot.

Her body didn't care.

A laser dot found her forehead. With fluid motion, she fell to the floor and whipped Trev's sidearm from the pile of used-to-be-man. Plasma blasts ignited copper stench, singeing flesh, exploding console, pockmarking paneling. The brunette cried out in agony, gripping her shoulder. A spray of blood arched toward the ceiling.

A hit!

Not precise, but a hit. It was enough to send the brunette's shot high and wide, but failed to knock the weapon from her hands. The brunette clung to the sniper rifle like life itself. Through gritted teeth accompanied by a throaty grunt, she heaved the weapon level for another shot.

Celia pumped her legs as fast as she could, running toward

the nearest guard who was still shaking, paralyzed with fear. The sniper rifle laser dot gave chase, trailing inches behind her. In full sprint, Celia edged to her right, trying her best to keep the other security guards in the brunette's line of fire.

A high-pitch shriek tore through the confines of the control booth. Celia's UI lit up with an emergency warning milliseconds before the shot tossed her up against the blast door. She twisted in mid-air, feet landing on the wall, and used her forward momentum to defy gravity for mere seconds, running perpendicular to the floor. She leaped at the nearest guard, landed on his shoulders, and wrapped her legs around his neck.

"Don't!" he spat, grabbing at her thighs. He pulled at the figure four created by her interlocking legs that was clamping down on his neck.

Her leg lock was slipping. The guard managed to slide his fingers between her hold. Leaning backward, she let the guard's neck bare her full weight. He gasped, clawing at her.

Upside down, Celia reached for the nylon gun-strap across his chest and tugged. It fought her, snagged on something behind the struggling guard. She yanked harder as the guard gurgled for air and pulled at her legs. He flailed, a desperate struggle for breath, his complexion turning red to purple, the color in his lips fading to pale blue. She pulled harder on the strap. Something gave and the blaster rifle slid around his body.

As she reached for the weapon, a laser dot crawled up her forearm. She grasped the blaster rifle, finger sliding into the trigger guard. The now familiar sound of the sniper rifle echoed in the small confines. Celia sat upright, cradling the suffocating security guard's head, and sprayed suppressive fire at the brunette.

For the first time since the ordeal began, she noticed that the other security guard had been trying to pry her loose as well. The butt end of his blaster rifle raced toward her face. She twisted, squeezing her legs tight, but it was a losing battle. The butt landed on her thigh. A series of beeps sounded inside her head. A paint by numbers icon of herself lit up across her display—a red left shoulder, yellow right thigh, orange left ribcage.

The sensation wasn't pain. Not exactly. She knew she was injured, that her body was beginning to fail, that she needed to end this incursion soon, or she wouldn't have the wherewithal to see the mission to its end.

The guard beneath her fought for survival. Her thighs tightened around his neck. A choking, gurgling rattle escaped from the guard, as bits of spittle flew. That was a bad sign. For her. Moments ago, he hadn't been able to breathe at all. The desperate sputtering inhalations meant he was breaking free.

He dug his fingers into her legs, prying her vice-like grip from his neck. With an exasperated shove he ripped her away and held her at arm's length. She grabbed the black gun-strap and snapped the plastic buckle with a twist of her wrist. He shoved the writhing automaton away and gasped for sweet, sweet air.

The gun strap slithered from his chest, and the blaster rifle came with Celia.

A smile found its way onto the guard's face, as he sucked in air that had never tasted so good. He opened his eyes for a split second, and looked up into the barrel of his own blaster rifle. A burst of three plasma bolts cycled toward him.

Blood spatter war-painted Celia's face.

This was a brand new experience.

A new feeling.

Her database had a word for it, but she could not be sure that the feeling matched the description.

Pride, it said.

Satisfaction for a job well done.

She shouldn't be doing this. Pride was all wrong. She should feel bad. At least, she was supposed to feel bad. She was taking life. Not just *a* life. Multiple *lives.* Everything she had ever been taught said in no uncertain terms: taking life was a bad thing.

Yet, she didn't feel bad at all.

Her head sparked with life, creating new neural pathways, making new connections. Her actions were not her own. *Or was that just an excuse?* She was a passenger along for the ride, watching herself beat the life out of each guard that stood in the way of her mission.

And she was enjoying it.

She skidded across the floor, rolling to her side. She brought the brunette into her sights. A volley of superheated particles pelted the brunette, knocking her against the wall. The brunette's body shimmied in lifeless dance before crumpling to the floor.

A smile crept onto Celia's face.

She was *so* good at this.

Her blaster rifle click-click-clicked its empty battery charge. The last remaining guard brought his weapon around, shaking in desperation, praying for an escape. She gave him no more thought than to throw a snarl in his direction along with her spent blaster. The spinning blaster sailed at his head. Off balance, he ducked. Repetitive pulses in bursts of three sprayed wide of the target and tore through the ceiling. A panel of overhead lights crashed to the floor. Wires whipped out with coursing electricity.

Celia heard a noise, new to her, unmistakable to her UI. She turned. Sprawled out on the floor and bleeding everywhere, the brunette pulled back the bolt-action on her sniper rifle. Through the scope, a giant eye stared directly at her.

Celia dodged right, but never had a chance. The blast

connected at point blank range. Red and orange warnings flashed on her UI. A mannequin icon lit up in reds and yellows along its left side. But she didn't stop. She couldn't. She would fulfill her mission if it killed her.

The brunette staggered to her feet.

Amazing, Celia thought. *Truly amazing.*

The brunette was probably thinking the same thing. Why won't this kid, die? She hefted the sniper rifle, using her knee for leverage.

The deafening pitter-patter of tiny feet rushed toward her.

Celia plunged her fist through abdomen, clutching spine. The brunette looked down at the little girl, now hoisting her off the ground. Celia raised her above her head and turned toward the last remaining guard that was clambering for escape. Failing that, for his weapon.

The brunette gurgled. Blood poured from her speechless mouth and dripped down her chin. An expression of confusion lay plastered on her face. It didn't seem to Celia that the brunette was confused about the events that had unfolded. She had been aware—very aware. But her face was the kind of puzzled bewilderment that came only from ego—*This can't be happening—to me.*

The repetitive particle weapon bursts returned in threes. Only Celia had been ready for them this time. Her UI blinking in mostly reds couldn't take another hit. But they would not need to.

Nothing would hit her ever again, she thought. *Not ever.*

She spun, hoisting the brunette off her feet, absorbing the incoming blaster fire with her makeshift human shield.

A new mantra echoed through her head.

Never again.

A smirk twisted the corner of her mouth.

She charged the last remaining target, cutting loose a shrill shriek, drowning out the tension-wire blaster noise.

Every feeling she had ever been told was wrong, every indiscretion tallied as a problem she had caused, every indignity she had been forced to suffer for someone else's ego, every left over after thought that she had become in someone else's life, every variable that did not fit the formula—rippled through her and spilled out of her guts in a primal scream.

She charged with the brunette thrust out in front of her absorbing blaster fire. Petrified by the sight, the last remaining guard's blaster fell to the floor. His teeth chattered, eyes growing wide, focusing on the incoming attack he was helpless to prevent.

He heard a chunky crunch.

His eyes drifted down to his attacker.

She looked into his eyes.

His life ebbed.

It was hers now.

Hooded Sweatshirt slid through the crowd like an oil slick. Cutter tried to keep pace, bobbing and weaving, but the crowd seemed intent on constantly pushing him away from his target. He elbowed past a large man that was crossing in front of him just in time to see Hoody turn the corner into an access tunnel.

Great, Cutter thought as another pedestrian rammed into him, pushing him farther from the access tunnel. The man issued an apology to Cutter, the 'O' of his mouth poking through a shaggy beard. Cutter acknowledged the gesture, not with his eyes, but by shoving the bearded man out of his way.

Cutter ran down the corridor lifting his sleeve to his mouth. "Celia, he ducked into Access Tunnel D. Keep an eye out for him if he surfaces again."

Static buzzed an answer.

"Celia?"

Dammit.

He could have counted on Roy to be distracted by superficial technicalities. But he wasn't sure what could possibly keep Celia from responding. Her child-like bewilderment had kept her attention pinned to new experiences. In the short time he had known her, he had noticed that it was impossible for her not to ask questions about *everything.* Perhaps it was his fault. Maybe he expected too much from her. The Black and White programming should have helped, but what the hell did he know about bots, children, hell—anything really?

Cutter paused at a blind corner leading into the inner ring of the stadium. He leaned forward so that only a sliver of his body was exposed.

Cutter grimaced. The corridor was busier than he had hoped. People were shoulder to shoulder, moving like sludge, in queue to buy whatever crap it was they sold at the numerous concession stands and souvenir shops.

If he hadn't been distracted by a young blonde kid dropping a tray full of hotdogs, he would have missed Hoody altogether. Behind the kid, Hoody ducked into the men's room.

Cutter's entrance was greeted by the acrid stink of urine. Hoody was lined up at a stall, fly undone, hooded sweatshirt unzipped. Cutter's eyes drifted to an emblem on the left breast pocket, a circle with a corndog bisecting it. The pieces were all there. This wasn't Costas dressed up to look like someone that sold souvenirs and concessions at the stadium. This *was* someone who sold souvenirs and concessions at the stadium.

Sensing someone behind him, Hoody turned and caught Cutter staring. He was a year or two shy of forty. Acne scars pitted his cheeks, a much needed distraction from his dull sunken eyes completely devoid of life. With a disgusted look, he said, "See anything you like?"

"You're a vendor?"

"Get lost creep. I'm off-duty. Obviously."

"So you're what a wild goose looks like."

"Fuck outta here."

Bodyguards or not, Cutter assumed that Foster and his goons would be helpful at the very least.

Offloading goods. Cutter shook his head. *Assholes.*

He made his way back through the access tunnel to the arena. Foster paraded on the stage below, dead center, blah blah blahing about what a great Mayor he had been for the city. Yammering on about how he could make the city even better.

What's the hold-up, Ben? You've only had damn near two decades to do anything.

The absolute smugness in the Mayor's voice made Cutter seriously question whether or not he was someone worth protecting. "If you have been thinking about trying InSight, but haven't had the time, or hell, if you want to come down just to shake my hand, well then, by all means you have to stop by the official unveiling tomorrow."

What a complete pompous arrogant asshole.

Cutter made his way to the foot of the stage. Stadium security was accompanied by Foster's own personal detail, as well as a handful of uniformed L.A.P.D. officers that ringed the perimeter of the stage.

"I will personally be at the portside InSight operation. And

I expect to see you all—"

The forceshield bubble flickered.

Cutter watched the Mayor's expression change, faltering mid-sentence, suddenly conscious of the millions of eyes all focused on him.

There you go, asshole. All eyes on you. Bask in it.

Cutter's hand slid into his jacket, grasping the grip of his ZeroTwelve. His eyes flicked through the waves of supporters in the stands, briefly stopping on a man in a blue hat. No. They flicked to a woman flapping her arms with excitement by access tunnel B. No. Overhead. On the beams. Nothing.

Foster cleared his throat, regaining his composure. "I, uh, I will be at the harbor tomorrow…"

The blue glow faded. It wasn't a flicker this time. The entire forceshield vanished as quickly as the smile from Foster's face.

The stadium security turned out toward the crowd. A few looked up at the skybox control booth for signs of problems. Everything looked normal enough.

Foster's personal entourage stood slack-jawed by his side, weapons whipped from their shoulder holsters, looking like they hadn't a clue about what to do next.

Idiots.

The uniformed L.A.P.D officer on Cutter's immediate right was looking into an upper deck. Cutter slid past him and hopped onto the stage. The officer spun and yelled. "Hey! You're not allowed up there." He toggled the com on his chest. "We have a problem down here."

You sure do. And it isn't me.

Cutter charged across the stage. The officer pulled himself up and gave chase. Behind him, two more officers were climbing onto the stage to provide assistance. In front of Cutter, Foster's bodyguards turned to receive him with their weapons drawn, quickly finding a bead on their target.

"Move!" yelled Cutter.

But instead, they planted their feet, taking steady aim.

A high-pitch roar chimed with the resonance of a gong from somewhere to Cutter's right. The bodyguards turned at the deafening sound echoing through the arena, just enough of a distraction that allowed Cutter to barrel through the ape-like figures and reach the Mayor.

Thank God.

But the sound wasn't all sunshine and roses. In fact, Cutter had been fearing the sound even more than the armed thugs under Foster's employ intent on aerating his posterior.

Cutter tackled Foster to the stage, hitting with a thud, as a burst of blue-green energy blasted the podium to splinters. A second blue-green pulse exploded at their feet. Cutter grabbed Foster by his lapel and dragged him off the far side of the stage, away from incoming energy pulses.

Blue-green splashes of death rained from above throwing searing scraps of metal and chunks of wood at them.

With Foster out of sight, off to the side of the stage, the blue-green pulses focused fire on the bioscanner. A first hit punched a semi-circular hole in the casing at the top. It began to glow bright orange. Even from twenty yards away, Cutter could feel the intense heat radiating from the device. He looked up just in time to see an incoming second blast. Foster tried to look over the lip of the stage, but Cutter pushed him back down and covered him with his body.

The explosion shook the stage; pieces of bioscanner flew like shuriken and embedded into the concrete at Cutter and Foster's feet. Cutter threw an arm over his head as smaller debris tore into his leather sleeve. Foster had made a similar move, ducking under his suit coat, trying his best to protect himself from injury.

Cutter sat up on his haunches, ZeroTwelve held at the ready, and peeked over the lip of the stage.

The seats were abuzz with activity. Thousands upon thousands flooded the stairs and drained through the access tunnels in flight for their lives. It was damn near impossible to tell where the shots had come from.

Cutter sank down behind the stage. Two bodyguards flocked to Foster's side, manhandling him, checking for injuries.

Yeah, where were you guys three seconds ago when he was almost atomized?

Foster pushed the bigger bodyguard away and raised the back of his hand as if he were ready to slap him. Over the roar of screaming, rioting, fleeing crowd, Cutter heard Foster loosen a few expletives. He didn't sound none too happy about the day's events. After addressing the incompetence of his would-be protectors with a few choice words, he turned his attention to Cutter.

Spittle flew from Foster's mouth. "Where the fuck is he?!"

"There's only one place to shut down the forceshield."

"What the fuck are you waiting for?!"

It was a good question.

Cutter sprinted down the crowded corridor, barreling through panicking herds of people, fighting his way towards a door marked AUTHORIZED PERSONNEL ONLY. He swiped his thumb on a keypad and leaned into the door with his shoulder. Halfway up the winding stairwell he keyed his com. "Celia, you there?"

It was the third time he had tried to contact her with no success.

He had told her to use the com to contact him if anything—anything at all—seemed out of the ordinary. Maybe she had forgotten how to use it.

He hoped it was something as simple as that, but he had his doubts. He had given her step by step instructions. Showed her how to use it, practiced together. That should have been enough.

That and synths never forget.

He sprinted down the empty corridor leading to the skybox control booth, his footsteps echoing hollow thuds off cheap linoleum.

Everything was rigged from the skybox control booth: the lighting, the PA system, surveillance, and most importantly the forceshield. With any luck, he would also find Costas there.

He wished the control booth was closer. Not only would it give Costas less time to flee, but it would also give Cutter less time to think about the events leading up to this moment. The more he tried to make heads or tails of things, the less sense everything made.

How had the control room been compromised without Celia being able to alert him?

He chalked the dilemma up to one more piece in an ever expanding puzzle. With each new piece, the picture was falling further out of focus. That's not how these things were supposed to work.

Cutter grunted, pushing himself harder, concentrating only on his stride. Answers, at least some of them, were certain to be found inside the control booth.

He ran up the curving slope, as the heavy blast doors came

into view. He had expected to find the blast doors mangled, bent back, and pried open. Something stadium security assured him could never happen. But, in the past few days, a lot of things he had assumed could never happen had. Why should this be any different?

He stopped dead in his tracks. Every suspicion, every remote hunch evaporated like distant objects in a fog. In their place, another question with no answer surfaced through the haze.

In front of him, unblemished chrome sparkled with polish. Cutter ran his hand down the seam where steel door met steel door. They met in the perfectly symmetrical middle, forming a perfect seal, reflecting the hall fluorescents with the same perfect shimmering chrome sparkle he had seen when he exited these doors only an hour or so earlier.

The blast door was perfectly intact.

"What the hell?" Once again, he keyed his com, "Celia? Now would be a really nice time to answer."

Static hissed at him.

He paced to his right, hand hovering over the security keypad.

Whatever was on the other side of the door had disabled an entire security team, the forceshield, and his makeshift partner. He was keenly aware that the blast doors were protecting him as much as they were the assailant inside. Once opened, he would have no cover. Whoever was inside could hose down anyone bursting through the only entrance into the control room, safely situated behind any makeshift cover they may have jerry-rigged.

Cutter reached inside his leather jacket and unholstered his ZeroTwelve. He tilted his head down, looking at the security keypad and drew in a breath.

He closed his eyes.

And swiped his thumb.

The locking mechanism on the heavy blast doors clanked. A high pitched whine undulated with a repetitive whir. Cutter opened his eyes watching the doors slide apart, preparing for the worst.

A stench of burning plastic and decay wafted through the slit in the widening doors, carried on a rush of air that billowed past as pressure between room and corridor stabilized. Sparking wires swung down from the ceiling in Cutter's path crackling and whipping the ground with electric life. Inside, the air smelled of discharged particle weapons. The aftermath of a firefight was evidenced in blisters and pockmarks on the scorched walls. The wall of monitors on the left displayed static, save those that had caught a stray blast and now only displayed their electronic innards. A beam had fallen from the ceiling and was resting in a U-shape impression in the control console. Broken panels of ceiling insulation had been taken with it, burying switches and sliders under rubble.

On the ground to his right, a white and grey uniform with blue piping poked out from under fallen debris. A darkened liquid pooled beneath it. Cutter averted his eyes, only for them to fall on a gurgling fountain, still draining a similar substance from the neck of the fat camera operator who was slumped against the console. In a heap to his left, a tougher looking guard was minus his head. Beyond the sparking wires, sprawled out in the middle of the floor, a brunette lay on her back, sniper rifle just out of arm's reach.

Cutter entered, circling right, keeping distance from a writhing wire that snapped like a bullwhip. Moving to the console, he switched his weapon to his left hand and placed his right against the fallen beam. With some effort he shoved the collapsed beam off the console. It landed with a loud clang, taking much of the scattered debris with it.

Lights flickered on the control board, struggling to awaken. A few managed to regain full strength, while others found the fight too taxing and went dim. A series of beeps accompanied an automated reanimation cycle.

Debris shifted at his feet. He watched her eyes flutter open, pupils racking down to pinpricks under the harsh light. She struggled to swivel her head in his direction. Half her face was melted plastic; a surreal misshapen jowl drooped off her chin. Wires sparked and poked through her forehead. The other half of her face was pristine, a flawless china doll. Her body was a melted amalgamation of plastic and circuitry, fused to the front of the console, no longer looking like two separate entities—where the girl started and the machine ended, he had no clue.

His jaw fell slack. "Holy shit."

Celia looked up at him, eyes struggling to find focus.

He dropped to a knee at her side. Slowly, he reached for her unblemished cheek and cupped her chin in his hand. Her head fit so perfectly in the curve of his palm. He caressed the small patch of undamaged skin, smooth to the touch, soft, contrasting the sharp angles and protruding metal that poked through in patches like nettles. "Celia... What happened?"

"Jack..."

"Look at you, kid."

"I can't. I tried."

He shook his head. She wasn't making sense.

"You were supposed to warn me."

"I tried, Jack."

Maybe she had, but Cutter found that hard to believe. He was available at the click of a button and yet there had been no contact.

"Who did this?"

Her gaze fell to the floor, away from his. She silently stirred in place. He was about to press her for answers when he tilted his head looking at where she was sitting. She couldn't have picked a worse place to meltdown.

"You're on the forceshield controls. You have to move." He reached behind her, trying to pry her free.

She snapped out of her daze, her attention focusing back on Cutter. At his touch, she tried to help, tried to twist free.

"I—I cannot move."

Cutter grabbed her shoulders and began to pull her forward. "You're really stuck in there good."

He shoved his right arm behind her, reaching for the access panel. If he could open it, he could turn the forceshield back on, and maybe—

Searing heat torched the back of his hand.

Ow! God Dammit!

He whipped his hand back, clenching it into a tight fist. He held his hand close to his face, fighting the urge to shove the whole scolding thing into his mouth to cool it off.

As the initial shock of pain died down to a constant throb, he unclenched his fist, and painfully straightened his fingers turning his hand over to get a better glimpse in the light. Blistering skin bubbled on the back of his hand. He grimaced at the sight.

"Jack, are you okay?" Celia was looking at his hand.

What did she know about being okay?

"That is going to leave a scar," she said.

Cutter snorted.

No kidding it was going to leave a scar, he thought, but didn't have the heart to vocalize the sentiment. In fact, her reaction made him feel like an asshole for even having such cynically malicious thoughts in the first place. Here was a little girl, half her face destroyed, metal and sparking innards revealing her underlying construction—and she was more worried about a scar that might form on his hand.

For that brief instant, he couldn't help but laugh.

"Why the hell are you melted onto the control console?" he asked, his tone more conversational than seconds prior. "You're blocking the access panel. Who did this? Who left you like this?"

Celia cowered, rearing away from Cutter's raised hand.

"I did."

* * *

From his wide-eyed expression, she could tell that was not the answer he had been expecting. She ducked down, unable to meet his gaze.

"He told me to."

"Who?"

For some reason her thoughts weren't on the events at hand. She was thinking about Mommy and Daddy.

"Never leave me, Jack."

Even with her head down, she could feel Cutter staring at her; his gaze piercing through the top of her skull, as if he could see her thoughts.

"Celia, who told you to do this?"

She met his eyes, searching for signs that he would understand, hoping that he could.

"Ryan... I still feel him... In my head. He's still there."

"Costas? Where?"

Celia winced as he squeezed her shoulders tight.

"Celia, where is he?"

"Please do not leave me like this, Jack," she pleaded. "Please."

"Ceil, I need to know where he is. If you're able to hear him, he's transmitting a signal directly to you. I need you to backtrack to the source."

"I didn't want to hurt anyone."

"Ceil, we don't have time for this."

"But—"

"Backtrack the signal, Celia."

"I think…" Her voice came out small and distant as if the words belonged to someone else.

"I think… I liked it."

She watched Cutter's expression change and tried to interpolate meaning from the shift. Was he going to be upset at her? Upset like Mommy always got when she did something bad.

Moments prior there had been concern in his eyes. Now, she saw a glimmer she was far more familiar with—fear.

She could see disappointment as well. He had left her in the skybox to help and she had let him down. Not only had she failed the task she was given, but she was also the cause of the current predicament, the very root of the problem.

In the back of her mind she knew one thing—one thing that had been drilled into her core since the day Mommy brought her home from the factory—she was always the cause of the problem.

Initially, Celia had her doubts, but her role became abundantly clear after Mommy brought Jessica home from the hospital. If she was present, somehow she was always to blame. And when she couldn't vanish like she knew Mommy wanted, she spent nights alone in her room wishing she could, imagining how different, how much better things would be if only she disappeared. She knew, felt it in her very construction, that

Mommy would have been happier if she had never entered into her life in the first place.

That same look of fear, frustration, and disappointment, now stared down at her on the face of someone new. Celia's lips parted, words dangling from the tip of her tongue. She wanted to tell Jack that she had tried her best. But she knew what his reaction would be. Her best wasn't good enough. And in this case, she couldn't really blame him for being mad at her. Her best intentions didn't prevent five people from dying by her hand.

Maybe Mommy was right. She was just a screw up, not worth anyone's time or affections.

She felt Cutter shaking her back into focus. "Ceil, do you hear me?"

"I hear you, Jack."

"I need you to be a good girl, Ceil. Can you do that for me?"

At the sound of those familiar words—words she knew too well—her entire body drained of electricity. The very same words that had betrayed her so many times before.

"Do not leave me," she said.

"Ceil, can you help me or not?"

Celia looked up at Cutter. He no longer looked upset. Maybe she had been imagining it all along. He looked concerned. After all the mistakes she had made, after letting herself get taken advantage of, Jack was still coming to her, asking for help. Maybe she had been wrong about him. Perhaps, not all adults were like Mommy.

Stupid, she thought. She already knew, Jack was not like other adults.

"I…" She let the weight of her head rest in the palm of his hand. "I can help you, Jack."

"Where is he?"

Her HUD lit up through crackling static. The internal overlay blueprint of Staples Center faded into view across her UI. Green cones of light flickered and blinked as she quickly scanned for signs of Costas.

"Ceil, this is important!"

"I am looking, Jack."

Cutter's mouth snapped shut. His head bobbed with a small nod not directed at anyone in particular. Whatever was on his mind, whatever words he wanted to say to coax her into working faster, he kept to himself.

People were crawling across her scanners, ants marching in erratic lines, funneling through the exits in droves. Searching for Costas through conventional means wasn't going to work. However, amidst the rumbling chaos there was a beacon, a private conversation held in the middle of a stampeding thrum of feet and herding roar of spectators.

Something just for her.

She locked onto the signal and extrapolated position, rooting out the source. Two strings of numbers hovered across her UI, a longitude and a latitude.

She shook her head. The results didn't make sense.

A blue square pinpointed the location and overlaid it on the stadium blueprint. For these numbers to make sense, Costas would have been in the first tier of seating, section B, about fifteen rows back. They would have seen him. He would have been in plain sight of every single camera in the stadium.

Unless…

She pulled up the schematics of the stadium and rotated it from bird's eye view to elevation. She placed the coordinates according to the longitude and latitude values she had previously received. This time four blue targeting squares blinked in synchronicity, one on top of the other in a vertical line.

He wasn't in the seating area.

He was under it.

Celia started making adjustments to her code, rewriting the outdated program that lacked a Z-axis to take into account three dimensional space should she need the program in the future.

"Ceil? What do you got for me?" Cutter fidgeted, hovering over her.

She hesitated. She had the answer he wanted. She knew where Costas was. Why didn't she want to give Cutter the answer?

Wasn't he someone she could trust? Someone that had been upfront and honest with her. He had never hidden his intentions from her. He had been direct, blunt even, to the point of being rude. He had told her what had happened to her parents, invited her to accompany him, even provide assistance, and sparked her interested in detective work.

She swallowed, finding her voice, and then said, "Costas is in the tunnel leading away from the visitor's locker room. It looks like he is heading toward an underground parking structure."

"Thank you, Ceil." Cutter gently stroked her head, pulling a piece of hair that had been stuck to a puddle of melted cheek and swept it behind her ear.

Celia leaned forward resting in his arms. His embrace felt so warm, so right. This is where she belonged.

She felt him squeeze her tight. She could stay in his arms forever.

"Thank you, Ceil."

He placed his hand on her right arm, the only part of her body that remained free from the unrecognizable mass melted to the front of the control console.

And then he withdrew.

For a brief moment, she failed to recognize the significance of Jack's absence.

And then she reached out with her free arm and screamed, "Jack!"

But he was gone.

"Do not leave me like this! Do not leave me!"

Audio distortion mangled every plea; her damaged synth-voice-box shredded her screams. Her cries rang with a shrill pitch, echoing in the chaos and destruction of the control room, mixing with the sounds of snapping wires and raw sparking electricity.

She reached out with her free arm, straining, unable to free herself from the melted heap of plastic and circuitry.

"Do not leave me!" she screamed into the empty room.

5

Heaving breaths drowned out the rapid clickety-clack of designer shoes echoing through the corridor. Foster was in the lead, making distance on the bulkier men that trailed behind him.

"We have to get you to safety, sir," said one of the ape-like men trying to keep pace.

Foster turned about to tell him what he could do with his safety when the bodyguard vaporized in a puff of blue-green fire.

Foster threw himself against a wall as another blue-green pulse whizzed past. Without waiting to see if the last remaining bodyguard was still with him, Foster scrambled down the corridor and banked a hard right.

He put his back to the wall taking a moment to catch his breath. He jumped as a hand gripped the edge of the wall and a bodyguard pulled himself around the corner. Breath poured from the man like steam billowing out of a locomotive. He grabbed

Foster by the shoulder.

"Keep moving."

Keep moving? Foster was winded just thinking about all the day's running, and jumping, and bullet dodging.

He looked at the bodyguard. He was younger than Foster had anticipated. He thought all his bodyguards were in their late thirties and early forties—hell, even a few were retired ex-cops and ex-military pushing their sixties. But this man, well, Foster couldn't even call him a man—this was a kid, early twenties, shaggy blonde hair, built like a brick shithouse.

Foster had forgotten his name. That was if he had ever known it in the first place. He wasn't sure that he had. He had only really acquainted himself with Ron, the head of his bodyguard entourage—and even that was more personal than he preferred to get with men trained to lay down their lives for him. He didn't want to get attached. Or so he told himself.

But Ron was no longer with them. That's what he had been trained to say, *I'm sorry, but he is no longer with us.* The official version of events.

This young blonde man whose name escaped him at the moment was all that he had left.

"Is Yeoman in position?" Foster shouted over his shoulder.

"Haven't heard from him in a few minutes."

Foster's eyes drifted to the transparent curly-cue cord corkscrewing from the bodyguard's ear. Without warning, he slapped the bodyguard across the face. The burly kid didn't look too happy about it.

"That's not what I asked!"

Rubbing his jaw, the bodyguard said, "Should be. Ready, I mean."

"Should be? Should be?! That doesn't mean fuck-all."

Foster shook his head, muttering to himself. He ran toward the next intersection making another right in hopes of losing his pursuer.

The corridor dead ended into a single door. Foster pushed through it and entered into an underground parking structure. Overhead lights illuminated the main drag, but shadows gathered in unlit corners and between scattered rows of cars. From somewhere far off, a faint dripping punctuated the silence.

But Foster was more preoccupied by something else.

"He's not here," said Foster. "God damn it! He's not here!"

Yeoman had planned this escape route if another attempt on his life should take place. Better safe than sorry was Yeoman's model, but it was quickly becoming Foster's as well. The underground structure was a private VIP parking lot connected through a series of halls to the locker rooms. It had been built for athletes or presenters so they didn't have to park with the masses. Cause what an inconvenience that would be, right? The plan was devoid of the ever incompetent authorities, but Yeoman and Foster's bodyguards had never run any test trials, which in retrospect had probably been a mistake. Staring into the parking structure devoid of any other life than his bodyguard's and his own, Foster wished they had done some reconnaissance or pre-viz at the very least. Then he might have known ahead of time how ominous and poorly lit the underground parking structure was. Frankly, it was creepy as hell.

Foster paused at the threshold, unable to muster the courage to slink through the mottled light. A chill set him on edge. Danger lurked in every shadow. He felt the young bodyguard's presence hovering behind him, close on his hip. Foster slowly turned, looking at the empty corridor from which they had just fled. Rows of fluorescent lights illuminated the hall in brilliant sterile light.

"Where is he?"

The young bodyguard matched Foster's gaze. The hall was empty. "You mean Yeoman or the guy chasing us?"

"Either."

"Hell, if I know."

Foster spoke without taking his eyes from the hall. "He should be on top of us by now. Shouldn't he?"

"Maybe count our blessings?"

Foster looked at the bodyguard with an incredulous gaze. "You're not very good at this bodyguard thing are you?"

He shrugged in response. "You think we lost him?"

"Not too likely, is it?"

The bodyguard shook his head in agreement. No, it wasn't very likely.

"And where the hell is Yeoman?"

"We can't stay here," said the bodyguard nodding toward the glowing hallway behind them. "We need to move."

Foster found it hard to believe that leaving the light and slinking into the bowels of Staples Center, taking refuge in the dark and dim underbelly beneath literal tons of concrete and screaming panic was the best option at his disposal. He stood on the cusp of darkness, staring down the brightly lit hall, his gaze locked on the corner, certain that at any second an assassin would deliver blue-green pulses, a special parting gift just for him.

At the behest of the young bodyguard, Foster reluctantly tore his eyes away from the hall and crept into a new frightening danger of the unknown.

A long creaking groan of rusty hinges echoed impossibly loud as the door into the parking garage slowly eased shut behind them. The decision, right or wrong, was final.

They moved slowly, taking deliberate steps cushioning the sound of their footfalls. Intermittent dripping occasionally rose to the sound of a babbling brook, as they neared its source. They rounded a concrete pillar, and Foster saw a rusty rectangular pipe on the right. It funneled water onto the concrete from somewhere above. The runoff flowed back and forth in a concrete trough, siphoning into a drain in the middle of the floor.

Where was all the water coming from? It hadn't rained in—this was L.A.—it hadn't rained.

He should talk to someone about this. Seemed like such a waste of resources.

Foster shook his head, trying to shake free from the thoughts of responsibility and making the world a better place one leaky faucet at a time. It was so stupid, he thought, that he could be sidetracked so easily when he should really be scared stupid, frantic, running from the man that had wiped out his security team and twice attempted to assassinate him. Plus Yeoman was missing, bailing on the plan he had put together—plenty of thoughts to be worried about. But here he was lurking in the horror underneath Staples Center, and all he could focus on was the faint drip-drip-dripping of inefficiency.

Just then a loud clang thundered from the far corner behind them. Without warning, Foster was knocked off balance, laid out on his ass behind a Honda Civic. The young bodyguard hunkered low in a perched crouch behind the vehicle, one hand on his weapon, the other on Foster's shoulder forcing him to stay down.

"Do you see him?" Foster asked, peering up through the car's interior.

Scanning the depths of the structure, the bodyguard whispered out of the side of his mouth. "If I saw him, I'd either be shooting at him or dead."

Foster absentmindedly nodded. *Ask a stupid question...*

The garage was empty from what he could see. Apparitions of sound swirled around Foster. The low ceiling and wide sprawling layout magnified the smallest drip and the faintest crunch to haunting proportions. He tried to single out specific details from the buzzing silence, but his imagination amplified his thoughts and filled him with terror at every reverberation and distorted rumble.

Foster closed his eyes, straining to make out any sound that didn't belong.

Tires screeched a banshee wail from somewhere behind him. He snapped his neck around, nearly jumping out of his skin.

A white van tore around the corner, two of its tires struggling to keep firm grip on the road.

Foster held his arms high at his side, ready to throw them over his head, protect his face, do whatever his instinct screamed would help him get out of this alive.

The van drove past and painted black stripes of burning rubber on the concrete as it screeched to a halt in front of the door to the locker rooms some thirty yards behind Foster and the bodyguard. The driver's side door swung open and Yeoman exited.

The bodyguard nudged Foster and pointed at the van. "Yeoman's in position."

Foster glared at him. He could see that Yeoman was in position. He was *right* there.

Fighting the urge to slap the bodyguard again, Foster said, "Go check it out."

"Looks clear."

Foster gritted his teeth, emphasizing each word individually. "Go. Check. *It.* Out!"

Maintaining eye contact with Foster, the bodyguard let his head bob in agreement, but didn't move. Had he even heard what Foster had said? At the point Foster was ready to scream, the bodyguard stood up and scratched his butt with his weapon. "So you want me to go over there?"

Foster assumed this was a rhetorical question because the bodyguard didn't wait for an answer. Instead, he raised a hand and shouted at Yeoman.

"Hey! Hey you!"

Yeoman turned and arched an eyebrow at the suited wannabe surfer jogging toward him.

"Hey, Yeoman, right?"

"Yes," said Yeoman unable to conceal a hint of apprehension behind his rigid demeanor.

"Great. Perfect. Good. We're here." The bodyguard tossed a thumb over his shoulder in Foster's direction.

Foster shook his head, making a mental note that should he get out of this alive, he needed to hire people that weren't complete morons.

"We got out. Uh, so, you got him, right?" He gave Yeoman a smile and a thumbs up that quickly morphed into a finger gun. Yeoman tilted his head slightly askew. This was the closest Foster had ever seen Yeoman come to rolling his eyes.

"See, it's all right," said the bodyguard flapping his arms, signaling Foster to cross seconds before a blue-green pulse tossed him against the side of the van and carried his atoms away in aquamarine mist.

Shit.

Foster was already heading toward the van *with perfect fucking timing, as always.*

The word *serpentine* ran through his mind. He felt like an

asshole zig-zagging back and forth in the parking structure. He was pretty sure he looked like one too. But the next shot missed, so *serpentine, serpentine.*

Ducking blaster fire, he closed in on the van and yelled, "Yeoman, you better be ready!"

God damn it. He better be ready.

Under a constant barrage of gunfire, Yeoman jumped into the driver's seat and slammed the door shut behind him.

Foster dove behind the van and rolled into a sitting position with his back flat against the rear tire. The ridge of the wheel well dug into his back and he felt the cold smooth paneling above it. He looked down briefly, noticing his scuffed knee bleeding through a hole that had been torn in his designer slacks.

Blaster fire plinked off paneling, pitter patter like rain on a tin roof.

"Yeoman! You see him?"

"Not yet. But—" A high pitch wail rang out followed by a crescendo of shattering glass stifling Yeoman's words.

"Yeoman?" Foster raised up on his haunches craning his neck for a better view. He felt his ears perk, straining for any indication that Yeoman was okay. It wasn't a totally altruistic curiosity. He'd preferred that he wasn't the only one left to face down the mechanical menace Hell-bent on sending him to a fiery afterworld.

"Yeoman...?" Foster said, certain that no one was going to answer, but still, he had to try anything to break the silence and help calm his shaking nerves. "Are you all right?"

A metallic voice cut through the silence. "Quite a show you put on."

Foster stopped cold in his tracks. Instinct flooded in with a singular thought: *You are in extreme danger!* It took every ounce of self-control for Foster to hold his ground. His fight of flight response was pinging every nerve in his body. In mere seconds, he was riding an adrenaline high, senses sharpened, picking up every auditory and visual detail. He knew—fighting was not an option. He had seen this assassin in action.

Run!

Get the hell away!

Now!

Fucking stupid instinct, his brain calmly said.

I know fighting isn't an option, he said to himself. *Now shut the fuck up!*

Because flight wasn't an option either.

Fleeing would mean a blue-green pulse to the backside and a quick lesson in Newton's Second Law of Thermodynamics. He wished Mother Nature gave more than simple binary options. If he wanted to live, and he most certainly did, he needed an alternative to flight and-or fight.

He released the breath that he was unaware he had been holding.

"I try…" said Foster, peeking around the rear corner of the van. A blue-green energy pulse splashed across the fender, launching the taillight assembly into a nearby pillar.

"You there, Foster?" Heavy metal steps clinked toward him. "Pretty sure I didn't get you with that one."

Crouched low, Foster circled to the front of the van, feeling his heart trying to beat its way out of his chest. He debated whether he should respond, debated playing dead, but it wouldn't really matter if the assassin came closer to investigate, would it?

"Haven't hit me yet," said Foster. He braced his weight with his left hand on the paneling and pushed himself alongside the van. "Think you'd have worked on your aim a little bit before something like this. You know what they say about practice and all. Could always head to a shooting range. I got time. Or you could just give up. Could always give up. No harm, no foul."

Metallic laughter echoed off the concrete girders that supported the narrow slant and low ceilings of the parking structure. The tinny cackle enveloped Foster from all sides. There was no escape.

"No harm, no foul—how apropos. Such a high and mighty motto to live by."

Foster listened for footsteps. But they were gone.

He had been circling to his right. Now, he wondered if it was a trick, if his assassin had stopped with the intent of drawing him closer. He looked to his left toward the rear of the van, waiting and listening. Nothing.

"Not too talkative all of a sudden," said Foster, hoping for a response.

Somewhere to his left, the assassin said, "Scared?"

"Not exactly." Foster cautiously moved to his right, placing one foot after the other as silently as he could. His life depended on stealth.

He came around the front of the van. The windshield was a mosaic of spider-web cracks making it near impossible to see through. A hole had been burned through the windshield on the driver's side. Foster felt a lump in his throat. He moved along the front of the van, lining up the hole so that he could see into the driver's seat.

Jesus Christ!

He didn't think his heart could take anymore.

On the other side of the windshield, glittering glass peppered a mound of soft pink flesh. Crimson peeked through a torn designer suit jacket. A pink cord, like a belt, wrapped around

Yeoman's waist. Or rather, extruded from it, revealing his gaping innards.

Putting his forearm to his mouth, Foster fought back the bile rising in his stomach. He had never said it, but he had considered Yeoman a friend. A subordinate, yes. But one privy to the most intimate details of his life. In his book, that qualified Yeoman as a friend. And in truth, that made Yeoman both the nearest and dearest to his heart and also the only friend he had.

"You continually surprise me, Foster."

Foster bit back his rising hatred. "I aim to please."

"You brought a van? I expected a limo or in light of recent events a tank. But a plain unmarked van? You're beginning to disappoint."

"You have my sincerest condolences, I'm sure."

With his hands on the hood of the van, Foster leaned out for a glimpse of his pursuer when sudden movement in the driver's seat had him choking on his heart. He was two feet in the air, yelling out in a jumbled mix of curses and gibberish when he realized what had happened.

"You okay, over there?" A weighty footstep echoed closer to him. "Would hate for anything to happen to you. Yet, I mean."

Foster stifled his cries. Somehow, despite his condition, Yeoman was moving. He was still alive. As he turned in place, his intestines slid over his body leaving a snail-trail of blood on his pant leg. Foster cringed. *Don't move! For Christ's sake stop moving!*

Foster shushed Yeoman, holding an extended finger to his lips. Heavy lidded, Yeoman met Foster's gaze. He blinked in acknowledgment and forced the aching groans to subside.

Foster tilted his head back and projected his voice loud and clear over the top of the van. "What do you want?"

"Aren't you the direct one?"

"You've been trying so very hard to get my attention. Well—I'm all ears now. What do you want?"

"I want you to suffer."

"Fair enough. Got any reasons for that? Or was plain crazy reason enough?"

"I have my reasons."

Foster tapped on the hood, grabbing Yeoman's attention, and then pointed at him before raising his hand in a shrugging gesture.

Yeoman nodded with his eyes.

For the first time since the forceshield had dropped, Foster smiled his big trademarked smile.

Good. We may just get this son of a bitch, yet.

He held his breath, mustered his courage, and leaned into view of the far side of the van.

"Hey, so why don't—"

The assassin was nowhere to be seen.

Where the hell was he?

He stared in silence at the empty spot where the blackened metal Grim Reaper should have been. After a moment, he moved, dodging the rearview mirror on the driver's side that stuck out a good six inches from the vehicle. He paused at the door and looked in through the window. Yeoman had been tracking him as best he could. He managed a small head movement in the way of a nod.

Foster returned the nod, pointed toward the rear of the van, and continued his journey in silence.

He leaped around the rear corner, half-expecting to be punched in the face. The other half expected more of the same. The assassin was missing.

He didn't have patience for this death game of Ring Around

the Rosie. He had made a complete circuit around the vehicle.

"This is cute and all," Foster said, "but I thought you were the one chasing me. Where the hell are you?"

"Boo." Foster's skin crawled. The voice was hauntingly close.

He looked up. Crouched on the roof of the van, the assassin sighted down the barrel of a large pulse rifle. "Any famous last words?"

"Now!" Foster screamed.

The van shook knocking the would-be Grim Reaper off balance. The side panels fell to the concrete revealing the van's innards and giving the van a decidedly new appearance, that of a flatbed truck. At the corners, four large metal pillars bent towards each other, electricity arcing between them.

The assassin fell into the center. It climbed to its feet and ran, but with each step it looked as if it were trudging through molasses. The more it fought the force, the less it could move, until it snapped back into the center as if attached by rubber bands. Above it, a cross section of four electric beams converged, hissing and crackling, and spitting sparks.

It got to its knees, turned toward Foster, and fired.

For a brief few seconds, a pale sphere of yellowing energy lit up the parking structure like daylight.

Foster approached. He smiled listening to the comforting hum of raw energy that encapsulated his would-be assassin.

It fired again. With similar results. The blast from his weapon dissipated into a sphere of yellow energy.

"Go ahead. Keep firing," said Foster. "We brought this here specifically for you."

The assassin obliged. Shot after shot discharged, dissipating into rippling yellow sphere after rippling yellow sphere.

"What happened? You were so talkative a few minutes ago."

Foster circled, sizing up his catch.

"Well, that's fine I suppose." Foster shook his head, and then pointed toward the ceiling as if a random thought had just occurred to him. "You know, I can't believe you really thought I'd show up tonight without a contingency plan? The city needs me."

"Like it needs a hole in the head."

Foster laughed. A smile crawled across his face. "Well, it seems we haven't stolen your voice completely, after all."

Foster leaned in for a closer look, nose inches from the surging energy bubble. The horizontal slats over the assassin's right eye (or where the right eye should have been) were bent. Twice, it looked like. Once damaged by something that had penetrated the gap between the slats pushing the slats wide, and then a second time to bend the horizontal slats back into alignment, creating a rather wavy organic pattern. It didn't quite fit in with the rest of this thing's appearance of metallic rigidness.

"What happened there?" Foster asked, pointing at its face.

"Wouldn't you like to know?"

"Yes. I wouldn't have asked otherwise."

A strange repeating sound came from the assassin. It took Foster a moment to recognize it. The assassin was snickering at him. "Good luck getting anything from me."

Foster stopped circling. His smile grew wider. "I have plans for you, my friend. And none of them require your consent."

◗

At least his trail was easy to follow, Cutter thought as he hurdled another injured gorilla in a black suit.

Foster was supposed to have stayed with his battalion of security. There were plans to evacuate him under heavily armed guard should another attack on his life occur. However, no one had planned for the failure of the forceshield. Well, except Costas, of course. Failure of a forceshield was unheard of. Until tonight.

Great, here he was making history.

But when Cutter made it back downstairs, he discovered that it was not just devoid of civilians, but of Foster as well. A few officers had stayed behind to cordon off the scene. They could only answer his questions with shrugs and "I dunno's."

On the bright side, Foster's entire bodyguard division was missing. It was a safe bet that wherever he had gone, he had taken them with him. Another safe bet was that wherever they were, Costas was hot on their tail.

And thanks to Celia, he knew where to find Costas.

He sprinted through the corridors beneath the stadium passing a trail of bodyguards that bore the results of Costas's unmistakable handiwork. His hunches were turning out to be true. Maybe he should buy a lottery ticket. Might be his lucky day, after all.

At the next intersection, he was greeted by a smear of something that bore the vague resemblance to a man, a silhouette of atoms painted into the wall like a fresco. A faint ring of blue-green haloed the impressionistic work. He turned down the corridor away from the charred blotch.

The brightly lit corridor dead-ended into a single door. He pushed through it and out into the parking structure. Immediately, he fought the urge to sneeze as the familiar telltale scent of blaster fire forced its way up his nostrils.

He was too late.

The fight had already happened.

And judging from how many bits and pieces of bodyguard were left in the adjoining corridors, there probably wasn't much left to fend off the teched-out mercenary.

Why had Foster come down here anyway?

He might have figured that if Costas was in the skybox the best place for him was with a couple thousand tons of concrete between them. Or maybe he didn't trust the city or the officers to protect him.

The notion was somewhat ironic. The Mayor, a physical representation of the city in human form, a man that had devoted his entire life's work to the community, a man that spent countless hours and resources rebuilding the Los Angeles Police Department into something people could believe in, didn't have enough faith in its ability to protect him when his life was on the line. He had run away from everything he said he believed in.

Cutter heard a strange scratching sound. To his right, shadows danced on the concrete in rhythm with the faint scratches. He moved toward them, sweeping the area with his ZeroTwelve.

Foster was sitting on the concrete absent mindedly playing with a discarded plastic cup. He leaned against a support pillar, using it as a backrest.

Whether Foster was ignoring him or simply oblivious to his presence, Cutter couldn't tell, but it was probably a smart move to approach him as cautiously as possible. Foster's apparel showed signs that he had been in a struggle. His suit jacket was in tatters. Blood soaked a blotchy camouflage pattern on his right shin, a stylish accent to the frayed hole at the knee.

But Foster didn't look like a man scared for his life. He looked like someone that belonged in a room with padded walls.

Cutter slowed to a crawl, his senses in a state of high alert.

"You're alive?" Cutter asked, nudging Foster with his foot.

Foster looked up from his trance. He quirked a smile. "Those detective skills really are quite amazing."

Cutter grumbled. At least Foster wasn't crazy. Asshole, yes. Crazy, no. "Everything okay?"

"Peachy."

"We need to get you back upstairs."

Cutter reached for his hand, but Foster shrugged a shoulder and pulled it close to his body. Childish. Even for Foster.

Cutter's nerves were on edge. Foster was way too comfortable. He was familiar with both sides of Foster. There was a behind-the-scenes Foster that could lose his cool at the slightest hiccough. He had also seen the other Foster, the one with the frosty demeanor and tempered smile.

"What happened?" Cutter asked, still offering his hand.

Foster scoffed. "Well, for starters, I was shot at. Again. Someone was trying really hard to kill me. No thanks to you by the by."

"And you're fine, now?"

"Seems that way, doesn't it?"

Cutter looked back over his shoulder as the sound of running water rose. After a moment, it died back down to a trickle.

"Really should talk to someone about that," said Foster. "So inefficient."

"Where is everyone?"

"Dead."

"Where is he?"

Foster met Cutter's gaze and held it for a subjective eternity. "I wouldn't worry about it if I were you. We took care of him."

"We?"

"Well, not you. But yes, we."

"Why didn't you stick with your security detail?"

"I did."

"You know what I mean. Why didn't you stick with the

detail we assigned to you?"

"You mean, the same city appointed detail that allowed my previous decoy-bot to be assassinated?"

Cutter couldn't argue that point. If it had been his life on the line, he'd have made the same decision. But then again, had it been his life on the line, he wouldn't have shown up at all. Give bait a choice, and it'd prefer a warm hole in the dirt to dangling on the end of a hook.

"You're all alone," Cutter said. It was a statement of fact, but the question was implied.

"Don't look so shocked. You'd think you'd have a better poker face to mask your years of staggering incompetence."

"Helps when you stick to the plan."

"Also makes it easier for those that know the plan to exploit it."

"You think someone from the department is feeding this guy information."

It wasn't the first he had heard of it. Chief Parks had pointed out concerns that someone from the precinct might have been leaking information to Costas. More specifically, Parks had fingered him as mole informant numero uno.

"Don't you?" said Foster. "Hate to tell you how to do your job and all—"

Cutter doubted that. He could tell from the Foster's expression that he loved every minute of it. If he could tell every person in the city how to do their jobs, how to behave, how to live in a civilized society, he wouldn't hesitate to do so.

"—but that would be my first guess when my cases go ass up so quickly."

"I guess it's lucky for the city that you don't have my job."

"So who is he?"

Terrific question, Cutter thought. My ex-partner. That I don't remember. Who is he?

He had been asking himself the very same question.

Apparently, Foster was no slouch. He caught him looking away and to the left.

"Come now, Detective. It's obvious you know more about him than you're letting on."

"What makes you say that?"

"You seem more concerned about his whereabouts, than my well-being. What's in this for you?"

"Law and order and all that."

And the answer to a mystery that had been blazing in his head since the case started.

Costas had known him. And there wasn't a single thing Cutter could remember about Costas.

Foster snorted, running the back of his hand across his nose. "You? Law and order? Funny."

"Figure you gotta start some time, right?"

"I guess so, Jack. I just thought that sometime for you was never." He squinted at Cutter, eyes flicking from side to side. "So who was he?"

"Was?"

"Is… Was. Let's not play semantics. There's no big revelation to be discerned from past tense over the present one. We both saw him. He's not a synth. There's a man under all that tech." Foster wafted a hand, as if to add emphasis. "So I ask again, who was he?"

"Talk to Parks. You two are buddy-buddy."

"We talk."

"And what's he tell you?"

"Not enough, apparently."

Cutter was getting nowhere with Foster. Whatever he had seen, whatever had happened down here, he had buttoned up about it. Getting that information out of Foster now would be next to impossible.

Cutter radioed for backup. "I have Foster. He's safe."

He directed units to his position.

Foster quietly turned the discarded plastic cup over in his hands. Whatever he had done with Costas was his secret.

Cutter nodded to himself. If Foster wanted to play it coy, that was fine. There was one other person that could track down Costas.

REASSEMBLED

1

Chief Parks hadn't so much as mumbled a word in nearly five minutes. His head was buried in paperwork as he scratched and scribbled through a stack of papers several inches thick.

Cutter shifted his weight, stiffly turning, mostly with his eyes, for a better view of the bullpen. Outside the office, the precinct was alive with movement. Normally, it was so still Cutter wouldn't have been surprised if a tumbleweed meandered through the office. But after the events at Staples Center, officers were running from desk to desk, grabbing files, interfacing with the citywide database, answering phone calls, interviewing witnesses and possible links to the attack, and stirring up a general frenzy of motion.

Cutter quietly watched Parks fill out another form.

This was one time he wished he had busy work to tend to. Anything to keep him out of Parks' office.

But Parks had something in mind.

So far, watching him fill out paperwork was the extent of it. But Cutter was positive Parks interest in him wouldn't end there.

That'd be too convenient.

"She's slated for recycling," Parks finally said.

Cutter nodded. He had expected as much.

Looking up from the paperwork, Parks tapped his pen against the desk three times. "Something still doesn't track."

"Oh?" said Cutter, intrigued.

"You say you were up in the skybox."

"Yup."

"And our perp wasn't there."

"Just the remains of his handiwork."

Parks jotted a few notes and then repeatedly underlined something. After a moment, he looked up. "How could he have cleared out the security team in the skybox and been on the floor firing at Foster at the same time?"

Cutter shrugged. "Maybe he blew the forceshield on a delay?"

That wasn't so far from the truth. Costas *had* set up a delay allowing for a better firing position when the forceshield went down.

That delay was named Celia.

But telling Parks wouldn't get him anywhere, except in trouble.

Parks nodded to himself. "The crime scene techs went over everything. Neither the console, nor the controls had been tampered with internally. They said someone had physically damaged the device causing the forceshield to fail."

Cutter held his gaze, locked in a quiet stare-down with Parks. After a few long seconds Cutter broke the silence.

"I feel like there's a question here."

"You want to tell me how that's possible?"

The assassin had hijacked a synthetic little girl's body by remote control and commanded her to disable the forceshield. Then he told her to melt herself on top of the access panel, preventing anyone from reactivating it.

Cutter had been at the scene. He knew it would be difficult for forensics to determine who had done what. Although there wasn't much physical evidence pointing to Costas, Celia's handiwork bore his familiar and devastating trademark.

And besides.

He needed her.

She was his only link to Costas.

To his missing memories.

Cutter shrugged. "I'm not much of a tech guy. If that's what they say, that's what they say."

Parks *mhmm'd* and scribbled his initials at the bottom of another page.

"About the bot…" said Cutter.

Parks barely lifted his eyes from his paperwork.

Uh oh. He had been expecting the inquiry.

"You mean the bot," Parks started. "Excuse me—the evidence from another case that you were using as your personal Black and White after I had explicitly banned you from using any Black and Whites? That bot?"

"That would be the one," said Cutter, trying to keep sarcasm from his tone. He wasn't sure he had succeeded.

"What about her?"

"I don't think recycling is the best idea."

"Oh? And why's that?"

She was linked to Costas. She had tracked him before. Hopefully, she still could.

Instead, Cutter said, "She may have seen something. There might be something in her memory we can use."

Parks grunted and returned to his paperwork. "We searched her memory. Every file, every memory bank, every circuit. If she had any memory of the incident, it's gone now."

"Gone?" Cutter heard himself repeat the Chief, but failed to find meaning in the word.

"Pinkerton was in every nook and cranny of her programming. He had so much electricity racing through her system that if the memory had been in there it was probably cooked after all our tampering."

"How is that even possible? Synths never forget."

Parks lifted his gaze and glared at Cutter through a partially squinted eye.

Seconds turned into minutes.

With a sweep of his hand, Cutter brushed the paperwork off Parks' desk. Pages fluttered to the floor scattering in all directions.

Parks glared at him. The subdued reaction wasn't exactly what Cutter had been expecting. Parks pointed at him with the back of his pen.

"Jack, there is nothing left. And I'll be damned if I let a subordinate tell me how to run my precinct."

"Maybe you should."

"Excuse me?" said Parks, rising up from his chair.

Cutter leaned back, touching the back of his neck in a casual manner. "All I'm saying is that it's impossible she was wiped clean after the incident."

Parks walked around the desk, stepping over fallen papers. Cutter's jaw tightened. Stopping inches from him, Parks sat on the edge of the desk, arms folded. His shirt was rolled up to his elbows, giving Cutter a nice view of his forearms, a reminder that Parks had been a force to be reckoned with in his day.

"For not being a tech," Parks said, "you seem awfully knowledgeable on this subject."

He wasn't an expert per se. Or at all. He just knew that Celia wasn't simply a witness to the events that took place in the skybox. She had caused them.

Telling that to Parks would guarantee recycling.

For Cutter, the case no longer had anything to do with Costas or his attempts on Foster's life. It had become personal. This was about his missing memories. Somebody had been mucking around in his head, tampering with his memories and he wanted to know why.

With Celia scheduled for routine oblivion, the last remaining clues to the person he had once been but couldn't remember, would be lost forever—which would be perfect for anyone…

"You…" said Cutter.

"Me, what?"

"You're in on it."

"What on God's green Earth are you babbling about?"

"That's why you don't want me on the case. That's why you're burying Celia and our only lead."

Parks furrowed his brow and locked on Cutter like a lion staring down a gazelle. His left eye twitched.

Almost immediately, the silence was interrupted by rumbling, gut-rolling laughter. The walls shook in sync to the bass rhythm.

Momentarily stunned, Cutter tracked his reaction. He thought getting chewed out was bad.

But laughter? Much worse.

"I don't think it's all that funny," said Cutter.

"You don't know a God damn, do you, Jack?"

"You've kept me in the dark on this whole investigation."

"Maybe it's because I was afraid you'd botch it from the very beginning."

"Yeah, because I'm such a terrible detective."

Parks glared at him, his mouth an expressionless horizontal line. If Cutter didn't know better, he had spoken the very words Parks had been thinking.

"Seriously, Chief?"

"You said it. Not me."

"Wait, you're serious?"

"You haven't exactly been on your 'A' game lately, Jack. Or ever, really. In fact, it's been years since you've actually done any real detective work of note."

"That's a good one." Cutter scoffed.

"Really, Jack? You really think you're such a great detective? You just accused me of having something to do with the assassination attempts on Foster with absolutely no evidence. Just gut instinct. What were you planning? To browbeat a confession out of me? That's some real good detective work there, that is."

"I, uh—"

Cutter's chest tightened. Thoughts of Celia slipped away, as he lingered on the career he could hardly remember. A career built out of intimidation and skirting regulation. His modus operandi was to browbeat confessions out of scumbags and scuzzos. But that had been him bucking the norm—or so he thought.

But Parks had known all along. He had used his vigilantism as a tool. Cutter wasn't a rogue, just another extension of the authority he thought he was skirting.

"You used me."

"Hadn't thought that far ahead, Jack?" Cutter shook his head in disgust. "No surprise there. Look at the facts—"

"I'm looking."

"You're an investigator and you don't even have the slightest clue."

"It explains why you keep assigning me Black and Whites instead of a real partner. Real officers might have some moral resignations about what you and Foster are up to."

"You don't even know how wrong you are." Parks looked far too relaxed sitting on the edge of his desk with his arms tightly folded. "I don't want to keep assigning you synths. You cost the department a small fortune in damage and repairs."

"Then why keep doing it?"

"You can't honestly be that thick?"

"I guess I am. So why don't you go ahead and explain it to

me."

"No one wants to be your partner, Jack."

"That's…" He wanted to say it wasn't true. But looking back at his career, his partners—human and synthetic alike (those he could remember anyway), he had trouble punching holes in Parks' logic.

"It is, Jack." Parks settled back in his chair. "You aren't the super-cop you seem to think you are. You never were. More often than not it is me cleaning up your messes. And before that it was your partners. You were assigned synths because nobody—nobody at all wanted to work with you. The only reason you've stayed on payroll is that no one had the heart to let you go. Not after what had happened."

"Costas?"

Parks' eyes narrowed to slits. "You remember Costas?"

Cutter snapped his head to a side and stared obliquely across his cheek at Parks. "How do you know Costas?"

Apparently, he was quite the comedian because Parks was fighting back laughter once again.

"How do I know one of my officers that was gunned down in the line of duty? What is wrong with you, Jack?"

That was the million dollar question. What was wrong with him? He couldn't have been so off on things, could he?

He assumed Parks had seen Costas at the mall. Assumed that Parks had fallen under whatever hypnotic spell had erased his own memory and expunged Costas from it. But he hadn't forgotten Costas. In fact, he seemed surprised that Cutter knew Costas, recognized the name, could put together that Costas had been a part of his past.

This was one time assuming made an ass out of you and just you alone, thought Cutter.

Parks surprise didn't come from the fact that Cutter knew who Costas was. Rather, Parks was surprised he had remembered in the first place.

God damn it.

Tracking down Costas to dig deeper into the details of his past would be much easier if he had the help of the department. But Cutter wasn't sure that he could trust Parks.

If Parks was in whole hog, he was in for some real trouble. And he'd tipped his hand. He knew who Costas was, at least in a superficial sense, and he told Parks after being convinced that Parks was a part of a larger conspiracy.

The pieces were staring him in the face. Why couldn't he see the bigger picture?

Maybe Parks was right. He was a horrible detective, and always had been.

"But…" Cutter trailed off. He looked down at his hands clenched into tight fists. "If I'm such a colossal fuckup, then why'd you assign the case to me?"

"We've been over this. You brought in the drive."

"You could have handed the case to anyone. Stetler had nothing going on and everyone loves him."

"Maybe I should have." Parks shrugged. "But that's irrelevant now. The case is closed."

"Wait, what? For all we know this guy is still on the loose gunning for Foster." Cutter watched Park's expression for the slightest shift that might give away that he knew something more. Something that could tip Cutter off to his allegiance. Anything. Anything at all.

Jesus, he felt desperate.

"He's not," said Parks, his tone neutral. "We sent a couple officers to the hospital to get Yeoman's statement. He was conscious enough to give us a detailed run-down on the events."

"Which was?"

"They handled it."

"They?"

"Foster's people. They took care of the problem."

"Where's the body? Where's the tech?"

"They kept some of the parts as a souvenir of sorts."

The tech? What could Foster possibly want with the assassin's tech?

"And that's regulation?" asked Cutter.

Parks rubbed the tip of his nose. "You're one to talk. Look Jack, far as I'm concerned, this is one mess that I'm glad I don't have to deal with. If Foster wants a couple souvenirs from the psychopath that's been tormenting him, frankly, he can have at it."

"You can't do that."

"He's not the only one I've turned a blind eye to regulation for."

Cutter bit his tongue. "No. He's not."

Cutter wore the title well—the department heavy. The walking thug with a badge. The idiot detective so terrible at putting clues together that he was just now beginning to realize the only reason he even had the job was because everyone took pity on him.

"Jack, I know you're all kinds of thick, so let me drill this into your skull—I don't want to hear that you're still monkeying around with this."

Cutter shook his head. "There's not a single shred of evidence that this is over."

"Except for one thing, Jack."

Cutter raised a brow. "Yeah, what's that?"

"It *is* over. Do I make myself clear?"

Cutter slowly nodded. "Crystal."

A dull hiss emanated from a pocket incinerator. At a glance, the open mouth of the device seemed almost inviting. Like a living creature situated in the corner of Pinkerton's workshop hissing a constant reminder of its need to feed. A glimmer of nearly invisible flame revealed the nature of the device. Molten metal pooled yellow-orange in the catch basin.

Cutter always thought the pocket name was a bit of a misnomer. The thing was huge. Sure, it wasn't something you'd find in an industrial steel mill, but for its function, the thing took up the entire rear of Pinkerton's workshop.

Its belly consisted of three chambers. The main chamber was readily visible inside its open mouth. Two smaller chambers bubbled off either side, giving the appearance of bulbous ears. Inside the ear chambers, plastic was filtered from metal.

A constantly rotating conveyor belt fed bent bolts and busted circuit boards into its gaping maw, a never ending effort to quell the beast's insatiable appetite.

At the end of the treadmill runway, a heap of melted plastic, protruding wires, and bent metal was piled in a plastic disposal bin, inching forward on a slow march toward oblivion.

Undaunted by the increasing temperature baking his skin taut and crystallizing salt on his cheeks and around his eyes, Cutter approached the hell monster and its motorized feeding trough.

He reached into the box of unsalvageable spare parts on the conveyor belt and slid his hand under congealed plastic. Debris fell away as he twisted a familiar remnant. Its hazel eyes looked up at him, lifeless. He delicately caressed the underside of her chin. The conveyor belt constantly inched forward. She slowly slid through his fingers, until there was nothing left to hang on to, and she limply fell back into the disposal tray.

He had already run the pros and cons through his mind. The cons exponentially outnumbered the pros. It hadn't been a debate at all.

The cons, for starters, included losing his job. Kind of a catch twenty-two—to do the job, he had to sacrifice the job.

There was also the question of rebuilding her. She looked— *not good to put it bluntly.* The right corner of Cutter's mouth turned upward, breaking an otherwise straight line. An old memory of his mother, a phrase she used to say. *My better days are behind me.* He feared Celia's were as well.

And that didn't even begin to address the many other questions that tortured him. Could he find someone to put her back together? Could she even be rebuilt in the first place?

Hell, if he knew. Quite literally. If tech didn't involve weaponry, he didn't have the foggiest. He never saw any incentive to learn, either.

When a technoperp fired a weapon that melted skin to bone through heavy combat armor—that was important information to know—but when that same technoperp was a malfunctioning synth on the fritz, a bullet worked just as well as a technician's knowledge to remedy the problem.

And he already knew how to fire a gun.

The pros were one.

She might know something.

Quite frankly, that single reason didn't instill him with overwhelming confidence. His hopes hung on the edge of a perhaps. A maybe. An 'I dunno.'

He sighed. There wasn't much else to fall back on.

With Costas missing after the attack and Foster seemingly unconcerned—except when it came to publically ridiculing Cutter and the department—he wasn't left with much of a choice.

If he wanted answers to his past, to who Costas was, and why he couldn't remember, he needed Celia.

If he wanted to keep his job, he needed to leave her on the belt.

Stupid decisions. He wished decisions like this, the tough ones, the kind that tore up your guts, were automated. He lived in a technological society of ever increasing advancement. Why couldn't decisions be a rote choice already solved for the user through some outside algorithm, complete with all variables pre-entered? *When X happens, do Y. Else if Y happens, do Z.*

It would make things so much simpler.

He snapped his head toward a pattern of soft thuds coming from the corridor. His pleas for a society in which his toughest choices were precognitively solved would have to wait.

Outside the door, footsteps clomped on linoleum, growing louder with each approaching step. He looked at the door, at the silver deadbolt, flipped up in the unlocked position. There was still time to lock himself in, but not enough to cover up his rushed manhandling of the equipment. The footsteps (and whoever they belonged to) would be well aware of his presence inside Pinkerton's workshop should they encounter a locked door. His face warmed over with anger, but curses and self-flagellation wouldn't help.

If he pulled Celia off the belt, the places to hide would be even more limited. And pulling her off the belt would be a dead giveaway to his tampering. He could leave her on the conveyor belt, but that was a terrible idea. If whoever was coming decided to stay long enough, Celia would become the pocket incinerator's next meal while he sat in hiding, idly watching.

Besides, that wasn't his style.

Neither was wishful thinking, and yet—

Maybe the nearing footsteps were an officer on the way to the morgue. Maybe they weren't heading toward Pinkerton's tech filled den.

And he wasn't even sure that saving Celia from recycling was the right decision. In fact, the timing, the circumstances, his own career advancement, everything—told him that saving Celia from incineration was the wrong decision.

The thundering footsteps might as well have been stomping directly on his head. The rhythmic clomping, like a stampede of cloven hooves on tile, weren't passing by as he had hoped. Just as he was certain that they were coming for him, the footsteps stopped.

A jingle loud as an alarm rang out, followed by a metallic *ka-chunk-ka-chunk-ka-chunk* like machine gun fire in distorted slow motion. The silver doorknob slowly turned.

Without thinking, Cutter tossed the disposal tray on top of a mobile handcart.

"We're getting you out of here," he said to the pile of scrap he had once called Celia.

The door creaked open. Cutter wheeled the handcart between two floor-to-ceiling racks overflowing with electronic brick-a-brack. The narrow aisle between them was only secluded by an overabundance of clutter. Through the electronic debris hanging from the shelves, Cutter watched the silhouette in the doorframe. A glint of light reflected off an all too familiar eye loupe.

Cutter held perfectly still.

Pinkerton didn't dawdle at the door. Holding his ground, Cutter watched in silence. If Pinkerton found out what he was up to…

The thought was interrupted by Pinkerton's approach. He was heading straight for him.

Every muscle in his body tensed. Without a sound, he lifted a large metal pipe off a nearby shelf. He raised it over his head, poised for Pinkerton to round the corner into the aisle.

Instead of coming face to face with Cutter and a cart full of Celia, Pinkerton continued toward his workbench in the corner.

Carefully, Cutter lowered the pipe. As Pinkerton walked past at a brisk pace—an arm's reach away on the other side of the shelf—Cutter inched the handcart forward allowing piles of junk to obscure him from Pinkerton's view.

Pinkerton slid a high stool from under the workbench and perch atop it like an egret. His head swiveled from side to side and suddenly froze as he locked on to his target. With a sweep of his hand, he snatched a wire-wrapped ball of metal not much larger than a baseball off the workbench. Holding it up, he flipped his eye loupe down with his left hand and leaned in for closer scrutiny.

On tip-toe, Cutter silently pushed Celia and the handcart to the end of the aisle. Reaching out with a speed that would make a sloth impatient, Cutter laid the metal pipe on the shelf. He froze, grimacing at the faint clink of metal kissing metal.

Pinkerton turned at the noise.

"Who's there?" He craned his head from side to side. "Stetler, I told you yesterday you can't use the wrist mod without going through Parks first." When no response came, Pinkerton exhaled and rose from his stool. "C'mon, Cory. I don't have time for games."

Cutter hunched down pulling the handcart away from Pinkerton's approach. A bead of sweat dripped over his brow. With the back of his sleeve, he wiped it away, reassured his grip on the handcart, and wheeled it quietly between the aisles.

An extended foot and Pinkerton's flowing lab coat came into view. Cutter forced the handcart around the corner.

"Cory?" From the sound of his voice, Pinkerton was in the aisle, occupying the space where Cutter had been only seconds prior.

Cutter peeked up, watching Pinkerton lift something off the shelf. With an eyebrow raised, Pinkerton examined it, before delicately replacing it.

Pinkerton's eyes swept the remainder of the room. Cutter ducked down, leaned his back against the rack, and slid to a sitting position.

It was probably a safe bet that Pinkerton wasn't so certain on his assumptions that it was Stetler dinking around in his workshop. The device Pinkerton had been examining was a wrist mod made for augmenting grip strength. Cutter knew this because he had brought it in, apprehended the technoperp it had originally been attached too.

Cutter turned toward the door on his right, a mere five feet away. He gripped the handle of the handcart tight, not realizing how much sweat had been pouring out of him. The cushioned grip tape wrapped around the handle was clammy with moisture. There were wet smears from his hands along the bars and on the disposal tray. Everything he had touched was tinged with his sweat.

Gross. He wiped his hands on his jeans.

The close proximity to an exit was a tease. The few lights that illuminated the room were focused on Pinkerton's workbench and the exit. Cutter couldn't book it for the door without being caught—especially not with a bucket full of Celia to haul out with him.

He tilted his head to the left, listening for signs of Pinkerton's approach. The room was utterly silent, but that made him more aware of Pinkerton's presence, rather than less. Had Pinkerton been up to his normal routine, there would have been sounds, the normal noises one makes adding to the ambiance of the surroundings, tipping him off to Pinkerton's whereabouts. He should have been able to hear the key aural indicators that one is not alone, despite having no other senses than sound alerting him to the presence of another.

The absence of such indicators, despite knowing Pinkerton was lurking around the corner wasn't helping Cutter with his sweating situation any. A small bead carved a rivulet from his temple, over cheekbone, to his chin where it clung for dear life.

Cutter set his jaw, clenching it tight.

He wanted to peek around the corner—just one quick peek—to see if Pinkerton was closing in on him. He wanted confirmation. One look would be all he would need. And that glance would most assuredly expose himself and his whereabouts.

The sound of something sticky, perhaps half dried lubricant, making contact with the rubber soles of a sneaker betrayed Pinkerton's movements.

The little voice in Cutter's head shouted, *Now or never!*

He stood up, shoved the handcart forward, and accidentally gave himself the Heimlich Maneuver as the handcart refused to budge.

A black cable, thick as a vine, had snagged a protruding handle on the front of the handcart, holding it in place. Cutter huffed an expletive and tugged on the cable. The force banged the handcart into the shelf.

Pinkerton's voice rang through the electronic junk. "I know you're there. I can hear you."

Cutter pulled the cart back and shook it, trying to wrestle it free from the clutches of the cable. An older model bot that was little more than a torso with arms toppled from the shelf entangling itself with Cutter.

He leaned forward, and thrust his arm into the bot torso, pushing it off the cart. The torso fell to the floor yanking slack out of the cable. Something drawn taut and swept his feet out from under him.

The realization that the cable had been between his feet didn't help him regain his balance. He grasped for the handcart, seizing the metal bar just below the handle. His sweaty hands couldn't find purchase on the slick metal.

Cutter went down taking the handcart with him and scattering parts of Celia across the floor.

"Great Stetler. Now I have to clean up your mess too," said Pinkerton, rounding the corner.

Cutter looked up at him. He waved and put on the best smile he could muster. "Uh, hi."

Pinkerton was shaking his head, but he wasn't looking at Cutter. His eyes were locked on the handcart and its contents. After taking visual inventory of the theft, his eyes flicked back to Cutter. His face pinched together.

"Oh no," said Pinkerton. "No way. No way in hell, Jack!"

"You don't even know what I'm going to say."

"The answer is still no."

"I need her. She's the only one that can help."

"Guess you're shit out of luck."

"They're going to melt her down. Did you know that?"

"Of course I knew that. Who do you think put her on the incinerator belt?"

Mouth agape, Cutter twisted his tongue in his mouth. He gently bit down on it. "Here I was thinking you were this high and mighty equal rights for synths guy. Little did I know that you only relate to them because you are as equally devoid of a heart."

Pinkerton looked down at the melted mess of circuitry and hydraulics peeking through the visage of a little girl.

"You're a real asshole, you know that, Jack?"

3

"Just put it here."

"That doesn't go there!"

"Hurry up already."

"You want to do this? By all means, be my guest."

"Just get her up and running."

"It's not like I can flip a switch and repair all the damage she's sustained."

Darkness gave way to static. A mosaic arrangement of pixelated pigment blotched the visual.

She could see again.

Celia's voice crackled with electronic distortion. "Jack…"

"Well, that's a good sign," said Pinkerton. "Voice recognition is working."

She felt someone holding her hand, gently squeezing it. She pivoted toward the feeling, but her body fought her. Something kept her pinned on her back.

She opened her eyes and discovered Cutter looking down at her. But her hand wasn't clasped in his.

"I'm here," he said, giving her a cursory glance before returning to pester Pinkerton.

She tried to respond, but her voice wavered. It played a meek tune, lost of resonance. Trying to clear her throat, she coughed, but her voice never came. The best she could manage was something small and distant. Something that sounded far off even to her ears.

"You left me."

"Everything's going to be fine," said Cutter without looking at her. "We're putting you back together. You'll be good as new."

"We? How about me?" said Pinkerton. "*I'm* putting her back together again."

Once again, she felt her hand gently squeezed. She looked down and saw Pinkerton covering her hand with his.

Why wasn't it Cutter?

She stared at the back of Cutter's head waiting for him to meet her gaze.

"You left me…"

And still Cutter ignored her.

She felt pressure on her head as if she were submerged, the entire weight of the Pacific Ocean pressing down on her. Light smeared across her visual scanner in distorted bright whites. A halo glow rimmed Pinkerton. He stood amidst a black void of endless dark shadows.

She was starting to remember.

She had been improperly shut down. Sometimes after an improper shut down, programming subroutines got stuck in endless repetition, sending the same signal time and again, until the subroutine wore itself out or another took its place.

You left me, echoed in her head, mingling with background clinks and an occasional high-pitched whir. She shifted her eyes, finally taking toll of her surroundings. A single light was aimed at her, illuminating a small section of the otherwise darkened room.

What had happened to her? How badly was she injured?

A splash of static lit up her UI. She tried to bring up a diagnostic report. The erratic buzz of electricity crackled in her ear. With a brief flicker, her internal display fizzled out.

"Don't do that, sweetheart," said Pinkerton.

"What?" Cutter glared at her. "What's she doing?"

"Sorry," said Celia. Audio distortion shredded her meek inflection. Cutter grimaced. Pinkerton shivered. Her voice made nails on a chalkboard seem pleasant.

"She's running a routine diagnostic check," said Pinkerton. "She'll probably try to follow it with a maintenance routine, which wouldn't be all that great for me."

"Why's that?"

"I could lose a hand," he said, nodding in the direction of his hands. Celia couldn't see where they ended.

She stiffened as a sudden chill shot through her. Something ice cold emanated from somewhere near her fusion core. For a second, she thought it was a physical manifestation of her feelings for Cutter. For her abandonment. An empty freezing cold that left her hollow.

Three high pitch oscillations whirred, strange noises that seemed to belong more to a Nascar pitstop than a police station tech-room.

Cold metal brushed against her blinking innards. Followed by a strange after-sensation of warmth. The warmth came from Pinkerton's hands. The cold chill that tapped her insides with frigid sensation was a pneumatic tool he was guiding through her. She felt pieces of her insides pried back, as the pneumatic tool jabbed at her with a frozen kiss. An occasional bump sent fever chills through her body. Electricity arched between circuitry systems never meant to touch. Although it wasn't comfortable, she didn't blame Pinkerton for her discomfort. His hands moved with the precision of a surgeon, movement neither accidental, nor reckless. But not as painless as she would have desired. Pain, the kind that had never been catalogued by her programming ripped through her in pulsing waves.

Above her, Cutter yammered at Pinkerton with a look of determination that had little to do with her. She thought it obvious that his mind was on something else. Something besides her. Inside, she felt the warmth of fury rise, insulating her from the chill of abandonment.

She had trusted him. Him and everyone else that eventually wound up abandoning her. Time and again, the same patterns repeated themselves. Someone cared for her, or so she thought. And she too cared for them. But it was momentary, fleeting.

There were always words that betrayed her. Sweet promises whispered in her ear of a life she was unable to claim. Words that haunted her. Words she was tired of hearing. Empty words.

She was a good girl.

She let out a wail. Cold so intense it burned, spread through her chest.

Pinkerton softly shushed her. She barely heard him say, "We're almost done."

Cutter had made her feel something she dreaded. Something she tried her best to avoid. Something that humanity seemed eternally destined to make her feel.

Worthless.

She frowned, and let her head limply fall to a side on the workbench. She lay completely motionless, only tracking the movement of Cutter and Pinkerton with her eyes.

In contrast to Cutter's dismissive attitude, Pinkerton had a hundred and ten percent of his attention focused on her. And another ten percent devoted to swatting Cutter away like an annoying housefly.

An internal subroutine tried to raise the corner of her mouth in a smile. She consciously fought it. Forced her wavering mouth back into a straight line.

She couldn't help feeling that it was only a matter of time before Pinkerton would betray her as well. Better to not get attached in the first place. Better to not have these feelings at all.

"How much longer, you think?" Cutter asked, craning over Pinkerton's shoulder for a better look at her insides.

"She's missing too much." Pinkerton dodged a few errant sparks that spat from her chest. "Too damaged to say for sure."

"I thought you were the expert."

"With all the people that have been screwing around with her, I'm not even sure how she's operational. Her fusion core is a mess. The circuitry is spaghetti. There's too many pieces missing to get her on her feet."

"Can I talk to her?"

"I don't know. Can you?"

Cutter set his jaw. He flexed the rigid muscle in his cheek, causing the soft roundness of his features to disappear. He looked like he wanted to slug Pinkerton upside the head for the remark.

Celia caught him sneaking a peek at her from the corner of his eye. He held his gaze for a solid ten count before taking a deep breath and facing her.

"Ceil, can you hear me?"

"You left me, Jack."

"I did," he said matter of fact. "I need you to track down Costas again."

Betrayal piled upon betrayal. And now it wasn't even veiled. People wanted something from her and expected her to perform. Expected her to service every whim. And what did she receive in return?

No one thought about her wants, her needs, her desires.

She wanted compassion. That was all she had been hardwired for. She was designed to love and to be loved. It seemed only half of the bargain was ever fulfilled—the half that was her obligation to provide—the empty space in others' lives she was supposed to fill.

She met their needs, and they repeatedly failed to meet hers. Time and again.

Cutter turned to Pinkerton. "Did we lose her?"

Pinkerton smacked the side of a small box that blipped with vibrating green lines. "I don't think so."

"Ceil," Cutter said with urgency. "Can you hear me?"

"Loud and clear, Jack." A dry monotone had taken the place of the childish tone her voice once had.

"Do you still have a link to Costas?"

She brought up her UI.

"Yes, Jack. I feel the signal. It is faint, but I can find him."

"Great. Do it."

Pinkerton glared at Cutter. Celia saw it. She was convinced Cutter hadn't noticed. Of course he wouldn't. So oblivious to those around him.

She said, "He is at Los Angeles Harbor."

"The harbor?"

She nodded. Confirmation, and nothing more.

"Why the hell would they take him there?"

Pinkerton raised his eye loupe. "That's where all the facilities are."

"InSight?"

"Uh, yeah. And the opening is tomorrow."

"So?"

"The whole InSight going free to the public opening. Channel 5 says people are lining up already."

"Yeah, and?"

"Look, I don't know, Jack," said Pinkerton wiping sweat from his forehead with the back of his forearm. "You're the detective. You do the leg work."

Cutter steepled his fingers, leaned forward, and delicately placed his chin where his index fingers met. "You know what? You're absolutely right."

"I—what?"

"You're right. Get her on her feet. I'll be back for her in an hour."

"It's late, Jack. I need to get home. Celia will be fine for now. I can work on her in the morning."

"She's coming with me."

Pinkerton snorted. "Good luck with that."

"What the hell does the department pay you for? Do your job."

"As much as I'd *love* to help you, which is not at all, you don't have much say in the matter. I don't have replacement parts to get her on her feet again."

"What about Roy?" Cutter pointed at the scattered parts on the workbench.

"Roy?" The semi-infrequent whirring of the pneumatic tool stopped completely. The incinerator roared with a fiery hiss filling the silence.

Pinkerton turned to his right. Roy was a pile of discarded parts pushed into the corner of his workbench. His eyes were dark hollows. The opening in his chest cavity revealed a nest of wires and insulation.

"Roy's a bit more heavy duty," said Pinkerton. "I mean, he was made for combat. This one's a consumer model."

"I thought you were good at this."

Pinkerton threw his hands in the air, but the cord on the pneumatic tool yanked them back down. "I'm saying the parts might not be compatible."

"Just get her fixed. I'll be back in an hour."

Cutter's back was to her as he slinked away. She fought to roll onto her side, but her body wasn't responding to her commands. She could only reach out and watch the door swing closed.

"You left me."

4

"He's got a brain behind all that armor," said Reynolds. His eyes gleamed. The subtle hint of crow's feet appeared at the corners. "It's the most elaborate mod-job I've ever seen."

Foster felt his left eye twitch. Tomorrow was going to be a busy day, the busiest of his campaign. His lids were half-mast. He was leaning forward, nearly nodding off, needing to shake himself awake every few seconds only to have to repeat the process.

The facility had a bathroom where he could splash water on his face. But he didn't want to confront the image he was certain to see in the mirror. A strange bloated version of himself, hair askew, eyes sunken and bulging, the hint of blue piercing through barely open slits propped up on puffy bags of skin. He needed his beauty sleep. Yet here he was, in the middle of the night dealing with... *this.*

At this late hour, he had a hard time reconciling the jubilant juxtaposition that was Reynolds. He looked rather chipper skipping back and forth between his operating table and a tray full of strange looking medical implements.

Foster fought the urge to growl, finding Reynolds' demeanor all kinds of irritating.

"Come see," said Reynolds, hurriedly waving him over.

InSight had introduced them several years ago when the company realized they would need the help of a city official. Foster should have said no. Not because he knew what he was getting into, but because he was going to have to deal with people the likes of which he couldn't stand. The socially inept, the awkward, the dorks, and the geeks. He knew they were the ones that ran the show, that made it all possible, but he was a face. He liked interacting with other faces, usually in the most visible manner possible.

Reynolds wasn't the visible facade of InSight. He wasn't in charge of the company in any monetary capacity. Foster doubted more than half a dozen people even knew how important Reynolds was to InSight behind the scenes. He had met a few of the board members that had no clue that Reynolds even existed. Their business ran, as if by miracle, and they put no more thought into the people below them than that.

Reynolds was in charge of practically everything at InSight's main facility—from early construction, to general ambience and layout of the treatment rooms, to designing the drug cocktail and the treatment itself.

Reynolds hunched over the operating table, viciously jabbing at his new patient with a large metal tool that looked like a crowbar with a sharp hook end.

Foster shook his head. When they had first met, he had expected someone with a little more class and decorum. Not an overzealous grade schooler hungry for Thursday's zoology class because it meant he could poke at dead things with his fingers.

When it came to appearances, Reynolds didn't seem to try. He was balding with a frizzy laurel of hair propped up by his ears. He wore a white lab coat, unbuttoned. Between the open flaps Foster could make out a T-shirt that bore the name of some tourist town in Hawaii, its name mostly spelled in vowels. On it a surfer rode the nose of a longboard in silhouette against a large orange circle (presumably the sun). Reynolds' style was a complete lack of style. How did he live a life so oblivious to the perception of others?

Buy a comb.

He watched Reynolds giddily run back and forth between patient and the strange array of tools on, what amounted to, a medical tray on a pivoting arm. He couldn't help but wonder where Reynolds' assistant had gotten off to. Typically, there should have been someone handing him his needed implements. Someone assigned to monitor his process, keeping him in line, as much as they were there to assist him.

Foster scanned the room again, hoping that his assistant was hiding in some shockingly well-lit corner.

His assistant's name was Philips. Whenever Foster could manage, he scheduled his meetings to coincide with Reynolds' absence. Philips was a timid man, devoid of Reynolds' apparent raw genius. Apparent, Foster thought, because he was certain that those in charge had equated Reynolds' bizarre eccentricity with genius—because if it wasn't genius, it was surely madness. And genius looked better on the company manifold than certified loon.

Foster also preferred Philips complete lack of rambunctious attitude. Philips was more or less the nerdy scientist stereotype and Foster preferred his stereotypes as stereotypical as possible. Otherwise, why even bother categorizing them in the first place?

But Reynolds—Reynolds was a kid at play. The lab, science, engineering, mucking around with bio-chem, altering the face of humanity, crazy concepts for interior design, all were his turf.

Foster tugged at his collar loosening his tie.

Metal clanked against metal. Reynolds dropped the large crowbar tool on the medical tray. His hand scattered various odd-shaped implements and seized one that looked like an icepick. He skipped back to the operating table and ran a hand across sleek black tech with a touch usually saved for lovers.

Foster exhaled, somewhere between a groan and a sigh. "I'm well aware of what it is."

"It's really quite remarkable," said Reynolds. "The tech is all custom. It wasn't built and then attached to him. Whoever built this, built it specifically for *him*."

"Yes," said Foster. His tone was dismissive, but he found it far too late to care. Even decorum had to get some shut-eye every once in a while. "But do you have any inroads on getting him out of it?"

Reynolds leaped at Foster with a crazy gleam in his eye. "Do I? Do *I?!* You bet I do!"

Before primal fear could register in Foster, Reynolds had spun back to the operating table and jammed the icepick into a seam at his patient's neck.

Foster gave himself a minute for his heart to settle down before making the agonizing walk over to watch Reynolds work.

He kept wanting to call him Dr. Reynolds. Given the surroundings, the patient laid out on an operating table, the overhanging fluorescent lights on adjustable arms, the sterile dodecahedron room, it was easy to get the wrong impression. But he wasn't a doctor, at least not in the sense that Foster thought of one. He was a PHD. A mechanic. An engineer. A chemist. An earner of a doctorate. All of those. But not a Dr. Doctor.

"I don't think you understand," said Reynolds, hammering the icepick with the heel of his palm. "The tech is grafted into him. He's not modified. It's not an extension of him. It *is* him."

Semantics, Foster thought. But he was a politician. Everything was semantics. Semantics and bullshit. He had built his entire life around being able to cut through it while shoveling plenty of his own.

"Is he... online?" asked Foster.

"He's awake."

"Wonderful." His tone reflected no emotion at all. "That is wonderful."

The icepick slid a fraction of a millimeter under the neck plating. Reynolds pried it up, leaving a dent in the metal ridge. As he leaned into it, applying more pressure, the icepick popped out and skidded across the plating leaving a white scratch across the black finish.

Reynolds stepped back and cocked his head to a side. "Not exactly sure how I'm going to get through the faceshield, though."

"Have you tried asking him to open it?"

Reynolds froze.

Foster pursed his lips, biting his tongue. For a certified genius, certified something or other was more like it, Reynolds wore a dumbfounded expression like a seasoned professional.

Foster huffed. "Why don't we start with the basics?"

Reynolds nodded, hopped back to the operating table and craned over his patient. He raised a fist and knocked on the faceshield.

"Hello! Anybody in there!" He turned his head, putting

his ear to the horizontal face slats like a cowboy, ear to the rails listening for an approaching train. "Care to open up?"

Foster's head fell into his open palm. He slowly grinded his forehead back and forth across it.

"Knock, knock," said Reynolds. "Anybody home?"

A tinny voice came from behind the faceshield. "Who's there?"

It had a certain childish tone. A tone Reynolds wasn't picking up on.

"It's uh…" Reynolds looked at the mod with a raised eyebrow. "Reynolds," he said sounding like he was asking a question rather than answering one.

"Reynolds who?" the mod asked.

"Me." He thumped his chest. "Reynolds."

"Aren't you glad I didn't say orange?"

"What?"

Foster rolled his eyes.

"Well, that is certainly interesting," said the mod. "Was sure this guy had a sense of humor judging from how he dresses himself. Tell me Foster, is sense of humor no longer a prerequisite for joining this circus?"

Foster couldn't help but smile. "Forgive me," he said. "It seems you know my name, but I am at a loss for yours."

"Seems to be the case."

Foster's smile drained. "It's been a long night. Care to make this easy? Open that thing you got strapped to your head and we can all call it a night."

"No thanks, but thank you for asking. I do so appreciate good manners."

Foster nodded. He hadn't expected much cooperation, but it didn't hurt to ask.

"Have it your way," said Foster. He twirled a finger in the air. "He's all yours, Reynolds."

"Oh good. I was afraid you were going to torture me with droll conversation." The mod lifted his chin and presented the side of his neck to Reynolds. "Carry on."

He didn't need to ask Reynolds twice. Or once for that matter. Short of sprinting, Reynolds leaped to the mod's side, icepick tool drawn back for a piercing gouge that Foster was sure hadn't been taught in any medical school on the face of the planet. As the swing plunged for the mod's neck, the mod turned.

"Can I stop you for just a moment?"

Foster always had time for words. He'd gladly wait to hear what this mod had to say. Reynolds, on the other hand, he wasn't so sure about. And more specifically, the icepick in blurring motion may not share his delight in casual conversation.

Reynolds grimaced, twisted his body, and sent himself sprawling across the patient. Face to face with the mod, arm outstretched over his head, Reynolds gritted his teeth and snapped his jaw in the mod's direction.

"Sure..." said Foster apprehensively. "There's always time to see things eye to eye."

The mod wasn't scared of the likes of Reynolds. Foster knew that much. But the abrupt turnaround did more to set his nerves on edge than provide reassurances that this was a sudden breakthrough or momentary change of heart.

"Who's the looker with the sledgehammer?"

A slender figure with silky dark hair stood inside the sliding doors with a sledgehammer held diagonally across her body. Her features were Asian, but her overall appearance was much more SoCal in style.

"That's Amy," said Reynolds. "She assists me when Philips

is doing whatever it is he does when I'm not around." Reynolds trailed off muttering unintelligible gibberish about Philips under his breath.

"This is all I could find," said Amy, holding the sledgehammer out to Reynolds with both hands.

"Fine. Adequate. Fine," he said in a tone that didn't reveal whether it was in fact fine.

With some difficulty, Reynolds hoisted himself onto the operating table, butt waggling high in the air. Once atop, he pushed himself off of all fours and nearly toppled over as he stood. Staggering, he stepped in the crevice under the mod's armpit, a valley between chest and arm. In a sloppy effort to regain balance he jutted his arms out at his sides like a surfer catching a wave. Once he secured his footing, he signaled Amy with a flap of his fingers against his palm. She nodded and strained to raise the sledgehammer to him.

Metal clanked against metal. Reynolds placed the head of the sledgehammer on the operating table at an oblique angle, letting the handle rest against his leg. He spit into his hands, rubbed them together, and heaved the sledgehammer overhead. In the same motion, he delicately pinned the mod's head under his foot like a croquette ball—the raised sledgehammer an accompanying mallet.

Foster cringed. He didn't like seeing such directly blunt assaults. From his experience, a more indirect tact seemed to offer better, longer lasting results. But they didn't really have time for anything so planned out or orchestrated.

If he wanted this mod out of his shell, he needed to use more forceful methods than he would have preferred. And Reynolds was the right man for the job.

The sledgehammer clanged down on the mod's head.

Despite his reservations against brute force, Foster watched with sickening fascination. The thought of turning away never crossed his mind.

"That kinda tickled," said the mod.

Reynolds' face went red. His nostrils flared spitting fire. He hoisted the sledgehammer and smashed it down upon the faceshield with primal force.

White scuffmarks peppered the faceshield's black finish. A small indentation formed where the corner of the sledgehammer had caught cheek plating.

"It may take some work," said Reynolds, "but we'll get you out of there soon enough."

A series of blows to the head later, Reynolds was dripping sweat, his entire body blistering red from the strain. He merrily grunted to himself with every swing of the sledgehammer.

"Foster?" said the mod. "A word?"

The smile disappeared from Reynolds at sound of the mod's casual tone. He grunted his dissatisfaction in Foster's direction, but Foster ignored him.

Foster approached the operating table, toeing a line on the linoleum just out of arm's reach from both Reynolds and the mod.

"How can I be of assistance?"

Another clang filled the room.

"I have this little problem."

"Oh?" said Foster. "And what might that be?"

"Just a little thing."

Reynolds grunted and hit him harder.

"Why go through all this trouble?"

"Right... Right. Well, you probably don't realize this yet," said Foster between sledgehammer swings, "but you are going to be the new posterboy for InSight."

"Oh… And me without my makeup."

Foster was finding it hard to dislike this mod. At every word, a constant smile naturally appeared on his face. In public, he always appeared to be smiling, but seldom were they genuine. They were a part of the business, the role of the politician. A tool of the trade, like a lumberjack with an axe or a coach with a whistle. A trait he had practiced and mastered over the years. But in the presence of this mod, he found he could forget his training, and rely solely on natural human instinct.

"It really is great," said Foster. "Can you imagine a better advertisement for InSight?" He spread his hands wide, as if showcasing an invisible marquee overhead. "Once a mindless killer. Soon to be a tame, domesticated, and quite possibly, productive member of society."

"One can dream, can't he?"

Foster squinted at the mod. "Yes. That's precisely it."

The mod turned and looked up at Reynolds who was about to deliver another blow to his face. "Hey Doc."

"He's not a Doc," Foster corrected. "He's a P—"

"Gotch yer arm!"

The chain-gang rhythm was broken by a bloodcurdling scream that filled the confines and shook the glass walls.

Foster cocked his head to a side, watching Reynolds pirouette face first into the steel operating table, briefly hold scorpion form, before tumbling ass over teacups to the floor.

He didn't know if he should be upset at the incompetence or congratulate the mod for relieving him of ever having to deal with Reynolds again. He simply nodded and cleared his throat with a faint *mhmm* noise.

Amy was a horrified statue. An expression was frozen on her

face only rivalled by those set in stone for eternity by Medusa. Or so Foster assumed, never having met the woman. He also assumed the effects on Amy were temporary, despite the lack of any indication that her face should return to normal in the foreseeable future.

He wafted a lazy wrist trying to get Amy's attention, and pointed at the human shaped lump lying in a smear of blood.

"Find Philips," said Foster. "Oh, and be a dear. Get that off the floor. And please, no more fuckups."

5

"I have to shut you down, sweetheart."

"But—"

"It'll be fine, I promise," said Pinkerton, soothing Celia with a soft whisper. "You're through the hard part. But I need to cinch up these connections before I can send you out. And it's much easier with you offline."

Celia batted doe eyes at Pinkerton, scanning for something he wasn't sure was programmed into her subroutines.

"Okay," she said after some hesitation.

"That's a good girl."

Odd, Pinkerton thought. A fraction of a second before he turned her off, he thought he saw a glimmer of sheer terror in her eyes before they went dull.

"How's the patient?"

He hadn't heard Cutter enter. His attention had been devoted to Celia. To repairing her. To getting her up and running again.

"What's this?" Cutter picked up a pneumatic caliper.

"Jack," said Pinkerton shooting a sideways glance at him. "You ever think of giving your personality a make-over?" He removed the caliper from his hand and hung it from a hook on the pegboard overshadowing the workbench. "You could definitely use one."

"Funny guy, Doc."

"Don't call me, Doc. Makes you sound like Bugs Bunny."

"She still offline?"

"Temporarily. I'm not a hundred percent how she'll take to the new gear."

"Just wire her up, and let's go. Parts be parts."

From the corner of his eye, he saw Cutter scanning the room looking for the next thing he could play with. He folded his arms, forcing a statue facade. Pinkerton knew better. He knew the posture. Cutter was fighting the need to touch everything within reach.

"She looks good enough to me. Close her up so we can get on the road."

Pinkerton chewed his lower lip. He edged a green wire past a circuitboard. Blue static arced from the board to the wire, shooting an explosion of sparks out of her chest cavity.

"Dammit!"

Cutter furrowed his brow and glowered at Pinkerton.

"You know, we're talking about a machine that thinks for itself here," said Pinkerton. "One crossed wire and she might use Roy's gear to punch a hole through a wall when she meant to shake hands."

With a sing-songy tone, irritating even for Cutter, he said, "The arm wire is connected to the—arm wire."

Pinkerton paused, looking up from Celia for a moment. He counted to ten in his head.

"Each part is different. They have to be sync'd on an individual basis. If her neural processor rejects the link, they won't work at all. If it's a partial connection, well, she might just decide she doesn't like it, and opt not to work either."

"You talk like synths have personality. They're built off a blueprint. That's the whole point. Interchangeable parts."

Pinkerton shook his head at Cutter. "You don't even have the slightest clue, do you?"

"Not the first time I've heard those words. Today."

"Her brain is not so different from yours or mine. A single pulse of electricity surging through a series of binary pathways can relay even the most complicated of instructions. That's exactly how we work. The only real difference is that biology is better at compression. We have far more two-way connections than can be socketed onto a CPU. But every second of every day technology is catching up."

Pinkerton pointed at him with a pair of rubber handled tongs. Cutter gave him a wary look. "And it's not like we use all of those connections anyway. Some of us less than others."

"Yeah, but I've got personality."

"If you want to call it that." He plunged his hands into Celia's open innards, pinning several bundles of wires to a side, and twisted her fusion core with the tongs. "You ever stop to think that the path in which electricity travels through your head is what determines personality?"

Pinkerton waited for a response. Normally, he wasn't interested in small chat, but he liked to consider the possibilities of his work. What it meant to be working on thinking machines. The delayed response gave him more time to reflect, but apparently Cutter shared his disinterest for banter.

Next to him, Cutter had his arms crossed, idly watching.

Pinkerton laughed to himself. "No, I guess you haven't have you? Think about it. The who you are, your soul if you let me be so bold, is nothing more than the arbitrary path that electricity chooses to carve through your brain."

"Preach on, brother-man," said Cutter, wry and disinterested.

"Make fun all you like. The vast majority of your brain is nothing more than a storage compartment for data. Accessing and interpreting that information has less to do with size and more to do with neural pathways—essentially the flow of electricity. The path electricity follows in your head obeys its own laws of chaos and randomness."

"I'm not here for a lecture on… whatever this is."

You barged into my workshop, my territory, in the middle of the night demanding that I repair a machine capable of independent thought that you put in harm's way—you're going to hear a lecture whether you like it or not!

"You ever have a car that runs a little funny? Not worse or better than anything else—just different. Haven't you ever heard someone say, 'Hey, that's got personality,' in reference to, I don't know, a toaster, a car, a synthetic."

Cutter stood defiantly silent.

"C'mon Jack. Think about it. You have first-hand experience. Was Roy identical to Carl? Or Sid? Or Steve? They all came off the same assembly line. All have the same schematics and programming. All had the same parts. Did they all behave the same?"

Cutter was stone, an expression that said much without saying anything. It put a smile on Pinkerton's face knowing that Cutter could never admit that someone else was right.

"Uh huh. I'm getting through that tough guy thing you got going there."

"Is she done? Seems I'm quite the distraction. And we have places to be."

"Almost done," said Pinkerton. He tapped her innards with the caliper, lighting up the right side. He placed the caliper down and picked up a screwdriver with a socket head. He fit it onto a bolt at her armpit, and twisted. Celia's new right arm moved with the motion.

"Weren't you the one complaining about Roy? How painfully direct he was. How any indication of foul play would distract him?"

Cutter sighed, closing his eyes. "It was a problem, yes."

Roy had been painfully direct to a fault. Cutter knew it. Pinkerton also knew that Cutter had exploited that fault.

Much like every synthetic he ever came in contact with. Cutter was extremely gifted in pinpointing the weaknesses, the infinitesimal differences from one synthetic to the next. Whether it was conscious or not, Pinkerton couldn't be certain. Sure, Cutter was a grade-A asshole. But he meant well. Even Pinkerton had a hard time believing anyone, even Cutter, could intentionally be as insensitive as appearances deemed.

No, the ease at which he seemed able to exploit one's weakness was much too natural.

Pinkerton paused, grinning ear to ear at Cutter. "I guess thought isn't something you're known for, is it?"

"You're forgetting one major difference."

"Oh?"

"I don't come off an assembly line."

"Don't you?" Pinkerton waved his hand toward the ceiling, as if pontificating on some grand notion that exceeded the confines of the room. "That great biological assembly line."

"Between every woman's thighs?"

Pinkerton grimaced. Sometimes he forgot how blunt Cutter could be. "I was trying to be metaphoric."

"Better off sticking to the tech, Doc."

He muttered to himself under his breath and then delicately placed a finger in the dead center of Celia's forehead.

"This one here didn't come off an assembly line. She was handmade. One of a kind. A DNA crossbreed of her parents…"

A shiver ran through his body. He faltered, midsentence. A thought hti him like lightning, leaving him dumbstruck—how easy it had been for Cutter to find and exploit Celia's weakness. Her need for someone to look after her. Her need for a role model and a teacher. Someone she could look up to.

A parent.

The thought lingered like white noise in an empty room. It had little to do with the speed, nor how naturally Cutter seemed able to isolate and exploit a person's being. What sent the chill through Pinkerton was the idea that Cutter did so without thought at all.

For him, exploiting others was automatic.

Pinkerton cleared his throat, stumbling over his words. "Her, uh… overall programming was specified to match her parent's desires for their child. And the—the initial learning programs installed into her are basic things, you know, things you and I learn from childhood to adolescence."

He stared at Cutter. "What makes her any different than you or I?"

But even that question wasn't wholly accurate. He was certain that there was more in common between himself and Celia, between man and synthetic, than the relationship Cutter had with humanity in general.

"I can't download the entire contents of Wikipedia into my noggin," said Cutter without missing a beat.

Pinkerton shook his head. "Not funny, Jack."

"That too. Don't hear her making wisecracks."

Pinkerton let the room fill with the hissing hum from the pocket incinerator. Both Celia and Roy had been missing large chunks of their chest. He had improvised a breastplate for her from pieces of Roy's back armor.

He placed the makeshift breastplate flush against the opening in her chest. The metal kept shifting and folding closed. Interlocking, overlapping sheets of metal allowed a wide range of movement, necessary for the back anatomy of most bipedal synthetics. But it also made the makeshift patch a royal pain in the ass to use as a cover over the chest. It demanded something more rigid.

With a thud, Pinkerton tossed the thick hunk of metal to a side. He yanked a pneumatic tool off the air hose and replaced it with a rivet gun. He once again picked up the large chunk of interlocking armor plating and spread it best he could concealing her blinking electronic innards. Air hissed through the nozzle of the rivet gun. It punched a hole through the toughened armor, inserted a metal rivet, and pulled the nail through it, crushing it into a perfect round nub.

Loud thunks filled the tech-room. Cutter cringed, hunching his shoulders.

"Not a fan of seeing how the sausage is made?" Pinkerton jibed.

The makeshift breastplate's right edge mirrored the hole, following a rounded path, like that of a ribcage. Pinkerton grabbed the inner edge and spread the interlocking plates to cover the gap. It didn't quite reach. He frowned.

He raised up on tip-toe, put his knee into Celia's chest and pressed his weight into the plate. It flexed enough to cover the opening. Half a dozen pneumatic thundercracks rang out.

Pinkerton inspected the work. It wasn't great, or even pretty, but it should work. And ironically, the patch-job was stronger than the original plastic polymer it was replacing. Any new holes she wanted to punch through herself would have to find a different point of entry.

He placed his right thumb on her hip and held three fingers in a claw shape, pushing into specific points on her back.

Color returned to Celia's eyes.

"How's that feel?" asked Pinkerton.

"Different."

Pinkerton nodded. "You'll get used to it."

"So, that it?" said Cutter.

"She's up and running, but there's no guarantee that she won't malfunction again. I think you should leave her here so I can run a full diagnostic. Make sure everything is functioning normally."

"Don't worry about it. If she gets out of hand, I'll put her out of her misery."

"Nice Jack," said Pinkerton nonplussed. He held the pneumatic rivet gun in his hand, unsure whether he should put it down or aim it at Cutter. "You tug on my heartstrings to get me to put her together again and immediately threaten to turn her back into scrap."

"What can I say? You do good work."

Pinkerton glared at Cutter. Only one word came to mind. "Asshole."

5

"Well, well, well," said Foster, "isn't this quite the surprise."

Philips stood a good distance away from the metal man

strapped to the operating table. He wore a similar white lab coat to the one Reynolds had worn, except on Reynolds it looked more like a bathrobe—like he was continually *just* getting out of the shower. Reynolds' appearance was irritatingly casual. But on Philips, the lab coat was buttoned tightly and had a permanent crease that ran down the length of his sleeves. Philips was how scientists should look, Foster thought.

"So, uh," muttered Philips. "So… yeah. He's uh…"

Philips tucked his arms in close to his chest, like a nerdy Tyrannosaurus Rex. He hesitated to reach for anything, as if extending his arms too far would result in them being ripped free from his body. In any other case, he would have looked overly cautious. In this one, well… Foster couldn't fault the man for his meek demeanor.

"We removed the faceshield," said Philips. "So uh, there he is."

Foster started laughing. "Yes. There he is."

Philips jittered from side to side, staring wide-eyed at Foster. "Um… so, yeah. It's—he's everything you wanted, right? Hoped and dreamed?"

"Oh, this is perfect." Foster slapped Philips on the back. Philips swayed with the force. Foster didn't mean to hurt the man, but this was better than he could have ever imagined.

"Thank you, Philips. Great work."

"Do—do, uh, do you need me anymore?" Philips inched toward the exit. "Cause, uh, if you don't mind, I'd like to be leaving."

"No. I think we'll be quite fine."

As Philips made for the door he caught sight of Foster holding up a hand. "Oh, Philips…"

The frightened man stopped in the doorway.

"Yes?"

Foster beamed. "Thanks again."

After an awkwardly long pause, Philips nodded, and left.

"So," said Foster, taking a seat on the edge of the operating table. "To what do we owe the honor of your presence—"

He waited a beat before finishing.

"—Costas."

Costas smiled the way an alligator smiles—not to portray emotion, but because that was the set of his jaw—set with the illusion of joy. "Glad to see you remembered my name."

"How could I forget?"

Costas gave a small chuckle. "That's funny, all things considered."

Foster rolled his shoulders. "Never let them say I was a man without a sense of humor."

"Seems that you've pieced everything together."

Foster shook his head. "No. But at least I know why someone wanted me dead. This was all personal, wasn't it?"

"I wouldn't say entirely. Part of it was fun."

"How times change."

"How they stay the same."

"I wouldn't say that," said Foster. "Have you see what I've done with the city?"

"Have I? You're kidding, right?"

"Right. I guess that's why you're here."

"Still want me as your posterboy?"

"Most definitely." Foster steepled his hands in front of a grim smile. "It's almost poetic."

INSIGHT

1

Cutter felt an inkling of warmth on his back. The first rays of a rising sun crested over a mountain ridge chasing away the damp chill on the marina and the remainders of the night. Fingers of golden yellow reached out and grabbed a handful of shipping containers on an expanse of darkened tarmac. Beyond the shipyard, the ocean shimmered with the beginnings of a new day, bathing everything in a soft reflected glow.

Mornings like this had a life of their own.

Cutter raised a pair of binoculars to his eyes and chewed on the end of a cigarette. In the harbor below, amidst the multi-colored containers, a stage had been constructed. Given the surroundings, it seemed out of place. It was larger and more permanent than the temporary structure erected at M.J. Square. It reminded Cutter of a Grecian amphitheater crossed with a giant conch shell. One oddity, at least Cutter thought so, was that the seats turned inward, facing the shipyard, while the stage faced out toward the ocean.

The Port of Los Angeles sat on nearly four thousand acres of prime Southern California coast line. Jagged manmade inlets and peninsulas, like broken teeth, tore into artificially flattened water. A breakwall, barely visible on the horizon, kept the ocean swell to a bare minimum.

At the water's edge, half a dozen metal dinosaurs stood the test of time against corrosive salt air and the occasional lapping wave. None were currently in operation, but a large cargo ship several football fields long (like Los Angeles residents knew what a football field looked like) was coming in to dock beneath them.

The tarmac's outer perimeter was gated off by chain link fencing. Nothing fancy. No razor wire was needed to keep people out. It was more or less a simple boundary marking the confines of the shipyard.

Tents hugged miles of chain-linked perimeter, starting from two large gates that had been chained together. People were already gathering, ready for the early bird special.

Glowing orange fire hit the dirt. Cutter shifted his weight, grinding the discarded butt underfoot. The shipyard was of little importance. He was more interested in the new construction that had slipped into the harbor over the past few years.

A small rectangular building, like a grave stone, jutted up from the edge of the seawall. It was painted canary yellow with garish sea foam green trim. Above its sliding entrance doors, a sign spelled out its contents in cyan glow.

InSight.

The company with a vision for the future of Los Angeles. A company that had wanted to stay close to its ideal demographic. A company that needed a lot of land for its operation, and quickly ran into the dilemma that SoCal was both overpopulated and property ain't cheap.

Somehow InSight had convinced the port authority that their needs were all subterranean and that they would make sure construction would not hinder harbor traffic in the slightest. That—and they probably paid the port authority a shit-ton of money, as well.

Somewhere below the gently lapping surface, attached to the yellow and sea foam green eyesore, was a catacomb of dodecahedron chambers and an interconnected web of underwater tubes and airlocks.

Somehow, Cutter had to find a way inside without anyone

noticing.

Good luck with that.

"You left me."

Cutter lowered his binoculars and took a deep breath.

He fought the urge to look at the tiny synthetic to his right. Fought the urge to address her directly. He was still trying to figure a way inside the facility. Yeah, he thought, that was a good reason why he had to avoid eye contact.

He cleared his throat. "You're sounding like a broken record now, Ceil."

"But you left me."

"And I came back for you. Got you all patched up, good as new, right?"

Despite his better judgment, he found himself turning, facing her, looking down at the dark haired girl he was using as a partner. Her brows furrowed, lower lip jutted out. He had seen bulls staring at red with less intensity in their eyes.

"You left me."

Something jumped into his throat and tied itself into a knot. He wanted to think it was his stomach, but he had a hunch it was something closer to his heart.

"You left me!" she said again, punctuating the statement with a stomp of her foot kicking up a whorl of dust.

It was the first time he had heard her raise her voice. Probably the first time she had ever asserted herself. Or maybe it was only the first time he had noticed. As he thought about the past couple days, he doubted it was the first time she had ever acted out. There was a skybox full of people who could attest to that.

"You aren't going to go all crazy on me now?" Cutter asked, only half-joking. "Are you, kid?"

Another thought occurred to him. *Maybe that was why she*

had been abandoned in the mall in the first place. Little details he had taken for granted were starting to fall into place.

He tilted his head to a side and squinted at Celia. She glared at him, not the sweet inquisitive look he had grown to adore. This was something else. He could be wrong, apparently his detective skills and intuition were severely lacking—thanks to a new revelation—but Celia was looking up at him with hatred in her eyes. She was clearly fuming. And who wouldn't be?

A synthetic, he told himself.

That's who wouldn't be. In fact, it shouldn't even be possible for a synthetic to hold a grudge.

In a half-baked effort to lighten the mood, Cutter placed a hand on her shoulder. "Don't be so down. You look better than new. You look asymmetrically badass."

Despite reconstruction, she was still small in stature, carrying the overall appearance of a child. However, Roy's parts jutted out of her like a sword swallower with a thousand mouths swallowing a thousand swords. The bulkier parts, obviously made for combat, dwarfed the doll versions they had replaced. G.I. Joe had been built out of a Barbie doll.

He liked her new unsettling image. It made him think of a greasy haired, bloody knuckled biker that had tied a weathered teddy bear to the front of his chopper. It should have been cute, an ice breaker, a mood lightener. Instead, the hint of softness, the invitation to drop your guard, was all the more frightening.

He was glad she was on his side.

"You left me!" she said, this time shouting.

Or had been on his side.

He ignored her and raised the binoculars to his eyes, once more scoping out the shipyard.

"You're sure he's in there?"

She had already confirmed the location. He just wanted to fill the silence with something other than how he had abandoned her.

Next to him, feet shifted on asphalt, but no response came. Trying to covertly peek at her without her noticing, he flicked his eyes to his right without lowering the binoculars. He couldn't make out what she was doing. Under his breath, a low groan rumbled.

She was intentionally drawing out her response to upset him. He was sure of it.

He exhaled and lowered the binoculars. Celia sat Indian-style on the road, looking up at him.

"Celia." His voice was stern. "Is he in there?"

"Yes."

"I don't know why you do this. This isn't a game."

"This is not a game," she agreed.

"I'm not your father. I'm not here to take care of you."

"That is the truth."

Cutter raked a hand through his hair and swiftly brought it up under his nose in a fist. "Why do you have to make this so difficult?"

She glared at him.

"I need you on your A-game," said Cutter. "Whatever happened in the skybox, you need to forget it."

He realized his statement could be taken two ways. He had meant that she should forget about what she had done. The lives she had taken. That it wasn't her fault.

At least... she had told him it wasn't her fault. That Costas had taken control.

But she also said she had liked it.

Sitting on the edge of the road, she drew circles in the dusty shoulder. Yesterday, he couldn't have pictured her having the ability to hurt a single living thing. But that was the problem with synthetics wasn't it? It was impossible to tell what they were capable of, what was going on behind that plastic facade.

He didn't think it was right to ask her to forget that he had abandoned her. That was the right thing to say, wasn't it?

Or maybe he had meant both versions.

Forget it.

Forget it all.

Maybe that's why he had stated it so ambiguously.

He knelt down next to her. "Listen to me. This is important." He placed his hands on her shoulders.

"Ceil… You're a synthetic. You know that, right?"

Celia met his gaze. Something softened. Or maybe that was just wishful thinking on his part. He searched her giant brown eyes for signs that she understood. That it wasn't personal. He had a job to do, and if that meant betraying trust he had built, well, that's what he would do. She had to understand.

"You're a tool to be used as the situation requires."

The words came out harsher than he had intended. He forced a smile. "You understand, don't you?"

"Perfectly."

"Ceil!" Cutter yelled. Footsteps pounded behind her, but it was already too late. She was halfway across the open tarmac when Cutter ducked behind a shipping container for fear of being seen.

She marched up to InSight's yellow and sea foam green entrance. Beneath the glowing cyan logo, a not-so hidden camera swept the shipyard.

Even from this distance, she could hear Cutter breathing. Panting. Maybe if he spent more time thinking about her, her wants, her needs, instead of staring through his binoculars or telling her things she already knew, she wouldn't have gotten so far ahead of him in the first place.

The camera silently pivoted toward her. She saw it, but didn't bother to pick up the pace. Cutter's breathing stopped short. She knew he wanted to yell out, but couldn't. Or rather wouldn't, frightened that someone might hear. There was an awkward shuffling of feet, lurching crunches in the dirt and gravel. But they never got any closer. Cutter wouldn't let himself be caught on camera. Celia smiled to herself.

The camera finished its return sweep of the entrance. Before it could spot her, she had ducked around the corner on the far side of InSight's entrance. Her effortless stealth reminded her of all the times she had hidden from Mommy. Practice had, in fact, made perfect.

She ripped the metal face off a circuit box and tossed it to the dirt. Inside the housing, several bundles of lavender wires were bound together by a zip-tie. She reached in, tracing the path of a wire with her finger. The wire dead-ended into the third circuit breaker from the top. She yanked. A loud crack hammered the air like an anvil and showered Celia with sparks.

"What the hell were you thinking?!" Cutter had caught up. Finally, she thought. He was behind her, face red, breathing hard, doubled over with one hand on his knee and the other on her shoulder for support.

"You said you needed the door opened." She pointed at the open sliding glass doors leading deeper inside InSight's grave marker facade. "I opened the door. I also took care of the closed circuit cameras."

"That doesn't answer my question."

Celia nodded with certainty. "It does."

"You can't just go running… Hey, wait up a sec!" Cutter jogged behind her to catch up as she entered the building. "You have to think these things through."

"I am a tool. Nothing more. Nothing less."

The image of Daddy flashed across her memory. The same words he had said to her, but in a completely different context. *Mommy needed time alone with Jessica.*

Nothing more.

Nothing less.

Cutter grumbled. "I get it. You don't need to be all pouty about it, you know." He muttered something else under his breath. Her better than human hearing deciphered it: *It's freakin' me out.*

"I am not programmed to be pouty," she said and as an afterthought added, "Most people find that annoying."

She pressed the call button for the elevator.

Cutter's footsteps stopped. He stood motionless in the entry, looking out at the shipyard. A trio of seagulls took flight. A guy wire caught the morning breeze and clinked against metal in a semi-rhythmic melody.

Scanning the shipyard, he asked, "Think anyone saw us?"

"No."

"You seem awfully certain."

"No one is shooting at us."

Cutter pursed his lips together and tilted his head. "Good point."

He joined her inside the entry, waiting for the elevator, and pressed the illuminated button half a dozen times.

She noticed his deeply calloused hands and the gnarled

fingers attached to them, and wondered if they would stop assaulting the poor call button any time soon. Although she did not have nerves to speak of, if she had, Cutter most definitely would have been wearing them thin.

She grabbed his hand with what used to be Roy's. "That does not help. The elevator will arrive regardless of how many times you push the button."

Cutter winced at her grip, and rubbed his aching hand as she let go.

"Says you," he said. "Peace of mind always helps."

He pressed the call button three more times. And then a fourth for good measure. After a few moments of silence, he looked down at her.

"Celia..." He let the word hang like an hourglass on a loading screen.

She closed her eyes and inhaled. "What do you want?"

"Are you okay?"

"I am operational."

Her HUD had offered different responses. Many better suited for her apparent age. Her programming informed her such a choice was one a human might make out of spite. She assured the voice in her head that her decision had most definitely not been made out of spite.

Cutter patted her on the arm. Rather Roy's arm that had been shoved into her. "That's not exactly what I meant."

The elevator door slid open.

Cutter went in first. Celia followed close behind, and slammed into the doorframe. The walls shook from the collision.

Cutter's eyes were saucers, brows sky high. "Uh, I know I just asked this, but are you sure you're okay?"

"One hundred percent functional."

"You just ran into a wall."

"It was a doorframe."

"Okay… You just ran into a doorframe."

"I am fine."

Cutter slowly raised his head, the first half of a nod, and glared down his nose at her. "If you say so."

Celia turned, facing out. Even synthetics had this needlessly pointless piece of elevator etiquette hardwired into them. She rolled her shoulder, checking to make sure nothing was damaged. With a slight tug on her arm, she brought up her system diagnostics.

She could hear Cutter nervously fidgeting next to her. Her UI suggested that she should probably comfort him. She disagreed.

But humans aren't prepared to treat synthetics like real people, it argued. *You should do something to set his fears aside.*

Why? He's never done so for me.

After a minute of arguing with herself she finally caved.

Fine!

Facing forward, she said, "It is the new Black and White parts. I am not used to them yet."

"Uh… right." Cutter couldn't hide the apprehension in his voice. Not from her, nor her programming. It flashed his probable emotional state across her UI in big red flashing letters.

She made mental note, hoping that her internal programming would read it. *Now you listen to me! He's not comforted anyway! Feel free to save any future suggestions for someone else!*

Yes, talking to her onboard programming was ridiculous. But at least it made her feel better and also seconded the notion that she was not crazy. That everyone else telling her what to do and who to be were just mirror reflections of what they wanted. They could all go to Hell. Her programming included.

She let her left hand linger on her right arm. And turned looking at it with closer scrutiny. Her new arm felt familiar, but foreign at the same time.

She checked her internal UI, a wireframe grid of her contours. *Let's put you to good use—for once,* she thought. Other foreign oddities lit up in greens and greys throughout her body, displaying where she wasn't herself any longer.

She sent an electrical signal pinging each of her new parts. Despite feeling like they didn't belong to the whole, they instantly responded to her commands. The most disconcerting part was the speed at which they responded. They did what she told— what she commanded—even faster and with more veracity than her old default parts.

It wasn't just her outlook that was new and different. Her body was as well. Roy's combat chassis and limbs were a part of her now. Part of the new being she was becoming inside and out.

Besides the mental incongruity, the bulkier nature of Roy created problems her wiring was having difficulty reconciling. She had noticed it on the way out of the precinct. She kept banging her elbow into corners and objects that her previous, more slender frame would have fit through. The wider bits and pieces were slightly longer—responsive, but not existing in the same space she remembered.

Only one of Cutter's brows had returned to its normal position. The other was still saluting the sky.

The elevator doors slid shut.

A rush of air filled the chamber.

"Where do you think this goes?" said Cutter.

"Down," she said coldly.

Something loud and metallic clanked into place. Before either of them could utter any resignations, the ground fell out from beneath their feet. The functionally ugly concrete structure gave way to an endless sea of Los Angeles sewage on all sides, as they fell into it.

From all appearances, they should have been swimming. Air swirled around them in soft puffs like pillows cushioning their fall, ushering them through a glass tube on their journey to the bottom of the harbor.

Celia placed her hand flat against the tube as they rushed past. She stared through her splayed fingers into the murky depths of Los Angeles Harbor. Rays of light desperately tried to penetrate the rippling ocean surface in a kaleidoscope of natural beauty. The all too short-lived moment ended with an abrupt halt.

At the bottom of the tube, the elevator doors swept open revealing a glass room, dodecahedron in shape. Three tubes branched out from the main hub—two on either side and a third dead ahead.

Cutter stood next to her holding his stomach. "Glad I skimped on breakfast."

"I do not eat."

"Yeah. We've been through this."

She ignored Cutter and stepped into the room.

"Hey, where are you going?"

"You wanted to get inside," said Celia. "We are inside."

The mystery intrigued her. She checked the signal. Costas was down here—somewhere close.

With Mommy and Daddy, the idea of being anything other than their daughter never crossed her mind. But here with Cutter, and even without him, she could picture herself working in law enforcement. She wanted to hunt down those that wanted to harm others. It only seemed right.

And recently, she added those that let harm come to others to that list, as well.

Celia took two steps forward, stopped dead in her tracks, and gawked at the spectacle. Above her, the geodesic dome of glass and steel protected them from a silent world. Daylight danced in the swirling waters, refracting into warm colors, cutting through cool blues. Looming like a rain cloud on a swift breeze, the darkened silhouette of a cargo ship drifted along the surface. A spiraling vortex twisted behind, marking its path like a trail of breadcrumbs. She watched for a prolonged moment, until a stingray cut across her vision and glided along the surface of the structure, before disappearing into a bed of seaweed.

Cutter leaned forward and placed his hand on her shoulder. She clenched her jaw at his touch.

"We need to find Costas," he said. "Figure out what they want with him."

"What about what you want with him?"

"What do you mean?"

"The case was closed. The only logical reason we are here is because you want something."

"So what if it is? Can you track him down or not?"

"Of course I can." Celia smiled. It wasn't her innocent childish smile. Not anymore. She felt pride, a sense of worth, and a bit of snark.

Just a tool. We'll see.

"Well, do it before somebody realizes they have company down here."

Cutter jumped at the sound of a blaring klaxon. Red and orange lights flashed down the corridors and in every interior corner of the dodecahedron structure.

Cutter threw his arms into the air and let them spasmodically flail like a ragdoll in the wind. "Well, so much for that."

"Seems they are aware of an intruder."

"Gee, you think?"

"Yes." Celia nodded. She most certainly did.

"I thought you jammed the cameras when you let us in."

"I did." Her internal UI once again popped up with a less terse answer. It was a response that gave a possible list of outcomes and reasons why they had been discovered, while proving that she had in fact disabled the cameras. It urged her to share those with Cutter.

But Celia saw no reason to.

If he wants to know something. He can ask. I can only do what I've been told. Isn't that, right? she rhetorically asked her CPU.

"So how do they know we're here?"

"Heat scan?"

"Right…" Cutter slipped into a thousand yard stare. "Heat scan."

"You only have yourself to blame for that one."

"Very funny."

He choked on the word 'funny,' like he hadn't wanted to say it at all. His eyes drifted down to her. "Never mind. It's not funny at all."

The walls thrummed with a jarring beat, like a million hammers pounding the metal grates that passed for floors. From the central corridor, the thundering drone grew in decibel with each passing second.

Celia snapped her head to the sound. She could only see thirty-five feet down the corridor to where it dead-ended. Her snarky bravado faded, and she began to feel vulnerable, exposed. "What do you think they are sending?"

"That's your department, sweetheart." Cutter grabbed her

hand and sprinted down the east corridor at a pace just short of dragging her.

"My department?"

"The Black and Whites do that. Assess threat and provide feedback and reconnaissance on possible incoming attacks. Profile offensive and defensive capabilities of the attackers, how many, provide suggestions for countermeasures, that type of thing."

"Oh."

"Yeah, so you might want to get on that ASAP."

Celia looked back over her shoulder, stumbling in the process. Cutter raised his arm and set her back on her feet. She clung to his hand for support and asked, "Why the east tunnel?"

"I didn't hear you making any suggestions."

"Costas's signal is coming from the west."

Cutter stopped. He looked down at her and shook his head. "Seriously?!" He looked back over his shoulder. At the flashing red and orange lights. Listening to the blaring klaxon and the percussive beat of approaching footsteps. "You've got to be kidding me."

"Nope."

"C'mon."

Cutter wrapped his arm around her midsection, lifted her to his shoulder, and doubled back toward the elevator. He skipped across the center corridor as a small battalion of men and women clad in matching InSight security uniform thundered out of it. They wore plasticized combat helmets with tinted visors and carried stun rifles. As the front row poured out of the center corridor, Cutter barreled straight through knocking the first two guards to the ground and shouldered past the next row on a dead sprint.

"Think they saw us?" asked Cutter.

"Yup."

"So how's that Black and White programming coming?"

She had managed to access the training files and pull up the required programming. A large portion had already been downloaded at Staples Center, but she hadn't had time to explore its more advanced options.

Her UI lit up with familiar red and yellow targeting reticles. She cringed at the memory. At what they meant. At what she had done the last time she had used them.

"Celia?!"

"Twenty."

"Oh. Only twenty," said Cutter, scurrying into the west tunnel as a barrage of stun blasts hit the wall behind him. "That's nothing."

Thirty five feet ahead, the corridor dead-ended into a T-intersection. Cutter hefted Celia onto his shoulder so that she faced backward, allowing him to pick up his pace.

The guards rounded into the west tunnel, hot on their heels.

"They are behind us," said Celia.

A stun blast hit overhead, raining sparks and part of the track lighting unit down on their heads. "Hadn't noticed."

Another blast hit Celia in the shoulder. The force pushed Cutter forward. Stumbling, he fell to all fours, and managed to push himself upright with his forearm without breaking stride. "Jesus Christ! You okay?"

Celia checked her internal UI. The wireframe grid outline of herself lit up in faint blue. She was shocked. Her previous encounter with pulse weapons had left her damage reports in reds and yellows.

"It hit Roy's parts," she said. "I think I am fine." She double-checked her display, still amazed by the lack of damage she had sustained.

Another stun blast plinked off her forearm. Not a single scratch. She grabbed Cutter by the neck and pulled his ear to her mouth. "Is this how all your investigations end up?"

Cutter grumbled under his breath. "Not all."

They turned the corner, a momentary relief from the spray of blaster weapons.

"Am I heading in the right, direction?" asked Cutter.

"Huh?"

"Costas. Am I heading in the right direction?"

"Oh, yeah. Right."

"Right?" Cutter threw a quick glance back at Celia. "Right way or what?"

"Checking."

"Take your time, why don't you?"

Concentric yellow lines pulsed on the overlay of subterranean twists and turns. Blaster fire exploded, as the security guards surfaced from a blind corner.

"Take the next right."

"Right?!" Cutter yelled having already run past it. He spun on his heel, heading directly at the oncoming tide of pissed off security, and jumped into the corridor.

Cutter grabbed Celia's hand and tugged on it. "Could you, I don't know, give me a head's up on the directions *before* I run past them?"

"I can." She had meant to tone down the snarkiness, but she couldn't help herself. Cutter had it coming.

"Please, do!"

She checked their location against Costas's signal. "We are close, Jack. Only a couple more corridors. He is up ahead and to the right."

"Ahead and to the right. Check."

The corridor was a straight sprint for a hundred yards with no adjoining rooms or hubs that she could see. A blast pushed Celia into the back of Cutter's head. She turned to see the guards charging after them in hot pursuit. Boots roared like an ocean of crashing waves against the metal grating.

Celia spun around on Jack's shoulder, kicking his head in the process.

"What are you doing?" He swatted at the back of his head.

"I have an idea."

She leaned forward, bent over his shoulder, and let her upper torso hang down his front. His jacket wildly flapped, swatting at her hands. She pinned the right side with her left palm, reached into his jacket, pushed the leather safety strap from the holster and removed the ZeroTwelve.

Cutter grabbed at her hand—"Oh no you don't!"—but she was too quick. She spun, sitting upright on his shoulder, facing backward.

"Celia! That is not a toy!"

Two of the three guards in the lead stopped in their tracks at the sight of Celia perched on Cutter's shoulder wielding an illegal blackmarket pulse pistol. The one on the far right had his head down, sights set a little too intently on capturing his target.

A spray of superheated red particles tore down the corridor, ripping through the oblivious guard's shoulder armor, and tossing him against the wall. The other two dove for cover, while the rest of the battalion came to a hard stop. Those that could, backpedaled into the safety of the adjacent corridor. A few were knocked to the ground, shoved by the ranks in the rear that were still running forward.

Celia laughed and laid down suppressive fire in haphazard

bursts. The nearest guards retreated to the safety of the adjoining tunnel, dragging the unconscious shoulder blasted guard by his boot.

Firing wildly down the hall, the powerful pulse pistol leaped in her grip, threatening to bounce out of her hands with each recoil.

They had made it to the end of the corridor. A single guard peeked around the corner making sure it was safe. And then disappeared from view as Cutter turned a corner heading for Costas.

"That was fun!"

Cutter shook his head. "Christ, kid. What the hell were you thinking?"

Celia pushed out her lower lip. "I was making a suggestion for countermeasures."

"Gimmie that!" Cutter yanked the ZeroTwelve from her hand. In one fluid motion, he spun it on his finger and slid it back into its holster. Celia was impressed by the move.

"Next time suggest it first," said Cutter.

"It worked, did it not?"

Cutter stopped. He reached up, holding his palm out to her. She placed her hand in his and he lowered her to the ground. She assumed he needed a few seconds to catch his breath, but they didn't have much time. The guards would catch up shortly. All she had done was given them an extended buffer.

"The signal is straight ahead."

But Jack wasn't moving. He was staring at a door to his right. It looked like any other door they had run past. A cyan InSight logo was stamped over a square reinforced window.

"Jack?"

Cutter stared at the door, as if in a trance.

"Jack… Costas is at the end of the hall."

"I recognize this," Cutter whispered.

"Jack, the guards are coming. I can hear them. They will be here in seventeen seconds."

Cutter opened the door and cautiously pushed inside.

3

Red blood cells pounded out a heavy metal rhythm and hop-scotched across Cutter's eardrums. He strained to hear anything over the beat of his own heart.

He stood inside a dodecahedron cage that held Los Angeles harbor over his head, a manmade bubble of serenity on the bay floor. At its center a long square box made of glass and black metal rods was surrounded by six larger rods that stooped over it. Large hoods flared atop the six monoliths. On the far wall, a giant display monitor slowly blipped with white text on a cyan background.

Celia brushed his hand with her elbow, as she stepped into the room. She gave it a quick once over, before turning towards him. "What are we doing in here, Jack?"

"I've been here before."

He didn't know how or when. He simply knew. He had been here before.

Celia looked toward the door, then back at Cutter. "The guards will be here any second."

The statement dropkicked his senses back to reality. Without hesitation, he swept the leg of a chair, spun it towards himself, and wedged the back against the only door in or out. Here he was in one of the most advanced facilities he had ever seen, and he was propping a chair against a door, using it as a makeshift barricade.

The irony that he had chosen the most low tech solution possible didn't escape him. In fact he appreciated the simplicity.

"That should hold them," said Cutter. Just then, the handle rattled. Through the reinforced window, he saw bobbing helmets and tinted plastic. He took a step back from the frenzy of motion on the other side of the door. The chair held, as several loud thuds echoed into the room. There was a brief pause and then a red spot appeared inches from the door handle. "For now."

Cutter retreated into the room, only to find Celia cycling through dozens of screens on the display monitor at a pace he couldn't follow. "What are you doing?"

"Going through their files," said Celia. "I confirmed Costas's location. Now I am…curious."

"You're curious?"

Celia shrugged and continued plugging away at the display interface.

While the room looked like some sort of medical facility, the rod and glass contraption before him looked like a medieval torture device. He ran his hand down the metal edge and stopped at a pair of leather straps on either side.

"The hell is this thing?"

"Jack…" Celia said. "I found something you should take a look at."

"Something that can tell us what the hell all this is?" He scrambled to the monitor, nudged her out of the way, and took over the keyboard.

"No," she said. "I found you."

On the display was a picture of himself. A younger version, probably from his rookie years. He shook his head in disbelief.

"What is this?"

He felt a tug at his sleeve, but found it impossible to tear himself away from the display.

"Why do they have information on you?"

"Do you think I know the answer to that?"

She didn't respond, but that was answer enough.

There were hundreds of files dedicated to him. His past, his present. Charts, graphs, infographics. Past medical history, vitals, score on his Academy entrance exams, and more information than he could internalize even if he had hours to go through it all.

He was looking at more than his personal history.

They were tracking him. Recording the results.

"Why the hell do they have all this information on me?"

"It is not just you," said Celia. "Costas is in there as well. As is Parks and Foster."

Celia tugged at his sleeve. "Jack…"

"Not now!" He threw off her hand.

"What do we do about them?"

"Them?" Cutter looked down at Celia and followed her gaze toward the door.

"Right." The red spot had become a rectangular outline around the door handle. "Them."

He put two fingers to the bridge of his nose and closed his eyes. There was so much here. So much he didn't know or understand. And they didn't have time to go through it all.

"You need to hide," he said, almost on autopilot.

Celia arched a brow. "You want me to leave you here?"

"Yes! You need to hide. You need to remember all of this and get word back to—" It donned on Cutter that he probably couldn't get word back to Parks. "We'll figure it out. But for now, I need you to hide. Get somewhere they'll never find you. And no matter what happens, do not move until I come and get you. Do you understand?"

Celia reluctantly nodded.

Cutter tussled her hair, and swatted her behind, nudging her away from the entrance. "Good. Now go."

"What are you going to do?"

Cutter bit his lower lip and tossed a worried glance at the door. "I haven't figured that out, yet."

The door handle fell to the floor. With nothing supporting it, the chair followed suit.

Cutter turned to urge Celia to hustle, but she was gone. Quickly scanning the area, he searched for any trace of her.

"Good job, kid," he said under his breath.

The doors burst open and a dozen uniformed InSight security guards surged into the room and surrounded him in a semi-circle. Every blaster rifle gave a plastic rattle as the guards leveled them squarely at him.

"Okay guys," said Cutter. He raised his hands over his head. The gesture was more reminiscent of a shrug than surrender. "You got me."

"Weapon! On the ground! Now!" the lead guard shouted in broken fragments. A scruffy red beard poked out from beneath the helmet's built-in visor.

"Okay. Don't get your panties in a bunch there, Trigger."

Cutter let his jacket flap open so they could all see the ZeroTwelve in its holster. The room went deathly silent. Cutter felt the tension like an overstretched rubber band. He preferred not to test its breaking point. With glacial movement, he lifted the ZeroTwelve out of its holster with his index finger and thumb, letting the barrel hang down at the floor. And dropped the weapon at his feet.

Before Trigger could instruct him to, he kicked the ZeroTwelve across the room. It stopped a few feet shy of the nearest InSight security guard.

"No reason to panic. We can talk this out like civilized whatever we ares."

Trigger barked an order, and before Cutter could react, they swarmed him. The last thing he remembered was the butt-end of a stun blaster.

4

"Jack…" said Foster. "Why am I not surprised?"

Cutter opened his eyes. He was lying on his back staring at the ceiling. Brilliant white teeth glared at him. So did the man they were attached to.

"That makes one of us," said Cutter. "I'm surprised as hell."

"That too is not surprising," said Foster.

"Kinda going in circles, aren't we?"

Cutter went for a swing at the pretty face, but his arm didn't respond. He struggled to prop himself up. Faux leather straps at his wrists and feet bound him to… something.

"Look, it's too early in the morning for this," said Foster. "I've been up all night and I'm tired. I appreciate you coming to us. It makes things that much easier."

Cutter surveyed the room, trying to get a better view of the contraption he was tied to. "Where is everyone? Your goon squad with the matching outfits?"

"I don't think we'll be needing their assistance, do you?"

He was elevated. A little over five feet off the ground, putting him nearly at Foster's eye level. Twisting against the restraints, he could feel a grid of hard squares, maybe four inches wide pressing into his back. He was lying on some sort of rack suspended over a tank containing liquid far too blue to be water.

"What is this place?"

Foster rolled his neck in a big sweeping motion, taking in the contents of the room as if he had never seen them before. After a moment, he turned toward Cutter with a twisted smirk and glinting eyes. "Why, it's the future, of course."

"Damn. How long was I out?"

Foster's tight smile blossomed into a dopey toothy grin. A rumbling like the starting of a motor boat mixed with the purr of a cat set the hairs on Cutter's arm upright. Foster was cool, calm, collected, and worst of all, he was laughing.

"You can be quite entertaining when you want to be," said Foster. "So what can I do for you? You're a little early for your checkup, but we should still be able to accommodate you."

"No," said Cutter automatically. "No checkups."

Foster nodded. "I see."

There was something unsettling about the container he was tied to. It was long and deep. It reminded him of a coffin. A warped post-post-postmodern artist's take on a coffin of the future. Steel and glass with a water feature.

Accompanied by a familiar feel.

Everything was oddly familiar.

The water-filled coffin.

The room.

The bright lights.

Los Angeles harbor's crushing presence.

He knew what this place was. Even if he couldn't remember it. He had been here before.

Foster ran a finger across Cutter's cheek. Cutter cringed. He leaned back as far as his restraints would allow, but Foster simply followed with a clammy touch.

"It's great seeing you and all," said Foster, "but I don't have time for anything too lengthy. I have a campaign to run. An unveiling in an hour or so. You understand?"

"I know what you're up to."

Foster nodded. "I should hope so."

"You're brainwashing people."

"It's part of the packaging, Jack. It's what they sign up for. Not exactly a mystery."

"Kind of hard to know that you've made a bad decision if you can't remember it in the first place."

"That's kinda the point, isn't it?"

"I—uh—what?" Cutter balked.

"Wow. I really…" Foster shook his head in disbelief. "This is hard to believe. Well, maybe not that hard. You are a civil servant after all."

"Speak for yourself."

Foster glowered at Cutter.

"Peace of mind, maybe?" said Foster. "And just in case you're confused, no maybe about it. InSight is about peace of mind."

Foster leaned in. Despite a somewhat haggard appearance, haggard for Foster anyway, Cutter could still smell traces of his cologne, remnants of the care to which this man took to present himself to the world. He smelled good. Really good.

"C'mon, Jack. You can't be that naive. This is what people want. They want to live a life they don't have to think about. They want the simplicity of joyful bliss. Of being happy. They want someone to make all the difficult choices for them and not have to be reminded of the consequences of those decisions."

"And you're just the self-appointed man for the job."

Foster wriggled his shoulders and straightened his collar. "Thank you, I couldn't agree more."

Through gritted teeth, Cutter spat, "It wasn't an endorsement."

"Not yet," said Foster. "But it will be."

Once again that gleaming toothy smile appeared on that overly manufactured facade. Cutter wished his hands were free so could physically rearrange it.

Somewhere in his gut, none of the events were making sense. But that wasn't wholly true.

All the reasons why he couldn't remember his partner, why Parks memory of Costas was foggy, why the archives would have records that he couldn't recollect—it all pointed to an entity that manipulated memory. What had happened to him made perfect sense.

What wasn't adding up was the *Why?*

"Why would they brainwash their officers?" asked Cutter. His tone came out more cynical sounding than he had meant. But seriously... why the hell would anyone be mucking around with the memories of their employees?

"Why do you think?" said Foster.

"I honestly couldn't tell you."

"I guess that's a side effect of the treatment. You have no idea how important you were to all this, Jack. I mean, literally. You have no idea."

"So fill me in."

"We aren't forcing anyone's hand. This is all optional. All on a volunteer basis. If you don't like what InSight has to offer, there is no obligation to sign up. No obligation to take treatments. Nothing is forced."

"Yeah, tell that to the gaps in my memory."

Foster cut loose roils of laughter. Cutter writhed in his restraints, as if punched in the kidneys. His hands clenched into fists, tugging against the leather straps.

"You'll have to excuse me," said Cutter, finding an icy calm.

"But I don't see what's so funny."

"I forgive you for not seeing the irony, Jack."

"I mean every word of it. You put the memory-whammy on me. You didn't do me any favors."

"That's not what you said before."

Cutter opened his mouth, searching for some wry bit of banter, but—"Wha' the hell are you talking about?" was the best he could muster.

"Not even curious?" asked Foster. "This one's a freebie." Foster circled the tank like a shark. "You came here because you *wanted* to forget. You volunteered."

"Bullshit."

Brainwash myself? My ass.

To his ears, *bullshit* fit perfectly. However, the surety of his words were not backed by his inner voice. His response was the kind of reaction he was supposed to have. A foul-mouthed quip on the fly. But something deep inside tugged at his conscience, vying for attention, whispering in his ear, that maybe, maybe he should listen to what this Foster guy had to say.

There were a whole lot of things he had done that were unaccounted for but tallied and tracked by the precinct's archives and vidfiles. Things he couldn't remember doing, for reasons completely unknown to him.

Of course he had to have been brainwashed. Brainwashing had been the only thing that made sense. But that didn't solve the mystery. It didn't answer any of his questions. His problem wasn't the events or the results. His problem was the reasons behind them.

Because you did it to yourself.

You volunteered.

You wanted your mind obliterated and the past destroyed.

Foster nodded, and shrugged his shoulders. "Whatever you say, Jack. The truth of our realities is a subjective thing, isn't it?"

"What do you get out of this?"

"Me?" Foster's voice pitched up slightly. He pointed to himself in a girlishly coy manner. "You mean aside from the betterment of mankind, of course?"

"Yeah, 'sides that. Pinnacle of bleeding altruism that you are."

"Those at the frontlines of a new revolution should get to reap the rewards, don't you think?"

Cutter couldn't argue there. That sort of fit in with his own personal modus operandi. You put in the time, lay the groundwork, bust your ass, you should reap the rewards—assuming there were any.

"Believe what you may about me, Jack, but I've always used my position for the people. I've never taken advantage of my office. I haven't always made the best decisions, but they've always been for the people. For the betterment of this city. For the livelihoods of those living here. Think about what the world of tomorrow will be like, Jack. No one having to worry about making bad decisions. Past indiscretions won't come back to haunt decisions of today. People can simply live for the moment. For the now. Living lives filled with bliss, unburdened by worry."

"There's a saying that fits here perfectly," said Cutter. "I'm having a little trouble with it, though. It goes something like— Ignorance is… I'm drawing a blank here. Help me out with that last part, will ya? Ignorance is… Come on, Foster. It's on the tip of my tongue. I just, you know, can't remember. Ignorance is… something. Ah hell, well it probably wasn't important anyway."

"Like I said, Jack. You can be very amusing."

"I've learned some things in my time, Foster. I've seen things repeat endlessly. The world is what it is. There isn't the time to fix things. To change things. To make the world a better place. There aren't enough people that want the world to be different. And to be honest, I'm not convinced people really want things to be different than they are anyway."

"Aren't you the unsurprisingly pessimistic one? Oh, Jack. Like a broken record. Things can't be fixed, so why bother."

"You got me wrong. Go monkeying around and things could always be much, much worse."

"Luckily for me, the department, Police Chief Parks, the city council, to put it simply—*everyone*—disagrees with you on this one. A society with the ability to choose to forget their past, to live without regret, to make choices unburdened by history is where this city is heading, whether you like it or not. And you've seen the rallies. The support. People love InSight. They love what it does. They love how it changes their lives. Who are you to take that away from them?"

"Just a guy strapped to some watery coffin." Cutter raised his arms to the extent the restraints would allow. "Not exactly a ringing endorsement on doing the right thing."

"Yes. I admit, there are certain complications that have arisen that need tending to."

"So I'm here for moral support?"

"Not exactly, Jack. You were the first. The guinea pig. The trial run. You were the ringing endorsement that convinced L.A.P.D. to implement InSight for its officers in the first place."

"Why the hell would I do that?"

Foster tilted his head. Cutter shied away, refusing to meet the gaze.

"I can't answer that for you, Jack. Only you can." Foster briefly paused. "But why would anyone erase their memories?

Peace of mind, Jack. That's the only reason I can think of. Peace of mind."

"Right, so strap me to a death table like some James Bond villain."

"First off, it's not a death table. Second, we have a small hitch."

"Costas?"

"So you remember?"

"Was curious if you knew him," said Cutter. "Thanks for that."

"It's very important that nothing happen to dissuade people from signing up for InSight in the first place. Popular opinion can be so fickle."

"So I get a few rounds in the human dunk tank?"

"I'm very sorry about this Jack. But we can't have you running around telling everyone you know about our other problem."

"Why not just kill me? It'd make things so much neater."

Foster smiled his trademark toothy grin. "Why would I kill you when I can have your vote?"

Foster activated the machine. A small motor began to hum. Steel support girders vibrated to the rhythm. Cables groaned over rusted pulleys. Struggling against the faux leather restraints binding his wrists and ankles, Cutter arched his back in a desperate attempt to free himself from the contraption slowly lowering into a water filled coffin.

"See you later, Jack," said Foster.

On his approach to the exit, Foster paused in the doorway and casually raised a finger, turning his head in profile. "Oh, and if I forget, thanks for your continued support."

The doors slammed shut, echoing with finality.

"You fucking asshole!" yelled Cutter. But he might as well have been shouting at thin air for all the good it did.

He whipped his head from side to side, trying for a better glimpse of the vat of cyan liquid that he was slowly sinking into. The cool water soaked his back and crept up along his sides. He had expected it to be freezing, but it was merely brisk. If he hadn't been so concerned about losing every inkling of his self to the soothing waters, he might have even found it refreshing.

This was how it would end. By not ending at all. Not some machine crushing the life out of him. But by making him forget. Transforming him into a living machine of sorts—a man to be reprogrammed at will.

He had forgotten his past once before. Everything that had been important to him—or so he assumed—he couldn't really remember if what he had given up had been important or not. His past life was a mystery, wreckage of some vessel long swallowed by what appeared to be calm waters.

Everything was gone.

His eyes went wide.

Almost everything was gone. How could he have forgotten?

Cutter twisted in his restraints and rolled onto his side as best he could manage. He peered through the viscous liquid, through the glass walls of the tank, and into the surrounding room. The world outside was tinted cyan.

A medical tray with odd implements on it blocked his view of half of the room. Beyond the stand holding the tray upright, six craning lamps peered down at him, bent at their midsection like ancient men. Blinding light blasted through the waters, refracting in shimmering sheets.

He searched frantically along the walls for his target. Rows of blinking machines, some beeping in semi erratic pattern, lined the glass walls that separated the room from the murky harbor outside. In a tight crevice between a chattering machine and an industrial steel counter he saw what he had forgotten.

They made eye contact.

"Celi—"

Cool fluid flooded into his open mouth, hammering the back of his throat, a karate chop to his trachea taking his voice with it. He gagged on the fluid forcing its way into his body.

Though it looked vaguely like water, the taste was syrupy sweet. He clamped his lips tight, trying to prevent the fluid from further penetrating the seal of his body. But it was too late.

The fluid pushed up his nostrils, exhaust vents he couldn't force shut. He felt the overwhelming urge to sneeze. Violently shaking, hanging on the edge, he fought through sheer force of will to shove the foreign substance from his body. Somewhere in the back of his mind, an instinctual compulsion took over. He wanted the endless tickle to complete. To finish. The little voice was practical. It said things that made sense in soothing tones. It politely asked him to stop fighting.

It knew.

And so did Cutter.

He had no chance.

The soothing fluid funneled through his sinus cavity, coating internal crevices and pockets of air, filling his throat, and seeping behind his eyes. He no longer felt as if he was floating in the substance, rather that he was a part of it. More than that. He belonged to it. He was no longer an obstacle for the fluid to fill. Rather the fluid was something that flowed through him as if he wasn't there at all.

Euphoria swept through him sending an electrical tingling sensation throughout his body. The world was right. The moment was singular, forever and always.

His lungs burned, but he no longer felt the searing pain torturing him for breath. He merely acknowledged the pain as part of the condition of his current existence.

His head lulled to a side, bobbing to the gentle currents of the saccrin fluid swirling within his new home. Floating blobs of browns and purples and pinks rippled in a pattern to his left. The blinding light that had been there only moments prior, now haloed the floating colors.

Celia!

Cutter writhed against the straps, trying to free his arms. He wanted to get her attention, to signal that he needed her help. She could still save him.

But shouldn't that be obvious? She was standing over him now. She had come out of her hiding spot and towered beside the vat. Couldn't she see him struggling?

Or had he given up already? Had he given in to the effects of the fluid? Given in to the echoes of his inner voice telling him not to worry, that everything was going to be just fine. That the world could always be as peaceful as he felt right now.

No!

That wasn't right. Nothing was easy. Everything was always a fight. He couldn't submit. Not now. Not being so close to his answers.

Celia stood watching.

"Get me out of here!" Cutter screamed under the constant pressure, but he couldn't hear anything more than the muffled bass of his own voice. Had he even shouted the words in the first place or was it merely a figment of his imagination, a desire to be saved from a predicament beyond his control?

His grunts, while expressive, weren't enough to articulate his current problem to the floating blobs of color that arranged themselves in peculiar fashion; an impressionistic little girl. His problem should have been obvious to anyone standing at the outset, watching him struggle.

But the pigment stood still. Large brown orbs watched, a distorted hoot owl in the night.

In his imagination, he screamed again. Or maybe he really did. It was so difficult to be certain.

Maybe she couldn't hear him?

Or maybe it was something else entirely.

She was a machine, a tool built to service mankind as it saw fit. She needed direct and exact input. She needed to be guided and told what to do to perform even the simplest of tasks. Tasks like saving him from drowning. Saving him from losing himself.

He mouthed the words, forming over-exaggerated shapes. *Get help!*

Through the rippling waves, Cutter could make out her expression—a complete lack of one. Celia was looking right at him. Staring right through him.

What the fuck, Celia?!

Get help!

Celia!

Get help! Get help!

But she only watched.

If he hadn't been drowning, desperate for rescue, he would have found her lifeless stare creepy. No, even drowning, struggling for air, grasping for life, it was still creepy.

More so, he thought.

He needed to hang on.

He needed to remember.

Costas was here. There was something he needed from Costas. Already, the reasons were slipping away. Something Costas knew. About him. Something from his past.

Costas was the key.

The reason why he had been tangled up with InSight in the first place.

Now, what replaced oxygen was his own willpower to stay conscious. His body wanted, needed, demanded breath. It began to accept the fluid filling his lungs.

Fight! Don't let it win!

As if it had a consciousness of its own that defied his willpower, his body began to shut down, trying to conserve as much energy as it could.

No! Live God dammit!

He struggled against the restraints. Faux leather cuffs dug into his wrists. In his ear, his own voice empowered with the knowledge that he couldn't break free transformed his will to survive into a constant reminder of the inevitability of his struggles. His animal mind screamed for survival, a convincing counterpoint to the rational side of his brain that just wanted it to shut the fuck up.

Just let it happen.

He wouldn't give up.

He reached out, clawing at smooth glass. Fingers slid leaving oily smudges.

Celia!

His body went limp.

5

Somewhere in a suburban backyard in Pasadena, a girl of six or seven played with her dollies under an oak tree, oblivious to the man watching from the backdoor. A brick courtyard had been built around the oak tree. Bricks near the base protruded at odd angles. The roots beneath grew through the manmade landscape changing and distorting it.

The courtyard opened out to a two tiered backyard. Agapanthus lined a gravel driveway winding through the lower tier. Impossibly tall rose bushes stood shoulder to shoulder like soldiers, guarding a stone wall that held back the sloping grass hills of the upper tier. At the peak was a stand-alone tree house with a slide. Another oak tree, this one much larger than the teenager in the courtyard, dominated the far corner of the yard. From its branches hung a makeshift swing—a knotted piece of rope pierced the center of a wooden slat.

The girl wore a pink dress with frills that matched the dress of her dolly. She gingerly lifted a miniature tea cup to its mouth.

The man walked into the courtyard and looked down at the little girl. Still, she was unaware of his presence.

"Carrie...?" said Cutter.

The girl looked up at him. "Yes?"

"Do you know who I am?"

The girl nodded. "What a silly thing to say, Jackie."

Cutter caught his reflection in the patio window. He was no longer the hardened grizzled man he saw daily in his mind's eye. He was a boy.

"What is this place?" he asked.

"What do you mean?" Carrie looked up at him with a

puzzled expression. "It's my home. I live here. We play here all the time."

"Right… right."

This home hadn't existed in twenty years. Not like this, anyway.

The girl went back to playing with her dollies, hardly paying notice to Cutter. He watched for a prolonged moment, trying to put together what he was doing here.

His thoughts were cloudy.

He remembered swimming. Or rather drowning. But not much else.

A freestanding door stood on the edge of the courtyard. Cautiously, Cutter approached and tried the knob. It rattled and failed to turn.

Cutter pointed at the door. "Any advice on this thing?"

"What thing?" asked Carrie.

"The door."

"What door?"

"Right…" Cutter's head absent-mindedly bobbed.

He tried the knob once again, but the results were the same. He circled the door, but the backside was identical to the front. Jutting out his jaw, he thrust his lower lip over his upper. "A freestanding door in the middle of nowhere. Scratch that. A *locked* freestanding door in the middle of nowhere and no deadbolt on either side." He nodded at the door as if the situation made perfect sense. "And now, I'm talking to myself."

He tried the knob on the backside. It too was locked. With a grunt he vigorously rattled the knob.

"Yup. Perfect sense."

He leaned back and tilted his head at the door, as if a tilted head would provide answers he couldn't readily see. He circled once again, but regardless of how many times he tried, both sides remained locked.

On his fifth pass, he accidentally brushed his front right jean pocket and felt something he hadn't remembered putting there. He reached in and pulled out a key.

It was a key unlike the Swipe-Pass, Ret-Scan, or Voice-Reco devices in primary use these days. It was a large iron skeleton key—the kind of key that was used long before his childhood, like something straight out of a fairytale.

The key grinded into the lock. It felt as if something had grabbed it from the other side and held it in place. Cutter hesitated. Did he really want to see what was on the other side of the door?

He had a hunch that the door was locked for good reason.

Counting to ten in his head, he held his breath, and turned the key. The door opened.

In contrast to the wide open spaces behind him, the inside was a labyrinth of twists and turns. Overhead, darkness hung like a ceiling.

Carrie was in here too.

Only she was older and had grown out of the gawky preteen stage and bloomed into something breathtaking. He had forgotten how beautiful she was. Her flowing brunette hair cascaded down her back as she turned toward him. Her eyes were green and had a feline grace that gave her otherwise natural beauty an exotic twist.

Her left eye was purple and swollen. He tried not to, but he could remember how she had gotten it. There *was* good reason this memory was hidden behind lock and key.

"Jack..." she said.

"Please don't. I don't want to remember."

"But what about the good times? We had so many good

times."

Cutter reluctantly nodded. "We did."

She smiled at him. He remembered that smile. A smile that could illuminate the world. "Don't let the good times become a casualty."

"You're not the reason I'm here." He didn't know why he was here, but he knew he didn't really want to talk to her. To rehash the past. To live out old memories.

Carrie turned her back on Cutter. In front of her half a dozen paths led deeper into the darkness. "You don't want to go in there, Jack. You put us in here for a reason."

Cutter felt his lips draw taut. "I know."

He walked past, brushing her shoulder as he moved. "There's something that I need."

"You need it all," said Carrie. "It's all important. Wrong or right, this is who you are."

Cutter had been here before. He knew this place.

It was where memories went to die.

On previous excursions to this cave of darkness, he had dropped off memories that would never see the light of day again.

He felt Carrie's hand slide around his waist. Warm breath caressed his ear. "Take them with you this time."

Stalactites appeared out of the darkness as if by magic. Cutter reached out to his right, placing a hand on the wall for support. He ducked under a mound of dripping darkness that hung from the ceiling. The smooth surface under his fingertips didn't match the rocky cavern that was being painted over the darkness in his mind's eye. He could barely see the solid protrusions jutting out at him, making the corridor nearly impossible to navigate. Tracing his hand along the wall, he tracked his progress into the pitch black cavern.

His nose led the retreat as he slammed face first into solid blackness. "God damn!" he yelped, rubbing the pain out of his eyes with the flat of his palms.

To his right, orange fire light flickered. He cautiously approached the threshold. The path wound tightly down before him ending in a circle of full dark. On either side, archways opened up into adjacent corridors. Light blasted in from some while darkness receded into others.

A shriek deafened him as he walked past the first opening. He spun on heel, hands raised into fists, ready for any nightmare that wanted to throw down. A funnel of wind blew from the opening, accompanied by another foul shriek.

But nothing came.

He saw darkness and nothing else.

Something was in there. Breathing. Beckoning him.

He gathered his nerve, fighting against his better instinct to never turn his sight from this opening and locked his gaze on the darkness at the end of the path. The shriek wailed again. He closed his eyes and focused on his breathing.

With each footstep, he drew closer to the next opening. A brilliant green light blasted in from the left. A raging red light danced with it on the right, colors mixing together in a muddy combination that briefly stirred his stomach with nausea.

He slinked sideways down the corridor bracing himself for another sensory assault. Diversions branched from the main path pleading for recognition. Halfway down the hall, a voice that he thought he knew whispered something so softly in his ear that he couldn't make out the words. He veered toward an opening on his left that was masked in darkness. He gritted his teeth and fought against his own footsteps leading him astray. His feet felt as if they had been dipped in concrete, each step toward the darkness at the end of the path weighing him down.

He could stay here. Find out what was behind each and every opening. It wasn't his own inner monologue that told him these things. Or maybe it was. He was inside his own head after all. Maybe his subconscious didn't want to reach the other end either.

A nagging compulsion tugged him deeper into the cave, pulling him toward the darkness at the end.

He cautiously approached the end of the corridor and reached out into the darkness. There wasn't an opening as had been the case for the twists and turns behind him. He was staring at a large dark portal that could lead anywhere. Skimming the surface with his open palm, he felt an energy, something almost magnetic, pulsing from the strange void. It made the hairs on the back of his hand stand on end.

Why was the portal so different than the openings behind him? Was this how all the prisons for his memory started out? As mere gaping voids hungering for the next delicious memory to give them life?

Was this where he was to leave his newest memories? To lock them away and never be remembered?

He was here. One way or the other he had to know.

He stepped through.

Light blinded him. As his eyes adjusted to his new surroundings, he noticed that the light hadn't been all that bright to begin with. Just sheer contrast to the darkness he had left behind.

A soft morning glow filled the room. Unlike the claustrophobic heat of the cramped corridors he had come from, this room was cool, deliberately kept at a comfortable temperature. A man with a piece of paper and a pen in his hand was hunched over a hospital bed. Machines blipped with an occasional tone.

Cutter noticed the man's leather jacket. It didn't show its age yet, but he could recognize that jacket from any time and place. It was his.

He was watching himself cower over another man asleep in a bed. The younger him, the echo of his memory sat down on the edge of the bed. A tear rolled down his cheek.

There was only one person he'd be visiting at a hospital.

No!

He knew this place. Why he was here. Who the patient was. He didn't dare get any closer.

Twisting his body in a wild motion, he fled for the full darkness of the corridor behind him only to discover that the entrance was gone. A solid hospital wall resided where he was sure the portal had been. Instead of a void into nothing, he was staring at a wall adorned with a few medical dispensers and a plastic sheath containing a medical chart.

No!

He clawed at the wall. The corridor had to be here, somewhere. Anywhere. His escape. He couldn't stay here. He couldn't watch. He needed to be anywhere else.

He looked back over his shoulder in desperate panic, cringing at the younger him standing over the man asleep in the bed. Both were equally broken.

I shouldn't be here! I can't be here! I need to get out!

As the tear fell from the echo of his memory he felt a tug at his neck and shoulder. His entire body felt like it was being stretched, pulled toward a singular point somewhere behind him. This must be what it feels like to be on the edge of an event horizon of a black hole, he thought. To feel your body pulled apart at an exponential pace through time. The parts closest to the echo felt as if they were already light years away from the parts of him that were scratching at the walls, grasping for escape.

Tendons of light gripped him, reaching out from the echo of his memory. His feet slid across the linoleum floors. A force tugged at him, pulling him backward against his will. He grabbed at the counter, trying to find purchase, to hold on, but only knocked over a glass container and scattered tongue depressors into a sink. He snapped back into the echo of himself like the recoil on a slingshot.

On the bed before him, Costas was sound asleep. No, he knew better. Costas was in a coma.

Despite wanting to turn away, he couldn't. He was a passenger within himself, along for the ride.

The echo of his memory unrolled the piece of paper and placed it by Costas' hand. He noticed the uniform language of the document, text too jargon filled to be anything other than legal and binding. Beneath it, the elements of old, a spiraling sprawl of black ink bled into the page guided by a rigid and perfectly horizontal line.

He could feel the pen resting in the cradle of his hand, held between the index finger and thumb of another. Ink bled, scarring the surface, agreeing to strict formalities printed in courier font.

Signed and dated.

With a name that wasn't his.

Ryan T. Costas

He felt queasy…

The world spun around him. He was unsure if the nausea belonged to him or the echo of his memory. Perhaps both.

When he regained his senses, he was no longer in the hospital and Costas was nowhere to be seen. *Probably for the best,* he thought.

Did he think that? Or did his memory self?

He couldn't tell the difference.

...for the best. Probably.

Cutter was in the middle of a glass dodecahedron structure. Light refracted through murky water, casting shimmering reflections on the corrugated steel floors. He shielded his eyes from the light's disorienting effect. Six craning lamps spotlighted a tank filled with fluid too blue to be water at the room's center.

Cutter jumped as he felt a tap on his shoulder, but the body he inhabited hadn't reacted at all. It had been expecting the touch. He didn't like the way his body failed to respond to his thoughts. They responded to someone else. To another him. A version from his past that he felt distantly removed from.

You shouldn't be here! Move! Get out of this place!

"You sure this is what you want?" came a voice from behind him. Cutter wanted to turn, wanted to see who the voice belonged to, but his body, the memory of himself stared into the tank of swirling blue liquid.

"Yes," he said.

No, this is not what I want!

"Once we start there's no turning back."

"What about Costas?"

"Doctors said he woke up in the middle of the night and signed his paperwork."

"When he wakes up, will he remember?"

"If he wakes up, you mean?"

"When," Cutter's body said.

Foster appeared in his line of vision and looked at him apprehensively. Behind Foster, Reynolds methodically typed into a computer. Foster held eye contact for what seemed an awkwardly long moment, before nodding to himself. "Costas consented to have the memory of his attack and the subsequent medical treatments erased. He'll be well taken care of. But we're here for you. There's no going back after we do this."

"Then what are we waiting for?"

You fucking idiot! Cutter shouted in his mind's ear. But it wasn't listening.

Without a word, Foster raised a bar and guided Cutter onto the rack mounted over the liquid-filled tank. His body placed a hand on the ledge, lifted itself up, and laid down facing the ceiling.

Move! Get up!

But he silently laid still as Foster secured the faux leather straps at his wrists and ankles.

"So…" said Foster, briefly searching for something to say. "Anything you want to say before… Before we do this?"

"I don't want to remember anything."

God dammit! No!

Foster simply nodded and gave the contraption a final shake. "You should be fine. I just… I want to thank you, Jack. This is a very brave thing you're doing."

All he could see was the ceiling—rather the ever shifting light piercing through the harbor waters. To his left, he heard Foster say, "It's time." Reynolds responded with a grunt, followed by two pairs of footsteps and a sliding door shushing closed. The gentle hum of the motor lowering him into the water-filled coffin was the only thing that broke the silence.

That and his voice screaming in his head.

Get the fuck up! Move! This is not what you want! You want to remember! You need to remember!

But his body remained still.

The world suddenly appeared cyan and he felt euphoria sweep through his body.

He had been wrong.

This wasn't the place where he was to come to find his answers.

He was the new memory. This was his final resting place, to be dropped off and sealed away forever. The hospital room had been a previous memory's final resting place. This coffin of cyan blue would be his.

No! I can't let this happen!

But his body had a different agenda. It lay perfectly still awaiting a time when it would wake up refreshed, without the bothersome worry of a past it no longer remembered. It was shedding itself of him.

In contrast to the serenity and stillness that his body felt, his mind writhed, bouncing off the inner walls of his own skull, drop-kicking his brain in the hopes that he could jumpstart the body it was supposedly attached to. Out of sheer frustration, he screamed.

Fragments of light split into component colors and radiated in all directions through the room's geometric shape. To any outsider, it would have seemed all was right with the world. To the newly formed memory that was to be locked away forever in this dodecahedron prison it was its last fleeting moments fighting for survival.

Above him, he heard a ratcheting tapping noise. The sheets of glass holding so much Los Angeles sewage at bay exploded into a mosaic of spider web cracks and fractures. Cutter held his breath hoping that the crackling glass would stop expanding. This was not how he wanted to be forgotten—left and abandoned inside his own body. He didn't have much time to think as a salt smell assaulted his nostrils. Rivulets of moisture began to pour down the interior walls. The dodecahedron gave a final groan and the murky waters of Los Angeles harbor burst into the room with violent elemental force.

◗

The tinkling sound of faeries, chimes blown in the wind, lulled Cutter from an eternal slumber. He felt more refreshed than he could remember. After a moment, he recognized the chimes as shards of glass sprinkling against corrugated steel, but had no context to understand why he was hearing the sound.

Cool pressure drained from all sides, until the only sensation left was a brisk kiss of air on his skin. His nose was the first to break the surface, an iceberg hinting at the larger form lying beneath. Small puddles of fluid gathered on his exposed chest and stomach. Aided by gravity, brooks trickled free from the pool of fluid and wrapped around his body like cyan tattoos. The waterline receded down his sides, and a full body continent rose from the waters.

A faint click plucked the air as if it was a string on a harp. The chafing at his wrists relented. He raised his hands and felt edges of a metal rim lining his current resting place.

It was time to wake up.

Cutter pulled himself upright. His head groggily lulled into his chest. In what would have been an otherwise serene and dreamlike moment, he began gasping for air. Though his body violently heaved, his mind simply acknowledged the hacking coughs and sputtering spasms as something necessary. Something that would pass in time—like all things.

When the coughing fit subsided and his breath returned, he pulled himself out of the glass tank, placing his chest on the metal rim. He strained to hoist his body, but his arms felt weak.

He managed to twist his way out, balancing his bulk on the metal rim. Facing the ground, he reached out to try and lower himself, but slipped and fell with a thud to the steel operating room floor.

The stench of bleach bore into his brain. Six lights shined down on him with blinding luminance. Mustering his strength, he pushed himself upright. He felt a sharp twinge of pain in his left palm. He held the hand in a fist, and got his legs under his body, and managed to sit upright. He held out his hand and inspected it in the light. Something shimmered with a reddish tint. He dug out a small chunk of glass from his palm and placed it on the floor beside him.

Footsteps approached from somewhere behind, but he didn't have the energy to turn. A pair of pink Converse stepped into view. Frilly pink socks were shoved into them. Stout little legs, with perhaps the hint of remaining baby fat, trailed up into the small form of a little girl.

She seemed out of place in this medical facility. Someone so young, so timid. On closer inspection, Cutter noticed that she wasn't a girl after all. She was something else. She looked as if she had an accident with a construction site. Steel rods poked in and out of her. She stood over Cutter, silently waiting.

Who was this girl in front of him? He searched his memory.

Giant brown eyes stared at him in bewilderment. Something dark dripped off her hand and twisted around her wrist. Reaching for her hand, he nodded his head, trying to indicate that he would not harm her, that he was merely curious. She put her hand in his. He rolled it over and smeared away the blood coiling around her wrist. No cuts or marks were present on her inner wrist. That was a good sign, though he wasn't sure it would have mattered anyway. He flipped her hand over and saw only superficial cuts and scrapes on her knuckles and backside of her hand.

He looked up meeting her endless gaze.

"Celia…" he said.

He wrapped his arms around her, nearly collapsing on top of her with his full weight, and hugged her tight.

"Thank you," he said, his voice barely a whisper. He repeated the words again and again. "Thank you, thank you, thank you."

When the echoes of his voice finally faded into the ambience of the room, he leaned back and looked into her eyes. "Why?" He struggled to understand. "Why did you save me?"

She stood before him without expression and said, "So you will never forget."

RESET

1

Clinking chains fell to the tarmac releasing a sea of limbs. Unable to hold the line against the tidal wave of elbowing InSight supporters, the front two barricade guards exchanged glances. Without a word between them, they had come to the same conclusion. Nodding, they stepped away from the barricade and let the crowd through. A voice cried from over their shoulders. It belonged to their supervisor, and it sounded pissed. The right guard turned and simply raised his hands over his head, as if to say, "The hell you want me to do?"

Signs of support for Foster and InSight waved overhead, carried by the surge of supporters heading for the conch shell amphitheater like leaves on a stream. A banner spanned the entrance tunnel welcoming the flood of supporters with a message that read: INVEST IN YOUR FUTURE—REELECT MAYOR BENJAMIN FOSTER. Streamers of red, white, and blue waved in the morning breeze.

Onlookers were still funneling into the amphitheater, crowding the aisles, many having to settle for seats there as well, as Foster's charismatic timbre echoed over the PA.

Slicing the air with a firm chop of his hand, Foster silenced the crowd. He smiled. It was difficult not to appreciate the power he commanded with a single gesture.

"Good morning all," said Foster casually adjusting the lavalier microphone on his lapel.

Banners and support posters in varying quantities of red, white, and blues decorated the curving backdrop. Dead center behind Foster, a large self-portrait towered forty feet overhead.

His name was etched in capitals at the bottom, each letter standing taller than him.

Foster paced center stage. To his left a large shape was covered by a grey tarp, standing slightly overhead.

"So this is the moment we've all been waiting for. Today marks an historic moment for Los Angeles. Through a program I've been working on for the past several years, what was only available to the rich is now available to everyone."

The crowd roared with approval, taking to its feet in a thunderous standing ovation. A catcall cut through the ruckus and banners and signs of support were vigorously waved, rattling the air with sounds of celebration.

"Well, I'm glad to hear such an enthusiastic response. But I know, some of you have your doubts." Foster grabbed the corner of the grey tarp, slowly pulling at its edge, teasing the audience with the surprise beneath. "Fret not my fellow citizens—"

With a snap of his wrist, he whipped the tarp off the hidden object like a magician yanking a tablecloth from under a dinner setting. A metal skeleton hung from a circular ring, like a twisted cybernetic version of Da Vinci's "Vitruvian Man." His arms were pinned to the ring above his head and his legs were secured at the base. Costas dangled before the crowd in ultramodern cruciform.

In front of Costas, a tank built out of black metal rods and glass was filled to the brim with fluid too blue to be water. Foster moved within the nook of Costas's body, daringly close.

"This—" he said, showcasing the unconscious Costas, "—is the man that's been trying so very hard to end my life. Perhaps you've been following the news lately?"

Costas jumped to life, lunging at Foster. A unified gasp echoed through the amphitheater. His body arched forward, wrists and ankles pinned to the restraining ring.

Inches from the snarling Costas, Foster dismissively waved to the crowd. "No, no. Don't be afraid. This here is our friend. Believe it or not, but under all of this, he's human."

Foster cupped a hand on Costas's cheek. "Can we—uh, can we get in closer?"

Watching one of the display monitors as the shot pushed in to a close-up on Costas, Foster pointed to the screen. "There. That's better."

The faceshield that had hidden Costas' identity and protected him was gone, leaving his only remaining humanity exposed to the prying eyes of onlookers in the crowd.

"As you can see, this isn't your ordinary monster. He's a man, just like you or me. Well, maybe a little bit more aggressive than you or me. Dissatisfied with his lot in life, he's been trying to get my attention in the most negative manner possible."

Foster shook his head and *tsk*'d at Costas the way he would a child. "Such a shame. My office doors are always open. All he had to do was come down and we could have a friendly chat."

"You having fun?" asked Costas. His voice carried to Foster, but not much farther. He wasn't mic'd, preventing the spectators from hearing him. Foster had thought of everything.

The gleam of pearly whites issued Foster's official response.

"It's about to come to an end," said Costas. "You must know that by now."

With a move that seemed perfectly natural, Foster brushed his hand across his lapel, blocking his microphone, obfuscating any sound with clothes rustle. Through a perfect smile, he said, "Only for you, my friend. Only for you. I'm about to be immortalized."

"Want to bet on it?"

For a fraction of a second, Foster's smile faltered. He was

sure no one in the audience had noticed. He allowed his smile to once again grow into the practiced trademark of his profession. Raising his arm with a flourish, he presented Costas to the fans itching for a first taste of InSight.

"What better candidate for the peace of mind that InSight can bestow than the poor broken soul who saw my murder as the only way to find his salvation?"

Foster ran the back of his hand down Costas' cheek in a loving manner. This time his smile was something sinister. "Poor thing. But I am preaching to the choir. Everyone here today, is here because of the benefits of InSight. You are ready to receive. Well, I must applaud you. Bear with me. Today's event is being live-streamed for those still on the fence.

"After this demonstration, however, I am convinced that all doubts will be banished from your minds. This man, Ryan Costas, has twice attempted to end my life. Twice has he tried and failed to rest the turmoil of his soul with the destruction of another. Today, friends we will witness the benefits of InSight."

The ring Costas was attached to rotated, whining like the aching joints of an old man. Positioning Costas face down over the vat of cyan fluid, the contraption shuddered and snapped into place.

Foster felt a warmth swell in his chest. All the time and effort he had put into this campaign, all the struggle he had overcome jumping through political bullcrap was about to pay off. He basked in thoughts of the adoration that would be showered upon him for ushering in a new era of peaceful bliss. And at the same time, reveled in his own brilliance that he had ensured his place forever at the head of this new era.

Foster watched the ring lock into place. A small motor hummed and cables groaned over rusty pulleys. With Costas as a shining example, his place would be cemented in the history of Los Angeles for time immemorial.

2

"He tried to erase my memory!" Cutter said, hammering the elevator call button.

"Again," Celia reminded him.

"He tried to erase my memory, *again!*"

At Cutter's feet, light swirled on the corrugated steel in flickering waves illuminating the room like something drenched in a cyan dream. Thoughts frothed like foam on the rolling waves of an endless ocean. Through tempestuous waters, he caught sparse glimpses of a man he used to be.

He tried to ignore the images, but they imprinted themselves across his vision. Too many. Things he had forgotten.

How many times had he reset?

Memories flooded back with the damp chill of an Arctic breeze.

How many times had they erased his memory?

How many different lives had he lived? An entire world of the past was lost to him.

A muzzle flash. A barrage of fists. Blood. Pools of it. Months, years, decades worth. Broken bones. Dirty streets. Dirtier secrets. Glimpses of faces flittered into sight. Some he knew. Others he recognized, but could not attach a name.

How many cases had he let go unsolved simply because he no longer remembered them? How many people had he let down?

He began to think about friends, about family, about things he hadn't considered in a long time.

Was he ever loved?

How many times had he been courting a woman, entrenched in a meaningful relationship, only to be wiped clean of the experience. Was she forever waiting by the phone for a call that was never coming?

Whipping wind lifted Cutter and Celia through the tube, away from the muck dredged floors of Los Angeles harbor. In his ear, the swirling breeze whispered a name over the deafening hum.

Carrie.

Bits and pieces were cracking through.

Her green eyes and brunette hair. A lifetime they had spent with each other—as children—as adults. The memories streamed back to his consciousness as little more than a feathered tickle. Warmth filled his heart. Tears glazed his eyes.

He remembered. He had loved her more than he thought possible.

But he also remembered… other things.

He remembered the nights he had come home late—the nights she was still up waiting. The look of concern in her eyes. The exact arch of her back, as she turned away hiding tears. Wiping them away where he couldn't watch.

Her concern.

And his lack of it.

Another memory sucked him back into his thoughts with the force of a riptide.

The things she said. That led to the fights. That led to…

Worse.

And she had been right. He had become so hardened by his job, by the city, so cynical about life, that he was unable to find meaningful existence with another human being.

Cutter paused, and watched Celia standing rigid as rippling

light flickered across her face. Darker thoughts stabbed his mind with previously unknown responsibility. After all she had been through. She was still here. By his side.

He felt stupid.

Really, really, really fucking stupid.

It was too late to apologize. Too late to say sorry.

To both of them.

And yet there she was. Still here. Looking up to him, hazel eyes brimming with wonder.

Until he had broken his promise to her. He had abandoned her.

And yet... she was still here.

Whether or not things had happened in some rose-colored fairytale version of his past or not, InSight had taken away his memories. They took away his past. His perspective.

Cutter clenched his fists into tight balls and watched the digital readout rapidly count down as the elevator rose to the surface. With a chime, the elevator doors slid open. Cutter barely waited for them to part as he barged through the InSight entrance and stomped onto the shipyard tarmac.

He held his head low, barreling toward the conch shell amphitheater. Winds of change exposed new thoughts, revealed like treasures once buried in the sands of time. His consciousness rose up and shouted over the memories lingering in his mind. *Nobody fucks with my head.*

Celia brushed his arm. "Are you okay?"

He looked down at Celia's battered face. Half of a perfect china doll stared back at him, the picture of innocence—the other half, a mechanical monstrosity, hard and cold, like his worst nightmares come to fruition. Biting his tongue, he found enough inner calm to respond. "I asked you that same question, didn't I?"

Celia nodded.

"And what did you say?"

"I am fine."

"Yeah, me too kid."

"I know what it is like, Jack. I remember everything anyone has ever done to me. I cannot forget."

Cutter stopped cold in his tracks. It was stupid, but he had never really considered what his actions did to others. Hell, he barely considered what his actions did to himself. But now, deliberate steps he had taken, his own cowardice, and refusal to face the mistakes of his past, had allowed him to become the test subject for a project that was going to rob the city of its memory.

There wasn't much left to say.

"Yeah, it sucks."

Breaking eye contact, Celia scanned the ground. She kicked a loose pebble and sent it skittering. "Foster gave you a chance to pretend those memories were gone."

"Pretend, nothing," said Cutter. "He got rid of them completely."

"Did it work?"

The sea breeze carried an aroma of salt mixed with a smoky chemical stench. Overhead, cargo cranes like giant four legged monsters creaked, busily unloading a cargo ship. A ribbon of smoke spouted from an exhaust stack.

There were things he didn't want to remember. Things he had deliberately forgotten. But even the fleeting memories that skirted recall, he still felt.

Cutter ran a hand through Celia's hair. "No," he said, letting a few strands slide through his fingers. "It didn't."

The entrance to the amphitheater was oddly devoid of InSight's security detail. Foster's normal goon squad entourage was nowhere to be seen either. Security had taken a broader position throughout the shipyard, guarding and lining the perimeter. A barricade had been established at the entrance gates. A team of five or six, wearing the cyan blue uniforms of InSight, guarded the entrance in full combat gear. The handful of remaining guards were scattered throughout the massive expanse of blacktop, pacing a circuitous route through the stacked towers of primary colored containers.

Cutter reached down and took Celia's hand, leading her into the amphitheater. "Stay close."

They were quickly greeted by the outdoors once again. The amphitheater's inner ring was nothing more than a ticket booth and a few souvenir and concession stands. Cutter raised a hand shielding his eyes from a sun that was climbing into a sky unmarred by clouds. Maneuvering around InSight supporters sitting in the aisles, they made their way down to the stage.

Foster was grandstanding, proselytizing a crowd hungry for freedom from the drudgery of their lives regardless of the cost. Next to him, a very familiar tank was filled with cyan fluid. A circular ring pivoted over the contraption. Cutter recognized the man strapped to it.

"Costas." Celia pointed.

Cutter clenched his jaw.

"What is he doing?" asked Celia.

Cutter knew all too well. "He's going to make an example out of him."

"Why?"

"Because it's a hell of a product endorsement."

Still holding Cutter's hand, Celia twisted, scanning the crowd. Everyone in the audience was on their feet waving banners and signs. "There are a lot of people here."

"Yes." Cutter nodded. "There are."

The foot of the stage was swarming with men in cheap suits that had rather large bulges in their jackets. Translucent white cords corkscrewed out of their ears. So this was where Foster's goon squad had gotten off to. They were barely hidden from the crowd, piled in the gulley that ran between the stage and front row. From their shifting eyes and sweat drenched brows, it was evident they were ready for trouble, despite Foster's casual stage-manner.

As Cutter and Celia approached the stage, Foster made eye contact. Somehow, the smile that was already present blossomed into something even brighter. Bile rose in Cutter's stomach. Without missing a beat, Foster waved to Cutter like they were best friends.

"He thinks I'm some mindless idiot." Cutter reached into his jacket and removed his ZeroTwelve. Before Celia could respond, he answered, "More so than usual, I mean."

"What are you going to do, Jack?"

He pulled back the slide on the ZeroTwelve, chambering a flashing round. "Give him a piece of my mind."

Foster ignored the first loud thunk.

The stage shook beneath his feet with a second thundering clang. Heads snapped toward the noise searching for its source. A third and a fourth thunk hammered the stage, followed by a distant hailstorm of clanking thuds.

Foster's permanent smile was unable to hide the fear in his eyes. He slowly turned toward the noises behind him.

Toward the tank.

And Costas.

His mouth gaped opened, smile lost forever.

3

Foster stood frozen in horror.

"No… This can't be happening."

Dangling from the restraining ring, Costas's disembodied left hand waved at Foster. Cybernetic limbs and assorted pieces of almost-man were scattered in a puddle of cyan liquid at the base of the tank. Costas inched along the floor like a caterpillar, pushing his disembodied leg forward with his chin.

"What's the matter, Foster?" said Costas. "Speechless? This is your big day. Let's celebrate."

Stopping next to his right arm, Costas rolled onto his side and snapped the limb into place. He dragged his dead weight toward the remaining body parts, reaching forward with his newly reattached limb, inching ever closer to Foster.

"I really should thank you," said Costas. He picked up his left leg and used it as a crutch before securing it to his hip. "I wouldn't have been able to do that had it not been for you."

Foster scrambled backwards, tripping over his own feet. He landed hard on his tailbone. Twisting and clawing at the ground, he scuttled for escape. "Somebody stop him!" he cried to anyone within earshot.

His personal goon squad was already in action. An army of cheap black suits climbed the stairs.

Costas stretched his arms over his head. Servos whined. The linked vertebrae in his spine split in two, revealing the plasma rifle beneath. Craning over his shoulder, the rifle settled into his hands. "Much better," said Costas, shuffling his shoulders. His finger slid inside the trigger guard.

A fan of red pulse blasts peppered the stage. Muzzles flashed bright. Squinting, Costas turned his head just in time to take a blast to the side of his head. Two inches to the right and it would have hit his exposed face. Chuckling to himself, he leaned forward and braced himself against the recoil of his weapon.

The entire left side of the stage exploded in a wave of blue-green energy. Limbs flew in all directions, a stunt similar to the one he had pulled off moments prior. Only, he was fairly certain these men wouldn't be able to put themselves back together again.

At the first sight of Costas breaking free of restraint, the crowd had become a writhing mass of unrest. Many had fled for the exits. But those that remained, unsure if it was all part of the show, had no doubts now. Signs of support were abandoned and trampled. A roaring frenzy of panic surged through the crowd. The curve of the amphitheater backdrop redirected shrieks of terror back to those that had produced them. Supporters pushed and shoved toward daylight.

Crawling on his hands and knees, Foster desperately scrambled across the stage, trying to join them.

"You aren't going anywhere," said Costas. Two swift strides and he was on top of Foster. Planting his foot on Foster's back, he stomped flat. He slid his foot beneath Foster and rolled him over like a flapjack. Costas bent down, haloing the Mayor's face with his hands.

Poor Mayor. His illusion of perfection was gone. Sweat spotted his forehead. Greasy blemish makeup streaked his cheeks. With his eyes clamped shut, he wildly swung at Costas, arms pumping the air, uselessly colliding with combat hardened alloy.

Costas leaned in close. "Look at me."

Like a child refusing to be spoon-fed, Foster writhed back and forth, arms flailing, legs kicking in all directions.

Costas tightened his grip. Foster's lips curled and his blues eyes bulged. A blood vessel burst, staining his left eye red. Frightened for his life, he held still. A hollow gaze dimmed the life in his eyes.

Costas snorted. The faint twist of a smile appeared. "Was it worth it?"

"Put me down," Foster muttered.

"All this power, all this control, and what has it gotten you?"

Foster hesitated. "I just do what they tell me."

"Maybe you should have done some thinking for yourself."

Costas dragged Foster across the stage and threw him against the tank. Slamming into the steel lip, he bent backward. Cyan fluid sloshed, spilling down the front of his shirt. His breath was heavy, his head fell into his chest, as he lay in a slumped pile. He could barely find the strength to lift his head, as a pair of metal feet clanked toward him. Towering over him, Costas reached out and released his left hand from the restraining ring. With a simple twist of the wrist, he reattached it.

He turned his attention back to Foster. "Where were we?"

A small spark of hope glimmered in Foster's eyes. "I can give you anything you want."

Costas squatted next to him, shaking his head. "What I wanted was for you to leave me alone. How hard was that?"

"I can do that! You'll never see me again."

"Somehow, I doubt that." Costas dipped his head in the direction of the cameras. "I think I'd still see a lot of you. You don't exactly strike me as the type willing to give up his position. Besides, look at all the people you've tricked."

Costas placed his hand on Foster's head and forcefully turned it. The audience had almost completely vacated the amphitheater. Those few remaining were busily shoving others through the exits. "We've got to set the record straight."

"What are you going to do?" Foster pushed against the mechanical monstrosity, trying to pull his feet beneath his body and make a run for it.

Costas struck him in the Adam's apple. Foster gasped, hands shooting straight to his throat. Staggering, he fell back against the tank.

"You wanted their minds," Costas snarled. "You wanted sheep. I'm going to make sure that never happens."

"But…" Foster blubbered, "…it's their choice." Snot bubbled from his left nostril.

Costas paused for a moment enjoying Foster's sputtering sounds, listening to him gasp for breath that wouldn't come. Running his hands down Foster's lapel, he removed the lavalier microphone and clipped it to his chest.

Rising to his feet, he picked Foster up by a mess of his hair. He held Foster out to the crowd, waving him back and forth, sweeping the stage with the tips of Foster's toes. He turned to a nearby camera, red light still illuminated despite the lack of a cameraman. He was going to make sure that the viewers at home got a good look.

"Here is your example," Costas shouted. The acoustics of the amphitheater magnified his voice. "Watch."

Costas slammed Foster head first into the tank. Foster splashed about, struggling against the synthetic arm holding him underwater. With his free arm, Costas tipped the lapel mic towards his mouth. "This is what happens when you try to take a man's mind from him."

He let Foster surface and cheated him toward the camera. "So tell me Ben, how do you like it?"

Foster heaved, gasping for air. "Stop."

"Ah, that's too bad."

Costas dunked him again.

* * *

"What are you going to do?" Celia asked.

Nothing was what he really wanted to say.

Cutter tapped the grip of his ZeroTwelve with his thumb. Flipping open his jacket, he slid the weapon back into his shoulder holster. "Looks like Costas has things locked up."

Celia tailed, a few steps behind. "You are going to let Costas kill him?"

Cutter bit his lower lip. Only moments prior, he had been ready to charge up on stage and do, well, not what Costas had done. In point of fact, he thought Costas' approach was much more effective than anything he could have dreamed up.

Cutter shrugged.

"You cannot let him do this, Jack."

"Why not?" The words came out glib.

"Because it is not right."

"I don't need you to tell me the difference between right and wrong. I know all about it."

Besides, what Foster was doing wasn't right either. He wanted to brainwash the entire populace to rig an election. Turnabout is fair play, or something.

The sounds of a splashing struggle came from behind him. Foster uttered something unintelligible, amidst gurgling gasps for breath.

Celia was right. He should go up there and stop Costas. Rather attempt to stop Costas, because good luck with that.

But the difference between right and wrong, wasn't why he was hesitant. Nor was the fact that Foster had used him.

The truth was—he was afraid.

He was always afraid.

Erasing his memory was just another reminder that his macho facade was a front. One more piece of evidence piled against him that he wasn't the brave tough-guy he saw in his mind's eye.

He hadn't volunteered to wipe his memory to become a hero. It wasn't to rescue the city from itself. There was no grand scheme for the betterment of a world of blissful perfection. He hadn't done it to protect Costas, or himself, either. Rather, he had volunteered because it was easier than dealing with the truth.

Celia tugged on his arm, spinning him around. Even from this distance, Cutter could see Costas' beaming smile. He had been waiting for this for a long time. To get even with the man who had forced him to go into hiding. The man that wanted to take away his memories, to try and appease his pain. Costas had sacrificed so much of his self for this moment.

And Celia brought Cutter back to reality like a lead weight. "Foster is being attacked because of what you did."

God dammit.

Why did she have to be so God damned logical all the time?

Cutter looked up at the stage. He pursed his lips and shook his head.

Cyan fluid dribbled from the corner of Foster's mouth leaving a smear on his chin. "No more," he whispered. "No more."

"Giving up already?" said Costas. "But I'm not done yet."

"Stop!" Cutter shouted. He cautiously moved up the stairs onto the stage with his ZeroTwelve drawn.

Costas spun on heel. "Jack…" He waved him over. "How nice to see you." He nodded toward Foster. "You want a free pot shot or two? I'll bet you're just itching to lay in a free one."

Cutter held his ground. "Stop."

Celia peered up at them from the gully between the stage

and front row.

"I see you brought your friend," said Costas. "How nice. This official police duty?"

"I came in for a checkup."

"Haven't you figured it out yet, Jack? What this is all about. What they've done to you. You're just a puppet on a string. You're acting exactly how they want you to."

"I'm no puppet."

There had been many things he had done that he regretted. But they had been a choice. His choice.

The more memories that flooded back, filling in the gaps of his past, the more he realized that every time he was faced with a challenge, faced with doubt, faced with a difficult decision, he made the wrong choice. He buckled.

Staring at the cybernetic Grim Reaper, for the first time in his life, he made the choice that was sure to place him directly in harm's way.

"It was me."

4

Costas turned, eyes set on Cutter.

"You don't know what you're saying, Jack." His voice came out as a high pitched squeal.

"It was me," Cutter said forcefully.

Costas took a step forward, stopped, and paced back toward Foster, looking lost. Normally, Costas moved with supernatural fluidity. But now he jerked and shuddered as if stop-motion animated. His head snapped around in Cutter's direction. "You don't know what you're saying."

Cutter leaned back on his right foot, securing his footing.

Readjusting his sweaty grip on the ZeroTwelve, he locked sights on Costas' exposed face. Sweat beaded on his forehead. He could feel heat building up in his torso. Inhaling deeply, he searched for a calm he was unsure he could find.

"It wasn't Foster that wanted to use you as a guinea pig," said Cutter. "It was me."

Cutter watched Costas' expression slowly contort.

"I volunteered *us*."

Costas screamed, charging headfirst at Cutter. "YOU DON'T KNOW WHAT YOU ARE SAYING!"

The blast ricocheted off blackened metal shoulder in a spray of fiery red. Cutter dove to his left, narrowly avoiding the incoming mod. Hunched over, he clawed at the stage, raising a hand in front of his body, as if the gesture alone could ward off Costas.

"What have you done?!" Costas roared. Cutter felt a hand on his leg and was yanked backward. His legs flew out from under him and he smacked into the stage, knocking the wind from his lungs. Rigid metal barred across his throat, pushing down immense tonnage behind it. Cutter put his feet up, kicking with every ounce of strength.

"I remember," said Cutter, through winded gasps. "I remember why I wanted it all gone."

"That's great, Jack! Really!"

Costas was levering his body down, crushing him. Rearing back an arm, he swung for Cutter's head. Cutter rolled out of the way. The blow connected with the stage splintering wooden panels, and Costas sunk down to his shoulder.

Climbing to his feet, Cutter held the ZeroTwelve in shaking hands. Costas was a wild animal. The only thing that could protect him from the enraged mod was a well-placed shot. A tiny opening on a ferocious agile moving target.

"You saved me," said Cutter.

"You think I don't know that, Jack?! I'm not the one whose brain they fried!"

"I couldn't deal with the guilt. I wanted it gone."

Costas stalked forward like a jungle cat. There was no doubt in Cutter's mind—he was the prey. "They came for me, Jack!" Costas pointed at his face with a mechanized finger. "Look at what I had to do to survive! Look at what I've become!"

"I thought you'd be better off…"

"You were wrong!"

Costas lunged at Cutter, wildly swinging and shouting. "You thought you'd be free of guilt? That if I couldn't remember, your conscience would be clear?" Cutter fired. Pulse blasts deflected off rapidly moving limbs that were quickly closing in on him. Cutter dodged, leaping off the stage into the gully below.

"And you…" Costas turned toward Foster who was running up the aisle. He pointed with his entire arm. A large bulge on his forearm snapped into place. "You made this all possible. A grant from the fucked-up foundation."

Foster looked over his shoulder for a split second. A U-ring hit him in bridge of the nose, momentarily dazing him. Another U-ring hit him in the ribs, while two more hit the wall behind him. He reached up to protect his face, and a fourth U-ring caught his hand, pinning it to the wall.

Foster tugged at his arm, trying to free it. Costas ran at him, going down onto all fours in an animalistic sprint.

"No!" Cutter yelled. "I'm over here. I'm the one that you want!"

Costas tackled Foster, ripping the U-ring from the wall. They tumbled together. Costas rose, holding Foster off the ground by his neck.

From somewhere over his shoulder, Cutter heard a commanding voice. The amphitheater should have been empty by now. In silhouette, a team of InSight guards ran through the entrance tunnel. The guard in front wind-milled his left arm, shouting instructions. Guards clad in cyan spread through the aisles and into the seating. Plasma rifles were steadied and aimed at Costas.

"Put him down!" the lead guard yelled.

Costas raised Foster over his head—"Here's your conscience, Jack"—and brought him down on his knee. Foster gave a short whimper; his eyes rolled back in his head. Arms and legs dangled, dead weight free of tension. Costas let Foster's corpse fall to the floor with a thud.

"It's your turn now, Jack!"

"Fire!" the commanding guard shouted.

A barrage of plasma blasts showered Costas with destruction. Raising an arm over his face, he twisted his back toward the incoming blaster fire, deflecting streams of superheated particle energy. Cutter saw Costas duck down. Seconds later he was in mid-air leaping over seats on a direct route for him.

"That's not good."

"What do we do now, Jack?"

"We run."

Cutter grabbed Celia's hand and cornered up the opposite aisle away from Costas. Costas wasn't as slowed down by the gap, as much as Cutter had hoped. The mod simply skipped through the seating with acrobatic grace. Blaster fire pinged off his cybernetic parts, slowing him down more than any positional requirements.

Cutter turned back, looking over his shoulder. Terror gripped him. He pushed Celia to the floor.

"Get down!"

Costas collided. They left an imprint in the wall and went down in a flurry of swinging limbs. Costas had both hands on his wrist, smashing his hand to the ground, trying to force his grip on the ZeroTwelve. Cutter drew back his free hand and punched Costas in his face. He felt solid contact, flesh against flesh. Bone gave and a tooth flew across the aisle landing at Celia's feet.

Over Costas' shoulder, Cutter could see the InSight guards lining up, rifles lowered, ready, but for some reason, not doing a God damned thing.

"What are you waiting for?!" Cutter yelled. "Shoot him already!"

The air sizzled with blaster fire. Not his smartest of ideas, but what choice did he have?

Costas turned away from Cutter. His back opened, revealing his weapon. As it craned into position, Cutter grabbed it. Instead of stopping the weapon from deploying as Cutter had hoped, the motion flung him over Costas' shoulder. Landing on his back in front of Costas, he saw him glance down for the briefest of seconds. A sneer curled the corner of his mouth.

An aquamarine pulse roasted the air above Cutter's head. It plowed through the amphitheater tossing seats in all directions. Cutter covered his head as debris rained down on him.

"Jack!" Celia reached out toward him.

"Go, get out of here!" He pointed toward the exit.

Wisps of blue-green static crackled around a smoking muzzle. Costas dipped it toward him. "Where were we?"

Cutter spun, sweeping Costas' legs out from under him. Another blue-green pulse sailed into the ceiling. It connected with a crossbeam, atomizing a large chunk in its center.

A low bass sound groaned. The entire amphitheater shell began to shake. As if the beam itself was shouting for the guards below to look out it screeched, before falling on top of them. The other half of the beam peeled from the ceiling and dragged a line of destruction through the seating area. Running out of momentum, it toppled over on its side, a large crescent, cutting off the remaining InSight guards.

Cutter grabbed the barrel and pulled Costas towards him. Close quarters combat was not exactly ideal, but neither was getting his molecules rearranged at point blank range.

"Jack!" Celia screamed.

"I said get—"

Costas punched him in the ear. Blood dripped down the side of his face. His world was spinning. He was able to make out Celia's tiny form running for the exit.

He faced Costas, accidentally meeting the next punch with his cheek. He staggered forward. Clatter, as large sections of catwalk fell all around them. From the looks of it, the amphitheater wasn't going to be upright much longer. But he wasn't sure that mattered. Because neither was he.

Disoriented, Cutter flailed, trying to block the next incoming blow. He deflected a lot of the force, but it still connected sending him reeling.

Costas laughed, shaking his head at Cutter. "Pathetic." He pointed. "You might want to take a look at this."

Cutter followed the length of his arm. He was pointing at Celia with a grim smile plastered on his face. "She's not going anywhere, either." The U-ring launcher snapped up from his forearm.

"No!" Cutter shouted. Dizzy, world spinning around him, he got to his feet. He staggered forward, reaching for the outstretched arm. It wasn't pretty, but he fell into the Costas.

The U-ring sailed through the air, hurtling end over end towards Celia. It flew inches over her head.

It had missed.

Celia was outside.

Safe.

Trying to compensate, Costas continued firing U-ring after U-ring. Using what little strength he had left, Cutter twisted Costas' arm behind his back. A stray U-ring caught Costas in the left arm. Stumbling away, from Costas, Cutter crawled along the aisle, heading for the exit.

Costas lunged forward, only to be tossed to the ground. The U-ring had burrowed into the fallen crossbeam, pinning his left wrist to it.

Cutter pushed himself upright, slinking away from the mod. The building was coming down around him. He needed to move faster. He could hear Costas raving incoherently, a trapped animal sensing its imminent demise.

Celia was at the exit, screaming for him to hurry.

The ceiling rained debris. The sound of a whip crack caught his attention and Cutter dodged to the right. A stage light bigger than he was smashed into the aisle. Hot glass shards pelted his exposed skin, face and hands taking the brunt of it. He climbed over the backs of chairs, eyes set on the daylight streaming in from the exit.

He couldn't hear anything over the roar of the building collapsing around him. A fog of dust clouded his vision. Rays of light streamed through it, pointing toward salvation so close.

With arms outstretched, he felt her touch. He wrapped his arms around her and lifted her into the air in a spinning embrace.

He was outside.

5

Heat rose off the blackened tarmac in visible ripples. Hand in hand, Cutter and Celia trudged across it. Celia felt him stop at her side. She turned to see Cutter raising a hand to his brow, a makeshift salute, shading his eyes from the sun. He stared back at the destruction behind them. The shell portion of the amphitheater had fallen over, taking the entrance with it, stirring up a cloud of white and beige debris. The sea breeze scattered it into smaller wispy plumes, blowing a patchy haze throughout the shipyard.

"It's over," said Cutter.

A half smile found its way onto her expression. She wanted to believe him, but the voice in her head wouldn't allow it.

Celia...

"We'll be okay now," said Cutter.

Bring him to me, Celia.

"No!" Celia shouted.

Cutter snapped his head in her direction. Celia could see the questions dancing behind his wide eyes. "Costas wants me to lead you to him."

"Oh... Right. You can still hear him?"

She nodded. White noise that had been present since her first run-in with Costas buzzed in her ear.

Cutter's features blanched white. He grabbed her by the shoulder and quickly hunkered down behind a red shipping container. Leaning around it, he stared at the collapsed amphitheater.

"So, I take it he's still alive."

"Yes. He is tracking my signal the same way I tracked his."

"Right. So we can't exactly hide."

"Jack, he sounds really angry."

"I'll bet."

Nervously fidgeting, Cutter rubbed his hands together. His left foot jittered kicking up small puffs of dust. "Okay, kid… You stay here."

Celia grabbed his hand. "Jack…" She clamped down tight on his sleeve.

"Just listen. You stay here—"

"Do not leave me."

Cutter paused. She could see him struggling for words, searching fruitlessly for something to say. Was he looking for an excuse? A way to appease his guilt? Erasing his memory wasn't a choice anymore. Not after today. He would have to live with the outcome of any future decisions.

After what seemed like an eternity, Cutter said, "I won't."

He held eye contact, looking directly at her. Her innate programming told her people did that when they were telling the truth. When people lie, they tend to break eye contact and look to their right or left.

Unfortunately, the Black and White profiling programs said exactly the opposite. People looked left or right because they were lost in thought. That didn't necessarily mean they were lost in the fabrication of a lie. Furthermore, when a suspect locked eyes, it was usually so that they could confirm whether or not the person they were lying to believed them.

Celia didn't know which theory to believe.

"You need to stay here in the shipyard. It'd be even better if you stayed as far away from the exit as possible. Lead him around by the seawall."

She wanted to believe Cutter. She wanted to believe that he

wouldn't abandon her. Not again.

"Don't make it too easy for him to catch you. Run around. Do what you can to evade him. I need time."

Time to run away, Celia thought.

"You got all that?"

"Do not leave me."

Gritting his teeth, Cutter reached out to pat her on the shoulder. Halfway through the motion he stopped and instead withdrew.

"Celia, don't make this harder than it has to be. I don't know what I can say to make you believe me." He placed his hand over hers and delicately pried her fingers from his jacket. "I will not ditch you."

She had resigned herself to her decision. She wanted to have faith in humanity. In Cutter. She wanted to believe that despite overwhelming evidence to the contrary, she could trust people.

But this time, she was prepared to be let down.

She nodded.

As Cutter reached out to once again tussle her hair, she leaned away, avoiding his touch.

"I believe you, Jack."

But deep down, she was ready to be betrayed again. At least this time, she'd see it coming.

Wavering, his mouth formed a broken frown. He returned her nod before disappearing into the labyrinth of shipping containers.

Where are you, Celia?

"You know exactly where I am." There was no child-like wonder in her tone. She was too busy preparing herself for the inevitable to care how she came across.

It's okay. I'll come to you.

Chills ran down her spine. She was sure he would. The sonar blip of his signal pinged louder with each passing second.

Celia peered at the collapsed amphitheater entrance. A cloud of dust was settling. The faint caw of a seagull rose over the ever present droning roar of the ocean. The day seemed to pay no mind to the destruction the morning had witnessed.

The signal pinged louder. Costas was on the move. She scanned the shipyard for traces of his approach. Palm fronds on the trees that marked the shoreline danced to a slight breeze. The world stirred with occasional motion, calm and serene, in direct opposition to everything she felt.

Somewhere, closing in on her location was a man possessed of a singular goal. A man with a vendetta against those that had made his life a living Hell. And she was his only link to exacting revenge.

The tone pinged. She jumped in shock at the volume. Much louder than before. He had to be close. Somewhere nearby. She scoured the landscape, the shipyard, the amphitheater, but Cutter was nowhere to be seen.

Make this easy on all of us, Celia.

The tone blipped again.

Bring him to me.

Dangling from a crane, a container swayed in the breeze. Apparently, the crane operators and dock workers had abandoned their stations as word spread of the attacks in the amphitheater. Now the cranes were lifeless monsters frozen in time. Celia wanted to join the workers. And Cutter. Fleeing was a good idea.

The tone blipped again.

A very good idea.

Instead, she was stuck in the middle of a gorgeous Southern California day. The sun shone high and bright and warm. Not a spec of cloud in the sky.

Blip.

The tone. Loud. So close now.

And there was no indication of Costas' approach.

His voice sounded as if he was standing behind her softly whispering in her ear.

There you are.

Without hesitation, Celia bolted for the seawall. She didn't stop to think. His voice was so soft, so close. The signal, so loud. No time for thought. Only time to flee. To react.

Blip.

Running as fast as her legs could carry her, she could not escape the tone. It constantly grew in decibel until she felt it, more than heard it, vibrating in sympathetic response to her construction.

She rounded the corner out of sight of her previous hiding spot and slammed into something rigid, knocking her to the ground. She clambered in the dirt, trying to get her feet beneath her.

The intimidating form of blackened metal forged into the likeness of a man stood before her. She could see his pink fleshy face. He barely looked at her. His eyes flicked back and forth, scanning the surroundings.

"Where is he?"

All Celia had was the truth.

"He left me."

Costas grabbed her by the neck and raised her to eye level. He cocked his head inspecting the shoddy patch job. She felt his gaze resting on her disfigured face.

"What have you gone and done with yourself?"

"You should know. You told me to."

Costas squinted, gazing across the shipyard, searching for movement, signs of life, anything.

"Jack!" Costas shouted. He held Celia out at arm's length. "Kind of a pattern, don't you think? First me. Then Roy. Now this one. You hide behind all your partners? The noble sacrifice is jumping on the grenade, not pushing your partners onto it and high-tailing it to safety."

"I told you, he left me." Celia kicked Costas in the chest.

That was enough to grab his attention. He looked down at her. "Aren't you an angel?"

"Not today," she said.

"Jack! Let's end this," Costas yelled, his voice carrying over the tarmac. Echoes were the only reply. "Foster's dead. All that's left is you. All these years, and it was you all along. I guess that I can't say it's not personal. It is."

Costas scoured the shipyard. Now, it was his turn to be privy to the delights of a Southern California day. But he had other things on his mind than soaking in the warmth, sun, and serenity.

"Okay, Jack. We do it the hard way."

Costas stroked Celia's hair. "My apologies. But this is going to smart."

Before she knew it, she was a hundred meters in the air. Her body flailed under the force, rag-dolling as she came to the apex of the climb, a victim of the effects of gravity. From this height she could see the entire shipyard. Not that the perspective helped. Cutter was just as absent in the twists and turns of the shipyard maze from this view as any other.

She hurtled toward the ground, spinning, trying to right herself, and cushion the inevitable impact. Before she smashed into the ground, Costas leaped up at her, and met her with his foot. She rocketed through the air, skipping twice off the tarmac, before colliding into a green shipping container.

The container buckled at its midsection. Celia groaned, resting in the dented center. Staggering, she pushed herself up onto all fours. The impact should have caused more damage than she had sustained. She was reminded of the skybox control room at Staples Center. In that attack, her body had barely been able to hold together.

But today, her new body held. She felt different. It wasn't just Roy's parts either.

"Jack…" Costas' voice carried across the shipyard. "I don't know how much of this she can take. You might want to get over here while there's still something left of her to salvage."

Costas skulked toward her. He watched her struggle to sit upright with sickening fascination. After a moment, he returned his attention back to their surroundings, staring across the shipyard. There was something odd about Costas. Despite how in control of the situation he had been, he had a strange look on his face.

He was surprised.

She wasn't.

She heard him make a sound that seemed too organic, too human, to be emanating from something that was mostly machine. He sighed and slowly turned toward her.

"He really abandoned you, didn't he?"

Celia hung her head. By the time she looked back up, the plasma rifle had already craned over his shoulder and was resting in his hands.

"I'm sorry," said Costas.

5

Blue-green light emanated from the tip of the barrel. Celia sighed, nodding to herself. If disappointment and betrayal was all that life held in store, she didn't want to live it anymore. She was perfectly happy to be atomized by the incoming blast.

A creaking whine of rusty metal on metal shrieked over the thrum of building particle energy. A blur of red flashed before Celia, followed by what she could only describe as a single instant of thunder. The world around her exploded. Rotten cabbage stink permeated the air, while everything glowed in blue-green reflection. Sound drowned in the rush of a deafening cymbal crash.

In front of her, a red container stood in place of Costas. Overhead, a hook snapped back and forth on the end of a cable relieved of the strain it had been under. She traced the cable to its source, the crane arm arching out over her. Twenty-three meters above her head, the arm was mounted beneath a box of plexiglass windows that housed the crane controls and its operator. Poking his head out of an open window, Cutter shouted at her.

"Run!"

In a daze, her senses came back to her as if in slow motion. A tittering repetitive tapping came from inside the red container. As she got to her feet, the container split in half, launching metal shards. Two main portions flew in opposite directions. Celia's feet slid across the asphalt, kicking bits of gravel. She ducked, lowering her body, reaching forward and jumped out of the way as a shard bigger than a car spun past her.

Costas stood in the middle of what looked more like an exploded party favor than a shipping container. A noise came from him. A roar. A cry. Words may have even been mixed in. Celia couldn't tell. But it was primal. He bellowed to clear skies with a ferocity that shook the ground.

Turning toward her, he swung his plasma rifle in her direction. There was nowhere to run to avoid the shot.

But it never came.

She tossed a glance over her shoulder. Costas was throwing a fit. He ripped the plasma rifle off his back and tossed it to the ground at his side.

"Jack! He's coming!"

"Run!"

"I am!"

"Faster!"

Costas looked up at the crane. At Cutter. His face scrunched, angry wrinkles appeared above his nose and around his eyes. He pointed at Cutter and the contraption on his forearm snapped into place.

"Jack!" he yelled. U-rings assaulted the plexiglass container along with a barrage of verbal assaults. Roaring with anger, Costas charged toward the base of the crane.

Cutter had his foot on the ladder heading back down to the ground. But at the sight of Costas climbing the crane like an irate baboon, he thought better of it. He slammed the hatch shut, twisted the wheel lock, and hoped against hope that it would be enough to hold Costas at bay.

Cutter slid open the plexiglass window and climbed out onto the crane arm. Inside the control booth, the hatch smashed into the ceiling, torn off its hinges. Costas appeared seconds later. Ducking down, Cutter flung himself flat against the crane arm.

He heard metal steps clanking on the steel flooring inside the booth. As the sounds crept closer, he inched back along the crane.

Costas peeked up over the sill. Cutter backed away, reaching into his jacket, grasping for the ZeroTwelve that wasn't there. He stared down at the empty holster.

Costas climbed through the window onto the crane arm. Metal shards sprung up off his body, sharpened to a razor's edge.

"It's over, Jack."

Cutter always imagined that he would have felt panic or fear at his impending demise. But that's not what he felt now. At first, he couldn't quite place the emotion. It wasn't that the emotion was unfamiliar, more that it was out of place. Staring at Costas, at his ex-partner, facing the truth that had finally been exposed, Cutter felt relief.

Costas raised his arm, blades glinting in the sun. As the swing came down, something plinked off the side of Costas, causing him to stagger forward.

Costas looked down. Beneath him, Celia held a handful of rocks to her stomach. She reared back her arm and threw another. Costas leaned, letting the stone pass unmolested.

"Kid's got some heart," said Costas.

He aimed at her. A U-ring caught her wrist and pinned her to a container.

"Jack!" she yelled. She pulled against the U-ring, but it wouldn't budge. "No, Jack!"

Jack needed her. He had kept his word. He hadn't abandoned her. He had saved her.

Now it was her turn to save him. He was outmatched by Costas. He could have fled and saved himself. Instead, he had stayed behind.

Celia tugged at her wrist.

She could do this. Maybe she couldn't release the U-ring,

but that didn't mean she couldn't free herself. Costas had done it. And so could she.

She was just a machine.

She leaned back easing her full weight onto her wrist. Servos whined beneath the surface. She could feel wires drawing taut. Her hand spasmed, as electrical signals became erratic. Plasti-flesh split at her wrist, revealing her underlying mechanical innards. Wires sparked and snapped. She could see gears slipping, being pulled apart, teeth no longer interlocking. Bits of metal and plastic, things she probably needed were falling out of the open crevice in her wrist.

Her internal UI lit up in reds. An alarm sounded in her head. Her internal programming yelled at her to stop. She was damaging herself, it screamed. She already knew. She didn't need her onboard UI flashing, nor the voice in her head telling her that. She could feel it.

She could feel pain. Felt herself being torn apart. Could feel her body resisting. Stupid body. Give in. Break.

She leaned forward and snapped her arm back, twisting her entire upper body as hard as she could. The wires holding her wrist together snapped.

She was free.

"Jack! Hold on!"

Above her, she saw Cutter put his hands up in surrender. Costas raised his arm. With one swipe he split Cutter from shoulder to groin. Cutter stepped forward, but the rest of him didn't follow. He fell to the tarmac in separate pieces.

Tears streaked down her cheeks, giving a plastic shine to her otherwise human features. She dropped to her knees at Cutter's side.

"No…"

It couldn't be. He couldn't be dead. He had sacrificed himself for her.

The cry of a gull was carried on the wind.

Before her, Cutter lay in two pieces. The flesh exposed by his wounds, black cherry red peppered by black pinpoint dots, had been cauterized by the Costas' tech. His arm lay next to him, connected to his disembodied leg by a flap of skin. The attack had missed most of his torso.

Celia put her hands together, placing the heel of her palm at the base of his sternum. "It's… it's not as bad as it looks," she said.

But it was.

She pumped his stomach. Once. Twice. And stopped. CPR was pointless.

Two pairs of glassy eyes stared up at a spotless sky. Closing hers, she could make out the faintest breath. She put her ear to his mouth, but the sound was different now—a constant hiss of air escaping from deflating lungs.

She laid her head on his chest. Her tears wouldn't stop.

"Do not leave me," she sobbed. The faint lub-dub of his heart thumped a final beat.

"…do not leave…"

She laid there in silence. Waiting. Hoping for one more beat.

In the silence she could make out a faint hum. A high pitched vibration that had been with her for a while now. It wasn't coming from Cutter. It was coming from inside her. She recognized the frequency. The link that Costas had established.

It worked both ways.

"You cannot leave like this."

There was a long silence. And then she repeated herself.

"You cannot leave me like this."

A voice broke the silence, caressing her with its smooth timbre.

It's done.

"Come back."

Goodbye Celia.

There was an audible click. Then the faint hum of static that had been buzzing in her thoughts since she first met Costas vanished.

She waited for a long time.

She told herself that her connection wasn't completely lost. It couldn't be.

She had already lost Mommy and Daddy.

Now Cutter.

And even Costas had abandoned her too.

She couldn't lose everything.

Waves gently lapped against the seawall. She heard the rustle of feathers, as a handful of seagulls took flight. For the first time in her short life, she realized that she was all alone.

Her sobs echoed through the empty shipyard. The dust clouds were settling, dissipating, revealing the otherwise pristine day.

She sat up. Pulled on the hair above her ears. Pulled hard. "No!"

She got to her feet and screamed. "No!"

"Ryan," she said, hoping that maybe the signal would

transmit, if only she spoke the words loud enough.

"Costas!" Her shouts were greeted with silence.

She had been programmed to act a certain way. To love and trust unconditionally. Programmed with the belief that her efforts would be rewarded. Perhaps not in ways she could understand. All she had ever done was love. And what did she get in return?

Mommy had been trying to kill her. Jessica had replaced her. She had loved Jessica too. But that didn't change Mommy.

Cutter found her and rescued her. And then abandoned her. Left her for dead. When she thought Cutter had abandoned her once again, he saved her. And now he was gone.

And Costas. Took over her mind and her body. And when he was finished using her, he had left too.

It was not fair.

IT WAS NOT FAIR!

She closed the distance in no time flat.

Leaping at him, she planted her feet in the square of his back, the full force of her body plowing into him.

Surprised, Costas scrambled to his feet. He lowered his guard at the sight of Celia.

With arms angled back, head and shoulders thrust forward, she screamed, "You are not going anywhere!"

He smiled at her. "You really are the most human of us all."

"You took everyone from me!"

"Sometimes that is just the way of things, Celia. When you get older, you'll understand."

"That is not how the world is supposed to work!"

"But it is. You want something. You take it. Foster wanted a city to mindlessly worship him in perfect uncaring bliss. Jack wanted to appease his guilt. He erased his memories. And tried to erase mine in the process. Both made the same fatal mistake."

Costas turned and walked away at a steady pace. He was in no rush.

Celia's UI lit up with targeting reticles. An overlay of her structure highlighted Roy's parts in dark green—combat status, capabilities, and durability. She reached out with Roy's arm that was now a part of her, grabbed Costas by his shoulders, and threw him to the ground.

Costas picked himself up and dusted off his arms and legs, belting out a half broken chuckle. "Once was cute Celia. Now it's just getting annoying."

There was a loud pop. Cartilage snapped. Blood poured from his left nostril. The force of the blow put him on his seat. He wiped his upper lip with the back of his hand, examining the smear of blood left behind. Fire ignited in his eyes. "What do you think you're doing?!"

"You took everything from me!" Celia swung at him again, but this time Costas was ready. He caught her fist, Roy's combat reinforced fist, and shoved against it, sending her sprawling to the ground. She skidded across the pavement and slammed into the side of a blue shipping container.

"Come now, child. That's getting rather annoying. You don't want to start this."

"Start this?!" Celia screamed, pulling on her bangs. "You started this! You!"

She put her head down and charged.

Costas jabbed at the air. A barrage of U-rings flew at Celia. She leaped into the air and jumped off the first U-ring. Tucking her feet up under her body, she grabbed the second U-ring in midflight and whipped it at Costas. Eyes bulging with surprise, he ducked, barely avoiding his own weapon.

She reared back her arm. Costas spun with her movement,

grabbing her extended arm, and wrapping his arms around her. She squirmed in his grasp. "Let me go!" Fighting for control, he palmed her head like it was a basketball and held her away from his body. She swung wildly, trying to connect with anything.

"Ah, isn't that cute," Costas said. "Give up Celia. Sometimes you are just out of your weight class and there's nothing you can do about it."

"We will see about that." She jabbed him in the face the stump of her arm. Broken shards of plastic and metal dug into his flesh. Sparking wires sent small shocks of electricity through him. Costas howled in pain.

"You little bitch!"

He grabbed her by the waist. Her hands raked over the top of his, hitting the pressure plate on the back of his hand, releasing the fiber optic cable.

He threw her. Celia held on tight to the fiber optic cable. Reaching its full length, it snapped taut.

Costas ran at her like a derailed locomotive. Fury burned in his eyes. Metal folded from his body, large blades snapping into place, the same blades that had taken Cutter away from her.

She jammed the fiber optic cable into the back of her neck. Electricity surged through her access port.

Costas froze in place, his fist inches from her face.

"I can't move! What did you do?!" His face contorted, as if he thought his over exaggerated expressions could compensate for his body's lack of movement.

"I am in control now," said Celia.

Frozen in a runner's stance, Costas shook his head violently. His body refused to respond.

Celia stood up. Costas mirrored her movement. For an infinitesimal second, Costas thought his motor control had returned. He scrunched his features, as if trying to operate his limbs with his brows.

"What are you doing?"

"I am tired of people messing with my head. I am taking control." Celia walked forward. Costas' body walked toward her. When they were so close that she could reach out and touch him, she curtsied. Costas dropped to a knee, putting them face to face. She stared into his ice cold blue eyes. "I am tired of living for everyone else. I am done being a puppet."

Celia raised her arms parallel to the ground. As did Costas. She slowly brought her hands together in front of her chest until they were several inches apart. Instead of mirroring her, Costas' hands came together on either side of his head.

"This is what it is like!" Celia shouted. She slowly closed the gap. From four inches to three.

"Don't do this, Celia!" Costas' hands clamped down on his head like a vice. Servos in his arms cried out under the strain. "I'm a human being. Flesh and blood! You can't do this!"

She watched his face turn from red to purple. Watched sweat instantaneously bead from every pore. Watched the vein in his forehead throbbing, blood pulsing under immense pressure, an underground volcano ready to explode.

"Stop!" Costas cried out in agony. "Celia, please! You don't know what you are doing!"

A calm washed over her face. She tilted her head, locking eyes with Costas.

"I know exactly what I am doing."

Her hands met.

8

Pinkerton's workshop was brightly lit, looking more like a recovery room at a hospital than the dingy tech-filled den that Celia had become used to. She was lying on top of several pillows that had been pushed together into a makeshift bed. Along the wall to her left, a row of display screens squiggled with green lines that tracked her vitals.

In the corner, Pinkerton tinkered on a robotic arm. This one was different than the ones she had seen before. It was smaller and had a softness to its appearance that was missing from the combat reinforced limbs that Pinkerton normally worked on— those belonging to the station's Black and Whites.

Pinkerton lifted a can of lubricant. Its conical shape looked prehistoric to her robotic eyes. It squeaked as he greased up the elbow joint. He set the can aside and folded the arm, holding it at shoulder and wrist. Working the joint loose, he flexed the arm back and forth until it operated with fluid motion.

He brought it to her side. With a loud click, the arm snapped into place.

"How's that?"

Celia looked down at it, almost as if she were afraid to move it. Afraid that perhaps it would no longer be under her control. "I don't know."

Pinkerton reached out and with a huff, said, "Oh my God. Try it!"

Celia shrugged her shoulders. Her new arm responded. She brought it to her chest like a weight lifter pumping iron. Only, she was examining her parts, feeling its range of motion.

"So..." Pinkerton asked, his eyes wide with anticipation.

"It is good."

"Please, child. It's better than good. That there is perfect."

Celia smiled and held her arm close to her chest as if it were a prize possession. "It is perfect."

Pinkerton was still shaking his head as he ran a diagnostic check at the computer terminal. "Good?" he muttered. "That arm won't even be on the market for another six months. She says 'Good.' Unbelievable."

Celia beamed at Pinkerton. It felt good to have someone taking care of her, watching over her, actually concerned about her well-being.

"How's our little patient?" The voice came from somewhere behind her. She turned toward it and saw him framed in the arch of the doorway.

"Jack!" she cried.

"She's never been better," said Pinkerton. He spun a diagnostic monitor toward Cutter. "Check for yourself."

Cutter ducked under a hanging cable and approached the workbench. Celia threw her arms around him. "You are all right!"

Cutter chuckled to himself and tussled her hair. "Why wouldn't I be?"

Holding her head slightly at a tilt, Celia peered across her cheek at Cutter. "How are you feeling?"

"I feel fine, kiddo. The real question is how are you feeling?"

"Pinkerton says I am perfect."

"Well la-dee-dah."

It was so good to see Jack in one piece. She had thought that she had lost him forever at the shipyard. But apparently, the rescue team had been able to get Cutter to the hospital in time to save him. They would have had to replace his arm and leg with synthetic ones, and probably a few of his organs as well, but as least he was alive.

Cutter pinched her cheek. "Pinkerton get you all put back together?"

"Yeah!" She bounced with excitement and pressed her arm up against his. "Now we're the same!"

"Yeah? How do you figure?"

"Your arm."

Cutter looked at his arm.

"Yeah, it's my arm. What about it?"

"Yours is synthetic now too!" Celia said excitedly.

"You got some imagination, kid." Cutter chuckled.

Her bouncing enthusiasm halted. Was he joking? She had always found it difficult to grasp sarcasm. It came down to the slightest variations in tone and rhythm. But, to her ear, it didn't sound like Cutter was being sarcastic. Not this time.

His reaction didn't make sense.

"The damage you sustained," said Celia. "The only way you could have survived is if they replaced your injuries with synthetic parts."

"Knock it off, Ceil." His voice was gruff. He tried not to be short with her, especially after all she had been through. "I'm not in the mood for games."

"But… your scar."

"What scar?"

"On your hand." She reached out for his hand, taking it into hers. She rolled it over and caressed the smooth skin on the backside of his hand. "You burned your hand when you reached behind me to shut off the forceshield at Staples Center." She turned his hand over and over, searching. "It is gone."

"Seriously, Ceil—you're creeping me out."

Celia shook her head in disbelief, trying to put the pieces

together. "I do not understand. You sustained fatal injuries after Mayor Benjamin Foster had been killed."

"Ho-boy." Cutter elbowed Pinkerton in the ribs. Pinkerton let out a grunt. "Thought you said she's never been better."

Pinkerton's brow bunched together, as he rotated the diagnostic monitor. "Everything checks out."

"What?" Celia said. "That does not make any sense."

"The mayor's fine," said Cutter.

"But… I saw Costas kill him. And then he went after you and I, and—"

Pinkerton and Cutter looked at her with blank expressions. No, it was worse than blank expressions. They were looking at her like she was crazy.

"Who is Costas?" asked Cutter.

"He…" Celia was at a loss for words. "I…"

So many incongruent thoughts ran through her head.

"Ceil, see for yourself. The Mayor's giving a speech right now." Cutter walked over to the corner and turned on the TV.

That couldn't be true. How could it?

She turned to Pinkerton, searching, hoping that he could straighten out the dissonance she felt. But he simply nodded, seconding Cutter's statement.

On the TV, Mayor Benjamin Foster, was addressing a small crowd. He looked polished and perfect, an American icon standing in front of a slowly wafting American flag. At every pause, he flashed his pearly whites to the camera.

Celia found herself shaking her head at the image of Foster on the television screen.

It didn't make sense.

Unless…

And then she saw it.

"Celia?" Cutter asked. "You okay?"

Cutter turned back to Celia, but she was no longer looking at him. She was looking at Mayor Foster on the television screen.

Cutter kneeled down next to her. He followed her gaze, hoping he could figure out what she was looking at. Maybe it would answer why she had been acting so peculiar.

But following her gaze didn't help.

He checked and rechecked, his head bobbing back and forth from Celia to the TV monitor. For whatever reason, she was fixated on Mayor Benjamin Foster's eyes.

His cold black eyes.

FUTURE RELEASES

If you enjoyed DAMAGED GOOD, don't miss out on Cutter and Celia's next case, **FOREVER SIX**.

FOREVER SIX - Concerned that Costas' lingering programming might still be present and affecting Celia, Cutter vows to teach her right from wrong.

But when a criminal that has been terminating synthetics targets Celia, Cutter will do whatever it takes to protect her. Even if that means breaking the law and undoing everything he has taught her.

CONTACT INFO

If you need a social fix, J.E. Mac usually trolls Facebook and Twitter. You can sling comments his way @J_E_Mac or on Facebook.

Be forewarned, once you're his friend, he may or may not write inanely stupid things on your newsfeeds. You have been warned!

And as always, **REVIEWS** are a big help. It allows me to get the Ramen with shrimp flavoring. Oh-la-la.

The best place to speak your mind about my books are AMAZON and GOODREADS.

Also keep an eye out for the first book in a new series—

TERMINAL EXPERIMENT

All Kinsey wanted was to be a normal teenager. That's a little difficult when you are a genetically engineered super-spy with telekinetic powers.

After a botched mission, the clandestine organization she works for called The Clinic has plans to scramble her DNA and see if they can get better results on the next go-around. In short, kill her.

Narrowly escaping their clutches, she settles into a rural Colorado community, and finds a perfectly normal high school, where she can fit in as a perfectly normal high school student. Despite years of spy training, she quickly discovers that blending in at high school is more difficult than she had anticipated.

Her presence brings The Clinic to town, forcing her to shed her assumed persona and fight off the forces that created her or risk bringing harm to her newly made friends.

ACKNOWLEDGMENTS

The first thank you goes out to my mother.

So often is she overlooked. (I know, what a bad son I am!) But we really think alike. When I was twenty-five I often found myself wondering where my sick sense of humor came from, and then one day my mom said, "I'm going to write a memoir and call it 'Rat Poison Casserole and Other Family Recipes'."

Oh, right.

Thanks Mom!

And thanks for the endless support and unconditional love. It finally outweighed my seemingly endless pessimism.

Thank you Nick Porreca to whom this book is dedicated. To the guy that has read all my crap from its very crappiest, to what it has become today. And I'm talking earliest screenplays, comicbooks, work from long before I even had the notion to write a novel.

Thank you for sharing your novel writing aspirations with me, and your manuscript, and trouncing my pessimism by showing me that writing a novel-length manuscript wasn't limited to super-powered beings, and was attainable by us mere mortals.

And I also have to apologize—and deeply thank you.

I see the longing in your eyes, the lifelong desire you have always had for writing and literature. And the superhero strength it takes to put those dreams aside and support a family in their stead.

Yes, I know you've supplanted old dreams with those of the new, of family, and child, and what the future holds in store for them, and yourself.

But still, I see the look. When you say nice things about my writing, I can hear your inner monologue (Yes, I read minds now, it's a thing. I went to see X-Men: Days of Future Past and someone spilled teriyaki chicken on me, and gave me their fortune cookie as an apology, and now I can read minds. That's how it works in the movies, right?)... I know that you wish you had the time to devote towards writing. To honing your craft. To becoming the writer you always saw yourself as. I know you love your family, and you're a true inspiration there as well. I know you wish you could do both, and have trouble finding the ability to do so.

It'll work out. We'll figure something out. I'm always plotting and planning—usually to overthrow the government, but that'll help right?

In part, I thank you for the dream.

Thank you Eric Hoffman. In part for letting me borrow your best friend, Nick. But also for sharing parts of yourself, and introducing me to Max Barry's work, as well as Brandon Sanderson's.

Thank you Vanessa Haney and the Haney clan. There's been some really rough times in my life, and you've always seemed to pop-up when I needed you. Not a singular 'you,' but an all-inclusive y'all.

To Vanessa specifically, also thank you for straightening out my nose. My mom says it looks better—so there's that.

Thank you Shivang for being a shy-guy like me. For making me realize how simple it is to pick up the phone and say, "Hey, you wanna hang out?"

Stupid, right?

How easy that is, and how we as adults (well, you know, the age of adults, I wouldn't really consider us adults :p) can forget that it takes two to be friends.

A big thank you to my father.

This seems like an easy one for most people. But those that know me, know this is a tough one. My father and I didn't always get along, and a big reason for that was how I measured myself in his eyes. I always felt that I was never good enough (see, even this is a cliché'd tale). In the process of writing this book, in my own struggle with the discipline of writing, of learning how to write a novel, he said one thing that stuck with me and helped me muscle through.

"I am going to take away all your excuses."

It was a heated statement. I'm not sure he meant it how I took it. But it was freeing.

And he was right.

There are no excuses. If you want to accomplish something, you take the steps toward your goal, and simply do it. Everything else is just an excuse.

There are some obvious thank you's—thank you's that anyone self publishing will already know. Hugh Howey and Joe Konrath, you two are the "Thank You, Jesus," to my any-award-show-championship speech. The thank you that goes without saying, but still I feel compelled to say it.

There are the not-so obvious thank you's.

These are the people that had a more profound effect on me than they probably know. The people that we interact with via the technology of social media. The people that our modern language doesn't have a name for. They aren't friends exactly, nor have we met face to face, but they have been inspirations none-the-less.

Thank you Ray Dillon. I knew you before I knew you. And then I met Emily Henke and felt I knew you even better. And yet we've never met.

Thank you for the cover. It is AWESOME! If anyone picks up this book in the first place, it is because of that cover. That cover is pitch-perfect. Enticing, eye catching, hints at the story between the covers, connotes genre. And has a little bit of that

Mona Lisa type smile going on.

Just… perfect.

Thank you Bill Cunningham and Pulp 2.0, you were an inspiration and an eye opener. I doubt you know it, but you were the one that made me think taking this venture would be even remotely economically feasible.

Thank you Matthew Mather. For sharing your success both indirectly and directly via email.

Thank you Susan Kaye Quinn. I love batting ideas back and forth with you.

You probably don't know this, and probably have no idea as to the weight or significance of a simple act. You posted on my Facebook page. It was the first time someone who I didn't know, whose name I recognized from other sources had posted on my Facebook wall.

Only days earlier I had been flipping through a copy of Open Minds in a Barnes & Nobles store (These were a thing, kids. Actual physical places that sold books! I know! And to have your book in there was actually a big deal!)

I was contemplating how to get my books into such a store. And only days later there's a 'like' and a comment on my Facebook about something clever or stupid I said. (Probably stupid. I usually say stupid stuff on Facebook. I mean, that's what it's for, right?)

I look forward to years of sapping inspiration from all of you!

And I'm sure many of you are muttering under your breaths, "Oh, great, that guy," and locking your imaginary front doors, pretending you're not home.

"Hey, guys! Want to build a snowman?" (I love that line).

In short, thank you.

THANK YOU ME

This bit here is for me. It may come off as incredibly self-indulgent, pretentious, and/or egocentric. If that is not your type of thing to read (and trust me, it's not mine), I urge you to stop reading here.

I thank you readers greatly for getting to this point. And hopefully you enjoyed the journey.

But this is for me.

A message, a thank you, from present me to past me—in the form of a time capsule that future me may one day look back on, and go, "Ah, yes, I remember when..."

Asides aside.

I think it is easy to forget the time and effort needed to attain a goal, to chase a dream. It is easy to write off the will and determination it takes to accomplish a task that was only fragments of ideas, scraps of imagination, whispers in an ear, and place them on a page, not for mere record, but in the hopes that others can also enjoy the fantasy.

It is easy to forget the first steps. The misfires. The words, sentences, paragraphs, scenes, and entire chapters that met the delete key.

It is easy to forget the hopelessness of the middle, the constant fight for a never perfect opening, and the ending always seeming so close, yet so far away.

* * *

I am not a very disciplined person.

Writing is difficult. It takes a determination and a strength of will that, honestly, I don't possess. (Or didn't. Now, it's a meek sort of thing. But we're strength training. Doing some cardio and endurance training as well).

I am also a person plagued with the inability to finish.

I don't even really know what that means, or why. I don't know if that's a real thing. All I know are the results. All I see are the piles of started and uncompleted projects.

Things I abandoned. Things I no longer have any hope in their ability to be of a certain unreachable quality or standard that I set unbelievably high for myself. A standard it seems impossible to attain.

Despite these hindrances, you've managed to muscle through.

Thank you.

Thank you for setting aside time each day to write. To achieve your goal. To chase your dreams.

Thank you for repeatedly getting back on the horse after falling off.

Thank you for facing the blank page, willing your fingers to move, despite how horrendous the outcome.

Thank you for fighting through the discouragement of missing personal deadlines, not by giving up and quitting, but by continuing anyway.

Thank you for learning the ease of the rewrite and the power of the delete key. That words have to be on the page first before you can make them good (or even passable).

Thank you for finishing. At all costs. Despite however awful the prospect of inflicting the finished project on others feels. Despite convincing yourself that you are the worst (Worst what?—THE worst. Oh, right).

Thank you for ignoring doubt and moving forward.

Thank you for acknowledging imperfection and muscling on anyway.

But most of all—

Thank you.

For without you, there are no dreams. There's only figments of the imagination.

It's easy to rest on the laurels of our friends. To co-opt their successes. It is an entirely different monster to unabashedly seek personal success for yourself.

It's easy to give up.

Easy to write off personal desire as selfishness and never pursue it.

It is much harder to live a life for yourself. To carve a piece of fantasy out of the real world.

Thank you for never giving up.

Made in the USA
San Bernardino, CA
04 October 2015